SHE KNEW TOO MUCH

by
Victoria Weisfeld

Cover Designed by: GinnefineArt.com

ISBN: 979-8988533368 - PAPERBACK
ISBN: 979-8988533375 - EPUB

Published by:
Audecyn Books, LLC
Upper Marlboro, MD USA

Dedication

To Neil, who makes all things possible.

Acknowledgements

So much kind support has been given me as I worked on this novel, it's inevitable my overstuffed brain will forget someone truly important. I hope not.

First, my publisher, Austin Comacho and the team, who took a chance on a newish novelist; my editor, Barb Goffman, from whom I learned so much and who is a genius at diagnosing a wide range of fictional maladies; and my cousin Jola Edwards, a brilliant proof-reader—so valuable when I had long passed the point of seeing any errors. As authors always say, and I appreciate why, any errors are my own.

When it comes to writing in general, I gained much from the kind tutelage of acclaimed author Lauren B. Davis and her "Sharpening the Quill" workshops, as well as almost 15 years of monthly critique sessions by my writers' group, Room at the Table. Ironically, we had such a loyal membership that there hardly ever *was* any room at the table. I've met many fellow authors through writers' organizations and conferences and can attest to what a supportive environment they provide throughout the nerve-wracking process of creating, polishing, publishing, and marketing the words herein.

Finally, I think apologetically about the many family conversations that have stalled while I drag my brain home from Rome or Perugia where my characters are struggling to figure out their lives. That my husband Neil, especially, puts up with all my blank looks is why this book is dedicated to him, endlessly generous in giving me the space I need.

SHE KNEW
TOO MUCH

CHAPTER—1

Sunday, October 14

Text from Genie Clarke to her brother Robbie:
Home soon.
Presents!
Miss u. xo.

Genie on Twitter:
#Rome's Palazzo Doria Pamphilj—fabulous private art collection most tourists miss! #ILoveItaly #traveltips.

GENIE

How did I get so lucky? So many people spend their workdays staring at computer screens and breathing stale air in oatmeal-colored cubicles. Not me. I'm paid to travel the world and write about it. Every day, I thank the ancient gods of travel. Here in Italy, that's Mercury.

I was reflecting on my good fortune at the end of a ten-day trip, as I leaned on the stone parapet of one of my favorite places in Rome, the Pincio Overlook. Warmed by the late-afternoon sun, I admired the perfect vista of St. Peter's dome, hazy and pink in the distance. The views, the distinctive bells of different churches, the lively people, the perfect October weather. That day, I'd soaked it all in, one last time.

The writing part of the assignment was nearly complete too, and tomorrow, I'd fly home to Virginia. Already, a small lump of early-onset nostalgia made my throat ache. Below, at street level, the bustling Piazza del Popolo offered a tempting pair of *caffès*. A bitter cup of espresso would revive me.

I trotted down the steps to the Piazza and threaded the narrow path between *caffè* tables and a tight row of motorbikes. One bump and they'd all go crashing, like steel and chrome dominoes.

At the first *caffè* I passed close by three lean young men who I guessed were the owners of a couple of those bikes. At least they dressed the part—all in black, leather jackets punctuated by steel zippers and snaps. Hunched over a small table, they looked like a trio of ravens, pecking at their smartphones. One looked up and scowled at me. He was strangely pale, with spiky blond hair like wheat field stubble. He was close enough to grab my arm, and for some reason, I shied away, in case he did. I shivered, remembering what Dad always said: Someone's walking on your grave.

Just beyond was a thick hedge of oleanders, and a much more inviting *caffè*. Up at the counter, I ordered espresso. I found a rickety table alongside the piazza, near the motorbikes, and breathed in the fruity scent of the blooming hedge at my back, tinged, naturally, with auto exhaust.

From my yellow leather bag, a find from this trip, I retrieved the thriller I'd bought at the train station. My Italian was better than fair, and I counted on the book to be entertaining language practice. Whispering the words as I read, feeling the shape of their sounds, tapping unfamiliar phrases into a list on my phone, I was totally absorbed.

A harsh scraping distracted me, and I glanced up. Movement at the edge of my vision drew my attention to the oversized side mirror of a red Mojito 50 in the long row of motorbikes. It revealed a man dragging a chair to join the three black-clad twenty-somethings on the other side of the hedge. The newcomer, who wore a suit and necktie, looked old enough to be the father of one of them.

Their low rumble of conversation remained part of the background noise until one of them, the older man, I guessed, because he had a weary, growling voice, said,

"*Maria Maggiore,*" a basilica I'd visited that morning. A litany of other prominent church names followed.

Maybe I was stereotyping, but these guys didn't strike me as churchgoers. Apparently, they intended to check out the churches as part of a Plan. The way they emphasized the word *Progetto,* it had that capital P. I wasn't eavesdropping, exactly, and before long, I heard the name "Cubellis." A sharp "*Chiudi il becco!*" followed. Slang, but it was unmistakably "Shut up!"

Whoa. I knew who Cubellis was. Everyone did. A mafia leader who eluded justice time and again. Narcotics, sex trafficking, extortion, murder, and the art form perfected by Italians, corruption. That was Cubellis. Now I really *was* curious, and I strained to hear more.

Much later it occurred to me they might have picked that *caffè* for a reason. With the constant traffic drone, they could hold a private conversation right out in public. Plus, most patrons sat close to the waiter's station, not at the periphery, like me.

"*Scuse, Signora.*" The waiter's loud interruption startled me. "*È tutto?*"

From behind came an angry "*Merda!*" followed by ominous silence. The oleanders rustled, and the waiter glared over my head at the shrubbery. The leaves rustled again. "*Americana!*" a man muttered.

Somehow, they always knew.

OK, I'd play the oblivious tourist. I swept the book into my bag to hide the shining gold letters of its title. Best case, they'd assume I hadn't understood a word of what they'd said. In my most distinct American voice, I said loudly, "No, thank you. Just the coffee," and stammered a half-Spanish "*Gra-see.*" I handed the waiter a twenty euro note, smallest I had. "I'm afraid I need change. Sorry."

The voices behind me subsided to a hiss. The Mojito's big mirror showed the black-clad men shifting in their seats, big boned and alert as panthers. In the center of the reflection, the older man relaxed, exploring his teeth with a silver toothpick. Even through the shrubbery I sensed his hostility, an attitude so ancient, Romulus and Remus would have recognized it: the detached yet alert regard a wolf with a full belly gives a stray sheep.

A cell phone chimed. The man who answered wore a skimpy ponytail. "*Marco*," he said, listened, and tossed the phone to the older man, who broke off his fixed attention on my invisible back.

Where was that damn waiter?

The phone conversation was low at the outset, but soon the man's commanding voice broke through a lull in the traffic noise. He was trying to set a date and place for a meeting of some kind, but the young men kept arguing with him. They rejected anywhere *troppi soldati?* 'Too many…' the next word blurred. I could look it up, if I could guess the spelling. Forget it. They obviously didn't want anyone knowing their business. "*Sì, problema! Americana!*" the older man said, before the conversation faded again.

That was too much. I jumped up and grabbed my bag. I'd intercept that sluggardly waiter at the front of the restaurant. But here he came, winding his way among the chairs and smirking in a way that obliged me to count my change.

I pulled out a green Michelin guide—an ordinary, clueless tourist on an ordinary Sunday afternoon and left the *caffè* and the menacing patrons behind.

Thick with pedestrians, the Piazza del Popolo earned its nickname as the "people's plaza" that day. I tried to lose myself in the crowd, conscious that my red sun hat and bright yellow bag were poor camouflage, *if* the men were watching me, which I assured myself they were not.

I crossed the one-way traffic to reach the Piazza del Popolo's spacious central rectangle. People ambled toward one or another of the half-dozen streets that converged on the Piazza or to the steps leading up to the Villa Borghese Gardens, where I'd spent the afternoon. I was aiming for the Via del Babuino, street of the Baboon, which got its name from a particularly hideous sculpture. In a few blocks, that street ended at the Piazza di Spagna and the always-crowded Spanish Steps, a half block from my hotel.

On the far side, I again negotiated the circling rush of traffic and chanced a look behind. *What the hell?* The spiky-haired blond had crossed the first stream of traffic. Now he jostled through the crowd, coming straight my way. He was tracking me, and he didn't care if I knew it.

I was in trouble. And, if I didn't want to believe my eyes, the hair on the back of my neck confirmed it. I picked up my pace, walking as fast as I could in my flimsy sandals.

Dozens of times I'd traveled the few blocks connecting the two piazzas. Now this familiar street radiated hostility, and the stones of the Sunday-shuttered buildings reflected no warmth. Surely something, some business, would be open. I sped past my favorite stationery store, the gallery whose owner I'd interviewed. Shut tight as oysters.

Why hadn't I asked someone near the piazza for help? Could I have made myself understood? Would they have agreed to get involved? I shook my head in frustration. No time for second-guessing.

The usually busy street was unaccountably deserted. Where *was* everybody? I reached a corner and again glanced behind. He wasn't running, but the distance between us was closing.

How was this happening? To me? As a seasoned traveler and, I believed, savvy woman of the world, I told my readers how to have fun while staying *out* of trouble. Thousands of them relied on my advice. They emailed and tweeted and messaged to tell me so.

My gaze darted left, right, looking for refuge, a person in a doorway, help of any kind. A side street to the left was jammed with parked cars. *No people.* On the right, a *trattoria* a few doors down. *Closed.* Even the cats slept. Hearing the clomp of boots from behind, I kicked off the annoying sandals and ran.

The sound of the boots grew louder, faster, racing my pounding heart. My mouth filled with the metallic taste of adrenaline. Another few strides and, ahead on the right, was the Anglican All Saints' Church. I *knew* that church. I'd been there!

I dashed across the Via di Gesu e Maria—*Thank you, Jesus and Mary!* Through the church's main doors and into a hallway alongside the nave.

"Hello?" I panted as I streaked past unattended offices. Silence. Desks abandoned. Phones stilled. Empty on Sunday? Nobody counting the collection, choir practice—*nothing?*

A hint of incense and candle smoke lingered in the sanctuary. My hopes clung to that last word: sanctuary. Sun streaming through leaded windows stained the brickwork bloody. The tile was cold on my bare feet. "Hello? Anybody here?" After a few seconds—where the devil was that priest? I pulled out my phone and punched in the emergency number, 113.

Frantically I looked for a place to hide, as the emergency line rang on, unanswered. Then I saw it. The church's side door. It opened onto a narrow park that connected to the next street. If I could slip out that way, I could disappear.

I dashed to the door. Its new-looking deadbolt turned easily, but the heavy brass doorknob resisted. *Come on!* I tucked the phone into my shoulder to free both hands. Sweating palms didn't help. The blond man would be inside the church any second, while the emergency number rang unanswered. I wrapped one hand in my skirt and grasped the knob. *Hallelujah!* It turned. I rushed outside, blinking in the sudden brightness.

I sensed movement to my left, and a heavy blow struck the back of my head. I lost my handbag and phone, and my straw hat sailed to the ground. Dazed, I turned toward my attacker to ward off whatever was coming next. My arms flung up to protect my face, knocking off his mirror sunglasses. He seized an arm, squeezed, and crushed me against him.

"*Fatti i cazzi tuoi!*" he spat.

Dizzy, I swayed, staring into eyes pale and hard as silver coins. My knees gave way, and I slid down his chest. The foul odor of sweat-stained leather enveloped me. A zipper tore my cheek. I was yelling, or trying to, but he was undeterred. With one hand he held me up by the armpit, while his other fist found my face, stomach, ribs.

My brain kept repeating his warning. "Mind your own fucking business, mind your own business, mind your ..."

I squirmed and twisted but couldn't break free. Our bodies were locked too closely together, my face buried deep in the rancid jacket. I tasted blood. I tried to call out again, but he knocked the wind out of me, and I could barely gasp. I stomped on his instep—futile in my bare feet—and foolish—his boots heavy and rigid. One of those boots connected with my shin, then stepped hard on my bare toes. I yelped.

Vision blurred, perceptions clouded. I shook my head, trying to clear my thoughts. A tattoo of a blue and green snake's head covered the back of his hand. It coiled around his wrist and up under the jacket's leather sleeve. Confused as I was, I could almost believe it was the snake attacking me. Mesmerized, I followed its black eyes as the hand disappeared into a pocket and came out holding a knife. The flashing blade broke the spell. In a desperate surge of energy, I tore myself away from him and screamed, "No!"

"Impicciona! Puttana!"

I heard shouts, running feet. As I fell into blackness, the blond leaned over me. "I *will* kill you. Just not today."

MARCO

The young man with the thin ponytail was channel-surfing. The front door to his one-room apartment flew open and the pale blond bolted inside, slamming the door behind him. He leaned against it, blood-spattered and wild-eyed.

"Take care of it?" Marco sounded only mildly interested. He tossed the remote onto a low table.

"Got her good," Nic said. He pushed off from the door. At the kitchen sink, he took a drink from the faucet and spat it out. "She won't bother us now, man."

"But is she dead? You heard Umberto say 'take care of her.' You know what he meant. He doesn't fuck around."

Marco followed Nic into the kitchen area. He was scuffed up, but not bleeding. The blood must be hers.

"She's *not* walking and talking."

"Seriously? So, is she dead?"

Nic opened the refrigerator and pulled out a Peroni. "Listen. I was ready to do it. I grabbed my knife. But then a priest came running, and he got a good look at me, man. I had to take off. I can't be up on a murder charge with a priest as a witness."

"Yeah. You're too pretty for jail. What priest?"

"I caught the bitch coming out of some church. If he hadn't shown up, it would have been perfect." Nic mimed a stabbing thrust, in and up.

"But he did, and you *did* tell Umberto you'd take care of it." Marco moved dirty plates and cups to the sink. "Glad I'm not you."

"I couldn't help it, man. The fucker *saw* me." His Adam's apple bobbed as he drank half the beer.

Marco took a clean T-shirt from the closet and handed it to Nic. "Here. Wash up." He got a beer for himself. When Nic returned, they sat sideways at the plastic-topped kitchen table, backs to the wall. "He's coming at six, you know."

"Who?"

"Umberto. That psychopath. So glad I'm not you."

Marco's door latch clicked, and Umberto stepped into the unlocked apartment, red-faced and overheated, wearing a sweatsuit. Marco guessed he'd come from the gym, "keeping the temple in tune," the older man liked to say.

"*Ciao,*" he puffed.

"Hey. So are we going out for pasta?" Marco asked, attempting to steer the conversation. "I'm starved."

"*Certo.* After Nic tells me how he killed the American."

Marco locked eyes with Nic. His palms-up gesture said, "I tried."

"I beat her up pretty good and was about to stick my knife in her gut when a priest came outta nowhere and I took off. She was already on the ground, out of it. Bleeding and shit."

"So she's not dead."

"I don't know. Might be." Nic's glance darted to Marco. "She might be."

Marco went into the kitchen. He stared out the window at the blank wall opposite. A grunt and a crash and Nic was on the floor, howling and clutching his stomach. Umberto never went for the face when he roughed up his men. He might break their ribs, but he needed them presentable. "My guys can't look like losers," he once told Marco. "Makes me look bad."

"Hey, we can fix this," Marco said loud enough to capture Umberto's attention.

"Oh yeah, how?" Umberto kicked Nic's back hard. He'd be pissing blood for sure.

"If she's hurt as bad as Nic says, they'll stick her in a hospital. We can get to her there. In bed. Easy." Not as easy as he pretended, but still.

"I'd like to fuck her up good," Nic gasped.

"Yeah? So why didn't you?" Umberto landed another kick. Nic howled.

Marco hurried on. "Think about this, we don't even know if she heard anything. Or speaks Italian. She *is* an American, and you know how stupid they are." One of Umberto's favorite topics.

"For damn sure," Umberto said.

"So we can take care of it. In the hospital," Marco said.

"Fuck, yeah!" Nic coughed.

"Not you, *stupido*," Umberto said. "Marco will do it. If he needs help, he'll take Lama."

Marco grabbed another Peroni from the fridge and took it to Umberto. He stepped between the two men, helping Nic up off the floor and into a chair. Umberto occupied the sofa.

"*Va bene*, OK, what hospital would they take her to?" Marco asked.

"Forget it," Umberto said. "I know how to find her."

CHAPTER—2

Tuesday, October 16

GENIE

My eyes squinted open. An unfamiliar white room. Midday glare making the walls pulse with every heartbeat. My head, a melon chopped in two, the shrieking light magnifying the pain. White sheets and white cotton blanket. White curtain screening the left side of the room. Outside the open window, a sheer layer of smog bleaching the sky to bone. I squeezed my eyes shut again.

When I next woke, the room was dimmer, my mind possibly a little clearer. A pungent odor of disinfectant couldn't mask cloying, sticky-sweet nastiness. A hospital. Was it a real hospital, or …? Could I be in some gangster clinic? Well, if I was, I couldn't do a damn thing about it. I could barely move.

I tried to sit up, but a piercing pain in my left side stopped me. I lowered my head to the pillow as gently as if it were an unexploded bomb. Starting with my toes, working my way up my body, flexing joints, tensing muscles, I tried to find places that didn't hurt. There weren't any.

Left foot and both legs, sore and restless. The touch of the sheet on my right leg made the bruise there throb. My lower back? A towel being wrung out by giant hands. Moving my left arm produced shooting pains in my side and an immediate, excruciating cough. Broken rib? I lay still, recovering, before resuming my survey.

A gauze bandage half-covered my right forearm. Peeking at the bloody scrape underneath made me light-headed. It looked awful. With the gentlest touch possible, I used my right hand to explore the base of my skull, looking for the source of the pounding headache. Through matted hair I found a tender lump several inches long and something prickly. Stitches. I inhaled deeply—big mistake.

I needed to think, and I struggled to push aside the thick curtain of pain. What happened to me? The horrible headache was my first clue. Something hit me. Not something. *Someone.* I cranked the film backward. The stubborn church doorknob, the deserted sanctuary. The panicked, barefoot run along the empty street. The jostling crowds at the Piazza del Popolo. The *caffè*. The gangsterish men. Yes. Them.

Immobile in my white cocoon, I took shallow breaths until I stopped shaking inside.

When will someone come for me, and who will it be?

In and out of sleep, I woke when a young nurse stepped around the fabric screen. She twirled her stethoscope and crossed to the window. The sky was melting into the good-bye hues of twilight. Then she looked my way.

"You are awake!"

As she took my vital signs, I asked in Italian, voice croaking, "What hospital is this?"

"*Ospedale Fatebenefratelli.*"

A real hospital, thank god. On an island in the Tiber. Site of the ancient temple of Aesculapius. God of healing. At least the memory worked.

"How did I get here?"

"Probably an ambulance brought you." A literalist.

"I mean, why am I here? What happened?"

"The police have the details."

"The police?"

"They will come again."

"My head feels broken." That wasn't the right word, but damn close to the truth.

"*Commozione cerebrale.*"

Cerebral commotion? Perfect. "*In realtà,* everything hurts."

"Yes," said the nurse. "Four broken ribs. One punctured your lung. Your back is badly bruised. You were kicked."

I slammed my eyes shut, not remembering, and glad of it.

"You have a tube to drain the lung. That must stay. Also an IV and a catheter. Now that you are conscious, in the morning they can come out."

I waited while the nurse counted my pulse, icy fingertips to my wrist. When she finished, she wrote a long note in my chart. But she couldn't tell me anything useful. Not about the assault, my treatment, or how long I might be in the hospital.

"What day is it?" I suddenly wondered. "The date?"

"*Martedí. Il sedicesimo ottobre.*"

Tuesday? The sixteenth? I'd missed my flight home! Unconscious two whole days? "Are you sure?"

The nurse grunted. "One thing more." She opened the cabinet drawer and removed a hand mirror. She held it behind her, and the corners of her mouth drew down. "Regrettably, *Signora,* you have on your face many bruises. A bad scratch. Our plastic surgeon says it will heal without stitches, and she applied butterfly bandages. In time these marks will fade."

Oh, please. I'm not *that* vain. I thrust my hand out for the mirror. But no warning from the nurse could have prepared me to see a face whose only recognizable feature was a pair of ambiguous gray-green eyes. I flipped the mirror over and pushed it away. Those eyes were filling with tears.

I was far from home. I knew that. The people who cared about me most were many hours and an ocean away. I knew that too. What I hadn't known was that my own familiar self had abandoned me too.

When I next groped my way toward wakefulness through the pain and the drugs, the hospital was silent. Dim light from the hallway spilled into the room. Funny how the pain was still there, and how I knew it was there, even when I couldn't feel it. A disturbance of my aura, my massage therapist would say.

My phone—screen unbroken, miraculously—read midnight. Six p.m. in New York. Good time to call Wally, before he went to dinner.

Among the many travel magazine and guidebook editors I worked for, Wally—Charles Wallace—was my favorite. He would worry if I missed our Wednesday lunch date. I was in Rome in the first place because we were talking about Italy one day, and he'd burst out, "Let's see everything new! Rome may be the Eternal City, but let's freshen up our readers' thinking!" On this trip I'd scouted gallery openings, visited new shops and restaurants, and interviewed under-thirty creatives for tips on nightlife and the social scene. It had been fun. Until …

While I waited for the connection, I cleared my throat and practiced a few low notes. I wanted to sound strong, capable. I wanted him to believe I was, as always, coping.

Wally answered on the second ring. He sounded like the call had interrupted something important. "Who's calling?" A warm New York greeting.

"Wally?" My voice cracked.

"Who's calling?"

"It's Genie." And cracked again.

Immediately, he was transformed. "Genie? You sound awful! Are you sick? Where are you?"

My lower lip trembled. Every broken, bruised, and scraped part of my body clamored for attention. I could picture Wally's Manhattan office, him in his oversized swivel chair and the killer view of midtown buildings piercing the sky. If only I were there. "Still in Rome."

"Weren't you due back yesterday?" He would be mentally calculating the balance in my expense account.

"I was—mugged."

"Oh my god! Are you all right? When are you coming home? I'll send a car." Wally to a T. Natural kindness at war with extreme thrift. I almost smiled.

"I'm in the hospital." My voice, thin and high, was annoying as hell. "I don't know when I can come home." *Worse and worse.*

"Oh my god, Genie. Is your brother with you?"

"Robbie never leaves Virginia."

"The farmer. I remember. I'm so sorry! For god's sake, what happened? Never mind. Don't bother about that now."

"I'll miss our lunch."

He snorted dismissively. "Rest. Think healing thoughts. And I will too. But keep in touch. Let me know how you are. What I can do. Every day."

"I will. Thank you." When I disconnected, I couldn't decide which made me feel worse—my injuries or the vulnerability I just demonstrated. "Hate that," I muttered.

Who else could I, should I, reach out to? My brother Robbie had my itinerary. He'd be expecting my return too. I composed a bland text:

Hurt my leg. Cant sit hours on plane. Back soon.

In our most recent conversation, he'd teased me mercilessly, as usual, about my constant travel. I'd even broken our customary silence about our parents. Without thinking, I'd said, "They're why I do what I do."

He was silent, caught up short, maybe. Then he'd said, "That life, their kind of life, it's gone, Genie. You can't find it again."

"I know that! I meant—What I meant is—" What *had* I meant? "I meant I'm carrying on their spirit, how they loved to just pick up and go. Me too."

"Meanwhile, I stay put." He sounded far away. I waited. "Avoiding land mines."

He had me all wrong. Even at some artfully buried level of my psyche, I surely wasn't searching for our lost childhood. I wasn't using my career to avoid establishing a real home, like he said. Sure, there was some truth to his joke that my house in Arlington was merely a place to do laundry and store suitcases. But did he think my whole life was an attempt to replace the irreplaceable?

That was wrong, I was sure of it. I loved my work—hearing people's fascinating stories, trying their foods, seeing their art, roaming their neighborhoods, then writing about everything so compellingly that my readers would want to see, hear, and taste these worlds for themselves.

That was my life. It was exciting, challenging, lucky. It was all I needed.

That, and a redo of last Sunday.

CHAPTER—3

Wednesday, October 17

GENIE

Early the next morning two police detectives in rusty black suits shambled into my hospital room. The older one, baggy as his clothing, made a perfunctory introduction and glanced about for a place to sit. His junior retreated into the unknown territory beyond the curtain and reappeared with a chair upholstered in sticky-looking greenish vinyl, which he dragged next to the bed. From an inside coat pocket he retrieved notebook and pen and strolled to the window, where, as far as I could tell, the street outside captured his full attention.

The seated detective finally spoke. *"Come va oggi?"*

I disliked him instantly. He must have known I was a foreigner. Either he assumed I spoke his language or didn't care whether I understood him. I suspected the latter.

"Meglio, grazie." Better, thank you.

His eyebrows shot up. Was he surprised I spoke Italian or disappointed he'd actually have to interview me? In an accusing tone, he said he'd visited my room several times, but each time, I was unconscious.

I shrugged. *Right. Blame the victim.*

He asked about my attacker, and when I described him, he sighed like a punctured cushion. "He could be half the *teppisti* we have in Rome. *Tipico.*" With every wheezing exhalation, a sour cloud of espresso and cigarette fumes drifted in my direction.

"But he is *not* typical. He's incredibly blond."

The detective waved me off and repeated, *"Tipico."*

Struggling to hide my irritation, I changed the subject. "How did I get here?"

"A priest from the church saw you. He ran to help and the *violento* fled. Then he called us. But he knows nothing. We know nothing." He leaned closer and said in a confidential tone, "Undoubtedly a thief! They prey on lady tourists." He waggled a finger at me. "You should be more careful."

I could only glare at him. *Outrageous.*

"Did he take your money?"

"I don't know. I haven't looked."

"You have not looked?" His astonished tone suggested I was some bizarre species of tourist outside even his vast experience.

"If you would hand me my bag, please ..." I indicated the cabinet. He took out the yellow bag, the tender leather badly scuffed on one side now. Money, credit cards, camera, everything intact. I pulled my passport out of the zipper pocket. "Everything is here."

He held out his hand for the passport. He looked at my photograph, then at me, then the photo again. I felt my face flush. Evidently, he had trouble reconciling the picture with the bruised and bandaged visage before him, distorted by swelling, the lower lip puffy and scabbed, that long, livid scratch, hair like the nest of an especially angry osprey.

"*Allora,*" he said, returning the passport. "Are you married?"

"No."

Understanding brightened his face. "If you permit me to repeat myself, *Signora,* these hoodlums, they prey on lady tourists. Lady tourists who, ah—present themselves— alone." He waggled his eyebrows.

Did he think I flirted with that creep?

Under the covers, my broken fingernails dug into my palms. I tried to explain that the attack was not random, was *not* an attempted robbery. He made a show of listening, his indulgent smile edging toward a smirk.

"I was followed after overhearing a specific conversation," I insisted.

"And, this conversation so important, it was …?"

I described what I'd heard, and even to my ears, the men's conversation was full of holes and ambiguities.

"Who knows what all that meant?" He showed his yellow teeth.

"I'm sure they were planning something …" What was the right word? *Dammit!* I pulled my hand free of the covers and made an emphatic gesture. *"Criminale!"* Even that didn't capture his interest. My head pounded. "I made notes." I reached for my phone, where I'd tapped in some of their slang and confusing phrases. He shook his head and waved me off. I continued, "They mentioned the man Cubellis."

"Did they? My partner and I mention him every day. Are we criminals?" He chuckled.

Wouldn't surprise me.

I tried to mask my anger with a smile. I could bare my teeth too.

"Who knows what they meant? Or what you heard, really?" He patted my hand and cued the detective at the window. The pad closed, the pen clicked. He hadn't written one solitary word.

"If it was nothing, why did they come after me?" I tried to recapture the detective's attention as he eased out of the chair.

"Why do they do any of the things they do? My advice, *Signora*?" he said as he backed around the curtain, *"Lascia perdere."* They were gone.

"I will *not* forget about it," I quarreled at the empty room. I might be alone and far from home, but I wasn't helpless. Not totally. Was I?

My phone pinged. Robbie responding:

Leg hurt bad?

I longed to tell him the truth. I longed for his sympathy, for one of his bear hugs. But he was thousands of miles away and worrying him was pointless. I texted:

Nope

Shut my eyes, and refused to think about the useless detectives and the challenge of getting home again.

Mid-afternoon, hearing low voices, I blinked awake. Silhouettes of two tall men mostly blocked the bright window. They weren't doctors. No white coats.

Now what? My sharp inhale drew their attention.

One said, "I'll leave you now," and moved away.

"Thank you, Oliver, I appreciate it," the second man said. He pronounced the name "oh-*leave*-eh." I couldn't guess who he was, yet the low rumble of his voice resonated deep in my battered chest.

He came quickly to the bedside. "*Buon giorno*." He introduced himself as Leo Angelini from the *Polizia di Stato*.

"The police were here already," I responded in Italian, not hiding my irritation. "If you've come to tell me the same things they did, save your breath."

He looked taken aback. "What did they tell you?"

"They said forget the whole thing. Well, I *won't* forget it. I'm sure I wasn't the first person that guy has assaulted, and I won't be the last. I can't ignore it!" Saying so much, with so much emotion, winded me. I grabbed my phone. "Sorry. I don't know how to—" I tapped "curse" into my translation app, and a tinny voice said "*bestemmiare*"—"*in Italiano*."

"I could teach you." He looked amused.

"Seriously?" I laughed, then winced. "I can't just let it go."

"Nor should you. I agree with you. My friend Oliver Harmon—he left a moment ago—" he gestured toward the curtain—"said I should talk with you myself. He is worried about you."

"Why?"

"Why is he worried, or why did I come?"

"Both."

"As a priest, he makes daily rounds at this hospital. This morning, he heard the detective talking to you. The questions did not sound right to him. *Insufficiente*. He thought the detective may have missed a few things."

"He pretty much blew me off. Does 'blew me off' make sense in Italian?"

"Not really."

"Ummm. *Ignorato*. They ignored me. Didn't take me seriously."

"Ah. My sense as well. The older detective is near retirement. He believes the chance of concluding an investigation before you leave Italy is remote. A waste of his effort. The other one finds it easiest to follow along."

The pounding in my skull had returned full force. "They're so wrong! How does that help anything? What about the next ..." I didn't know the word I wanted and reached for my phone.

"*Vittima*?" he guessed. "I agree. It would be infinitely preferable to me to prevent crimes, rather than be faced with solving them. And when you said, 'They're so wrong' you meant—?"

"I meant I *would* stay, or I *would* come back if I could help put that horrible man in prison." *Carcere*, an unexpectedly useful word from my thriller. I massaged my forehead. My words were braver than I felt at the moment. Still ...

Detective Angelini took out his notebook. "Perhaps you would tell *me* what happened?"

"Well then, please." I gestured toward the disreputable-looking chair, moldering in a corner. He was certainly easier on the eyes than my previous visitor and, like me, hovering around forty, not sixty. Too bad I looked a complete disaster.

He set the chair down next to the bed. As I told him what happened, he impressed me as a careful listener, interested in my descriptions of the men. He asked probing questions about the mention of Cubellis, and he was obviously dismayed at the ferocity of the attack.

When I finished, he said, "Thank you for that comprehensive report. Your observations were excellent."

"That's what I get paid for."

"Observing?"

"I'm a travel writer. Observing *and* reporting."

He smiled. "Then I am sure you are an excellent one. So here is my impression. Most certainly you heard more than you think you did or less than they believe. If they would risk assaulting an American for having this information, it tells us how important it is to them, also that they are dangerous men, not petty thieves who prey on 'Lady Tourists.' Then there's the mention of *Signor* Cubellis. Did it sound like they knew him or was it just a mention, like they might name a pop star?"

"I can't say."

"No. Then for now I would not make too much of it." Though his words were reassuring, a deep frown creased his forehead.

"You would know best about that. American movies have convinced me that every crime is the fault of the mafia or terrorists."

He laughed. I sensed him sizing me up as carefully as I was assessing him. If he believed in me, maybe he would really investigate. I'd like nothing better than to put a stop to those gangsters and their *Progetto*.

"Could you write down exactly what the men said? As much as you remember?" He indicated my bandaged arm. "Can you write?"

"Of course." I could certainly try, and I was grateful for an assignment. A thought danced at the edge of my awareness, but I couldn't bring it center stage.

"Soon, if possible," he said. "It may help us understand why they did this. Knowing why would help us determine who they are."

"It will take a while. May I wait until after my afternoon nap?"

"*Certo.* I will return this evening. Meanwhile, you may reach me here." He handed me a business card.

So. He wasn't an ordinary *investigatore*. Leo Angelini headed Rome's main detectives' department in the *Polizia di Stato*.

"Your friend Father Harmon came to see me around dinnertime," I said, when Detective Angelini returned. I pressed the button to raise the head of the bed and, with difficulty, shifted into a sitting position.

"Allow me." He adjusted the pillows to give more support. "Oliver? And what did he have to say?"

"A lot."

Leo used a word that sounded like his accompanying chuckle. "*Un chiacchierone.*"

"What?"

"He likes to talk."

Being so much on the same wavelength with this man was reassuring. "He found me, you know. Outside the Anglican Church. I should say he saved me."

"Ah. That is why he is so concerned about you. That is a forever obligation, you understand."

"On my part or his?"

"Both, really."

That put my conversation with the priest in a different light. One I'd have to think about. "I asked him about the blond man, the one who—. He couldn't describe him any better than I can." The thought that eluded me earlier had come into focus while I was writing down the men's words. What if they came looking for me? I said, "I have to find out who he is—"

"Oh, now, *Signora* Clarke—" He held up a hand.

"Genie."

"—you are stepping into my territory, Genie. In Italy, we have a division of labor. Here the police investigate the crimes."

He said it pleasantly enough, but I bristled. So much for same wavelength. Looking after myself was not something I could hand off, despite my current limitations. "You mean, 'no interference from Lady Tourists.'"

"That is not the issue."

"That is exactly the issue. I will assume you are hardworking. Hardworking and well-meaning. But no one in Italy is more determined to find that man than I am. Not those detectives this morning and not you. And you *will* need my help, like it or not."

His eyes narrowed. "And to help me, you were going to write out the conversation you overheard, correct?"

"Yes." The nurse had put my papers on the bedside table out of reach. I tried to grab them anyway, wrenching my sore side.

"Please, let me."

Again he listened with seemingly infinite patience as I walked him through the transcript. I sensed all the holes and despaired.

But he didn't. "Interesting. May I?" He held out a hand for the pages. The worried expression reappeared as he read.

"What's wrong?"

Immediately he smiled broadly and adopted an encouraging tone. "Do you like it here in the hospital, Genie?"

I took in the room's brain-scouring whiteness, the lack of color extending to my untouched dinner: pallid broth and a viscous, phlegm-colored pudding. An aide had delivered the tray while I napped and placed it where I couldn't reach it, even if I wanted to. "I hate it."

His deep laugh was beautiful. "Is there someone you can stay with while you're recovering? Family?"

"My only brother is back in the States and doesn't travel, and *Dottor* Immormino says I can't fly for a couple of weeks. Punctured lung." Mentioning it cued a stab of pain.

The detective sounded surprised. "No family here? Friends?"

"No. This was a business trip." His questions were making me nervous. Something lay behind them.

"In that case, we must find another option."

"What do you mean? Yes, this room is awful …" Unbearable, in fact. But what was the alternative? "I'll be fine." Probably he heard the tremor in my voice.

He took my hand and seemed to weigh his next words. "To be honest completely, I am a little worried about your being here. Now, I could put a guard on your door, but that also succeeds in calling attention to you. Or, you could move to a more private location. But you say you don't have anyone to stay with."

Hearing him put my unease into words, I panicked. "Surely the hospital is safe!" Despite the warmth of his hand, mine was like ice.

"So many people coming and going. I regret to frighten you. But remember how we talked about the importance of preventing crimes? You Americans have the phrase 'just in case.' You are reasonably safe here, but 'just in case,' I wish you were somewhere less public."

"My hotel?" That was impossible, given my medical situation, but it was all I could think of. I pressed my scabby lips together to hide their trembling.

"Similarly insecure for someone in your condition. You need support." He was silent, gazing over my head. At last, he said, "I can think of one possibility. A woman from my hometown has an apartment near the Villa Borghese park. She lives alone. Best of all, she is a nurse and absolutely trustworthy."

"But—" When had I ever depended on a stranger's help? I couldn't begin to list all my objections. It was an incredible imposition, barging in on a stranger like that. I'd have to rely on this woman for decent meals—the untouched hospital dinner reminded me it would be hard to do worse—for clean sheets, for quiet. In the hospital, I could—I would complain if something wasn't right, but in someone's private home?

"I can't—" My itching forearm reminded me that just glimpsing that bloodied scrape made me feel faint, and it would need to be tended. There was the drain for my lung, and stitches, my medications, my need for rest. I couldn't manage all that on my own. I'd have to accept help or stay in the hospital.

"Agostina cared for my late wife, when—" He coughed.

"Oh, I see." Widower. That was a distracting piece of information. "Still—" OK, the woman was a nurse. But how could I repay this nurse? And what would I tell Robbie? When I started to feel better, I'd need company too, and what if she was a screaming bore? I couldn't escape her. I felt myself gearing up to dislike the woman, and we hadn't even met. The idea was impossible. "I don't think so."

It would be infinitely easier to stay where I was. I was exhausted, and my mind felt as blank as those glaring white walls.

I glanced around the room. Not one aspect of it made me feel comfortable, capable of healing. Her apartment had to be better than this. Maybe I was being unfair. The woman might be quite pleasant. And skilled. After all, Leo had entrusted his wife to her. Maybe she would be just what I needed.

"Let me call her," Leo said. Before I could respond, he pulled out his phone, checked the screen, and said something I guessed was one of those swear words I didn't know. "I use this thing too much." I heard *batteria*.

"Use mine," I said. I'd just made a decision.

Dottor Immormino, young and in a hurry, appeared around the curtain. The detective excused himself.

"How are you?" asked the doctor.

Before I could reply, he began talking about the latest X-ray of my lungs. He had the same answer for every question: "You are healing nicely."

Leo walked back into the room and thanked the doctor. "Such a good report! When can you discharge her?"

"Not for several days—"

"No sooner?"

"No sooner?" I echoed.

"We would not want to risk complica—"

"Ideally, I would agree," Leo said, "but this is a special situation. I cannot reveal police business, but you know she was the victim of a criminal attack."

Oh, boy. Testosterone war. Dottore Immormino might have his own way in the hospital, but Detective Angelini was accustomed to having his own way, period. He muttered vaguely about "protective custody." It would have been entertaining if they were discussing anything other than me.

I coughed. "*Signore, Dottore*." My interruption startled them. "*Scuse, per favore*. I know I'm a little fuzzy with medication, but isn't the most important thing for me to get better, stronger, as quickly as possible?"

"That goes without saying," Immormino said.

"That will be difficult if I must constantly worry about my safety. I could not rest. Everything considered, although I will miss the excellent care I have received here in the *Ospidale Fatebenefratelli*, I believe I must accept Detective Angelini's recommendation of safe haven. And, *Dottore*, I could keep appointments with you at your office. Couldn't I?" I directed my question to the detective.

"Naturally. Whatever is necessary." He handed Immormino his business card. "In case you have questions." In victory, gracious.

Immormino dropped the card into my medical chart, shifting it from one arm to the other, and said, "In the morning, one more X-ray. Then, if she feels strong enough, she can go." He disappeared behind the curtain.

Once he'd gone, I said, "There is another problem."

"Oh?"

"The nurse tells me your people have taken all my clothes."

He laughed. "That, at least, is easily solved."

In the stillness that followed Leo's departure, I hoped I *would* be strong enough to leave in the morning. I'd caught his apprehension, and I hadn't been exaggerating its effects. That night, every noise, every brush of air kept me awake.

CHAPTER—4

Thursday, October 18

Genie to Facebook friends:

Out of hospital. With friends & healing nicely. Love u.

Genie on Twitter:

Autumn sun on ancient stones. #Rome is gorgeous in October! #ILoveItaly #traveltips

LEO

The next morning Leo left Genie in the care of his trusted friend Agostina. On the drive to police headquarters, a heavy stone building that always seemed too massive for narrow Via di San Vitale, thoughts of the spirited American kept intruding. *When her bruises fade and that scratch on her face heals ... more important, when her damaged psyche recovers ...* the thought warmed him.

In the office, he sought out his most trusted subordinate, Emilio Bracci. "Possibly, it was an opportunistic attack," he told Bracci, "but I think not. Of course, if she is correct about the men, she remains in danger. Oliver Harmon heard the man threaten to kill her. She doesn't seem to remember that, and I didn't remind her."

"*Certo*, her story is worth checking out," Bracci said. "The snake tattoo might be a lead." His chair protested as he leaned back. "A gang mark?"

"Perhaps. Talk to the *caffè* staff. The men may be regulars."

"And I'll show her some pictures. She may recognize someone we already know. What do you see as Cubellis's role in this?"

"Who knows? Having him in the background is the most dangerous aspect of her situation, in my opinion."

"Then we agree."

"I have her transcript of the overheard conversation. I'll go around the corner for that." Around the corner. Outside the unit Bracci oversaw. "I need the young brain cells of our friend Sal. Not anesthetized by years in this building."

Bracci wouldn't take offense. Leo occasionally separated different aspects of an investigation, at least in its early stages, to avoid premature theorizing and maintain security. A brutal daytime attack on an American suggested high-level stakes. It would make people curious, and the less they knew, the safer Genie was. At least for now.

Leo found Sal hard at work. Not yet thirty, Salvatore Riccobono barely met the department's height requirement, but he stood far above the other young detectives in street smarts, creativity, and an ineffable charisma that attracted an embarrassing number of women admirers. In the department, he was still a floater, with no permanent assignment. He could be added to the team working on whatever case needed him most, a system that exposed new detectives to a variety of investigative styles and challenges.

"Sal, get an espresso with me?"

"Sure, Boss."

Sal gathered his notebook and pen and grabbed a jacket to hide the gun tucked in the waistband of his dark jeans. On their way to the elevator, Leo waved to Bracci and received a small salute.

At a nearby *caffè*, they found an outdoor table close to the street. There weren't many customers, and between the traffic noise and the pulsing electropop from the bar next door, no one would overhear them. A garbage truck geared down noisily as it approached a stoplight.

"This must be what it was like when *Signora* Clarke overheard the men at the Piazza del Popolo. She sat close to them, but what she heard was—" Leo circled a hand.

"How's her Italian?"

"Grammar good, reasonable vocabulary, a few idioms."

"Street slang?"

"None."

"Too bad."

"But smart. Very smart." Leo handed Sal the transcript. "I don't understand these young *teppisti* myself most of the time. That's your job."

Sal read a bit at a time, testing his interpretations aloud. "OK, the three younger men sound like the usual *bulli*. There's the blond, a guy with a ponytail, and one with a shaved head covered in tattoos. Then the older guy, who seems to be in charge. He was only about eight feet away from her, facing her back. She probably could hear him the clearest."

The older man was talking: "… Santa Maria Maggiore, San Giovanni in Laterano, San Paolo fuori le Mura, Santa Maria D'Aracoeli, San Pietro in Vincoli."

I remembered the names of these churches because I've visited them.

A swarm of motor scooters buzzed past, trailing a gritty cloud. "So, a list," Sal said, when the noise and fumes dissipated.

The one with the ponytail shifted into my view in the mirror and said, "Sunday. I'll check them all. Forget San Pietro, obviously, doesn't matter, the Plan [he emphasized that word] stays the same. We need [I missed a few seconds here] … one man, maybe two. One would be …"

"Sunday—which Sunday?" Sal mused. "Why forget St. Peter's? Why 'obviously'? Too many people? Swiss Guard?"

Sal was asking the right questions. If only they had the answers.

One of the young men asked a question.

"… Cubellis say?"

I recognized the name, of course, and they shushed him, which made me curious. So I started to listen more carefully.

"Bad sign," Sal said.

"Agreed."

Sal read the rest of Genie's report silently, then said, "OK, the key problems. They say something is happening 'within two weeks,' but we don't know when that clock starts ticking, or has it already? They're working with someone they don't exactly trust, but we don't know who that is or why they mistrust him. We have only part of what sounds like a name 'Gab-something Danzio,' which I can check out. And their 'twenty-two hundred' could be a time, or euros, or who knows?"

"Can we fill in any holes at all?" Leo asked. "Or will we mislead ourselves? But we need to move quickly. If they weren't planning something significant, probably soon, she wouldn't have been assaulted."

"We have a name: 'Marco.'"

GENIE

That evening, I greeted Leo from the depths of Agostina's sofa cushions. "Did I thank you for bringing my suitcase to the hospital? I'm afraid *Dottor* Immormino's extra dose of morphine may have damaged my manners." *Comportamento*, I said, then amended it to *maniere*.

"Easiest job of the day." He dismissed my appreciation with a flourish. "How are you here?"

"Deeply grateful the walls are not white." Putting myself in Agostina's hands had already brightened my outlook. "Your Detective Bracci visited. We looked at a lot of pictures, but ..." I dipped my head.

"It was worth a try."

"Yes. And Agostina insists you stay for dinner. Please do, or she will expect me to eat everything, and she's been cooking for hours." And, though I didn't say it, since he was trying to take charge of my life, I needed to know him better.

"Yes, stay," a voice floated from the kitchen.

Agostina's ground-floor apartment was one of four created from a 19th century three-story villa. Originally far from the city center, it was now in the heart of an elegant urban neighborhood. Through some convoluted property tax dispensation, which Agostina warned was best not looked into, the house had a walled garden enormous by city standards.

When I first arrived that morning, I'd only dimly taken in the large and airy public room where we now sat. Agostina had given me her bedroom because of the en suite bathroom, and she'd decamped to a second bedroom. French doors in the main room and my bedroom opened onto a pleasant patio and the shared garden, much of it shaded by a bay laurel tree. Flowering vines that I could never grow back in Virginia covered the garden walls, and terracotta pots overflowed with red, orange, and yellow blossoms in the season's last explosion of color.

Plus, the building had wi-fi. Between naps that afternoon, I'd sent out upbeat messages, pretending everything was normal.

Text to Robbie:

Beautiful day. In good hands here. Dont worry.

And to Wally:

On the mend. Friend looking after me. More soon.

I even tweeted:

#Rome #Italytravel #traveltips Don't miss digital photo exhibit at Museo di Roma Trastevere—fantastico!

Leo did stay for dinner. When I sneaked glances at him—*could I trust him?* I caught his dark eyes studying me. The smile that followed communicated something, I wasn't sure what. Was he trying to gauge my reliability in return? Was he looking at me like a policeman? Or something else?

He was handsome, all right, but what most attracted me was his deep, resonant voice. It was as if a piano string stretched from the crown of my head to the soles of my feet, and when he spoke, it vibrated every nerve in my body. I could imagine surrendering to that sound, but I couldn't, of course. I had too much at stake.

Leo and Agostina conversed amiably, as if everything were normal. They and Leo's late wife Liliana grew up in Perugia. I told them about the week I spent there researching an article about Umbrian art for an airline magazine. It turned out I'd patronized several of Leo's favorite out-of-the-way restaurants.

"Interesting, our art?" Leo asked.

"*Certo*. The Assisi frescoes are so well known, I searched out something different and discovered the ceiling paintings in Perugia's Banker's Guild—spectacular!"

"Leave it to an outsider to discover such things! I have never seen them," he said.

"Nor I," said Agostina. "They're beautiful?"

"Absolutely, though my opinion may have been influenced by the chocolate festival."

"Ah. Always our most persuasive export," Leo said.

I told them how my family had lived in Rome for a few months when I was five. I'd started school there. And how my mother had taken cooking lessons from our Italian neighbor.

"Did she?" Agostina sounded charmed.

"Unfortunately, *Signora* Capelli was a terrible cook. So, whenever Mom made a truly awful meal, Dad would say, 'Another *Signora* Capelli special?'" Laughter was painful.

Agostina went into the kitchen to brew a pot of espresso, and Leo's cell phone rang. He went out to the patio to take the call. I sat at the table being grateful.

After a few moments, he returned, locking the doors behind him and closing the draperies. His troubled expression stopped the conversation.

"That was your *Dottor* Immormino," he said, sitting down heavily. "I'm afraid it's … earlier this evening a woman, a patient sleeping in your former room was attacked. Since you also … he thought perhaps you were the intended victim."

Agostina moved her chair closer to me and placed a hand on my arm. "Surely not!"

"How could anyone find me there? Of course, we were afraid they might. But no." My words tumbled out as fast as the snare drum in my chest. I pushed my hands toward him, trying to push away his frightening news. "Not possible."

"Did they catch who did it?" Agostina asked.

"No one saw anything. I also talked to my detectives." He made a calming gesture. "I know this is frightening, and I am telling you not to alarm you unnecessarily, but to make sure you understand how serious this situation is."

"*Certo*," I said. "But it must be a horrible coincidence. Nothing to do with me." In the face of his apparent reluctance to speak, I added, "Right?"

"In the bedclothes, the police found a note with your name and room number on it."

Searching for me. Actually, really, honest-to-god searching. My voice shook. "Was the poor woman badly hurt?"

He leaned toward me and gripped my hand. "She is dead."

I lurched down the hallway, a long walk in my condition, steadying myself with one hand on the wall, the other clamped to my mouth. My eyes streamed. I managed to reach the hall bathroom and vomited into the toilet. The contracting muscles turned my broken ribs into spears. They might be doing damage, but I couldn't stop retching. I might just bleed to death on the bathroom floor.

A soft tap on the door was followed by Agostina's gentle voice. "Are you all right? Can I help?"

"Give me a minute," I croaked. With great effort I pulled myself upright, wincing, the pain bringing more tears.

I rested my forehead on the sink's cool porcelain, each sob an agony. At last, I was cried out. I rinsed my mouth and splashed cold water on my face.

Pale and shaky, with Agostina's arm around my waist, I returned to the living room. Leo helped ease me into a chair.

A stranger's chair. In a stranger's home. In a terrifying city. So far from home.

I shivered. Agostina fetched a sweater from my room.

Nothing I could think to say was adequate. Yet, my racing thoughts tripped over a nub of stubbornness. If I gave in to fear, I'd be declaring defeat. I pulled my spine straight and rasped, "Now what? What can I do?"

Leo and Agostina exchanged a glance. "First, let me make sure you are safe here," he said.

The house sat on a circular one-way street. Facing the street at the right front were three narrow garages belonging to the property, one of them Agostina's. She confirmed that tenants kept their garage doors locked and that the sidewalk gate locked automatically. Visitors buzzed one of the apartments to be let into the front yard and, then again, into the building. All the tenants were longtime residents, cautious about whom they admitted.

"Could a person climb the wall?" I fussed with the sweater sleeves, pulling first one then the other down over my knuckles.

"Broken glass in the cement at the top," Agostina said.

"*Chevaux de frise,*" I said. At Agostina's baffled expression, I added, "Medieval security system. Still works."

Leo had toured the apartment, inspecting doors and windows. "Your locks are better than most, Agostina. They would certainly slow down an intruder. Of course you must keep the patio doors locked at night and use the alarm."

"That's twice they've tried—" I was muttering and barely heard him.

"I requested a *poliziotto in borghese—*"

I looked up. "What?"

"—a policeman in civilian clothes. He will arrive soon, and he will observe the street outside the house. You should sleep undisturbed. After all, no one knows you are here." Despite the reassuring words, worry clouded his voice. "And, as long as the victim's identity remains a secret, she *is* you."

"What was her name, the woman I got killed?"

"Gemma Capuano."

I put my head in my hands. "Poor Gemma. What a mess." I saw the spiky blond hair and the silver eyes. Would he really murder me because of some thoughtless eavesdropping? I fought back another round of tears. Grief was an indulgence I didn't deserve, and, anyway, it hurt too much to cry. "It's my fault. That poor woman. Over such a stupid thing."

"You did not kill her," Leo said. "If you go down that path, the trail of responsibility is endless. If you lend a friend your car keys and she has a fatal accident, is it your fault? If you persuade your cousin to go hiking, and he has a heart attack, is that your fault? If you convince someone to skip her doctor's appointment and go on a long weekend with you …" His voice trailed off.

In my distress, I lost the thread. *What was he talking about?*

Leo coughed. "Someone decided to do murder and carried that decision into action. We must make sure he does not find you. Who knows—or could know—you are here, in Agostina's home?"

"My brother Robbie in Virginia knows I'm staying with a friend, but no more. And Wally—my editor—too. Why? They're in America."

"Please indulge me. Talk to them and insist they say nothing, not even in passing, that hints at your whereabouts. I doubt they will be approached, but you are known, knowable. Writers leave tracks. Bylines, biographies. Google is a great boon to criminals."

"That will frighten my brother—Wally too maybe."

"I hope so. It may make them more careful." Leo searched my face. "One more thing. You said you spent the day using the social media."

"Yes." I knew what he was going to say next.

"That must stop. You will be safe if the killer believes he succeeded. If he finds messages from you all over the Internet …"

"He'll know to keep looking." Cutting myself off from my network of friends and readers, from the constant low-level thrum of interaction and feedback—that rewrote my rules of engagement with the world.

"Exactly." He spoke slowly and gently. "Now, can you tell me more about the man who attacked you? Detective Bracci says the snake tattoo may be a gang mark. Can you describe it exactly?"

"Last night I dreamed about it so vividly, it woke me up. I'll draw it for you."

Agostina rose from the dining chair where she'd sat transfixed and went to my room, returning with my drawing pencils and pad. While Leo quizzed her about safety in the neighborhood, I sketched. I gripped the colored pencils tightly to keep the lines from wobbling too badly, and my hand was cramping by the time I finished.

Leo studied the drawing. "It is curious the way the snake winds up his arm." He folded the paper and slid it into his jacket pocket. "*Perfetto.* I will share this with Detective Bracci." He rose to leave. "If it is convenient, I'll check in with you again tomorrow evening."

"I have an appointment at *Dottor* Immormino's clinic tomorrow morning. Should I keep it?" I was pulling my sleeves down again, covering my hands to the fingertips.

"Yes, go," Leo said. "You also need to get well."

What I heard was, you'll need your strength.

MARCO

"You sure she's dead this time?" Marco's best friend Gianni asked. He slouched in the apartment's most comfortable chair, eyes half-closed. "Fucking tragedy Nic screwed up to begin with."

"Lama made sure." Marco shook his head sharply to dislodge the memory of the bloody bed. "You know what Umberto said?"

"He's crazy."

"No shit. He said, 'show me her head.' Like we could chop off her head and carry it around Rome. Lama took a picture with his phone." Marco lit a cigarette and snorted out the smoke.

"Sadistic bastard. Give me one." Gianni grabbed the pack. "We're losing control."

"It's Umberto's show now."

"But the plan is *ours*."

"I know it. You know it. Lama knows it. Even Nic, dim as he is. But Cubellis says Umberto's in charge, so we shut up about it." Marco couldn't hide his bitterness. So fucking unfair. "Maybe we'll get lucky and the cops will pick Umberto up. How's he out walking around, anyway, shit he pulls?"

"Turn him in?" A smile blossomed on Gianni's face.

"Tempting. But it would screw up our thing, and we're so close."

"I'm seeing my cousin tonight. Then, uh, I need a favor."

Always something. Marco folded his arms to wait.

"Can I stay here a couple days?"

"What's wrong with your place?"

"My sister Carla moved in to escape her bastard husband."

"Weeks ago."

"I know. She's not bad, though her boyfriend's an asshole. It's her damn cat, Bianca." He spat the name. According to Gianni, the cat was everywhere, lurking in corners—spying. Her long white hairs clung to the upholstered furniture and collected on the floors in pale, dusty balls.

Marco struggled not to laugh.

Worst of all, Bianca's white fur on Gianni's black wardrobe was a disgrace. Every day he brushed his clothing, trying to remove every last uncool, embarrassing reminder of that damned cat. As he told Marco this, he picked off a few fine white hairs clinging to his shirt. So, earlier that afternoon, Gianni tossed Bianca into the fenced yard his Rottweiler patrolled. He opened the kitchen window a few inches for a plausible alibi and left his sister a phone message saying he'd be away a few days.

"Can't go back there. Not until Monday at least. She'll be *una forsennata*." A madwoman.

VENIERI

Near midnight *Dottor* Pietro Venieri slumped at his desk, a ghostly figure in the blue-grey luminescence of his computer screen. Data printouts and drafts of scholarly papers lay piled around him, but the computer's devastating new numbers would consign them all to the recycling bin.

He could almost hear what his department chair would say. For two decades she'd ruled the Department of Biochemistry and Genetics at *Sapienza - Università di Roma,* and he knew her standard rebuke by heart: "Those of us fortunate enough to work at '*La Sapienza,*'" she would say, "bear many nonacademic burdens. We have a 700-year history. We are the largest university in Europe, the most prestigious campus in Rome, and each of us must keep it so."

She wouldn't mention the department's fierce competition for offices, laboratory space, staff—ultimately, for status—that led the faculty to become skilled backstabbers. Venieri's predatory colleagues would eagerly capitalize on this failure. He'd guaranteed that by bragging about an impending research breakthrough at Monday's faculty lunch. Why hadn't he kept his goddamn mouth shut?

He didn't know what he'd tell the Spellini Foundation. The blinking numbers on his screen could halt the generous checks that had supported his work—and him—for almost two decades. Before he reached thirty, Spellini had singled him out as a brilliant young scientist pursuing novel approaches to treating Alzheimer's disease. Back then, he spent sixteen hours a day chasing elusive *Signora* Alzheimer. She was the thrifty housewife moving slowly and silently in people's brains and turning down the lights, one by one, until she retraced her steps to shut them off completely.

When his university promoted him, gave him a lab and staff, Spellini tucked him further under its wing, and he settled in to pursue his most promising ideas. After years of unsatisfactory progress, the foundation's president last week gave Venieri an ultimatum. You want results?—Venieri laughed bitterly—*Well, now you've got them.* He lit a prohibited cigarette. Out of habit, he stretched across the desk to bat the office door closed. Smoke could contaminate the delicate brain tissue cultures growing in the adjacent laboratory. As if that mattered any longer.

Hesitant footsteps in the hallway of the deserted laboratory interrupted his dismal thoughts. The shadow of feet appeared in the bar of light under the door. The university's ancient security guard, checking on him. Venieri held the cigarette out of sight and fanned the hazy air.

"Pietro? Doc?" A young voice, not the security guard.

The door opened, and his cousin Gianni, one of a small herd of black sheep on his mother's side, walked in and flipped on the overhead lights. Venieri blinked. The two men shared a family resemblance with their dark coloring—though Venieri's hair was silver now—full lips, and slick good looks. But Venieri couldn't tolerate the di Landri men, that bunch of no-goods. Dull-witted in every other way, they were geniuses at exploiting vulnerability. He saved the incriminating report on his screen and switched the computer off.

Gianni slouched into a chair underneath a large red and black sign reading *"Vietato Fumare"* and lit a cigarette. Venieri skated the glass petri dish he used as an ashtray between the piles of paper for them to share.

"What's up?" Gianni asked.

"Finished for tonight. On my way home." Venieri shoved random documents into his briefcase and buckled the straps decisively.

Gianni tilted back in the chair and swung his feet onto the desk. "Got a problem, doc. Need a favor."

Venieri perched on the chair's edge, hands folded on top of the briefcase, staring at his cousin's heavy boots.

"Friend of mine, an old guy, has Alzheimer's—your racket, right? His doctor says it's on a fast track, but we need him in the business. Word gets out he's losing it, we've got problems. Know what I mean?"

He knew: La Mafia. Stay out of it.

Gianni's leather jacket creaked with every shift of his lean body. "My aunt says you're onto a new treatment. We need it."

Thanks, mama. Venieri protested, "My work is experimental. It needs years' more testing."

Gianni planted his feet on the floor and leaned across the desk. "My guy hasn't got years. If today's stuff don't help, we need tomorrow's."

"I can't. The treatment …" Venieri's mouth simply could not form the words "won't work." Instead, he said, "I can't just give it to you. It wouldn't be safe. Or legal," he added, choking on that last irrelevance.

Gianni raised his eyebrows and shoulders in a coordinated "So what?"

"I'd lose my funding, my career. Go to jail."

"So, it's a gamble. What fucking choice do we have? They're offering him nothing. We'd make it worth your while. You can do a lot of research with three and a half million euros." He squinted at Venieri.

"Not as much as you think."

"Yeah, but it's all for you."

Venieri scowled. In a dark corner of his mind, though, Gianni's proposition tinkled a bell. How far would three and a half million take him? "I'm going home."

"OK, but we're counting on you."

Outside the building, Gianni's habit of walking too close irritated Venieri. Bumping and nudging. The cousins separated at the parking lot, and Gianni cut across campus. Venieri watched him go, brushing the sleeve his cousin had leaned into.

He climbed into his silver Mercedes and started the engine, though he didn't put the car in gear. *Can I say no? Or will they kill me? What happens when they figure out my big discovery is useless?* He rested his forehead against the steering wheel and groaned.

CHAPTER—5

Friday, October 19

VENIERI

Pietro Venieri, still groggy after a rough night's sleep, drank a second cup of coffee and listened to the morning news—predictable governmental turmoil and insider dealing. This time, the head of the Supreme Court was dead, and his son was elected to succeed him, as if such an important post could be inherited like a family business.

He made a disgusted noise and riffled through the telephone messages his housekeeper had left. One was from an RAI Television producer hoping to book him for Sunday's early afternoon live interview program, *Telegiornale.*

Splendido! He downed another cup of coffee and returned the call.

The producer's idea, it turned out, was that because the Supreme Court president died of Alzheimer's disease— Venieri muttered a knowing, drawn-out "*Sì*"—the program wanted him, Italy's top expert—"*mmmmm*"—to describe for *Telegiornale* viewers "the state of the science in combating the disease and the promising studies under way at *Sapienza.*" In particular, Venieri's own research. Such media inquiries were rare and a godsend. His department chair would be ecstatic. He'd praise the Spellini Foundation. Repeatedly.

Venieri hung up, smiling. When the delayed action of the caffeine recalled to mind the disastrous revelations of the previous night, he was horror-struck. He *couldn't* discuss the dismal state of the science and *especially* not his own futile work. No matter what he said, his enemies in the department would use it against him.

The phone rang. His cousin Carla, Gianni's sister, sobbing. She related a long uninterruptible tale about how her cat escaped the house and was killed—'murdered'—by Gianni's vicious dog. Bloody clumps of Bianca's beautiful white fur were strewn around the yard, and to tell the truth, she was not at all sure Bianca's escape was an accident, because Gianni hated poor Bianca for no good reason.

Venieri barely listened. "Carla, calm down. That's how it is with pets. Always some calamity," he said, as the volume of her crying increased.

His career teetering, himself maybe slipping into the mafia's clutches—he didn't need this. "What do you mean, I'm not helping? Carla, I *am* very sorry … Yes, it's tragic … Let's get together soon. I'll take you to a nice restaurant."

Where was I? he wondered. The interview. He'd cancel. But, no, the producer said his department chair recommended him. She'd be disappointed. Ask probing questions, questions he didn't want to answer.

The goddamn investigative mind.

GENIE

The visit to *Dottor* Immormino wore me out. His nurse removed the annoying tube draining my lung, and he said I was "healing nicely," scribbled a prescription for pain, and handed me a business card on which he'd written his home number. "Call any time. I'll see you Monday." A flap of white coat, and he was gone. Now I was resting in a lounge chair on Agostina's patio.

"Are you asleep?" she asked, bringing a glass of water and my midday pills. I chuckled to think how all my worries about her had proved totally groundless. Agostina was a peach.

I opened my eyes. "Just thinking about my doctor. In such a hurry." I rubbed my sore side and wrapped my sweater more tightly around me. "Gemma Capuano's murder yesterday must have frightened him. That makes two of us."

"Three," Agostina said. "Four, counting Leo."

"Not him. He's used to it."

Agostina gave me a look and took the tray back inside. I spent some time sending carefully edited text messages to friends who expected me home already and stayed off social media. Around lunchtime, hearing Leo's deep voice caused my heart to hit a few extra-strong beats. *Don't do this*, I warned myself. *You're just a case to him.*

He came onto the patio and hovered. "Agostina says lunch is ready, and I hear your doctor visit went well." He looked tired, his eyes ringed with dark circles.

"Couldn't wait to get rid of me. Would you help me out of this chair, please?" I could walk—short distances, very slowly—but I sure couldn't hoist myself out of a lounge.

When his strong arms lifted me, I caught the scent of starch and cedar. The sudden change in position and a sharp pang in my side caused a minor dizzy spell. I gasped and for a few seconds leaned heavily into him.

"Sorry. It's the drugs." But he was smiling.

He gripped my elbow firmly, and I limped to the dining table. "Agostina and I are going to start taking walks. Partway around the block will be all I can probably manage."

He shook his head. "The perimeter of the yard only. The high walls will hide you from the street."

As I started to protest, Agostina hurried from the kitchen. "It's on the news! The patient killed in the hospital was a foreigner. Maybe an American!"

LEO

The harried public relations assistant at the *Ospidale Fatebenefratelli* had scheduled an afternoon briefing about the murder, and Leo could picture that spinning out of control. Media coverage, particularly in Italy's more sensationalistic news outlets—in his opinion, every last one of them—could be dangerous.

Before the briefing, he cornered the hospital officials. "A woman smothered in her hospital bed? A big story, yes. But you must withhold the victim's identity." He pressed on. "The surest way to protect *Signora* Clarke is for the perpetrator to believe she is dead."

"Nor do we wish the killer to return in search of her," the director said. "We will maintain the pretense. Certainly until the police find the dead woman's family. Then …"

Then, it might be impossible.

"Give me all the time you can," Leo said.

During the briefing, the hospital director skillfully evaded the journalists' questions about the investigation, though Leo was present to stonewall them, if necessary. He'd stationed himself near the exit, impatient to go upstairs and talk to the staff.

The director reviewed the barest facts of the murder and, with a furrowed brow and a tight grip on the lectern, expressed official sorrow. From her front row seat, the hospital's legal counsel straightened, alert for any hint the hospital bore responsibility for the tragedy. Hearing none, she relaxed.

The director explained that until they found the family, the hospital would not release any information about the victim. He would not confirm the patient's nationality. No, he would not share the name of the victim's doctor. No, he would not give reporters access to staff. "They are busy taking care of patients and, in any event, possess no information." By evening, clever headline writers would massage the lack of news into the news itself: "Alone in Life—and Death," read one.

While Leo listened, his mind repeatedly strayed to Genie's brave rally after the shock of the murder. He tried to recall the exact muted color of her eyes. Alas, those were thoughts he couldn't indulge in for long. He had too much to do.

With so few details, the reporters' questions quickly made a muddy mess of the facts they did possess, and the exasperated public relations assistant halted the briefing.

Leo raced up two sets of stairs to the second floor to talk to the afternoon shift—the same speech he'd given the night shift sometime after midnight and the early shift that morning—warning them not to discuss the case with anyone. Since this shift included the people on duty when the murder occurred, he came down hard on the dangers of even innocent sharing of information.

He met with them in small groups just inside the murder room, hoping that being on the scene might trigger a memory. Behind the police barrier, the stripped and bloodied bed was a shocking rebuke, and they moved uneasily, looking at the floor, out the window, some with tears in their eyes. He asked them to describe again where they were and what they were doing during the critical time period, comparing their words to the detectives' notes from the night before.

When the last group left, Leo tried to visualize what had gone on there. He pictured Genie in that bed. A heaviness began in the pit of his stomach, rose to fill his chest, and pressed against its walls.

A nurse's aide knocked softly. "Follow me," she said, and led him to the staff break room. "I should have said something last night." She indicated a dramatic arrangement of tropical flowers.

"What?" he asked.

"Flowers from that patient's room. Before the police arrived, I brought them in here. Maybe they would be in the way, and why shouldn't we enjoy them? Later I remembered they weren't in the room when I took in the patient's dinner. I asked the nurse, and she didn't see them delivered. Now I realize it might be possible that the murderer brought them."

"So, the investigating officers didn't know about these?"

She chewed a thumbnail. "No."

"No card?" Leo probed the arrangement.

"No."

"You are correct." His tone was icy. "You should have said something. I'll send someone to photograph this and dust for fingerprints. We will need yours, as well." The battery on his phone was low again, but he had enough juice for a few pictures.

Leo left the hospital lost in thought. He, the hospital director, and one or two others shared a secret. The medical examiner's report confirmed Gemma Capuano died of suffocation. A pillow, it seemed. But the killer hadn't been satisfied with squeezing the life out of her. He'd taken his knife and gone to work. He carved out her tongue and larynx and placed them alongside her head in a grisly tableau.

It was a message, and Leo had received it loud and clear.

At police headquarters, Leo met with the detectives reviewing the hospital security video. For the two-hour window during which Gemma Capuano was killed, they had tape from only one camera, located in the hospital lobby. They'd compiled a DVD of excerpts worth a closer look. Hospital staff on duty the previous evening might recognize and eliminate a few of these visitors, and they needed *Signora* Clarke to review it too, in case she recognized any of the men from the *caffè*.

Now Leo asked, "Did the tape show anyone bringing in flowers?"

"*Certo*. Several people."

He handed them his phone, with the photos of the tropical display.

"Oh, yeah."

"See who brought them in, and send me the clip."

Late in the afternoon, he again met with Emilio Bracci, whom he'd put in day-to-day charge of the case. Several inches shorter than Leo, Bracci wore a comfortable layer of extra padding he blamed on his wife's excellent cooking. Working with Bracci was *due per uno*. The amiable Bracci's sympathetic side reassured witnesses and drew out admissions more aggressive detectives could never obtain. Yet, he was tough-minded, incorruptible, and tireless when he had *un ragazzaccio* in his sights.

Bracci used a special key to open his desk's lock—one he'd installed himself to replace the standard-issue—and pulled out Genie's drawing of the tattoo.

"I agree it has hallmarks of a gang symbol, though I don't recognize it." He studied the drawing. "I gave copies to our liaisons in other departments, including the *carabinieri*. They're doing some below-the-radar checking. And I faxed it to Naples."

Genie had captured the snake's mesmerizing eyes almost too well. Bracci broke off staring at it with a quick shake of his head. "I didn't show this to anyone else in here yet." He slapped the desk in disgust and hissed, "Too many fucking leaks. But if you—"

Leo brushed away the suggestion. "We need to be much closer to him before we risk it. And right now ..." He did know one thing for sure. They were moving too slowly.

CHAPTER—6

Saturday, October 20

GENIE

"Leo should be here any minute," Agostina said on Saturday evening, as if I might need reminding. He was so damned appealing. Interesting. Smart. Sympathetic. But such awful timing. I glared at my bruised face in the mirror and asked myself, *What's important here? Really? Gemma. Dead instead of you. Because of you. Don't forget it.*

If Leo—even Agostina—knew how Gemma's death weighed on my spirit, they'd try to protect me, keep information from me. Leo might hesitate to ask my help with the investigation, while I was determined to provide it. True, I wasn't strong enough to contribute much—yet. No legwork. But it was also true I wouldn't stop trying.

"Would you fasten my necklace, please?" I handed Agostina the strings of multicolored glass bubbles bought from an artist I'd interviewed. "I still can't reach."

In the living room, a large vase filled with yellow alstroemeria glowed in the corner like a second sun. "You bought flowers! How pretty."

"*He* sent them." Agostina gave me an appraising look. I wore my travel-smart black dress, the colorful necklace, and a big smile. She said, "Leo is a very special man. Since his wife died, he's been lonely." She disappeared into the kitchen.

OK, Agostina, message received. However, a troublesome, banged-up foreigner would be low on his list of possible cures.

I tapped out a text to Robbie:

Dinner w lovely man tonite. Police detective, can u believe?

I didn't add, "A police detective barely letting me out of his sight." I fidgeted, wondering whether Leo's interest really was strictly professional and whether I should be working harder to resist my attraction to him.

It's these damned painkillers, I told myself. Can't think straight.

The gate buzzer sounded, and Leo's voice came over the scratchy intercom. In a moment, he arrived.

"Agostina, good evening! How are you and your demanding patient?"

"This afternoon she slept, how long? Three hours? Exhausted from our morning walk. Twice around the garden."

"The flowers you sent are beautiful," I said, trying to shift the conversation off my weaknesses. "So cheerful."

Agostina entered from the kitchen with a couple of pillar candles. "I'll just light these."

She had prepared another delicious meal. As a finale, she set out cups of espresso and a plate of chocolate-hazelnut truffles. "You've outdone yourself, *cara*," Leo said.

"Magnificent!" I inspected a truffle. "One thing in this house—the food is fabulous."

"Shall we sit a while? On the patio?" he suggested. "It was warm today."

"Good idea. I have questions for you."

He came around to help me out of the chair, saying, "I am certain you do. However, I do not have many answers." His sentence ended with a touch of frustration.

Once I was up, I brushed off his continued aid. "I can do it. I can walk. Agostina, I'm so sorry I'm no help to you."

She shooed us outside.

I lowered myself into a lounge chair, none too gracefully, and Leo brought a thick afghan from the living room. He dragged another lounge alongside.

"With your work, you must spend a lot of time away from home," he said.

"My brother Robbie says my suitcase *is* my home."

"You have mentioned your brother. Are you close?"

"Very. He and his wife live on a farm about an hour from me in Virginia. I'm so proud of the fantastic business he's built. He grows vegetables—*organico*—and sells eggs. Mostly to restaurants. I've spent a lot of time there, watching my charming nephew grow up."

"And your parents? Are they in Virginia too?"

"They died when we were children. They inspired my work, I think." The awkward exchange with Robbie flashed through my mind—"That kind of life is gone," he'd said.

"I am sorry. I did not know."

"Mmm." The air was warm, but I shivered and wrapped the wool throw closer.

"What troubles you? Tell me."

I rarely tell people my parents' story. Yet I wanted Leo to know it, so I began by explaining that my father was a career diplomat with the United Nations and worked in many sensitive posts. "I was born in Seoul and Robbie two years later, in Istanbul. This was in the 1970s. Our gypsy lifestyle, as our mother called it, eventually led us to Bern, Switzerland, when I was ten. We hiked, we learned to ski, and at Robbie's gleeful insistence, we rode the Chocolate Train." I smiled, remembering his delight.

I told Leo how one winter morning, sunny and blindingly clear, we went on a group hike—three couples and five children, ages seven to twelve, and a guide. In the mid-afternoon, we headed back down the mountain, and the guide led us on an unusual route, hoping we'd see a herd of chamois reportedly in the area.

"Robbie and I noticed dimples in the snow by some pine trees. We broke the guide's rule about staying together and ran over to see if they were chamois tracks. They were fresh tracks, all right. Lynx tracks. We were terrified!"

"I can imagine!"

Just then the guide shouted, also contrary to his rules. A glittering cloud of snow hid the hikers, as a ground-shaking roar and shouts and screams echoed off the mountain. When the cloud dissipated, only the smooth surface of the glacier and a long fresh crevasse remained. "Our parents and everyone were gone."

"*Mio Dio!*"

"They were walking on top of a deep fissure, camouflaged by the snow, and when the guide broke through, the snow bridge collapsed."

"I crawled as close to the edge of the crack as I dared. The glacier's blue-green walls glowed, but I couldn't see any people. No colorful jackets, no walking sticks, no red mittens. Nothing. Total silence, except for crumbling chunks of snow. Behind me Robbie started to cry.

"We were too far from the village for anyone to have heard and send help. Anyway, we couldn't wait. The sun was dropping closer to the mountain every minute. We had to get down. And somehow we did. I don't know how. Thankfully, we'd forgotten that lynx! When we reached the village, the alpine rescue team went out. They returned around midnight, with nothing."

The crack was scores of feet deep and the area too unstable to try to recover the bodies. "The town held ten funerals, with ten empty caskets. Robbie and I … clung together … we didn't ask what would happen to us. Our lives were gone. In a few days an aunt we'd never met arrived and took charge. She lived alone, never married, in Washington, D.C. We grew up there.

"We hated her. Most unfairly. To escape, we did a lot of sports—swim team for me, baseball and soccer for Robbie, and we competed in target shooting and tennis. We hid out in her attic and read to each other. Novels, history, poetry. That was our real education. Our inheritance covered college, and we've been on our own ever since."

Fatigue and regret were making it hard for me to continue. "Aunt Stevie was lots older than our father. She didn't know what to do with two kids dropped into her life. She kept telling us to put the accident out of our minds, which made us sad and angry."

Telling this familiar story in his language made it new again, newly experienced. I fought back tears. My mood matched the patio's flowers, cold and black under the moon's thin shawl of light.

After a moment, Leo said, "Children experience so much more tragedy than we like to acknowledge. Victims and witnesses to unspeakable violence, and these days we—we police—do try to get help for them. Like your aunt, we used to pretend they will forget, they will get over it, that it will not matter, but it always does." He reached over and squeezed my hand. "And now?"

"Now? Robbie doesn't travel, not ever, and I want people to see the world as we did when we were young. I try to be 'the good guide' my father believed in. I suppose he'd have a few doubts about me right now. Getting myself into *this* mess." I winced as I shifted position.

"Oh, I expect he would be proud of your strong spirit."

"There is a downside, or so Robbie says. All the travel has made me *too* independent—and opinionated." I tried to laugh.

"But that is what your readers expect of you, no? Your opinions?"

"They do."

"You know your own mind. It is refreshing."

"Not everyone thinks so, I assure you. But Agostina is tolerating me so far." Again my laugh sounded more like a cough. And hurt. Whatever Robbie thought, there wasn't a scrap of independence about me now. I knew it, and, worse, Leo knew it.

"Tell me about your family." I shrank into the woolly afghan.

His cheerfulness changed the mood. "Your family is so few, and mine goes on endlessly. At times, it seems everyone in Italy is related to us. Whenever I handcuff someone, I am tempted to whisper in his ear, 'Are we cousins?'"

"Afraid of the answer?"

He laughed again. "My parents would never forgive me if I arrested one of our relatives—at least the close ones. Yes, my parents are both alive and well and working hard to keep their three children in line, despite our careers, marriages, and for my sister, children. All the symptoms of adulthood, if not, in my younger brother's case, the disease itself."

"I'm sorry you lost your wife. Agostina says Liliana was a remarkable woman." The dim light concealed his expression.

"Yes. And a model of courage. As the end got closer, she spoke only about the good things in her life."

What memories were flowing through him? "You, for one."

"So she said." He made a dismissive gesture. "I'll always regret the time I spent working cases that weren't really important, rather than be with her. A futile attempt at distraction." I thought he might say more, but his glance strayed past me to the top of the wall where glass shards glittered, and he said, more lightly, "Married to the job now."

"Me too."

Over the years, several men had wanted to change that, and each time when they made me choose, I chose freedom. Now I couldn't picture what life would have been like with any of them. But the future? It crackled with uncertainty.

LEO

Genie shivered, and they moved inside, so Leo could describe for her and Agostina the progress of the investigation. He started with what the police had learned about Gemma Capuano. For the last six years, she'd lived alone on a remote farm outside the small valley town of Sommati, 150 kilometers northeast of Rome. She was touring the Vatican gardens when she fell and broke her arm, a minor mishap that landed her in *Ospidale Fatebenefratelli*. Local police were trying to find her family, but in a country so rich in relatives, Gemma Capuano seemed remarkably impoverished. The newspaper's "Alone in Life—and Death" headline had nailed it.

Leo's young detective Sal Riccobono had failed so far to locate a Gabriele or Gabriela Danzio, the name Genie thought she'd heard. He'd also probed the background of *Dottor* Immormino who, by consensus, was a hardworking, but not brilliant, physician from a modest family background.

"Why check him out?" Genie asked.

"Because you will continue seeing him."

Detective Bracci visited the *caffè* patronized by the men she'd overheard. When he asked about customers from nearly a week previous, the owner surveyed the crowded sidewalk with its dozens of tables and rolled his eyes.

The weapon that hit Genie on the back of the head was never recovered. The lab couldn't lift any fingerprints from the note found in the hospital room, the one with her name on it, or from the vase of flowers. A depressing litany of dead ends.

He didn't mention the disturbing issue of how the assailant knew Genie's name and hospital room number. Bracci's detectives had interviewed the hospital information desk and telephone operators, who claimed no one had inquired about her.

Mention of the flowers brought Leo back to them— "*Strelitzia,*" Genie said when he showed her the picture. "'Birds of paradise' *in Inglese.*" When Bracci's detectives reexamined the hospital security tape, they found who'd delivered them. Two men. The flowers obscured the face of the man carrying them, and his tall companion's face was hidden by a baseball cap. While initially their actions seemed innocent, repeated viewing raised doubts. Leo's detectives were canvassing local flower shops. "A *florista* might recognize them."

Knowing the approximate time for the flower delivery and that two men might be involved, Leo told the women how he believed the attack was carried out. Around eight p.m., when the men with the flowers entered the hospital, the staff was scattered around the second floor nursing unit, delivering medications and preparing patients for sleep.

Only one nurse was stationed at the desk closest to Genie's former room. The call bell of an elderly patient rang several times. His room was on the far side of the unit, out of her view. She waited a couple of minutes, and when the bell rang again, she went to check on him.

He was asleep. She made sure he wasn't lying on the call button and spent some time straightening his blankets, dimming the lights, and switching off the television, though she admitted she watched for a few minutes—a celebrity gossip program. She also chatted with another nurse before returning to her station. All told, it appeared she was away from her desk for at least twenty minutes.

By then, the assailants were gone. They apparently used the emergency exit, since the videotape did not show them leaving the hospital. The emergency exit bell rang shortly before eight thirty, but the security guard admitted he took his time responding. Too many false alarms.

"My theory," Leo said, "is that one of the intruders went into the sleeping man's room and rang the call bell. Then they waited for the nurse to respond."

"They could have had quite a wait," Genie said.

"This is one of your famous opinions?"

"No. Personal experience." She chanced a brief smile.

"I see. When they entered Gemma Capuano's room, they found her asleep and suffocated her with a pillow." Genie and Agostina didn't need to know the rest. The tongue ripped out. The savaged larynx. The blood. "Tomorrow, I'd like you to watch a DVD we've put together. See whether you recognize the men with the flowers or, for that matter, anyone else." He ran his hand through his hair. "I apologize. You are tired."

"I need to help," she said. "Tell me what else I can do."

He nodded and prepared to leave. What he wanted her to do might be impossible: stay out of harm's way.

CHAPTER—7

Sunday, October 21

Genie's text to Robbie:

TV here is awful! Oh, for some Breaking Bad reruns!

VENIERI

Plagued by nightmares about the impending television interview, Pietro Venieri woke early on Sunday. He set a cup of cappuccino and a stale roll next to his computer and opened the draperies. Thick gray clouds pregnant with rain covered the early morning sky.

He was determined to exorcise his nighttime demons through solid preparation. Having given so many talks about Alzheimer's disease, he had the basics down cold. If not for the recent setback in his research, he would welcome this interview.

Fresh information would juice it up. He switched on his computer. He could always find new research reports, yesterday-new, from that cornucopia of biomedical discoveries in the United States. Americans forever boasted to the media about their "breakthroughs," but how many of them came to anything? It would be just like an interviewer to ferret out one insignificant U.S. study Venieri hadn't heard of and make him look like a fool.

His thoughts strayed. *He* could go to the States. He could thrive in California and get rich on generous research grants and a few patentable discoveries. He could take Gianni's money and extricate himself from all his predicaments at once—his embarrassing career, the pile of unpublishable research papers covering his desk, the debris of his former marriage, and the crushing atmosphere of

Rome itself, with its whole mocking history of glory and ruin.

San Diego. La Jolla. Irvine. Los Angeles. Palo Alto. San Francisco. Except for the clumsy 'Irvine,' the names soothed like an incantation. His daydream traveled north along that golden trail.

The computer's rude beep refocused his attention on the problem at hand. Entering "Alzheimer's research 2018" in the Internet search window produced a dismaying 35 million results. Adding "summary" to the search term slashed the total to an equally unmanageable 2.9 million.

He swished cappuccino and contemplated the screen. He was going about this the wrong way. He should adopt the journalist's approach. His interviewer wouldn't be reading scientific articles. He would be reading what other journalists said about them. Venieri could almost see the plodder, squinting bleary-eyed at his computer screen and jotting notes about research that sounded important. But what would a reporter know? Nothing. Picking the wheat from the chaff, that was always the problem. And yet, that was exactly what Venieri could do. Maybe he could even parry any unwanted question with that same tactic. *"Yes, there are a few tentative*—emphasize 'tentative'—*findings about whatever-it-was, though really, the most significant new lines of research are ..."*

Off and running.

Venieri started over. He searched the major news sites, found a few recent stories, including an intriguing one on intercellular communication and cytokines that prompted him to retrieve and skim the original paper, written by researchers at the University of California. *Goddamn them.*

He called it a morning. New research, plausibly exciting, his ace in the hole. Any difficult questions about his own work, he'd simply deflect by inserting it into the long line of scientific discovery—*"links in the never-ending chain of biomedical research progress."* Almost too easy.

Venieri arrived at the television studio as the gravid clouds birthed a depressing drizzle. A production assistant met him at the reception desk and ushered him into a closet-sized makeup room. Seated in the single chair, he faced a large mirror surrounded by light bulbs.

Like in the movies, he thought. Except in the movies, you don't realize those bulbs are so damn HOT!

By the time the makeup assistant arrived, traitorous beads of sweat ran tickling down his spine. Despite the close shave he'd given himself that morning, his dark beard threatened to show. She applied a generous amount of off-color powder, especially to his chin and cheeks. She tamed his eyebrows and sprayed a smelly lacquer on his silver hair. In the cramped and stifling room, his skin became clammy. The young woman twisted away, opened the door, and fanned it back and forth. Cooler air floated in. He inhaled deeply.

She abandoned him there, door ajar. The tiny room contained no newspapers or magazines, not even any posted signs for him to study. Nothing to look at but the big mirror and his grimly powdered jaws. He looked like a corpse. At least the interviewer endured the same ritual. Acolytes coated his face with powder that flew up his nose. They sprayed his hair with asphyxiating chemicals. Sweat collected under his arms and soaked his waist.

He lectured his reflection: You know the material; you know how to control an interview. Don't fidget. Smile. All there is to it.

Five minutes before airtime, the production assistant arrived to escort him to the set. What on television appeared to be a comfortable living room, in reality consisted of two walls—a brightly lit L floating in the middle of the dark studio. On TV, the set looked so much larger. Surely it would have to be enormous to accommodate the egos of the *Telegiornale* guests, brilliant and engaging, bantering comfortably with the show's slightly dim interviewer.

Now he would be sitting there, with thousands— *millions!*—of expectant viewers. A horde of mice rampaged through his bowels. He straightened his posture and lifted his chin, face glistening under the makeup. The production assistant darted a glance at him and drew her brows together. He needed the men's room.

"Where's the m—" he began.

She held up a hand to stop him, so she could listen to instructions coming over her headphones. Still listening, she guided him up the two steps to the platform and the guest chair. The makeup room was an ice cave compared to the set and its blinding lights. No wonder the interviewer hadn't arrived yet. He knew to minimize this excruciating prelude.

Beyond the platform edge, the studio was black as deep space. The cameras were out there somewhere, gliding noiselessly and invisibly. He'd seen dozens of people on the production crew, but now he felt conspicuously alone.

Another black-clad young woman wearing headphones whipped onto the set and attached a pair of lapel mikes to his suit jacket. She asked him for a sound check, and "Where is the men's room?" was not something to broadcast to the entire studio. "One-two," his voice cracked. He coughed and repeated "one-two" until she motioned him to stop. The floor assistant relayed a one-minute cue. Venieri's fluttering heart tried to slip out from under his ribs. One minute? Still no sign of the interviewer. Where the hell is he? What if he doesn't come?

A striking blonde wearing an electric blue suit strode onto the set. Nearly panting, he asked, "Where's the interv—" before he recognized her. *Dottor* Rosa Lisi. Not the usual *Telegiornale* interviewer. Rosa Lisi was a physician-turned-journalist who covered health and science stories for a Milan television station and several newspapers. She'd been on CNN.

"Twenty seconds," the floor manager announced, as Rosa's mike was affixed and tested.

"Nice to see you again," she said to Venieri.

They'd met? What impression had he made? What did that smile mean? Venieri wiped his sweaty palm on his pants before shaking her cool hand.

The interview, a disaster. Later he told himself he was thrown off by having Lisi sprung on him. He'd anticipated a lay-language discussion, during which he could spend perhaps twenty minutes reviewing the preliminaries—capsule facts, like some 600,000 Italians suffer with Alzheimer's, it's Italy's second leading cause of death and rising fast, blah-blah-blah. Then plunge into the warning signs, usual course of illness, life expectancy—information interesting to the average viewer.

Unfortunately, Rosa Lisi summarized all that in two minutes before confronting him with, "So, *Dottor* Pietro Venieri, what are the most promising research developments on the horizon?"

He dithered. He stalled. Trying to sound measured, he succeeded in being dull.

"How much progress are you actually making?" she asked, eyes gleaming.

He nattered on about links in the research chain. He praised the work of his colleagues across Europe and wasted his ace by blurting out the intriguing cytokine findings.

"That research is being done in California, isn't it?" she pressed. "What about your research here?"

He smiled so much his teeth went dry. Totally out of character, he attempted to tamp down expectations about his own research. "… early days … work in progress … very much a research theory …" His chest tightened. She became a gleaming blue blur in front of him. His eyes darted in unexpected directions. Escape was impossible.

The interview dragged on mercilessly, but now she was winding it up. The overhead lights snapped off. The studio lights came on. The production assistant materialized to take him away. He mumbled a few words to Rosa Lisi. On his way out of the studio, he passed a man in a chair tilted against the wall, sound asleep.

What had he said during the last half of the interview? Had he extended words of comfort to the families of the poor souls stricken by Alzheimer's disease? He hoped so. For sure he'd forgotten to acknowledge the Spellini

Foundation, and what he'd said about the years of research they'd funded was hopelessly muddled.

Venieri, you are well and truly fucked.

The sparkle in Rosa Lisi's sharp blue eyes as she'd thanked him showed she knew it too.

MARCO

According to the Plan—the *Progetto*—it was Sunday when Marco visited Rome's churches. Dozens of multilingual guides created a distracting and most helpful confusion, and tourists swarmed around him to gape at coffered ceilings, photograph stone carvings, touch St. John's big toe for luck, and check the amount of time until the next meal.

They were all too preoccupied to notice an attentive, pony-tailed young man hiding in plain sight. Nor did they notice the unusual camera he carried, stashed in a canvas bag. It was a thermal imaging camera capable of detecting surface-temperature differences as slight as a half-degree centigrade.

In the late afternoon he arrived at his fifth stop, Santa Maria Maggiore. Although he'd lived in Rome more than a dozen years, he'd never been inside. He attached himself to one of the tour groups and, like any other visitor, gawked at the basilica's marvels.

The docent led her group down a curving stairway to the crypt tucked beneath the altar. At the bottom, she pointed out the kneeling statue of Pope Pius IX, marble fingertips touching in eternal prayer. While the nave was full of noisy activity, the crypt was intimate, peaceful. Its dark walls, lined with rich sienna-colored marble, reflected and multiplied the ranks of candles, flame upon flame, their waxy smoke hazing the air. There, in a niche at the back of the crypt, was a true prize.

"Is that the 'reliquary'?" an awestruck tourist whispered, pointing to the silver and gold vessel.

"Yes, exactly," the patient guide murmured. "A reliquary contains holy relics. This Nativity reliquary holds

five precious sycamore fragments, shards of Jesus's crib."
The visitors' cameras clicked. Through the reliquary's
crystal walls Marco glimpsed *some*thing, though he
doubted it was a collection of 2,000-year-old wood. Still,
the idea of the thing electrified him. *Perfetto.*

He fidgeted with the silk rope that blocked visitors from
moving closer. A heavyset priest knelt alongside him, head
bowed, mumbling a prayer. They were further separated
from the glass-fronted niche by an altar and a short expanse
of floor. When the guide marched her charges back up the
steps, Marco hung back. He'd have only a moment or two
to hop the barrier and get close to the niche before a new
batch of tourists arrived, and the priest was rising shakily,
rubbing his right temple.

"Are you OK?" Marco said. He grasped the older man's
elbow to steady him and, he hoped, move him along.

"Yes, yes, *grazie*. A headache coming on. But I wanted
to finish the special prayer for the crib. Would you like me
to recite it for you?" The priest still massaged his temple.

Are you kidding me? "Thank you, Father. Another
time."

The dazed man appeared unwilling—perhaps unable—
to leave.

"So this is where a poor man will find our Lord's crib,"
Marco murmured.

"*Sì, sì.*" The priest swept a hand toward the brightly lit
reliquary and, seemingly overcome with dizziness again,
grabbed Marco's sleeve. "Come with me," he said, hanging
onto Marco's arm and stepping over the rope. "This is the
unique glory of our basilica—the beginning. Christ's
birth." He planted his feet and leaned against the altar.

Without hesitation, Marco slipped behind the altar,
pulling out the camera. He ran it along the cinnabar pillars
that framed the niche.

"What—?" the priest began.

"What a wonderful thing." Marco spoke loudly. "To
think that after two thousand years, these holy relics exist
here, in our city."

"A miracle," the priest gasped. He backed away from the altar in shuffling steps, arms held wide for balance.

Marco glimpsed him stepping awkwardly over the rope and continuing to retreat. *Is he going for help?*

"Beautiful. So beautiful," he said, hoping to command the priest's attention, and took a few final pictures. Another tour group clomped down the steps. He dashed to the rope and cleared it. He moved alongside the wavering priest. "Thank you for letting me see it with you."

They climbed the steps, the priest gripping the railing. Marco paused with him at the top while he caught his breath. A small, tan-skinned man wearing an elaborate crucifix hurried past them down the stairs to the crypt.

"That's strange," the priest said, gesturing to the retreating figure. "He usually visits very early in the morning. I've tried to talk to him, to ask about his beautiful crucifix. It looks handmade. But I think he is a foreigner—a workman of some kind, given the state of his hands—and he leaves if I approach."

"A penitent?"

"As are we all." The priest gestured to Marco's infrared camera. "Your camera … I've not seen one like it."

Marco clasped it to his chest and covered it with his hands. "It belongs to my … *padrino*. Another relic, but not a holy one."

"Your godfather. How nice." As Marco prepared to leave, the priest said, "God go with you."

"And with you, Father." He nodded a farewell.

Marco had recognized the priest's irritating accent at once. A *campagnolo* from the south. In his experience, people who rose to unexpected heights—like a fat country-bumpkin priest who landed in Rome—wielded their authority, however limited, to inflate their good opinion of themselves. This type of man was easily intimidated, a fact that might serve them well.

He drifted to the gift shop, where he fingered the postcards depicting the crypt and the reliquary. He slipped a basilica map and several postcards into his pocket and left. From the front portico, he assessed the clearing sky. The

Plan—his and Gianni's—was now complete. Every time Umberto had pressured them to choose a target, Gianni and Marco said that for security, they'd pick it at the last possible moment. Did Umberto realize that was because they didn't trust him?

"Every church in Rome has something worth stealing," Gianni said. And he was right; Marco had seen plenty of precious objects that day. Making this final selection was the last shred of control they had.

Marco grinned as he drove the Vespa through the Piazza Venezia and past the alley where he and Lama—"Blade"— had stolen those crazy flowers. He could still hear Lama shouting over the engine's whine as they sped toward the hospital that night, "The wasp stings again!"

GENIE

"What an insufferable bore! He looked like a dog about to be kicked," Agostina said. As an early-afternoon diversion, we'd watched the *Telegiornale* interview of a noted Alzheimer's researcher.

"He certainly kept avoiding her questions. But *she* enjoyed it." I chuckled, setting my phone on the table.

I'd texted Robbie:

> *He cant even describe his work. Hope he wasnt expecting new investors!*

"Rosa Lisi? Nothing slips past her. She's so gorgeous and seems so refined, but let your guard down, and she plunges the stiletto." Agostina mimed the action, then picked up the television guide to see what was on next. "Nothing as interesting as the DVD Detective Bracci brought this morning."

"Those flowers were so distracting. Clever." Worryingly so.

"Who'd guess there are so many ways to make yourself look suspicious?"

The *Telegiornale* program credits ended, followed by news headlines:

"Officials at Rome's Ospidale Fatebenefratelli have identified the patient callously and viciously murdered in her bed Thursday night as forty-year-old Gemma Capuano, unmarried, who lived near Sommati, north of Rome."

The news reader creased his forehead with pretended concern.

OMG. There it was.

He continued:

"Police have yet to determine a motive for the slaying, and a hospital spokesman declined further comment. Rome weather for ... "

Agostina snapped off the television, and stood transfixed, as if the blank screen might yet deliver more bad news.

I fingered my necklace like a nervous penitent. "I knew this would happen. Now they'll start ... searching for me again ... I can't stay here and put you in danger, Agostina. I'll go somewhere ... back to the hotel."

"No. You'll stay right here."

"It's not safe for you. I can manage. I'm stronger every day. You know it." I'd rehearsed these words, in case I needed them. I wasn't at all sure I could live up to them. "We walked around the garden five times after Detective Bracci left."

"Yes, and then you slept for an hour." The telephone rang, and Agostina hurried to answer.

"Yes, Leo, we heard. How did they ...?" She listened. "Genie wants to move to the hotel ... of course not."

Agostina relayed Leo's message. The Sommati police had interviewed an elderly priest who recently retired, and he helped them locate one of Gemma's distant relatives. Hospital officials were supposed to coordinate any statements about the case with Leo or Bracci. But they hadn't, and whoever was in charge on a Sunday released Gemma's name to the journalists camped in the lobby.

"Leo thinks the hospital just wanted to get rid of the reporters," she said. "He says you're absolutely not moving, and he'll tell you that himself the next time we see him. Here, you are safe."

VENIERI

Water streamed from Pietro Venieri's umbrella onto the polished marble floor of the foyer. Through the study door, the answering machine's light blinked peremptorily. It was a toss-up whom he least wanted to talk to—his boss, a gloating colleague, or the Spellini Foundation.

Two messages. His department chair apologized for missing the interview. She was visiting her in-laws' home in the country, and television reception was poor. Venieri smiled until he listened to the second message: Cousin Gianni promising to call again. He did, almost immediately, with a query every bit as disquieting as one of Rosa Lisi's.

"You available tonight? I'll pick you up at 18:00. Someone wants to meet you."

Gianni hung up before Venieri could object. His cousin was a lightweight, but he worked for serious people. A scientist meeting a mob boss? How would that look? God forbid his department chair got wind of it. Though, really, how would she?

One thing he was sure of was that if the mafia wanted him to do something, they wouldn't give up easily. Of course, they might not be serious about wanting his drug. Maybe that was just his cousin's wishful thinking. Maybe the three and a half million euros was too.

He'd find everything out tonight. When he talked to Gianni's contact, he'd make it clear the drug was experimental. But if they insisted, fine. By the time they realized his great discovery didn't work, he'd be long gone.

Precisely at 6:00 p.m., a car honked. Venieri had just decided, for the twentieth time, that providing the drug was too risky and he somehow—how?—must refuse to hand it over. Gianni usually talked nonstop, but tonight he fidgeted silently behind the wheel. Venieri used the uneasy quiet to assemble his arguments, settling on the idea that "concern for the patient" was his most defensible position.

They followed a circuitous route through the darkening, rain-slicked city until they entered a narrow side street lined with drab flats. Though the rain had stopped, the trees shed icy drops on them as they approached a building whose unlit sign read "*Albergo.*"

The hotel's vacant reception area and Gianni's incessant jostling increased Venieri's nervousness. A pair of hulking men occupied the tired lobby furniture and stared at them. One followed them to the tiny elevator and pushed in behind them. He stood with his back to the doors, his wheezing breath filling the cramped space like static.

Two floors up, they all exited. With every step Venieri took down the bare, ill-lit hallway, he felt his body temperature drop. Not trusting the answer he'd receive, or maybe afraid of it, he hadn't asked whom he'd be meeting. When Gianni tapped a door at the end of the corridor, a robust little man of about eighty opened it. Gianni stepped away.

The man introduced himself simply as Cubellis. The tabloid name made Venieri's scalp prickle. Surely he wasn't the Alzheimer's patient Gianni had mentioned. This man moved with wiry energy, and his eyes weren't haunted by the panic Venieri observed in early-stage patients, their minds gradually slipping out of gear.

Cubellis motioned Venieri to the sofa and lowered himself into a chair opposite. One of the sofa's ancient springs poked Venieri's backside. He tried to appear at ease, crossed his legs, and cemented himself in place. No jiggling.

"Thank you for coming, *Dottore*," Cubellis's hoarse voice growled.

"I am honored, sir." Having grown up around his mother's family, Venieri knew the protocol. Polite, respectful, and as calm as possible though his heart threatened to scamper out of the room. He could never say no to a man like Cubellis, but maybe he could talk him out of wanting that drug.

Their conversation proceeded in circular slow motion—the opposite of the rapid-fire objections and pointed questions Venieri endured at the university. Cubellis pondered before he spoke, and Venieri emulated him. Don't rush it, he warned himself. Don't make a mistake.

"Gianni told you of our interest?"

"A new Alzheimer's treatment I'm researching—*starting* to research." He cleared his throat.

"Alzheimer's is a terrible disease."

"And unpredictable. I have known patients who go for years without serious consequences."

"They still have the disease."

"Yes. Though better treatments—a cure—are coming, maybe sooner than we expect."

"Some doctors are more pessimistic than you."

"And sometimes they are wrong."

"You have a treatment."

"The beginnings." Venieri frowned, as if at the formidable research tasks still before him. "It needs much more testing to know whether it works outside the laboratory *and* whether it's safe. Especially that."

"But you told Rosa Lisi it was coming along well."

Venieri startled. That damned interview! He recrossed his legs. The sofa spring jabbed him. "Oh. Well, yes, it is. Coming along. However. Imagine building a skyscraper. I've created a strong foundation. Now I must build on it. Many stories." *Stop babbling.*

"Rosa Lisi thinks differently. She said you are close to a breakthrough." Cubellis tapped his nose.

Venieri stammered. "I wish it were so. Of course I must sound optimistic when I talk to the media, in case any of my funders are watching." He chuckled humorlessly. "Scientific progress is always slow, even without setbacks." Venieri inhaled sharply, trying to suck that last word back inside.

"Setbacks?"

"Pebbles in the road, that's all. Not boulders. We need to amend our testing protocols." There. That sounded plausible.

"I am pleased to hear it." Cubellis leaned toward him. "I would not want to be disappointed in this."

A bead of sweat tickled Venieri's side. The broken spring goaded him mercilessly. After a prolonged silence in which that drop of sweat was joined by several others, Cubellis said, "I want that drug."

There it was. "I'm a *dottore in filosofia*, not a medical doctor who treats patients. There is much testing to do—in the laboratory, with animals, and, ultimately, with patients. Until that's complete I can't say what the right dose might be or how many doses are needed. And the possible side effects?" He blew air through his lips, a wordless "let's not even think about it." Venieri took a breath. "All that is several years away."

The old man laughed. "You misinterpret me. I don't want a few doses. I want the formula. If I ever decide I need your drug, one of my businesses can manufacture it. I won't trouble you. I understand you have more work ahead, but I would be grateful to have the formula now. For peace of mind. An insurance policy."

Venieri's confusion showed, and Cubellis continued, "What I'm asking for is not yet a drug. It is, we could agree, an idea, a possibility. Sharing an idea with a friend is not treating a patient."

"And all I have to give you is the chemical formula?"

"*Dottore*, when my sister makes an angel cake, she uses butter, eggs, flour, and sugar. You could say her recipe is the formula. But if I mixed together those same ingredients, even in the exactly correct amounts, I assure you I would not produce an angel cake."

What in hell—?

"So, I would need also to know the right process for manufacturing the drug. The right amounts, the right order, whether to beat the eggs first, you could say, the right temperature of the oven, and so on. You understand?"

"You?"

"Not me personally. One of my colleagues. A man who will appreciate the genius in what you've discovered"— Venieri attempted a modest demurral—"and how to reproduce it."

The complex process for assembling the molecule was outside the capabilities of most laboratories. It was highly unlikely Cubellis's "colleague"—Venieri pictured a university chemistry student running a meth lab—could ever replicate it. His hands trembled. For this, he'd get three and a half million. Another thought occurred to him. "And if the idea I shared is patentable?"

Cubellis waved away this concern. "Go ahead. I have no interest in patents. Our involvement begins and ends with this one transaction."

Venieri was carried away by Cubellis's convenient logic. Surely this proposal posed no ethical problem. What's more, he hadn't signed the university's nondisclosure forms, buried in the piles of paper on his desk. And surely that policy wouldn't even apply to research he might soon abandon. Was it actually possible this deal was risk-free? Except, "What if a drug company got hold of it?"

"My colleagues know how to keep your secrets." Cubellis anticipated his next question. "Did Gianni say how much we are willing to pay for this favor?"

Venieri's mouth went dry. "Three and a half million euros."

When Cubellis did not disagree, Venieri's attention dwelt on the convincing precision of the amount, not the likelihood it would ever be paid.

"Go home, give my request your consideration, and call Gianni when you decide. Today is October 21, my Aunt Teresa's birthday." Cubellis examined his veined and wrinkled hands. "A wonderful woman. Alzheimer's disease left her an empty shell." He locked eyes with Venieri. "By Tuesday, your answer."

MARCO

Late Sunday night, Marco watched television alone in his apartment, facing a forest of green beer bottles on the low table. A key rattled in the door and Gianni burst in.

"You OK?" Gianni asked.

"Yeah. Why wouldn't I be?" Marco propped a foot on the table's edge.

"You haven't heard?"

"What?" Marco stretched and yawned. "Want a beer?"

"The woman you and Lama killed. You got the wrong one."

"No way!" He gave Gianni his full attention.

"Vittorio Cima told me this afternoon. And if Cubellis's right-hand man knows, Cubellis knows."

Marco again saw the blood everywhere, the woman's ravaged throat. "No way! The wrong one?" He banged his forehead with a fist and swore.

"Yesterday when Lama told us what he did to her, I wanted to puke," Gianni said. "Umberto really got into it. Bragging about his 'team.'"

"He would." Marco paced the cramped room.

"Cima told him too. And now he's mad. Serves him right for making a big deal of it, but still—"

"Why didn't you call me? I'm sitting here, easy target."

"I know, I know. Why I came. So I can help."

"Does Lama know?" Marco grabbed his phone and punched in a number. "Cousin, hey, how you doing?"

On hearing Lama's response, Marco grunted, "Shit, man."

Gianni's foot tapped an annoying staccato, and Marco waved at him to stop. He made reassuring sounds and ended the call, saying, "I'll be there, soon as I can."

He shoved the phone in his pocket, and said, "Umberto's been there, and Lama can hardly talk. We're out of here."

Gianni went to the window and moved the curtain aside. "Too late. I see his fucking *carretta*."

"Stairs to the roof. I'll keep out of his way until he cools off."

They slipped out of the apartment and along the hallway, ears cocked for the drone of the elevator. Lazy Umberto would probably use it, even though Marco's apartment was only one flight up. But Umberto specialized in the nasty surprise, so Gianni listened for a moment at the stairwell door too. Then the elevator whined.

"OK," Gianni whispered.

Climbing the steps as quietly as possible, they scanned the stairwell behind them, watching for movement, shifting shadows. At every landing, they stopped to listen. Pipes thunked, the elevator motor whirred and rumbled, but no footsteps trailed them. Halfway to the third floor they rounded a blind corner. There stood Umberto, a couple of steps up, leaning against the far wall.

"Thought you assholes might come this way." Umberto's arm shot out, and he grabbed Marco by the shirt front. With surprising strength he lifted the younger man off the step, swung him around and smashed him into the wall before he could defend himself. The back of Marco's head struck with such force he almost blacked out.

"Wait," Gianni cried, "he can explain." He bobbed two steps lower, then back up, hopped down and up again.

"Oh yeah? It was your idea, Marco. And you fucked up. I don't care about the bitch you did kill." He slammed Marco into the wall again. "What I do care about is that American is still out there." He dropped Marco, who fell and rolled down to the landing. "And she'll be fucking impossible to get at now."

"We got lousy information," screeched Gianni. "It's not his fault."

Marco's head was ringing, and he couldn't keep Gianni's face in focus. He tried to talk and could only grunt.

"You and Marco think you're so smart, sucking up to Cubellis with your clever ideas. Well, *this* is what works. Every time." He drew his arm back and punched Gianni in the diaphragm, leaving him gasping.

Marco lifted one hand from the floor, trying to protest, but he had no power to stop this.

"The." Umberto hit Gianni. "Old." Again. "Ways." Again.

As Gianni collapsed forward onto his knees, Umberto clasped his hands and smashed Gianni's back. He lay next to Marco on the landing, moaning.

Umberto closed on Marco and kicked him in the ribs, then crouched over him. "I know you're the brains here, so I'll leave your skull intact, but this shit has to stop. You smart boys are fucking up all over the fucking place. You wanna be big shots? Get your shit together." He stomped on Marco's outstretched hand, grinding it into the concrete floor.

Gianni roused himself to tackle Umberto around the knees, and both of them crashed to the cement of the landing. Umberto broke Gianni's weak hold and clambered to his feet.

"You'll pay for that, di Landri, you little prick," Umberto said and spat. In no hurry, he clanged down the staircase. After a moment, a stairwell door slammed. Marco wanted to sit up, but wasn't sure he could. He clenched and unclenched his mangled hand, barely able to make a fist.

Gianni shook Marco's arm and gasped, "I hate that asshole."

Marco said hoarsely, "He knows it."

"Will he get Cubellis to kill our project?"

A slight headshake made Marco dizzy. "Too … much … money … in it."

Eventually, Gianni and Marco staggered back to the apartment, supporting each other like two drunks. Marco stuck his hand in the freezer, and Gianni called Lama to tell him his cousin wasn't coming after all.

"You know he'd be there if he could, man."

CHAPTER—8

Monday, October 22

MADOOR

The bell of Amit Madoor's antiquities shop tinkled farewell to the smiling pair of Americans, cradling their purchase. The young newlyweds had spent an hour in his shop on the Via in Selci, an unpromising, curving one-way street of auto repair shops and dusty storefronts near the Cavour metro station.

The shop bore a skinny vertical sign, painted to resemble a Roman column, that read *Antiquario*. Its display windows resembled museum cases. Their few objects rested on rippling Mediterranean blue velvet, and a few battered Roman coins clearly labeled "replica" lent authenticity to the rest. A card propped alongside the only genuine antiquity on the premises, a terracotta pot with faded black tracery, read "not for sale."

Madoor hummed as he reentered the showroom carrying a squat glass jug, a twin of the "one-of-a-kind" item he'd sold the Americans. The jug was fake, but what the couple truly bought was the romantic story Madoor had told them, redolent with orange-blossom-scented details, and the shared excitement of discovery. They left without remembering to ask for any proof of provenance, though he gladly would have supplied it, as inauthentic as the jug itself.

He put the replacement in one of the showroom's locked cases and settled at his desk, an imposing antique whose overall design and heavy carvings suggested hidden compartments and long-held secrets. In the shop's rear corner, velvet curtains filled the archway leading to the storeroom. The sun had faded their original black to the maroon of dried blood. The scent of dust and sandalwood hung in the air.

For Madoor, fake antiquities were an amusing sideline. Most of his attention was devoted to much more lucrative activities. Whenever the morning newspaper reported a shocking art theft, especially one attributable to one of the organized crime syndicates ringing the Mediterranean, he needed only to wait. Most likely, in a day or two, the buzzer on the back alley door would sound, announcing a client who required the discretion, speed, and top price that made him one of the preferred fences in Europe.

With his connections and skills, Madoor made certain kinds of theft much more lucrative, even thinkable. Stealing a valuable art object was child's play compared to selling it afterwards. A well-known work could be impossible for most thieves to dispose of at anything other than a bargain basement price. But Madoor had turned this business on its head. He matched stolen items to the tastes, resources, and appetite for risk of his carefully cultivated international buyers. They were convinced he worked for them, representing their interests in the art world's gray-to-black market.

On Mondays, Via in Selci usually had little pedestrian traffic, but already he'd had customers, and soon an unremarkable man in his late thirties—one who wouldn't be noticed in even a small crowd—entered the front door. Madoor greeted him effusively and showed him to a high-backed chair in front of his desk.

"How may I help you, *Signor* Cima?" Madoor treated the man with extreme courtesy, as if he were the principal in their affairs, not merely the emissary from the elderly head of one of Italy's top crime organizations.

Vittorio Cima wore a beautifully cut gray suit, like any prosperous Roman businessman. The extra padding around his middle did not signify too many pasta dinners; he wore body armor under his starched white shirt. The way his jacket hung told Madoor his visitor was prepared for all kinds of negotiations, even those requiring the extra persuasive powers of the gun hidden underneath. Between the two of them, it would not be necessary.

He offered Cima a Turkish cigarette and took one himself. Elbows on the desk, one hand resting on the other, cigarette pointing to the ceiling, his whole manner conveyed readiness to be of service.

Cima blew a stream of smoke and said, "In a few days, we expect to come into possession of a valuable item."

Madoor maintained a composed and mildly interested expression while his mind raced. The article wasn't stolen yet, and Cima wanted a sense of how difficult it would be to unload. But he probably wouldn't—couldn't—reveal what it was until Cubellis's people had it in their possession.

"Ah. Is it Italian?" Cima might tell him that much. Italy offered many treasures.

"Italian, yes. It should bring a high price—the highest you and I have ever dealt with. It will require a special buyer."

"Discreet." Madoor stated the obvious, to keep Cima talking.

"International."

So, an object they couldn't risk being seen in Italy. "Middle Eastern?"

"No." The man's prompt negative told Madoor the item was likely religious, and, this being Italy, most probably Catholic. There would be no market for it in any Muslim country.

"American?"

Cima shook his head.

Madoor agreed. Americans talked too much. "You're thinking ...?"

"Japanese? Chinese?"

"The East." Madoor's eyes half-closed. Wealth, discretion, and no qualms about appropriating the treasures of foreigners' religions. His right forefinger tapped the desk, and he contemplated the perfect knot in Cima's tie. He did business with several Japanese, as well as residents of Singapore, Hong Kong, and Shanghai. "Approximate value?"

"Priceless."

"But you have a price in mind?"

"A hundred million euros."

Though Madoor's eyelids lowered another millimeter, he did not blink.

Cima added, "More if you can get it."

Whatever he sold it for, Madoor would receive ten percent. It was Cubellis's rule, and it saved tense and potentially dangerous discussions. Occasionally, he earned his share easily; at other times, he assumed tremendous risk. The amount of risk depended on what the object was, how long he had to hold onto it, how easily it could be hidden and transported, and, most important, how badly the owner wanted it back.

"Oh, we can get the price," he said. "I can advise you better when I know what you have."

"Understood."

"A price in that range narrows the field of potential buyers." At the same time, men—and most often they were men—with that kind of wealth were among the world's most competitive. A discreet bidding war might make the deal easier to achieve. "We should perhaps consider South America too. Africa, no. Too unstable. We don't want your treasure emerging from the dust of a military coup."

Cima took a last drag on the cigarette and stubbed it out. "No."

"When do you expect to have it?" Madoor asked.

"In three days. Thursday."

Madoor met Cima's eyes. "Will you want me to store it for you and arrange transit to the purchaser?" If so, the difficulties he'd face would go a long way toward justifying the hefty commission. Cubellis created the ten percent rule, but Madoor needed Cubellis's people, the ones he dealt with, to accept it too, especially when his fee might be several million euros.

"Yes."

"With an object of such worth, the dogs will soon be sniffing around. It will be important to keep them away." His usual routine would accomplish that. "And quiet." That sometimes required more aggressive measures, but Cima and the old man accepted Madoor's methods, which kept their hands clean. Yet another invaluable service he provided.

"Understood."

VENIERI

A pimple-dotted twenty-year-old no sooner cranked up the steel shutter guarding an outlet of Affordable Computer and Electronics than his first customer arrived. Pietro Venieri picked this branch of Rome's omnipresent retailer for its location—far from the University and at the edge of a disreputable part of town where nosy colleagues would never stray. He bought ten multi-gig thumb drives and a powerful laptop with a fast processor. Nothing fancy, a workhorse.

He had a busy day ahead. He would copy files. He would telephone Gianni to arrange lunch. In the afternoon, he would work on the problems with his formula. Maybe he'd yet find an easy-to-fix problem—a slight miscalculation or wrong assumption early in the computation that rippled through catastrophically. He should be so lucky. Such a solution would protect him against retribution from Cubellis and his organization. Otherwise, he didn't want to be around when they figured out his drug was useless. If Cubellis wanted insurance, so did Venieri.

Near one o'clock, he drove to a suburban farmhouse restaurant whose few diners occupied tables scattered about a shady patio. A maple tree grudgingly surrendered fading golden leaves to the breeze, and in ones and twos, they floated onto the tables and flagstone floor.

His cousin was already seated. Cell phone clamped to his ear, Gianni signaled Venieri with the expansive wave of a Hollywood host. Seeing Venieri's glare, he abruptly ended his call.

Venieri appeared to study the menu carefully, though he actually was rehearsing how to broach this conversation. By the time the waiter departed with their orders, he'd settled on the direct approach. "I've decided to accept the offer."

Gianni's reaction suggested he never doubted it, but his laugh was cut short by a sharp intake of breath.

"Something wrong?" Venieri asked.

"Fell on some steps." Gianni rubbed his sore ribs.

Venieri raised his eyebrows. "You'll tell your boss my decision?"

"He knows already."

Apparently, Cubellis hadn't doubted it, either. A hard bean of resentment lodged in Venieri's throat. Taking him for granted. He choked it down, as a plate of linguine arrived. The next issue would be trickier. "About my decision, I would have thought you would feel …" He picked up his fork and set it down again.

"I feel on top of the fucking world, Doc. You've helped me show the big boss I can deliver. I told them you'd help us. And now …" Gianni spoke through a large mouthful of pasta. "Ha!"

"So, you owe me," Venieri said. He twined a few strands of pasta around his fork.

"*Molto, molto, molto!*"

"I need to cash in that debt."

"Hhuhh." Gianni's mouth was full again.

"I need a passport, academic credentials, and other identification, in a new name. It's all spelled out in here." Venieri pushed a large manila envelope across the table. Gianni's fork stopped halfway to his lips. "If you tell anyone I asked for this, our other arrangement is over. I keep the formula, and they will know you *cannot* deliver."

"You can't—"

"But I can," Gianni's anxiety prompted Venieri to sound more confident than he felt. "You need to find an *expert* who will create these documents and won't go over your head to your bosses. Do it quickly and quietly. I will keep my commitment. And you must do this for me."

"If they find out, they'll think—"

"Make sure they *don't* find out."

"But you can't abandon … He'll kill me."

"I will do everything he asked me to do. And he specifically did *not* ask me to stick around and be his doctor. He has doctors. If you're afraid of his reaction, that's another good reason to do this without shooting off your big mouth."

Gianni pushed his plate away and whined, "Who can I ask who won't tell him?"

"That's your problem. Make it worth their while. In here—" he pulled another envelope out of his inner coat pocket and flashed its contents at Gianni "—are thirty-five thousand euros." Almost everything Venieri had left after his ex-wife cleaned him out. "That should buy my new identity. And your silence."

He read Gianni's squirming as indecision. "You have to." As Gianni slowly reached for the envelopes, Venieri said, "One word to anyone and you're finished."

GIANNI

Gianni rode away on his Vespa, no destination in mind. He didn't like secrets. Secrets made people suspicious. And suspicious people were dangerous. Yet he desperately wanted the deal with his cousin to go through, to keep the newfound respect he'd gained from the men around Cubellis.

He cruised along the tree-lined road that wound through the Villa Ada. The people he could think of to ask for help would call Cubellis the minute his ass was out the door. But there was one guy; Gianni had driven Vittorio Cima to meet him a couple of times. Not a forger, but he would know one. Cima had a one-word description for him: "Fearless."

He found the storefront on one of the narrow streets near the Piazza Cavour, then drove around back. He pressed the buzzer, and a distorted voice came through the speaker: "A moment, please." He leaned against a pole, jingling the keys in his pocket. The security camera above the door pointed straight at him. He hoped Amit Madoor recognized him. The door opened.

"*Buon giorno*? I'm Gianni. I came here with Vittorio Cima? He—we—work for—"

"I remember." When Gianni didn't say more, Madoor asked, "Are you here *per suo conto*?"

Now Gianni doubted this plan. Madoor was an important man, and he was, he was what? "No, *Signore*, on my own business?"

Neatly stacked boxes crowded the shop's back room. Madoor gestured to chairs arranged in an open area demarked by a blue-black Persian carpet.

"I shouldn't bother you," Gianni said. A low brass-topped table sat in front of the ornate chairs.

"You are here."

Gianni plunged in. "I need identity papers ... a passport and ..." He put the envelope on the table and pointed to it, hoping the contents would answer Madoor's questions. "For my cousin. He's in a hurry, and they have to be good."

"I am a dealer in antiquities."

"I know. *Certo.* But I thought you might ... suggest someone. The people I know do jobs for ... and I can't—I don't—"

"You don't want *Signor* Cubellis to know." Madoor slipped the papers out of the envelope and glanced through them.

"Yeah." *He understands.* A muscle in Gianni's jaw twitched.

"And you can pay—?" Madoor made a circular motion with his hand, encouraging Gianni to provide a figure in the right neighborhood, whatever that might be.

"Ten thousand?"

Madoor snorted. "Ten? For ten, you might obtain a passport of low quality. But not one meeting today's security standards. For the whole set of papers listed here, twenty-five at a minimum."

"Twenty-five? Are you sure?"

"If it is cash. In advance."

It hurt Gianni to surrender such a large portion of his recent windfall, yet he was thrilled he could actually produce such a sum. He licked his thumb, counted out the required bills from the stash in the envelope, and held them out.

By a slight nod, Madoor indicated Gianni should put the money on the table. The young man flushed at his breach in etiquette.

"Where will the documents be delivered?" Madoor asked.

"I could pick them up here?"

"They will never be here."

"His office? He's a *professore* at Sapienza, in the biochemistry and *eccetera* department. The address is in there." He pointed to the large envelope.

"And all the necessary information is there too?"

"I think so."

Madoor spread the envelope contents across the table. He took the papers up again in a particular order, passport-style photographs on top. "They will find your cousin. Anything more?"

"No. Many thanks. I can't—"

Madoor held up a hand. "I am a businessman. You came to do business."

"And you won't tell …"

"Is this his business?"

"No."

Gianni stepped into the alley, and the door clicked firmly behind him. He congratulated himself for remembering Madoor. Climbing onto the Vespa, he muttered, "He's not afraid of anyone."

GENIE

"We can get rid of this," *Dottor* Immormino's nurse said, dropping the gauze and tape she'd removed from my still-healing arm into a waste container. "The arm is good." Maybe *she* thought so. I was glad to be rid of the itchy bandage, but the arm looked terrible to me. Red and still scabby. The small bandage on my left side, where the chest tube had been, also came off.

The nurse peered at the gash on my face, turning my chin this way and that. "Mmmm."

"*Significato?*"

"Better. The butterflies can go." She gently removed them.

She probed the tender stitches on my scalp. "Almost healed. But *Dottor* Immormino will want to leave these in for now."

When Immormino arrived, I complained about how short of breath I was when I tried to walk at anything like a normal pace. "Is my lung really improving?"

On his laptop, he called up the X-ray the radiology clinic next door had taken that morning. "Healing nicely." He gestured to the laptop. "Unfortunately, I don't have the earlier images from the hospital for comparison." He flipped through the thin folder. "They were supposed to be posted to the doctors' private website this morning. But they weren't, so my nurse called. The hospital cannot find your chart."

"Misfiled?"

"They say no. Missing." His fidgeting told me there was more. "The CDs in your hospital chart are copies. The images also should be in the Radiology Department's electronic files. Those are gone too. And your laboratory results." He raised his hands in a helpless gesture. "As far as *Ospidale Fatebenefratelli* is concerned, you were never a patient there."

"Try the billing department."

He shook a finger at me. "My nurse thought of that. You are erased from the system. Gone. If I had not seen you there myself ..."

Agostina broke in. "What are you saying?"

"Why would anyone want to ghost me?"

Was that idiomatic in Italian? But Immormino understood. "Removing your records creates confusion.

There is no way to connect you to the hospital, to that room, in case … there is ever a need."

He might as well have said, "in case something bad happens to you too." Like what happened to poor Gemma. A wave of queasiness hit, as I thought about people—Robbie—searching vainly for a trace of me.

"Wouldn't the nurses and other staff remember me? *You* do."

All too well.

"It's a busy place. Memories are short. And malleable, with the right incentives." He rubbed his fingers over the thumb. He closed the laptop. "I'll see you again Friday." And to Agostina: "Call that detective. Angelini."

LEO

To Leo, the missing medical records meant Genie's attackers were just as interested in her as ever. The case was becoming complicated, and he could no longer delay bringing in a *pubblico ministero*.

He pulled a few strings to get Maximilliano Tati assigned to the case. He'd worked with Tati before and knew he'd be satisfied with regular briefings as long as the detectives made progress. He wouldn't try to take over the investigation, like some public prosecutors. And if the case against Genie's attackers ever went to court, Leo trusted Tati to win it.

The detective arrived at the judiciary complex late Monday afternoon. Tati already had Genie's file open on his desk, and Leo reviewed the facts so far, in detail and without interpretation, omitting only his quietly growing and embarrassingly unprofessional admiration for her.

While Leo talked, Tati swiveled his chair sideways and leaned his tall, spare frame far back into thinking mode. He jotted occasional questions on a pad. An encounter with Tati was never hurried, but the questions kept coming, as his piercing black eyes searched for wavering, for inconsistencies, for gaps in logic. Leo called this approach

"Tati's steamroller," and he'd seen it flatten more than one courtroom witness.

"In sum," Tati said, "you believe the American is the center of the case, and the unfortunate Gemma Capuano was a 'wrong place, wrong time' victim?"

"Yes."

"And now the American is staying with someone you know?"

"She didn't have any family or friends here, and she is still recuperating. Agostina is a nurse and completely trustworthy. It seemed the safest choice, until today. And probably still is."

"Why wouldn't it be?"

"If they do have the medical record, they would have found Immormino's name and could be watching his office. The women could have been seen and followed."

"You have surveillance at the office?"

"Not yet." Leo made a note. "Emilio Bracci will set it up. I've put him in charge of the investigation."

"Out of curiosity, did the women believe they were followed?"

"They say no. *Signora* Clarke understood the potential significance of the missing record, and they left the office by a rear door."

"Where are they now?"

"Home."

Tati thought a while. "There is no reason to suppose *Signora* Clarke has made two sets of enemies since she's been in Rome?" Leo shook his head. "And you believe the same group who attacked her stole her medical record in case it contained clues that would help them find her?"

"Yes. And deleted her electronic records, perhaps to sow confusion."

"Or to make a case against them more difficult, because we would lack details about her injuries."

"We have pictures."

"Safeguard those. Though I prefer the authority of medical documentation. However, it seems there's no longer any reason to keep the hospital under pressure.

Cannot we confirm the death of the Capuano woman was a mistake? That the murderers sought a specific person, and killers are not roaming the halls of *Fatebenefratelli* in search of victims?" He pointed to the ceiling. "Calls are being made." The floors above housed the judiciary's higher levels of authority. Tati's bosses.

"I'll talk with the hospital director about how to handle it. I need to give him a difficult afternoon regarding two other problems, so at least I can offer him that."

"The missing medical record and yesterday's premature revelation?" Tati asked, and Leo nodded. "Return to the original exchange the American overheard. Do we have any idea what the men said that has caused so much trouble?"

"*Signora* Clarke could provide only fragments, and we're working on a reconstruction. The men mentioned the major basilicas, specifically excluding St. Peter's. But we don't know what we're looking for. Two of my detectives spent time yesterday at each of them. Saw nothing."

"Not St. Peter's."

"What the men said was, 'Forget St. Peter's—obviously.'"

"'Obviously.'" Tati rubbed his chin. "Have you contacted Vatican security?"

"I don't know what to tell them."

"Nevertheless, we should do so without delay." Tati possessed a special talent for navigating the byzantine Italian police bureaucracy. "Send them to me. Anything else I can do for you?"

"Possibly. My chief is getting restless about having a man watching Agostina's building twenty-four hours a day—"

"After two attempts on the woman's life? Is he *impazzito*? Does he want another fiasco involving an American?" He uttered an exclamation of disgust. "I'll take care of it. Is it full coverage?"

"Yes. Someone is dropped off for all three shifts."

"Where is your officer? On the street?"

"Yes."

"Consider whether that continues to be the best place. Or the only place."

Leo made another note.

"Is this a mafia situation, in your opinion?" Tati asked.

Leo knew the prosecutor would prefer to avoid involving the interagency Anti-Mafia Investigations Directorate, called the DIA. Competition and poor communication among the civilian police, the military *carabinieri*, and their various subagencies—who does what, who gets the credit—reduced investigations to slow-moving sludge. He said, "The mention of Cubellis, nothing else."

"Your thoughts?"

"Every pickpocket and pimp in Rome tries to clothe himself in some shred of Cubellis's presumed invincibility. There's no way to know yet what it means."

"Then we should not overreact. It raises anxieties in here and out there"—Tati gestured vaguely—"in the real world. *Signora* Clarke has more than enough worries without that."

After an uncomfortable visit with the hospital director, Leo drove to police headquarters and found a pile of messages, including a note from Sal. When he saw Leo headed toward his desk, the young detective grabbed a large envelope. "Something to show you."

They stepped into a conference room, and Sal laid out three large photographs. "I took pictures yesterday in the churches Capizzo and I visited. There's more than a hundred on my computer, but these were the most interesting."

He pointed to the two bottom pictures. "Santa Maria Maggiore, late Sunday afternoon. Crowded with tourists. But see this one guy." With the tip of a pen he pointed out a man wearing black leather talking to a heavyset priest. "In this shot, they're coming up from the crypt. Now here they are, standing at the top of the steps."

He pointed to the photo above. "San Giovanni in Laterano. Right after lunch. See? Same guy. Ponytail, black leather jacket, camera bag under his arm."

The detectives bent over the table.

"I went over every image full screen after I noticed this. He's the only person I found in more than one church. Coincidence? I remembered that black leather sleeve holding the big flowers. And the men at the *caffè* too."

"Good work, Sal." Leo examined the pictures again. "*Un ago in un pagliaio*, and we don't even know which haystack or what the needle is. Any progress with the transcript?

"Maybe. Didn't want to leave this on your desk." Sal pulled a sheet of paper out of the envelope. "The words in bold are hers. I filled in the rest. As best I could."

The older man: **"… Santa Maria Maggiore, San Giovanni in Laterano, San Paolo fuori le Mura, Santa Maria D'Aracoeli, San Pietro in Vincoli."**

Marco (possibly): "On **Sunday. I'll check them all. Forget San Pietro, obviously.** Which one **doesn't matter, the plan stays the same. We need** for this job **one man, maybe two. One would be** enough [not enough? better?]."

One of the young ones: "What does **Cubellis say?"**

They silence him with **"Shut your mouth!"**

"How much time do we have/need?"

"[We have to act] or [Something is happening] **soon.** [We can; Someone will] **deliver it within two weeks …"**

"Marco …" One of them addressing the man with the ponytail.

They notice her and lower their voices so she can't hear anything, and they may be talking about her. The phone rings, and the man with the ponytail answers, "**Marco.**" More evidence that's his name.

Arguing with the person on the phone, the older one says: "**We can't take** [chances?]. The *carabinieri* **station is too** close. I don't/We can't **trust him, anyway. He must come to us** ..." [This could be an expression of trust, but I don't think so, given everything around it.]

"Someplace not/That is **too obvious**."

On the phone: "**Yes, two weeks**! [We'll deliver it/meet him] **where we say**. Someplace **dark, but not isolated**. [We'll/It has to] be **quick**.

Still on phone: "... **Gab(?) Danzio** [A person's name?? Doesn't check out, so far] ... **twenty-two hundred. It can't be too late.**

He listened, then: **Yes, a problem! Americana**!

"Interesting," Leo said. "We can work with this. Excellent work, Sal."

"The key was when I thought about words that sound alike or have multiple meanings. Her *soldato* makes more sense as *isolato*, 'isolated.' I did try *soldato* for a while, but it didn't work with the rest. And, twenty-two hundred might be a time, because then he says 'late.'"

"Ah. Brilliant. Give Bracci a copy. This your only one?"

"Encrypted on my machine."

"In that case, I'll keep it. A question: Do you think your ponytailed man in the Sunday photos is *Signora* Clarke's Marco?"

"That would be a big step forward," Sal said.

"I'll find out."

When Leo entered Agostina's apartment, the women looked worried, and he offered an extra-cheerful greeting. "Good afternoon!" He pulled a chair to Genie's side. "I have something for you." He handed her a document. "A reconstructed transcript of what you overheard. My detective Sal Riccobono put it together. When you have time, see if it sounds right."

"I have nothing but time. We're perishing of boredom here, Leo."

"Well, when you can."

She glanced at the sheet and began to read. "As my mother would say, 'No time like the present.'"

"A woman after my own heart." He'd caught the edge in her voice. "We are trying to move quickly. I hope you understand we are following every lead."

She finally returned his smile, though hers was a little sad. "I do. And I know there aren't many. I just wish this was over with."

"The *pubblico ministero* we have now will be a great help."

"*Pubblico ministero?*"

"Similar to a prosecutor in the States," Leo said. "In larger crimes, public magistrates work in partnership with the police."

"Larger crimes?"

"Your assault became a larger crime when Gemma Capuano was murdered."

"Who is he?" Agostina asked.

"Maximilliano Tati. Already he gave me advice I believe we should follow. Because of the missing medical record, Bracci and I want to add a man inside the apartment. While the medical record doesn't provide this address, it gives other information. Immormino's name, obviously. We have an officer watching his office."

"I can't imagine he's happy about that," Genie said. "He already acts like I have leprosy. But here? That's so—"

"Our officer will be as unobtrusive as possible."

"If we need one, we will have one." Agostina was firm. "After all, Genie is safest here with me."

"Agostina, I—" Genie began.

"Don't apologize," Agostina said.

"I was only going to say—"

"I know you were, *cara*. I *want* to do this. We will keep our lives as normal as possible."

Agostina went into the kitchen to make espresso, and Genie read Sal's transcript. She said, "It does seem plausible. Good options in places. Nothing sounds off to me."

Satisfied with this small step, Leo returned the paper to the envelope and pulled out the photographs. "I'm told you haven't recognized any of the photographs Detective Bracci has shown you. Take a look at these two taken yesterday at Santa Maria Maggiore." He lined them up on the coffee table. "See the fellow talking to the priest? He shows up again in this third picture, from San Giovanni in Laterano, farther in the background."

"Those are popular tourist spots," Agostina said, returning with a tray.

Genie peered at one of the pictures from Santa Maria Maggiore. "He's holding an unusual camera there. Let me see the other one." Agostina slid it closer. "And here the priest is interested in the camera, and the man is covering it with his hands, almost like he's hiding it."

Leo examined them again. "Good eyes. We can try to see what that is."

"Do you know the word 'ponytail'?" she asked, pulling her own short hair together and miming it hanging down.

"*Codino,*" Agostina said.

Genie moved closer to Leo to study the pictures again. "The man has a—*codino?*—and I'm almost positive he was at the *caffè*. The one they called Marco."

CHAPTER—9

Tuesday, October 23

Genie's message to her editor Wally:

Working on fact-checking, then the Rome article is all yours. You'll love it! Great idea!

VENIERI

Pietro Venieri's mother was the first to call with the tragic news—her nephew Gianni di Landri, Venieri's cousin—was dead. Murdered! Venieri listened in shocked silence, while she wept in sympathy for her brother and the notion of a lost child, rather than for the weak-willed, easily misled petty criminal Gianni had become.

Venieri recovered enough to ask "How did—did—?"

Monday night, Gianni's sister Carla went to dinner with friends, his mother said. Her boyfriend had business to attend to and left the party early, but she stayed out longer, in order to avoid Gianni, actually. They had some quarrel going about her cat. When she arrived home, she found him dead. His parents—unaccountably shocked Gianni had died violently—wanted Pietro to give the eulogy.

After the call, he berated himself. Why did he draw Gianni into his problems? He should have known he'd fuck up. Gianni, with his grab bag of loyalties and no head for consequences, must have revealed Venieri's escape plan. Or, his mafia pals got hold of Venieri's papers and the money and drew their own conclusions. But if they'd done this to one of their own …

The eulogy was a bad idea. He'd be out in the open, the center of attention at the damn cemetery. Surrounded by death. He envisioned himself shot and falling into the open grave atop Gianni's casket.

He found a bottle of long-expired pain tablets in his desk and swallowed three of them dry. The phone rang. Carla, crying so hard he could barely decipher her words. "Gianni's dead. Really dead."

"I am so sorry—"

"It shouldn't have happened." Hiccupping sobs drowned her next sentence, but the word "fault" came through sharp as a spear in his belly. "Family should protect each other, not—"

"I'm sure no one in the family would—" What was he saying? Of course they would. "Who's with you?"

"My parents and brothers will never forgive—" a heart-piercing wail. "I shouldn't have called you …" Eventually, he extracted a little information. She'd slept the previous night at a friend's apartment. The police would let her back into the house now. Her parents and brothers were on their way, driving down from Modena. Four hours at least. Great. There'd be time to look for his envelopes.

"I'll be there as quickly as I can."

"Fault" was not a word he wanted to hear. Especially with Carla's simian brothers on the way.

GENIE

On Tuesday, finally, finally, finally, I felt well enough and had enough energy to do something productive. I spent the morning polishing my article for Wally, consulting my notes, surrounded by postcards and brochures for fact-checking.

I messaged him:

> *Article all yours soon. Just a couple of details to pin down. Yay, wi-fi!*

I scrolled through the draft, not satisfied. Those few details must have been knocked right out of my head. I didn't have the address for a new church opening in

November, and since it was new, no website. I couldn't remember the name of the *trattoria* near the Spanish Steps with the *straordinario* young chef, and if I'd made notes about a charming new shoe shop around the corner from the restaurant, I couldn't find them. Though I did buy three pairs of shoes. Agostina checked the boxes to see if I'd stashed my notes inside.

"Let's run over there," I suggested. "The church, then the Spanish Steps."

"We must ask Leo," Agostina said.

"He'll make us take—" I gestured toward the living room, where Bracci's man—a woman this morning—paced in front of the tall windows.

"Our baby minder." Agostina made a face. "What a *brontolona*."

"In English, we say 'sourpuss.' She hates being here with nothing to do. But if we finish this," I waved my list of loose ends, "we, at least, will have accomplished something!" Getting out of the apartment, even briefly, was a delightful prospect.

Agostina had her cell phone in her hand. "No Leo. Voicemail," she said. She left a cheerful message saying we were making a quick trip to the Spanish Steps and would be home—I mouthed "lunch" and patted my stomach—after *pranzo*.

When we explained our errand to Officer Torre, she said, "I cannot allow it. It could be a risk."

"How could we run into any problems on the Piazza di Spagna at a nice restaurant or, for heaven's sake, a ladies' shoe shop! Perfectly respectable and safe. And we have to eat. I need to get the facts right for my article, my work. I can't just let it go. People rely on me." I was learning the Italian art of piling on arguments from hearing Agostina on the phone with her sisters.

"As they rely on me. I will go with you."

Torre not only went, she commandeered the front passenger seat.

Verifying the address of the new church was easy, and near the Spanish Steps, we were three among scores of window-shopping tourists. At the shoe shop—notebook and pen in hand this time—I interviewed the ebullient owner. She was happy to answer questions, but dismayed to see my injuries, fading but still evident.

Where Via dei Condotti ended at the Piazza di Spagna, three competing restaurants vied for street space, distinguishable by the colors of their umbrellas—black, red, or green. "Black umbrellas. That's the one. *Il Girasole*." I wrote it down. "Can we have lunch there?"

"Not out here. Inside." Officer Torre gestured with her chin. The outdoor tables for all three restaurants were full in any case, with many people waiting.

"At least close to the French doors." I said a silent "Please!"

"*French* doors? *Portefinestre*, please," Agostina said.

"What I meant to say."

We climbed the four steps to the restaurant proper. With little room to maneuver between tables, I had to twist my torso to ease into a chair, which hurt, of course. I was immediately distracted by the lively scene below and the freedom of a lovely afternoon. "Excellent people-watching here."

Agostina, still studying her menu, agreed.

An affectionate couple strolled down the street. *That should be Leo and me*, I thought, and had an irrational pang of jealousy. Just then our waiter arrived, and I hastily ordered the first thing on the menu, sure my face was as red as the umbrellas across the way. I had no claim on Leo. He was an attractive man, and I wouldn't be the only woman to notice. Probably there *were* other women. The pointlessness of my infatuation hit hard, and the meal I'd so looked forward to tasted like dust in my mouth.

MARCO

On the side of the street opposite *Il Girasole*, in the hellish glow of sunlight filtered through red umbrellas, Nic and Marco lounged at a table that belonged to the least expensive of the three restaurants, their leather jackets slung over chair backs. Marco's head still ached from his encounter with Umberto, and he washed down a painkiller with beer.

"Where's Gianni?" Nic asked.

"Fucker's always late. I'm ordering."

Nic ran a hand through his disheveled blond hair, his nearly colorless eyes fixed on something across the way. "What the fuck—"

Following his gaze, Marco glimpsed three women who stood in the street, talking, then climbed the restaurant steps. "Isn't that the American?" he asked.

"Dunno," Nic said. The women took seats near the front of the restaurant, and one lowered a distinctive yellow bag to the floor. "It's her, man." Excitement colored his voice.

"You sure?" This time? was unspoken. Marco could almost believe the woman was a phantom. Not only did Nic claim to see her several times a day, but for days, Marco had believed he and Lama had murdered her. Maybe she wasn't meant to be killed.

"It's her. Two bitches with her." Nic was definite.

"I see them … I *know* one of them! The one in the white shirt. She's a fucking *poliziotta*."

"You *know* her?"

"She's Enzo Torre's cousin. He pointed her out to me at a concert. We didn't talk to her. 'Too embarrassing,' he said."

"Enzo Torre?"

They laughed to think this police officer was related to Enzo Torre, who committed at least one crime every day just on principle.

"Your call, Nic. Now what?"

Nic was in the most trouble about the American because Umberto said everything that came after was trying to correct his original failure. Even though Umberto roughed up Marco and Lama on Sunday, he later conceded they'd received bad information, and since that information came from Umberto's own source, he let the subject drop.

"I want another chance at her. Let's follow them."

The overlapping umbrellas screened them from the women's direct view. They ate quickly and settled their bill, ready to leave whenever the women did. When the women paid and left the table, they didn't reappear on the restaurant steps.

"Taking a piss?" Nic said.

"Don't they always?"

The delay lengthened. "Check it out," Nic said. "That *troia* would recognize me, man."

Marco grabbed his jacket and sauntered across the way, dodging tables and chairs, hands in his jeans pockets. Once inside the restaurant, he worked his way unhurriedly toward a rear door. It opened onto an empty hallway with two doors for the toilets, a third open partway, soda crates and cleaning supplies stacked inside, and at the far end, an exit.

He cocked his head to the ladies' room door. No voices. He pushed it open. Empty.

Now he moved swiftly. The exit door led to a small platform littered with cigarette butts. Metal steps descended to a narrow alley between buildings, and the alley led to the street parallel to Via dei Condotti. The women progressed at a leisurely pace up the alley and had almost reached the next street, where they could go in many directions.

He jogged back through the restaurant, bumping a waiter carrying a heavy tray of plates. Curses trailed him. Outside, he grabbed Nic's arm. "Next block!" They pinballed through the crowd of pedestrians channeled into the tight path between the restaurants' tables.

Peering around the corner of the next street, they couldn't see the women. "Must be somewhere close," Marco said over his shoulder, as they loped down Via delle Carrozze, the street where the alley emerged. The women might have gone into one of the shops. Or to a first-floor office. Across the street another much wider alley connected to streets where cars were permitted.

Marco and Nic idled near the end of the narrow alley, ready to duck into it if the women approached. Marco lit a cigarette and with half-closed eyes studied the pedestrians. In the wide alley across the way, a rolling metal garage door rattled up. Nic squatted behind a trash can, out of view. Marco slouched against the alley wall. A car emerged, turned, and drove away. The *poliziotta* up front, the American in back.

"It's them," Marco said. Nic popped up.

Side by side they watched the departing car. Marco had a plan in mind. Women liked his rough charm and, with an introduction from cousin Enzo, his next move would be easy.

GENIE

When our car rounded the curve of Agostina's street, Leo was on the sidewalk ahead, talking and gesticulating to the plainclothes officer. The man nodded, pointing at the car, and Leo's head snapped in our direction, every muscle of his face pulled into a frown. I knew at once why he was angry. We shouldn't have gone.

He followed us into the apartment barely able to control an eruption of words.

Once the apartment door closed, I said, "My fault totally. I needed a few small pieces of information to finish my article, and we ran out for just a short while … lunch …" Confronted with Leo's rigid expression, I rattled on. "Leo, it was the middle of the day. There were *tons* of people. It wasn't dangerous."

I pressed my lips together. "Tons of people" cut both ways.

Leo turned to Officer Torre. "And?" His tone would stop a charging bull.

"I saw nothing alarming. At the restaurant, such a large number of people …" She bristled and wouldn't meet Leo's eyes. "We left by a rear door. No one followed."

"Wait out there." He pointed to the patio. "Shut the door behind you."

I shifted foot to foot like a nervous schoolchild, as the scarlet-faced Torre left us. She'd made it clear guarding me was beneath her, and now the assignment was going to cause her trouble.

"And you?" he said to Agostina, who studied the carpet.

"I'm not sure … when I drove out of the parking garage, I saw a man in my rearview mirror. Across the street. He glanced in our direction, and when he turned away, I saw his ponytail. *Possibly* he's the man in your photos."

"I can't believe it!" Leo said. "How could you be so irresponsible!"

We were clustered in the middle of the living room, Leo's six feet looming over us.

"Please, Leo," I said, panicking. What if that really *was* the man from the photos? "It was all my idea. I'm so sorry."

Agostina sat down, and Leo leaned over me, his flushed face in mine. "You know you've endangered yourself and Agostina? If those men have connections, they will know where you are before the end of the day." His deep voice thundered.

"But how? They didn't follow us." My conviction wavered, gathered steam, and came at him. "We're not prisoners here. Or are we? Is *that* your job? Our jailer?" The rash words flew out of my mouth. I was being unfair and I knew it, which only made me angrier.

"The car has a *targa*," he said.

"A—?"

"Number plate. That's how they will find you."

Before that moment, I would have sworn I was fully aware of the danger hovering darkly on the distant horizon. Yet I'd let Agostina and Leo insulate me with their care and attention, built up a false sense of security. The dinners, the strolls around the garden, wi-fi—a parade of simple, familiar things—had created the illusion of comfort, of normalcy.

Now the immediacy of the peril descended like a hurricane. Nightmare scenes flashed through my mind. Not only was I vulnerable. Agostina too. Maybe even Leo. Taking safety for granted, for just a few hours, had been a dangerous miscalculation. The most painful realization was that even the people closest to me couldn't trust my judgment.

"Oh my god." The strength went out of my legs, and I deflated into a chair.

"We both decided to go," Agostina said quietly.

"I can't believe this." Leo paced the living room and chopped the air with his open hands. "How could this happen? Where was common sense?" He whirled toward me.

"Stop yelling at me! I *know* it was my fault. I *know* I made an awful mistake. I *get* that. You don't need to keep saying it." I was near tears. "Tell me what I can *do* about it."

"We can't undo it!" His arms flailed.

"I *know* that."

"But why did you do it?"

The question seemed pointless, but the distress within it intensified the storm of my emotions. "Because I want my life back! I'm tired of being in pain, tired of taking drugs that exhaust me, and really, really tired of living by other people's rules. Strangers' rules. I don't understand what these criminals want. I don't know them. Why are they in charge of my life? I want to do normal things in a normal way like a normal person without jeopardizing people I care about." Including you, Leo. Surely the look I gave him made that clear.

I struggled to stand. My hands were fists with nothing to strike. Though only across the room, Leo might as well have been a thousand miles away. Fear and disappointment burst out of me as anger.

"Nothing makes sense anymore, Leo. I hope you understand that." I took a ragged breath. "Right now I'm tired of everything. Mostly myself." I walked haltingly to my room and closed the door, knowing that two inches of wood could never shut out everything arrayed against me.

VENIERI

The vinegar tang of an apple orchard sharpened the late-season air of the neighborhood where Gianni had lived. Venieri surveyed the row of modest two-story houses, whose weedy yards stretched to railroad tracks running behind. A pale gold ruff of tall grass surrounded his cousins' house.

On the far side of the orchard, no more than a kilometer away, Ciampino Airport spread over many flattened acres, providing a backdrop of unceasing noise and explaining why Gianni could afford this place. Hoarse barking came from one of the yards, regular as a heartbeat. A man yelled. The barking sped up.

Venieri knocked, and the front door opened. He steeled himself and walked inside. Carla was sunk into the sofa, friends tiered around her. Her ever-present boyfriend lounged in the kitchen doorway.

Muttering apologies, Venieri broke through Carla's protective circle and bent to embrace her. Act normal, he told himself. Innocent. "Oh, Carla, *amore mio*, I'm so, so sorry. I know how much you loved him." He tilted her chin to study her reddened eyes. Again he embraced her tightly and whispered in her ear. "This was the fault of the criminals who murdered him. No one else's."

He said to the friends, "Do the police know ...?"

"No, *Professore*. They have told her nothing."

Guilt corroding his heart, he held Carla until her sobs quieted. When he withdrew, the circle of young women closed around her. He glanced behind him, found the stairway to the bedrooms, and edged over to it.

At the top of the stairs on the left was a sparsely furnished bedroom. Its sole decoration was Carla's clothing scattered on the unmade bed. To the right, past the bathroom, police tape closed off a short hall leading to Gianni's room. Venieri stepped over the tape and tiptoed to the doorway, where he encountered the dusty smell of a room too long shut up.

The police had made a thorough job of it. Dark smears of fingerprint powder marked every surface the intruder might have touched, including the bedside table, its empty drawer lolling like a tongue. The doorless closet held a few pieces of dark clothing and several tumbled-together pairs of shoes. No dresser. Folded underwear and socks were in surprisingly neat stacks on the deep windowsill. The police had stripped away the pillows, blankets, and sheets, and the dirty mattress lay askew, as if lifted for a search. Nothing was on the floor under the bed except clumps of whitish lint.

Venieri stopped short of entering the room. His envelopes weren't there. No papers of any kind. Somehow, Gianni had sailed through life without the mile-wide wake of paper that trailed Venieri. He stepped into the bathroom and shut the door. Hand wrapped in a towel, he opened the cabinets and reached behind the toilet. Nothing.

A sharp noise from the yard jolted him out of his thoughts, followed by a commotion and a wail that only his aunt could produce. Gianni's family and their grief filled the room below. At the bottom of the stairs, Venieri embraced one of the brothers. "I wanted to see where it happened," he said, explaining himself unnecessarily. "Such a tragedy." The brother stared at him, unblinking.

After an hour of commiseration and tears, he slipped into the kitchen and quietly searched it too. If the envelopes had been in the house the previous night, the killer—or the police—took them.

The afternoon dragged on. No one paid him any special attention. His confidence grew. It didn't appear Carla would accuse him to the family after all. He picked a white hair off his dark suit and decided he could decently leave.

Outside, the airplanes continued to roar, but at least that dog had stopped barking.

CHAPTER—10

Wednesday, October 24

MADOOR

"It's tomorrow for sure," Vittorio Cima said as Amit Madoor led him to the familiar chair in front of his massive desk.

"Already I have a few nibbles of interest," Madoor said, "and we will soon learn whether the big fish will bite."

"You're confident they'll keep quiet?"

"If they do not, *Signore*, they will have a hard time explaining to their national authorities why they possess certain artworks whose ownership is, at best, in dispute."

"Understood. One of our men will join us this morning—the one who will give your people the package."

A single thump rattled the door, it opened, and a third man stepped into the shop.

Cima glanced over his shoulder. "Umberto Ricci." Cima was sparing with words, but never rude. Madoor walked over to shake the newcomer's hand and lock the door. He studied the new man to learn why Cima so obviously disliked him. Madoor's success—and occasionally his life—depended on seeing beneath a person's public exterior. Underneath Umberto's bespoke suit, he detected a savage.

"I told Madoor it's tomorrow," Cima said.

Umberto sprawled in the chair beside Cima. He pulled a case from his pocket and extracted a silver toothpick, which he waggled between his front teeth. "We'll do our part." He jabbed the toothpick toward Madoor. "You be ready."

Madoor inwardly recoiled, though he kept his voice level. "And where will this transfer take place?" He put his fingertips together and tapped his lips lightly. "There's my place here, but it is not ideal."

"Too close to the *carabinieri* station," Umberto said. He crossed his legs.

"That is not a problem in itself. The problem will be getting your package out of the central city if everyone is searching for it. And will they be?"

"Oh, yes." The toothpick continued its work. "That's why we *will* keep it in the center until the main search moves away."

"You have a safe place?"

"Perfectly safe. I found it myself."

Madoor raised an eyebrow. "Why don't we do the transfer there?"

"Impossible." Umberto's quick response signaled a lack of trust. "The police will expect us to move fast. By nighttime they will be scattered. Airport searches, roadblocks. Meanwhile our little package has traveled only a few blocks."

"Little?"

Umberto made a rough size estimate with his hands. "Not too big."

"No, not too big. But yet, not small. If you don't give it to me here or at your place, where do you have in mind?" The wiggling toothpick reminded Madoor of the jerking leg of a half-swallowed locust.

"There's a little pull-off on Viale Gabriele D'Annunzio, above the Piazza del Popolo. Dark as pitch. Many roads lead away. Our people—yours too—can melt into the traffic."

Madoor knew the spot, directly under the Monte Pincio overlook. "If you will excuse me, that sounds insane."

Umberto's vulpine features sharpened. "It is unusual. That's why we like it. No one will suspect what occurs there."

"People are always on the overlook."

"Not so many after sunset, after tourist season. And that's what they are doing. Looking over. Looking to the lights of San Pietro, the piazza. Not looking at a couple of unmarked delivery vans below them in the dark." The toothpick caught the light.

Madoor asked Cima, "What do you think?"

"We tested it last night," Cima said. "The vehicles can park next to each other, staying mostly hidden. One of our men watched the tourists. No one paid any attention. There's one streetlight, and tomorrow night there will be none. The trees also provide cover."

Madoor offered his guests cigarettes. Cima took one. Madoor lit it for him and one for himself.

"May I ask how long the item will be in your possession?"

"What do you mean?"

"When—what time—do you plan to take it?"

"None of your business." Umberto's jaw thrust forward.

Madoor encouraged smoke from his cigarette to create a flimsy curtain between them. "The longer it's in your possession, the greater the chance you are found and followed. I won't send my people into a trap."

"We're taking it tomorrow, early afternoon. Tomorrow night, it's yours."

Madoor's workers would have almost two days to plan their own security measures. Plenty of time. But the transfer logistics were hazardous.

"And you cannot tell me what it is?"

Cima flung his arm across Umberto's chest. "Not yet," Cima said. "Despite the confidence of our friend here, the theft itself has risks."

"What type of vehicle do we need?" Madoor asked.

"A normal delivery van. Dark color. No windows." Umberto said.

"How many men will you have?"

"Four. I'll drive and stay in the van. We'll have a lookout and two men to move the package."

"I will send two men." Not counting himself, parked out of view around the street's sharp bend, his gun out of its hidden compartment, loaded and on the seat beside him.

"Where will you take it?" Umberto asked.

"That must be *my* secret," Madoor answered. "And the time?"

"Ten at night. Twenty-two, if you prefer."

"How will my men know you?"

"You want a password?" Umberto snickered.

"A precaution."

"'Santa Maria Maggiore.'"

Cima glared at him.

Madoor took a new burner phone from the top drawer of his desk and scribbled the number on a piece of paper. "Any problems, call this number." He handed the paper across the wide desk.

Umberto pulled out the slim silver case and stowed the toothpick. He waved at the cases of phony artifacts behind him. "Why do you take chances with this shit?"

Cima shifted in his chair.

After a pause, Madoor said, "If through some calamity the *polizia* ever have suspicions about me, one glimpse of my shop and they will laugh in my face." He shrugged, palms up, and adopted a shame-faced grin, a petty criminal caught fleecing tourists. "True, they might get an amount of cash from me, time to time. However, if I presented myself as a legitimate businessman, they might decide to dig deeper."

Umberto snorted.

"Let's go," Cima said.

Madoor closed the door behind them and locked it again. From a shelf he pulled a thick catalog of the splendid and irreplaceable ornaments of Catholic Rome.

GENIE

I woke Wednesday morning unrested and hungry. I'd skipped dinner and huddled in my room the night before, trapped in mental and emotional quicksand. If only I could start over. I laughed bitterly. Start over from when? Before the quarrel with Leo? Before our ill-advised outing? Before I precipitously left the hospital, exposing the innocent

Gemma to her killers? Before I decided to have that cup of espresso? Before I got on the plane to Rome?

I couldn't rewrite one word of that script, and the scenes ahead looked increasingly perilous. Gemma's murder proved what the gang members could do—would do—if they had a chance. And a chance is what I'd handed them.

I was trapped. I couldn't travel yet, and there was Gemma. I owed her. Even at home, couldn't the long arm of the Mafia reach out to me? Maybe I'd watched *The Godfather* too many damn times. But maybe it could.

Compared to all that, my confrontation with Leo and the rupture of the bond between us shouldn't have mattered, but it did, I'd counted on him to be a valuable ally in bringing Gemma's killers to justice. He'd make the arrests; I'd be the reliable courtroom witness. But yesterday I discovered how much he meant to me, and now our alliance was broken before either of us could get what we wanted. No matter what that was or might have been.

Agostina knocked and opened the door a few inches. "*Che diavolo!*" She stepped into the room.

I was standing in front of the open patio door, feet wide apart, toes pointed in, folded in half, the top of my head nearly touching the floor. "Yoga. I'm so stiff. My left side is a mess."

"Trouble sleeping?" She picked up the litter of wadded tissues by the bed.

"I'm sorry. Bad night. Agostina, I'm so sorry."

"Please."

"It was unforgivable. I fooled myself into believing I could behave like I always do, even though way over there"—I stood and gestured vaguely into the distance—"these men wanted to find me. Even after Gemma Capuano was killed, I couldn't *really* imagine it would touch me—much less you—like it has. I wanted to feel safe, so I convinced myself I *am* safe and walked right into this danger. Now I don't know what to do."

"Protecting us—both of us—is Leo's department."

I rotated my torso to face Agostina and lifted my arms toward the ceiling, Warrior One position. I could straighten my scabby right arm, but on the left, the broken ribs side, my hand barely reached my ear.

"See what I mean?" I winced. "I know you admire Leo, but we can't—" I rephrased the thought. "Leo's doing his best, I truly believe that. But we can't *only* rely on the police to sort things out. We—I—have to—I don't know—be thinking, be ready, *do* something, while not exposing ourselves, myself, to risk again."

Agostina studied me. "He wants us to, as you say, 'sit tight' for another day or two. This situation is not our fault. It's those beasts who are after you."

"I'm not good at waiting. I like doing."

"Um-hmm."

I turned toward Agostina and stretched out my arms into Warrior Two. "I can't face him."

"*Cara!* Leo understands we do not want to be prisoners here. We want to go out and enjoy our lunch and should be free to do so. He wants that for us. Just not right now."

"I've let him down."

"We are all on edge. He's frustrated he cannot find these terrible men, but he will. They must be stopped."

My warrior thought precisely.

VENIERI

That Wednesday morning, a pile of phone messages awaited Venieri in his office. Several about the funeral. A few from people with university extensions whose names he didn't recognize—his students, probably. Three from Rosa Lisi, the annoying journalist. With a snort he balled her messages and tossed them at the wastebasket. Missed. He switched on his computer.

A knock surprised him. He swung his chair to face the door. "*Entrare!*"

Rosa Lisi strode in carrying two paper cups. "Good morning, Pietro! I brought us coffee. It's from the Porta Maggiore, so I hope it isn't terrible." She placed a cup in front of each of them, slid her heavy bag off her arm, and settled into the visitor's chair.

"I phoned you yesterday, but you didn't return my calls," she said, blue eyes pinning him to his chair.

"I left early," he said. "A cousin died. I didn't see your messages until this morning." His glance flicked to the crumpled slips around the wastebasket and hers followed.

She smiled. "I want to know why you stonewalled me Sunday. You're Italy's leading Alzheimer's expert, yet you said nothing. My instincts are screaming, 'Venieri. You are hiding something.' Yesterday, when I couldn't talk to you, I talked to your colleagues, of course."

"Of course. Whom, may I ask?"

She waved the question away. "No matter. They all said exactly the same. You expected a big breakthrough last week. You were mysterious about specifics, but—what did they say?—'practically jumping out of his chair with excitement.'" Venieri was too busy berating himself to interject. She leaned in. "Why did you hold out on me? I tried and tried to get you to talk about your research, but you kept blathering—'chain of research' and all that crap. Come on, Venieri, up your game." From her bag she pulled out notebook and pen. "Now. I'm writing an article for *ANSA*. Redeem yourself."

"*ANSA?*"

"The news service, Pietro. Italian and English. Everybody knows it. Focus."

"English?"

"Yes. And other languages too maybe. Whatever, it's read. Widely."

"What do you want to know?" He tried to sound cooperative.

"Not about the chain of research, I assure you. What's your link in it? Specifically. What was the big breakthrough?"

Pedaling fast and going nowhere, he said, "I didn't talk about it on Sunday because I don't know yet what I have. Last week I did get new data, and when I'm finished analyzing them, I may have pieces of the picture, but the analytic process takes—"

"Venieri. I said 'no crap.' That's not jump-out-of-your-chair exciting."

"Yes it is. Really. We've been inputting data for months. This was the first output."

"And?"

He wagged his head side to side. "Inconclusive." It was the best he could do. "At first pass. So now I'm digging deeper. As I knew I would have to. And you *know* this, Rosa," he wheedled, "sometimes a treatment that doesn't work in the population at large will work for certain subgroups. If I can determine *why* it works for them, I can adjust the treatment so it works for more people. But I needed that big bolus of data first."

He pleaded. "Rosa, that *is* exciting. But would the *Telegiornale* audience understand that? What was I to say? We have a million numbers? It would be a disservice to your viewers, to people with Alzheimer's in the family, to hint a cure is imminent." *Like you did*, he glowered.

Rosa wasn't writing anything. "What are you hiding?"

"What's to hide?" He lifted his hands.

"What does the Spellini Foundation say these days? How satisfied are they with your exciting progress?"

Oh, she was smart. He gulped coffee. She waited, pen poised. Now he could say what he'd forgotten to mention on Sunday and pray she'd use it. "Smart foundations know basic research pays off long-term. If they want quick results, they build clinics or send vaccines to Africa or something." He avoided her direct gaze. "I am extremely proud of my long-term association with such a generous and far-sighted organization as the Spellini Foundation."

She rolled her eyes and pursed her lovely lips. "How does your treatment work? Or, rather, *if* it worked, how would it work?"

Venieri ignored the thrust. "Since the exact causes of Alzheimer's remain in doubt, we can't work on primary prevention yet. Instead, we must stop the disease as early as possible."

She puffed in irritation, and he continued, "In theory, we could stop it chemically, or biologically, with stem cells, maybe, or other genetic techniques. My approach is chemical, that's all I can say."

"Lots of chemical treatments—drugs—have been tried before. What makes yours different?"

"I'm sorry, Rosa." He mimicked disappointment. "Nondisclosure agreements. You know." He splayed his hands on the desktop, smiling. Somewhere in that mess of papers were the university's unsigned forms.

LEO

After the disastrous scene at Agostina's apartment, Leo stayed at his desk until nearly midnight, with little to show for it. Later, thoughts of Genie intruded on his sleep. Eventually, tired of tossing, he lumbered out of bed, showered, and dressed. He reached the *questura* before dawn on Wednesday.

When his detectives arrived, he learned they'd found the shop whose stolen flowers ended up in Gemma Capuano's hospital room. The deliveryman spat when they showed him the photographs. Those flowers cost him a week's overtime pay. Much as he wanted to, he couldn't tell them anything about the thieves.

At Leo's regular meeting with Tati, the magistrate tilted his chair and mused aloud. "You see these people?" He waved to the framed photographs lining his walls, pictures of famous people he'd met—famous in crime circles.

"I recognize a few."

"These are my unpaid assistants. Judges, attorneys, detectives, victims, suspects I've convicted. That picture on the end—" Tati pointed "—is me with the head of the U.S. FBI. They sent it after some work we did together."

"Your assistants?"

"Yes. They help me remember. Often a case we prosecuted long ago sheds light on some new situation. But when it comes to your American, my assistants are failing me." He paused, hands on his stomach, fingers tapping together. "What's their game? If these *furfanti* indeed saw the license plate yesterday, as you suspect, and they know where she may be, why are they holding off?"

"Our surveillance?" Leo suggested. "Waiting until she's more exposed?"

"If so, they would be watching the house. But your people haven't detected that."

"No."

"It's been only a day since the—shall we say 'security breach'—at the Spanish Steps. They could be working out a plan of attack."

"Or maybe *Signora* Clarke isn't their top priority," Leo said. This idea was the only possibly useful insight gleaned during his restless night.

Tati's eyes widened.

Leo continued, "Think again about what she overheard in the Piazza del Popolo. The men were planning something involving churches. And you've seen the pictures from the basilicas with the man *Signora* Clarke identified."

"Scouting them?"

"Maybe. Whatever they were planning was supposed to take place 'within two weeks.' That could be this coming Sunday."

Tati pursed his lips. "With their big project pending, they can't afford the distraction? Pursuing *Signora* Clarke now, if it went wrong, could jeopardize the other?"

"It's my best theory." His only theory.

"Then perhaps the other is what we should worry about."

Leo couldn't keep the frustration out of his voice. "The problem is, where to begin? And, will we know about 'the other' when it happens?"

Tati withdrew a folder from the stack on his desk. "See what you think about this case, brought to me yesterday afternoon. The summary will do."

Leo read quickly. "I know about this one. Gianni di Landri. A low-level mobster in the Cubellis organization. A couple of our detectives are on it. Nothing so far."

"I thought it interesting," the prosecutor said. "You will have noted the mention of the snake tattoo. This man, with many recent bruises, strangled in his bed. Gemma Capuano, smothered in hers. An unfortunate coincidence? Or must we Romans abandon sleep altogether?"

Leo guessed Tati had noted his haggard appearance. But the detective could only shrug. The gulf between him and Genie produced an almost physical, sleep-depriving pain. With as much energy as he could muster, he said, "I'll ask Detective Bracci to look for a link. We'll get pictures and show them to Gen … *Signora* Clarke." His mind had stuttered, thinking about the next time he would see her.

CHAPTER—11

Thursday, October 25

Genie's Message to Wally:

Big Rome news. Unbelievable. You published special article on SMMaggiore two years ago. Heartbreaking.

MARCO

At six a.m. Marco lay in bed, staring at the ceiling, anticipating the alarm clock's buzz. He could almost hear Gianni insisting he check and recheck his preparations, asking endless questions, bitching about Umberto. Gianni should have been here, Marco thought. He deserved to be in on the finish.

At six-thirty Marco left the apartment and traveled twenty minutes to a disused and dirty garage. He exchanged his leather gloves for vinyl ones and unrolled a large sheet of clean paper. He arrayed the tools they'd need in front of him—wiping down each one, testing its weight, and laying it on the paper. Useful items, carefully chosen and well maintained. Although they undoubtedly would do the job, he was beginning to wonder whether the job was worth doing, without his partner. As long as Gianni was alive, Marco kept his reservations at bay. But now …

A motorbike entered the alley and switched off. Soon a key tickled the garage's new side door lock.

"Turn on some lights, man." Nic stepped inside. "You here?"

"Yeah." A dim bulb barely lit his work area, and Marco patted the wall behind him to find the switch for the overheads. "Didn't want to show too much light."

"It's fucking morning now." Nic pointed to a weak glow from the garage's grimy window. He plopped onto a wooden crate and yawned. "What's all this?"

"Tools go in this bag," Marco pointed to the smaller of two oversized canvas carryalls, "and *gigante* is for later. We need to put something heavy inside to give it weight. See what you can find."

Nic hoisted himself off the crate.

"Gloves. Wear the fucking gloves." Marco tossed Nic a pair.

Grumbling, Nic snapped them on and toured the garage perimeter. He returned with a greasy, shapeless mass.

"What the hell is that?"

Nic bent over and let the thing clunk to the floor alongside the large bag. "Stripped down engine block from a Fiat 850."

"What's it weigh?"

"About twenty kilos. Flimsy piece of crap."

"It's filthy. Wrap it in something so we don't fuck up the inside of the bag."

Nic made another circuit of the garage and returned with a sizeable drop cloth. Paint-splattered, but dry. "Best I can find."

"OK. They'll be here soon." They wrapped the engine and crammed it into the larger bag. "Now we wait."

Nic played with a ratchet wrench, testing which finger it fit best. "You going to Gianni's funeral?"

"No," Marco said. The thought of it made him sick. Gianni was one of the first friends he made when he moved to Rome, and losing him—especially that way—

"You two were tight. What happened, man?"

Marco grunted. He didn't know who killed Gianni, or why. He suspected Umberto, but the man was so well connected within Cubellis's organization, he might get away with it. And he had to keep his mouth shut. Very possibly, the murder was a warning to him too.

Umberto, along with Marco's cousin Lama, arrived in a nondescript black van Lama had stolen overnight. It filled the garage's single bay.

The four men crouched, campfire-style, around the carefully packed canvas bags. Umberto barked out questions, double-checking what Marco had triple-checked already.

"You get the letter?" he asked. Marco didn't reply. *Asshole.* He put on a fresh pair of gloves before pulling a stiff envelope out of an inside jacket pocket. He showed the letter around. Printed at the top were the Vatican's unmistakable triple-tiered crown and crossed keys in gold and silver. The letter was purportedly from the Department of Technical Services, Building Services Division, Extraterritorial Properties Unit, and described emergency repairs that must be made *today* to the crypt floor of His Holiness the Pope's Basilica, Santa Maria Maggiore.

In the several hours before they would leave for the basilica, Umberto gave them niggling jobs. He set Lama to work changing the van's license plates. He sent Marco and Nic to trace the route from the garage to the basilica and back, checking for road repairs, detours, unexpected police presence.

"He's got a flea up his ass this morning," Nic muttered, as they climbed onto Marco's bike. Marco gave the Vespa a jolt of gas.

When they reported nothing unusual, Umberto sent them out again, this time to inspect the streets from the garage to the drop-off point they'd use that night. By the time they returned, Umberto and Lama had spread a new plastic sheet on the van floor and covered the seats with plastic bags. They'd remove them when they abandoned the van, leaving behind no Vespa tire prints and no hairs or fibers or other microscopic remains of themselves for the police to find.

Umberto lurked behind Lama at a workbench littered with different types of electrical wire. He watched the younger man practice how he would disable the crypt's alarm, getting used to working with the gloves on. When Marco and Nic came up on Lama's other side, he never broke concentration, but Umberto looked over. His narrowed gaze settled on Marco. What was Umberto thinking?

What Marco was thinking was that the way they'd avoided speaking of Gianni—his best friend always—made his absence even more conspicuous.

NIC

"Get a real spot, man," Nic said from the back of the van, when Umberto double-parked outside Santa Maria Maggiore shortly after noon.

Umberto growled. At that moment a black limousine pulled out of a parking place just ahead and stopped closer to the basilica. Umberto eased into the space. Several high-ranking members of the basilica staff—their black garb limned in red—climbed into the waiting car, which pulled out heedless of traffic and earned itself a few horn blasts.

Another flock of priests exited the basilica and walked away.

"Here we go," Nic said, as he and Lama clambered onto the pavement, wearing Vatican maintenance uniforms and hard hats. As expected, they found the basilica relatively empty. The tourists had mostly left for lunch, like a school of fish that had suddenly changed direction.

"Check it out," Nic muttered, indicating a lone priest whom he recognized from Marco's description. "We ignore him." When they set up safety barriers marked "Do Not Cross" atop both sets of crypt stairs, the priest ambled over.

"I'm Father Maratea. What are you—?"

"Good afternoon, Father." Nic grinned, delighted and upbeat. "We're here to repair the wiring under the crypt floor."

"The—?"

"The wiring under the floor."

"It works perfectly."

Nic turned serious. "Hard to tell, Father. The chief inspector stopped by last week with his voltage tachometer. He says there's an uneven current. It's only a matter of time until we have a fire or—"

"His what?"

"Voltage tachometer, Father." Nic sped ahead. "Only a matter of time until—"

Father Maratea held up a hand. "You said fire? This building is stone. Stone doesn't burn."

"Sure, the parts we see are stone, but underneath there's subflooring and sub-subflooring. Who knows what flammable materials they used hundreds of years ago and in all the renovations since? And there's the wires themselves. Fire can race along those wires until it finds something that *will* burn."

"But you can't do this *today*. It's the twenty-fifth, the monthly anniversary of Jesus's birth. People come specifically to see the crib. From around the world."

Who gives a fuck? Nic thought. Not him. "We have to do it today." He pulled out the magic letter and held it for the priest to read, not letting go. "Emergency work. Thursday is a light visitor day."

"Thursday may *usually* be a light day," Father Maratea frowned, trying to remember whether this was so, "but *this* Thursday is the twenty-fifth. Not light at all."

"We have to do it today. We can't expose hundreds of weekend tourists to the risk of a major combustion event. Toxic fumes."

"You must ask Monsignor Goodnard about this. He is out now, but he will be back—"

Nic glanced around and sniffed the air, frowning. "The quicker we get going, the sooner we're done," he said. "Noon is a good time. We should finish by about thirteen hundred."

"Before Monsignor Goodnard returns, then?"

"If you say so."

"Oh, all right," the priest said, clearly perplexed.

"Thank you, Father." The visitors each grabbed a heavy canvas bag.

"Just finish before he gets back. He won't like this at all."

Nic touched his hard hat in a respectful gesture, and he and Lama descended the steps, securing the plastic barrier behind them. Lama said loudly, "First we put up the dust shield."

They fastened a large white cloth across the crypt opening, completely blocking it. Pope Pius, marble hands folded in entreaty, now stared at a blank screen dragging the floor.

Hidden by the makeshift curtain, Nic and Lama unwrapped the old motor, spread the drop cloth, and unpacked the carryalls.

From outside the dust shield came a soft cough. "Excuse me?"

Lama's tool thumped to the floor.

"Yeah?" Nic said.

"Excuse me, *Signore*, but Monsignor Goodnard wants to see you."

"What?" His hands padded with thick work gloves, Nic moved the curtain slightly aside.

"Monsignor Goodnard." Father Maratea lifted his chin toward the top of the stairs. "He came back early, and he's in charge. Of the basilica."

Jesus fucking Christ. Nic stomped up the stairs, trailed by the priest. But when he approached the monsignor, he became ingratiating. "I'm awfully sorry we have to disrupt you, Monsignor." With the gloves on, it was hard to grasp the letter, but he handed it to Goodnard. "Our inspector stopped by last week. It's a shaky situation down there. There's old wires and potential combustibles under the floor—"

Goodnard interrupted. "I'm going to call this—" he studied the letter's signature, "'Aurelio Conti' and make sure this work is absolutely necessary. Today."

"*Certo*. He should be back in the office in an hour or two. When we left the shop just before noon, he was on his way out to a church in the *periferia*. Water leak," Nic confided. "Tough. Hard to trace." He proceeded cheerfully, "We'll leave our stuff set up until you have a chance to talk to him."

Goodnard studied him and handed back the letter. Clearly, it could be hours before he could talk to Conti. "Oh, go ahead. Get it over with."

"You're busy today, so we'll work as fast as we can." Nic had an inspiration. "There may be some noise, understand. But we'll try not to set off any alarms." He scanned the visitors drifting back into the basilica. "Lots of scrambled wires down there. You know how people panic. Wouldn't want to cause a stampede."

"I can shut the alarm off," Father Maratea said. "I know how."

Goodnard gave him a sideways look. "Never mind. *I'll* do it," he said. And to Nic, "Finish as quickly as you can. This is a terrible inconvenience."

"We will, Monsignor. With your help." Nic smiled.

Goodnard swept away, and the priest wagged his head in apology.

"Bureaucrats," Nic hissed, "the same everywhere."

Although Monsignor Goodnard had promised to shut the alarm off, Lama wasn't the trusting sort. Marco's thermal imaging camera had revealed electrical wires along a pillar to the left of the niche, and Lama shattered a thin piece of caramel-colored marble, got hold of the wires there, and disabled the system.

"Got it?" Nic bounced from one foot to the other.

Lama grunted an affirmative. They each grabbed glass cutters and tackled the large pane in front of the reliquary. Because of its size and thickness, they made a number of relief scores, allowing the glass to be broken off in sections and preventing it from falling backward and damaging the reliquary or tipping outward and crashing at their feet. They worked quickly, stacking the glass on the altar behind them. That done, they took off their heavy leather work gloves, leaving the vinyl gloves underneath.

Already twenty minutes had elapsed since they entered the crypt. Each extra minute increased the likelihood of an interruption. While they could talk their way past a dimwit priest up top, in the crypt with the niche exposed would be a different story.

Hands on hips, they studied their gleaming quarry. The crystal and silver reliquary glowed against the niche's carmine silk lining. Elaborate silver and gold embellishments sprang from each end, and silver swags looped between gilt cherubs. A fat baby Jesus reclined on top, his raised arm pointing to heaven. Windows on the reliquary's sides provided an indistinct glimpse of the wooden shards inside.

"Looks like a giant soup tureen," Lama said.

"I get my soup from a can," Nic grunted. "We need to make up some time here. Put your back into it."

He gave the nearest leg a test pull. It didn't budge. They couldn't tell whether the reliquary was fastened to its platform or simply much heavier than expected.

"Don't damage it," Lama said, watching Nic try to wiggle an arm behind. Nic scowled. Lama worked his arm behind the reliquary on the other side. Now they circled it. Straining, they kept their bodies close together. If the damned thing did break loose, their torsos could help support the weight. But in this ungainly position they couldn't take full advantage of their strength. Panting, Nic was on the verge of giving up when the reliquary shifted forward an inch or so.

"Stubborn son of a bitch," Lama said through clenched teeth. Now it shifted forward on his side with a terrible screech.

"Goddammit! You'll wake the dead," Nic said, then remembered where he was and laughed.

"Yeah? We've got to get this fucking thing out of here." Lama pulled hard again. "OK, OK, it's close to the edge on my side."

He shifted slightly toward Nic to add strength on the right, and again the reliquary moved noisily.

"If that priest hears …" Nic said.

"We're taking too long." Lama gave it a jerk, and it separated from its invisible fastenings.

"Watch out! It's tipping."

"I've got it." Lama puffed and shoved his chest farther underneath. "Not that heavy. But awkward as hell."

"Easy now."

They let the reliquary slide slowly down to where they had a solid grip on it with their hands. They hunched over it, shoulders straining.

"Set it here or walk it to the bag?" Lama asked.

"Walk it."

They shuffled over to the gaping canvas bag and eased the reliquary inside. "Tight."

Nic bent over, panting, hands on thighs. "Shit."

"What?"

"I wanted to wrap it in the drop cloth."

"Fucking thing's dirty now." Lama gestured to the engine, dripping oil onto the cloth from some deep internal injury.

Nic caught Lama's eye. Lama's eyes widened, and he grinned. They lifted the engine—easy after the other—and set it in the floodlit niche. They took a step back.

"Nice," Nic grinned. "Looks like somebody incinerated it."

Lama studied the reliquary. "It'll take both of us to carry it out of here."

Someone nearby coughed, and their heads snapped toward the sheet. A pudgy hand gripped its edge, and Father Maratea stepped inside.

"You should be nearly—" His glance went to the niche, where, instead of the precious reliquary, was a brightly lit black *thing*. "Oh," the priest gasped, eyes bulging.

Nic moved alongside Lama to block the priest's view of the bag. Maratea glanced from the niche to them and back, stuttering. "What—?" he gurgled. "The electricity—?"

Nic thrust a hand into his pocket and fingered his knife. The priest glanced down and must have seen silver glinting from the top of the canvas bag, because he pointed, saying "Oh!" He looked at them accusingly and took a step backward. "OH!"

In a flash, Lama crossed the space between them. He had the priest's neck locked in the vise of one elbow and pressed his mouth closed so tightly a trickle of blood escaped his lips. The priest jerked forward, trying to shake Lama off. Smooth as a boxer, Lama took advantage of the priest's momentum and moved him toward Nic. Under the thin glove, the shadow of a snake wound up Nic's wrist. A knife blade flicked out of its mouth.

Shock and fear lit the priest's face and his whole body trembled as Nic lunged. His thrust deeply penetrated the priest's chest. Nic and Lama jumped aside, escaping an arc of bright blood. Maratea crumpled to the floor.

He lay on his stomach, eyes fixed on the canvas bag. Blood poured out of him, and he mouthed something. Nic thought he heard "*Amen.*"

Leaving the dying man where he lay, Nic and Lama stripped off their gloves and safety glasses and shoved them into the big carryall.

"The tools?" Lama asked.

"Leave them."

They zipped the canvas bag from each side until stopped by the fragile decorations at the ends of the reliquary.

"*Fuck.* Now what?" Lama asked. The decorations stuck out several inches.

"We can't cover it with the dirty drop cloth. And anyway ..." Nic glanced at the spreading pool of blood under the priest.

Lama took off his fake Vatican jacket. "Here."

They covered the protruding silver and telltale gap, and each grabbed a handle. "Act casual and keep moving," Nic said as they climbed the wide marble steps.

"Yeah, yeah."

The distance between them and the basilica doors seemed to have doubled since they'd entered. They made good progress across the nave before hearing a loud "*Mi scusi, Signori,*" from behind. They glanced at each other and kept walking. The voice came closer, "*Signori!*"

"Set it down," Nic muttered.

They lowered the carryall. A priest approached, accompanied by a young woman. "This lady is a docent.

She conducts tours in the crypt below, the statue of Pope Pius IX, the Holy Crib, the Valadier reliquary ...”

Nic's head bobbed. *Get on with it.*

“She wants to know how long access will be blocked, because she can't—”

“I get it,” Nic said and smiled. “*Signorina*, as soon as we take our tools here to the truck, we'll be back to clean up. We'll get rid of the curtain and the barriers. All yours again.”

“Bless you,” the priest said.

“Hold it.” Nic waited for them to walk away, then tucked Lama's jacket around the reliquary more tightly. “Let's get the hell out of here.”

MARCO

Marco watched Nic and Lama emerge from between the pillars of the basilica's portico. “*Bene*. Here we go.”

Umberto pulled the van into position. Nic and Lama opened the back doors, slid the carryall inside, and climbed in after it. Once they shut the doors, Umberto started the van rolling.

Over his shoulder, Marco said, “How'd it go?”

“Your fat priest kept sticking his nose in,” Nic said.

“We had to take care of him,” Lama made a thrusting gesture and laughed.

“Shit!” Marco said. “Why do you always—”

“Hey, man, we had to. He fucking *saw* us with this damn thing.”

“I thought—never mind.” Marco faced front again. He closed his eyes a moment and took a slow breath.

“Shit!” Umberto said.

Marco's eyes popped open. “I see it.” Two police officers had set up a roadblock.

“Can't turn around,” Umberto muttered. “Not enough room and too suspicious.”

The cops were talking to some of the drivers and waving others through. “That wasn't there earlier, but it can't be about us. Too soon. It's something else." Over his shoulder, Marco yelled, "Get those Vatican coveralls off. Quick!"

"Yes, Boss," Nic said. His tone was sarcastic, but he was already sliding out of the disguise. They both were. By the time the van reached the front of the line, Nic and Lama were in jeans and T-shirts, sitting on the floor in back atop neatly folded Vatican work clothes.

One of the policemen strolled over, and Umberto rolled down his window. "*Buon pomeriggio*," he said, grinning.

"Papers." His manner betrayed extreme boredom.

"What's the problem, officer?" Umberto handed over his fake driving license and asked Marco to retrieve the stolen van's documentation from the glove compartment. Lama had said the van wouldn't be missed, but when Marco glanced back at him, he held his head in his hands, elbows on knees.

"Vehicle theft ring working the area," the officer said, studying the documents. "These names don't match up."

"Company van," Umberto said.

"And where are you boys going?"

"Back to our shop to get our motorbikes, then out for a beer. A long week already."

Umberto never sounded so cheerful.

"And where is your shop? What kind of shop?" The officer appeared interested in the plastic covering their seats, and he wasn't budging.

"Electrical repairs. Northeast *periferia*. How's traffic today? That drive can be a son of a bitch."

"No problems I know of. Open the rear doors, please." He stepped away to let Umberto climb out.

Umberto had no intention of leaving the driver's seat. He peered over his shoulder and said, "Open a door back there, guys."

Marco's heart froze. *It's no good surprising the cops with two men in back.*

As Nic moved toward the van's rear doors, Umberto's right hand reached under his seat and pulled out a handgun. He held it low, out of sight.

Jesus Christ. A sweat stain darkened Marco's shirtfront, and he pulled his jacket over it.

The second policeman walked over to confer with his colleague as Nic opened one of the rear doors. In the side mirror, Marco saw five or six cars lined up behind them. He could envision how the whole scene would play out. Umberto going crazy. Nic too, maybe. Witnesses. The arrest. Jail. *Big* time jail. The end of everything.

A driver behind them honked his horn, long and loud. Several others joined in. *Shit! The cops will really take their time now*. Marco craned his neck around to see the rear compartment, filled with light because of the open door. The police wouldn't like it that a couple of men were riding back there, but Lama had moved the carryall well away from the doors. If only they didn't check inside it.

The second policeman strolled toward the car that had started the honking. As he bent down to talk to the driver, he waved at the van and hollered to his partner. "Get them out of the way."

Take it easy. Marco motioned for Nic to close the door again. The first cop returned the papers to Umberto, who passed them to Marco.

"Everybody's in a hurry," Umberto shook his head.

"On your way," the policeman said, his attention on the waiting cars.

"*Grazie*." Umberto eased forward. The four men remained silent until the van pulled into the temporary garage, having just driven the longest few blocks any of them had ever experienced. Inside, with the garage door rolled down, they erupted with whoops and back slaps.

"Nearly pissed my pants," Lama said.

"Glad you didn't," Marco said. "DNA."

LEO

Leo unlocked the file cabinet in his office and from a folder labeled "Tourist Information" pulled out his notes on the Clarke/Capuano case—unconnected data, stray thoughts, nothing official. Obstinate facts refusing to come together in his mind.

Bracci's inquiries into Gianni di Landri's background revealed definite mafia connections, and the snake tattoo suggested a link to Genie's case … maybe. Problematically, such a link would require Tati to alert the antimafia investigators.

"When is *Signora* Clarke returning to America?" Tati had asked him earlier that afternoon.

The unexpected question jolted him. "Not until the doctor releases her, which could be in a few days."

"After that?"

Leo didn't like thinking about "after that," but said, "I don't know."

If only he could get a good night's sleep. An eruption of ringing phones outside his office made it hard to concentrate.

"Boss!" Sal stuck his head in the door, excitement sparking off him. "Did you hear?"

"Just got in."

"A priest was murdered at Santa Maria Maggiore, and some famous relic may be stolen. Maybe it was Marco and crew—the thing they were planning. I'm on my way over to check it out."

Leo was out of his chair. "I'll go with you."

"Not my call. The chief put Gilletti in charge," Sal said, his disappointment evident. Sal was available to whichever senior detective needed him most, and Gillo Gilletti would not have been his choice. No one liked the man—the first to undermine his officers and the last to give them credit. Gilletti would fight to keep Leo away from such a high-profile case.

Leo took a minute debating whether to step in anyway. Technically, he was Gilletti's boss, but boxes on an organization chart didn't tell the whole story. Right now, a face-off with Gilletti or the chief was a fight he didn't need. "OK. You go. You know what to look for?"

"Get as good a description as I can of the perpetrator. Listen for anything reminding me of *Signora* Clarke's transcript."

"Take these with you." Leo handed photos of Marco across the desk.

"Keep them. I have copies." Sal patted his pocket. "Grabbed them from my 'auto insurance' file."

Leo chuckled. Sal had adopted his own fake-file subterfuge. He and his detectives kept their desks and file cabinets locked because it was departmental policy, not because it protected against snoops. They could be opened with a bent paperclip. Despite Leo's complaints, the department higher-ups hadn't provided more secure combination-lock cabinets, and he preferred not to ponder why.

Another young detective shouted Sal's name from across the room.

"Stay in touch."

SAL

When Sal and two other young detectives arrived at the basilica, Gillo Gilletti was standing in the emptied nave with representatives of the Vatican gendarmerie. Their role was to protect the Church's interests, and Sal had found generally good cooperation between the law enforcement agencies of Church and state. Gilletti, though, had a gift for antagonizing people and appeared to be already putting his talent to work. Sal and the others walked up just as the group was joined by Monsignor Goodnard and a smooth priest who handled the basilica's public relations and reported to the Vatican.

Goodnard described what happened in a stilted, under-rehearsed manner. He'd gone to check on the progress of the workmen and noticed the barriers still blocking the crypt steps. Below, a crimson stain rose from the hem of the dust shield. As a former field chaplain in the Italian military, he knew at once what that stain was.

"When I saw the blood, I sent Friar Orsini to—" he paused "—to check."

To do the dirty work, Sal thought.

"Friar Orsini confirmed my suspicion, and said the—the—reliquary—is—" He choked and launched into a mumbling ramble. "I—I can't believe it! The crib pieces are fragile and deteriorating. If they don't have proper care—"

The public relations man put a hand on Goodnard's shoulder and described how the Monsignor had encountered "poor Father Maratea" after lunch.

"Yes. *Poveruomo*." Poor man, Goodnard said, reminded he had a dead priest on his hands, "so dedicated to our basilica." He described how the workman showed him a letter from the Vatican building maintenance office authorizing emergency repairs. He glared at the three Vatican police officers.

"Do you have the letter?" they asked.

"I gave it—he took it back."

"Do you remember who signed it?"

"*Certo*. His name is … something like … The first name starts with 'A.' And the last name is … some common name. Corso or Caputo or Castillo. You must know your own people!"

The officers shuffled their feet. Sal rolled his eyes.

"Whatever his name is," Goodnard rushed ahead, "he should be easy to identify, because he was out visiting a church with a water leak. There can't be too many men doing that on this one day!"

"And, who told you that?" a Vatican man asked.

Goodnard flushed. "The letter was on Vatican stationery!"

"Which you can buy online," Sal said. "Can you describe the men?"

"The one I saw wore a yellow Vatican workman's jumpsuit." Goodnard gave the Vatican detectives another piercing look. "Big plastic glasses, hard hat. Really, I couldn't see much of him. Light skin and eyes. Average height."

"Any distinguishing marks, scars, tattoos?" Sal asked.

"No."

"On his hands or arms, maybe?"

"Really, I didn't see any." Goodnard paused, then said, "He wore work gloves. When he took out the letter, he fumbled. The gloves."

Gilletti stepped in front of Sal and took over. "So, there's nothing you particularly noticed about him?"

"What I particularly noticed was that these men were blocking the entrance to the crypt on the most important day of the month, and they'd probably make a mess down there."

Sal coughed. Got that right.

"Show us," Gilletti ordered.

Goodnard led the police and the public relations man past the barricade. At the bottom of the steps, he refused to go farther. He grew pale, staring at the mottled red and brown stain fanning across the screen.

From the front of the group, Gilletti held up a bony hand. "The medico and forensics team will be here any minute. We don't go in until they finish. But we can look from here." They also were waiting for representatives from the Carabinieri Headquarters for the Protection of Cultural Heritage, known as the TPC, since the crib was a significant art object as well as a religious treasure.

Despite the crisscrossing lines of authority, Sal knew Gilletti and the *Polizia di Stato* would lead the murder inquiry and lend other investigatory help, but the TPC—and the Vatican—would be in charge of recovering the crib.

The Vatican officers peered around one side of the makeshift curtain, as Gilletti and his men used the other. Sal squatted for an unobstructed view. The body was face down, along the curtain. A paint-splattered drop cloth covered the floor. In the middle was an upturned canvas carryall. Tools lay about, and stacked pieces of glass glinted from the altar. The elegant silk-lined niche displayed an irregular black object. Sal sniffed something unexpected. Motor oil.

They trudged up the steps to wait, Goodnard leaning heavily on the marble handrail.

"Your priest is dead, and your relic is gone," Gilletti told Goodnard, lifting his chin. "There's a black thing in the cabinet down there, but whatever it is, it doesn't look like this." He flicked a nail against the postcard Sal had handed him. "What is this thing, anyway?"

An awful expression came over Goodnard's face, and his knees buckled. An officer caught him and eased him onto the marble floor. Friar Orsini hurried to get water. Gilletti chewed his lip, contemplating the unconscious priest.

"Oh, just a reliquary holding a few pieces of Jesus' manger," Sal said.

LEO

A dozen times Leo picked up his phone to call Genie, but didn't. If this theft was what she'd overheard the men planning, it was big, all right, big enough to warrant silencing an unfortunate eavesdropper.

Before he could warn her about that, though, he wanted to explain something, preferably in person. He wanted to say that to protect her, he needed—he must have—her cooperation. He wasn't angry with her. The other day, he would say, he overreacted. Naturally, there was more to it.

With events sweeping out of his control, involving someone he cared about, the normal ways he managed his emotions were useless. He hadn't felt such uncertainty since he'd paced the oncologist's reception area, awaiting results from Liliana's final round of chemotherapy. When summoned, he walked down a long corridor and into the doctor's office, the view of her desk blocked by the two tall wing chairs that faced it. He winced, recalling the first time he and Liliana had sat there, holding hands across the short gap between the chairs. How hopeful they were!

At each subsequent visit, a bit of that hope melted, its icy runoff seeping into his veins. For this final conference, not until he moved farther into the room did he see his wife already curled, birdlike, in one of those chairs—shrunken, brittle—almost unrecognizable as the robust young woman she had been. He hardly dared touch her. It was over. Her eyes said she knew it.

In that terrible moment, Leo longed to feel compassion for her, sympathy, the first pangs of grief. But he didn't, and it felt like betrayal. Instead, his overriding emotion was anger. At the disease. At the doctors. Even at her. Anger and guilt. He was lost before she was gone.

The pain of those days had diminished, but never disappeared. He'd believed the living, beating prospect for love was scorched out of him. Until he met this stubborn American.

Behind him, atop the file cabinet, sat Liliana's photograph in its rococo silver frame. He liked to think she had his back. He met her eyes now and wordlessly asked her about Genie. Liliana had packed a lifetime of caring into everything she told him those last weeks. Now his head filled with her voice and the words he hadn't been ready to hear: "Leo, you must have love in your life."

He'd found some bitter consolation knowing he'd been helpless in the face of his wife's cancer. But this situation was different. Genie's fate was in his hands. If anything happened to her—

A phone call rescued him. Sal, at last.

"Here's the scoop. A priest *was* murdered. In the crypt under the altar. Stabbed with a thin blade, like a stiletto. There's so much blood, it must have hit a major artery, at least. They'll do the post mortem tonight and give Gilletti final word tomorrow morning."

"Was something stolen?"

"Oh, yeah. The reliquary with pieces of Christ's manger, if you can believe it. Snatched right out of its special niche."

"Holy mother of God."

"Agreed. And get this, they put a dirty old Fiat engine in its place. Kinky. The Monsignor in charge here fainted once. I thought he'd go down again when Gilletti told him that."

Sal summarized the investigators' findings so far. "We guess they killed the priest when he interrupted them."

"We?"

"The other detectives and me. Everybody but Gilletti. He wants to think the priest was in on it and they killed him in some kind of double cross."

Leo snorted. "Descriptions?"

"The Monsignor talked to one of them. But he's useless even when he's conscious. Nobody else paid them any mind. They had on Vatican coveralls and jackets, hard hats, the whole business. Didn't leave much of themselves to see. One tall, one average height and build. I'll bet the lab won't find any prints or fibers or hairs, or whatever."

"Wasn't there an alarm?"

"*Merda*! I skipped the best part! Goodnard—the fainter—shut the alarm off for them. The Vatican cops gave him a real grilling when they found that flipped switch. He'll be saying Hail Marys till doomsday."

Leo shook his head.

"I showed the photos around—docents, gift shop, a couple of other priests—and nobody remembers Mr. Ponytail. But the priest he was talking to in the picture? He's the victim."

Leo considered this last information. "Is that it?"

"If you need me, don't call my cell. It doesn't work in the crypt. Plus Gilletti's hovering. Had to step outside to call you. One more thing. I got a message—helpful, maybe. There's a bank across the street from the florist shop where the hospital flowers—"

"Right."

"Well, the bank has an ATM facing the street, and the ATM has a camera. They're sending me the video from the evening the flowers were snatched. If we're lucky—"

"When's that coming?"

"Early tomorrow morning. I should have the blowups from Sunday—Marco in the churches—then too."

"Can you do something for me after that?" Leo asked.

"Depends on how things go here. What's up?"

"There's a funeral I'd like you to attend."

"Anyone we know?"

"Someone we may need to know."

Leo hung up, thoughtful. He *had* to rebuild trust with Genie, to protect both her and the investigation, which was growing more consequential by the day. The challenge was her independent streak. Over the years, a lot of women—men too—had seen him angry, and most didn't stand up to him. "I want my life back," she said. He wished he knew whether it would include him.

He wadded the paper on which he'd been doodling and threw it into the wastebasket with such force it bounced back out. He stared at the balled-up nothing, not really seeing it, as he replayed their past conversations, searching for a hook that would help him save her.

By the time the sky was fully dark, he thought he might have the answer. He had been working the way he always worked, trying to solve the case *for* her. That approach was a disaster in this instance. He would have to solve the case *with* her.

He needed her. She'd said that, and she was right. The several truths in that thought knocked him into another long reverie, out of which emerged a specific memory: the wistful way she'd said, "My brother says my suitcase *is* my home." Her brother. Home.

GENIE

Thursday evening I stayed in my room, turning the pages of a novel whose characters and plot left no more impression than a gnat's footprints. I tossed my phone onto the bed, determined to call Leo one moment and afraid of the possible result the next. This was too important to mess up.

I fretted and checked the time. I wrote a few texts, straining to be upbeat. I texted friends who wondered where I was:

Still in Rome. Dr hasnt released me yet--soon I hope. Am ok really!

I wandered to the patio doors, then to my bedside table. I gathered my postcards—studied them, sorted them, and spread them out again, tiling the tabletop. I consulted my phone. On, battery full. Just not ringing. From beyond the garden wall, church bells tolled eight o'clock. Another hour, gone forever. I rested my forehead on the cool glass of the patio door.

I grabbed the phone and entered a familiar number that rang in a Northern Virginia farmhouse. That's where Robbie would be—sitting at the kitchen table, his large hand wrapped around a can of Coke, the newspaper spread before him. He'd be on his mid-afternoon break. Before long he'd be helping the neighbor twins who made his restaurant deliveries. They'd wash and pack vegetables, fill egg crates, and load the van. He'd resupply the roadside stand for the late-afternoon rush, relieving Susan so she could cook dinner. So regular, so dependable, so different from her life—especially now, when she felt like a rabbit in a tissue paper cage, the wolves pawing and snarling just outside.

"Robbie, it's me."

"Hey, how are you? How's the leg?"

My lie intact. "Not running hurdles yet. But much better."

"Glad to hear it. I don't get the secrecy, though. Why can't we say where you are? Aunt Stevie might want to know."

"I'll explain when I see you. It's important, but nothing to worry about." What a liar I was!

"Hmmm. Are you ensconced with movie stars or some such?"

I laughed. "Some such."

"So, when are you coming home?"

I rested the phone on my shoulder a few seconds while I pulled myself together to respond. "I see the doctor tomorrow. He has to release me."

"You're not hanging around because of that detective? Leo Something."

"Angelini," I said. Even saying his name hurt. "No. Waiting on the doctor."

"I thought you liked him."

Robbie could always tell. "I did. I do. That's a big question mark now, though."

"Hmmm. One thing, you're sure off your itinerary."

"In every possible way."

LEO

Through the early part of that evening, Leo attacked the paperwork accumulating on his desk, half his mind on his task and half on his silent phone. No further word from Sal. With every passing hour, the pressure for action rose within him. Frustrating.

Bracci had assigned a pair of men to rotate between the Spanish Steps and the Piazza del Popolo, trolling for their suspects where they'd previously been seen. Leo wondered whether they were brazen enough to show their faces, especially the day of the theft, *if* they were indeed involved.

Anyway, those places were always crowded. Bracci's men might miss something. He decided to take a look himself. Have dinner. Try the trattoria Genie found. Anything would beat sitting and waiting for Sal to call.

Parking near the Spanish Steps was always a bitch, and he zigzagged the one-way streets near the top until he found an illegal spot in a construction zone. He left his radio in the car—the kind of thugs they were after would spot a radio. He strode the irregular blocks to the top of the Steps. Below, the three restaurants' red, black, and green umbrellas resembled a pixelated flag. The women had eaten at the restaurant on the right—black umbrellas—and he jogged down the steps toward it.

He snagged an inside table near the front. The food was fresh, and a glass of Barbero took the slightest edge off his jangled nerves. Around nine o'clock, a trio of young men began clamoring for a table across the way. If these weren't Genie's *teppisti*, they were their doubles. He paid his bill and left by the rear door.

He circled the block to approach the restaurant from the plaza side. The men had commandeered a table at the fringe of the outdoor seating area. Genie would know at once if they were the ones. He'd order a car that could drop her off at—what was the closest accessible place?—the top of the Spanish Steps, in front of Trinità dei Monti. At that distance, the men couldn't recognize her, and he would bring her down to the pedestrian streets by elevator, out of their view.

An unfamiliar female voice answered the *questura* number. He said, "This is Detective Angelini. And you are?"

She identified herself and asked, "Your name again?"

She asked him to spell it, and he did, irritation sharpening each letter. While the woman wrote at what seemed like a snail's pace, his phone gave the telltale beep of a dying battery.

"And you want to speak to—?"

"Sal Riccobono."

"Oh, Sal. Sure. I'll check."

Excruciating minutes passed before the woman returned to report Gilletti's team was still at the basilica. The phone beeped again. He pulled it from his ear and glared at it. He gave her Agostina's number. "My phone's dying. Call this number and talk to *Signora* Clarke. Tell her to meet me in front of Trinità dei Monti as soon as she can. I need her to identify a couple of men at a restaurant. Send a patrol car for her. And tell her..." but somewhere during those instructions, his phone died for good.

GENIE

I turned a few more of the novel's pages. What could I do to make Agostina and me safer? Could we get out of Rome? That would mean leaving *Dottor* Immormino, but so what? I was healing nicely, and didn't he say so? Every time I saw him? A cinch he'd be glad to see the last of me. But how could I mend fences with Leo? I couldn't, unless he was willing. And why would he be?

I cringed, remembering my outburst. Unfair, accusatory. Shouldn't I make the first move? Apologize? I grabbed the phone and had entered the first few digits of Leo's number, when the hall telephone rang. I waited. Agostina answered and, in a moment, came to my door. "Detective Angelini's office is calling."

I dashed down the hallway, startling her with my speed. "Leo?" I fought to keep my voice normal.

"This is the duty desk for the detectives' department." A woman's voice, speaking with deliberation. "Detective Angelini asked me to call you. There are some men he wants you to see—to see if you recognize them—they're at a restaurant. He'll wait for you at"—a crackle of paper suggested she consulted a note—"Trinità dei Monti—"

"The church at the top of the Spanish Steps?"

"In front."

I hesitated. "Officer Torre will have a problem with this." Of course.

"Have him call me," she said. "Detective Angelini is sending a car. Give it a few minutes." The woman disconnected.

At last! I thought. Maybe we could arrest those bastards tonight!

Excited, I put on jeans, dark turtleneck, and a bulky gray sweater. In case I *did* recognize the men, I didn't want them to recognize me. I slipped on sturdy walking shoes and tied the laces. I'd bought a tweed golf cap for my nephew Andy at Shannon airport and I pulled it out of its tissue paper. A little large, but I could hide my hair underneath, and it shadowed my face.

Agostina waited outside with me for the car, chatting with the policeman on duty, Officer Capizzo. It was chilly standing there, and I shuffled from one foot to the other. I checked my watch. Almost nine-thirty.

"Who is coming for you?" Agostina asked again.

"A police car, I suppose."

"You'll check his identification before she gets in the car?" Agostina said to Capizzo.

"Of course." He grinned.

"It should be here by now," I said.

Capizzo called the detectives' office, and the person who answered didn't know about the car. It seemed the woman who'd relayed Leo's message was on her dinner break.

"This is taking way too long." I put my hand on Capizzo's arm. "Let's walk." The shortest route was through the Villa Borghese and I knew that park well, even a few shortcuts, especially near my favorite spot, the Pincio Overlook.

Capizzo called the *questura* again and learned it would take a patrol car considerable time to get to us. The police were busy manning roadblocks and checking train stations and airports, hunting a ring of thieves. He couldn't raise Leo on his cell phone, but left a message and sent a text.

"If I don't go soon, the men will leave the restaurant before I get there. I can go by myself—"

"I can't let you do that," Capizzo said. "Walking might be fastest, if you can do it."

"Take my car," Agostina told him.

"Against department rules. Anyway, the car connects her to this house. *Maybe* we escaped that problem once, but we can't risk it a second time. Detective Angelini said 'only to the doctor,' and he meant it."

"All right. We'll walk." A boost of adrenaline assured me it was possible.

"It must be about three kilometers," Agostina protested. "Just circling the yard a dozen times and you need a nap."

"So, I'm rested. I can do it."

Capizzo still looked uncertain.

"Haven't you all decided no one's watching the apartment? There's no one to follow us. And why would anyone look for me in the park? Meanwhile, Leo's waiting."

Reluctantly, Capizzo pulled out his radio to tell Officer Torre where we were going. Her exasperated response trailed me as I took off down the street. That woman wasn't going to stop me.

LEO

Even this late in the evening, quite a few people sat on the Spanish Steps and loitered in the Piazza di Spagna below. Tourists flowed around the plaza's baroque fountain and strolled the fashionable shopping streets that ended there. Leo paced at the top of the Steps, in front of the church. The crowds would provide good camouflage for him and Genie. If only she'd get there.

Already it was half past nine. Maybe she needed to get dressed. Or maybe she was in the middle of dinner when the office called. He pushed other, more disagreeable maybes out of his mind, like maybe something happened on the way, or maybe she refused to come. Not having the use of his phone was a damned nuisance, and he didn't trust that woman on the desk to get his message right.

Someone sitting about twenty steps below him glanced up in his direction—one of Bracci's plainclothes officers. Leo knew this one. The detectives called him "Pacino," a dead ringer for the American actor in his younger days. Smart and a bit of a smartass, Leo knew. He discreetly signaled, and Pacino rose, stretched, and climbed to the top in no particular hurry.

"Where have you been?" Leo demanded.

Pacino scanned the crowd below, unconcerned. To an observer, it would seem they were having a casual, even chance, conversation. "Did you park up here?" Pacino asked. "You came from this direction on your way to dinner. So, how was *Il Girasole*? I like their fish."

Leo gave him a sharp glance.

"Did your call go through?" Pacino continued. "The way you shook that phone! Probably I shouldn't mention it, I won't say I was offended, but when you passed me on your way up, I thought you'd say hello. And, why the pacing?"

"All right. I get it," Leo fumed. "You've got things under control." He said, "I saw men in one of the restaurants—"

"Three of them. At the red-umbrella restaurant, the table on this side. Not nearly as good as *Il Girasole*, in my opinion. Their main courses arrived, and the waiter brought another bottle of wine. Those men?"

"Yes. Sorry." He was embarrassed. "Do you have a phone?"

The man handed it over. Leo grimaced to see the full battery. He called Agostina's number. No answer.

He tried again a few minutes later.

"*Buona sera?*"

"Agostina, it's Leo. I've been calling."

"I was outside."

"Outside? Has the car come for Genie yet?"

"The car never came."

"It never came?" He knew that woman was an idiot!

"Genie's walking to meet you, through the park."

"Walking?" He almost shouted.

"Yes, with Officer Capizzo."

He heard her defenses rising, so kept his voice even. "When did they leave?"

"About twenty minutes ago. They expect to reach you shortly after ten."

He took a deep breath. This wasn't Agostina's fault. "Is someone there with you?"

"Yes, Officer Torre is here."

"Right. Good." He thanked her and disconnected. His watch read nine fifty. They'd allowed about thirty-five minutes. That seemed optimistic. Why hadn't the car come? The robbery, he thought. Of course. Leo pursed his lips and scanned the park's unrevealing dark face.

Reluctantly, he returned the phone to Pacino. "The American is meeting me here. If she identifies those men, I'll want you to follow them. Can you do that?"

"Our scooters are close by. Between my partner and me, we can tail at least two of them. Should I call backup?"

"Stay low profile until we figure out who they work for. Find out where they go, if you can, but don't alarm them." Leo remembered his place in the investigation. "What does Bracci say?"

"Same thing."

"Do you need to alert your partner? Is he at Popolo?"

"He's down there, sitting under the green umbrella closest to the suspects, drinking a glass of wine with his girlfriend. He has his back to them, and she's watching them for him."

Leo grimaced. "His girlfriend?"

"Officer Lorenzo."

Leo clapped Pacino on his shoulder. "Good work." His attention already strayed back to the dark and wooded park. So many routes wound through it, he couldn't predict where Genie and Capizzo would come out. What he most wanted to do—rush into the park to meet them—would be futile.

GENIE

I was pleased (OK, a little surprised) at my pace through the park. Of course, it was downhill. Capizzo scanned ahead and behind like human radar. I led him more or less straight to the bridge over Viale Muro Torto. I didn't want to admit it, especially to myself, but by then I was flagging. Capizzo took my arm as we reached the well-lit Napoleon I Square. At its far end was the Pincio Overlook, the spot I loved so much. We were still a couple of blocks from Trinità dei Monti.

A few pedestrians ambled across the square, and more people draped themselves along the parapet of the Pincio, enjoying the view. I forced myself to keep moving as Capizzo and I skirted the left side of the square. We had to reach the path leading to the "Polish poet" street—Adamo-something. We'd be at Trinità dei Monti in perhaps ten minutes. Perhaps.

When we did reach the path, I stopped. Wheezing, I put a hand on my heaving chest and bent over partway.

"You OK?"

"Let me rest … a minute." I had to sit. A children's fair was set up a short distance past the turnoff to Viale Adamo Mickiewicz. Colorful half-sized versions of popular rides—a carousel with a grinning blue Aladdin at the center, swirling multicolored teacups, a three-car train on a figure-eight track—were melancholy at this hour, with no laughing children, no music or colored lights. At least it offered benches.

We'd moved as fast as I could, and still it took nearly a half hour to reach this point. "I'm slowing you down," I panted. "Go on ahead—let Leo know—we're nearly there."

He pointed to the benches. "Sit right there. Are you sure you can't make it? I don't want to leave—"

"Go." I waved him away. "Let me catch my breath." And get this pain in my side to stop.

"Be right back." He hurried away.

I drifted toward the benches placed around the edge of the fair. But the city view drew me irresistibly, and I took a few extra steps to join the string of tourists at the overlook. I leaned heavily into the parapet, took off the cap, and fanned myself with it. The thick wool sweater was good camouflage, but too warm.

The familiar vista through the trees and across the city rooftops to St. Peter's—the unmistakable shape of its dome echoed by the smaller domes of lesser churches, children to their *pater familias*—perfectly captured one of Rome's many faces. I rubbed my sore ribs.

On the street below, a vehicle door slammed. Glancing down into the gloom, I saw the glint of moonlight on the roofs of a couple of dark delivery vans parked side-by-side. Men shuffled and murmured. When the rear doors of the van on the left creaked open, an interior light switched on, illuminating the area.

"*Merda!*" someone said sharply. "*Muoviti!*" Move it!

Two men struggled to remove a large carryall from the van. A cloth on top snagged on the door and pulled away, and I glimpsed a shiny object inside. A man with white-blond hair slouched nearby, smoking. I recognized him. I would know him anywhere. One of the men jerked the cloth cover back in place and slammed the van doors. The light went off. Shadowy figures transferred the carryall to the rear of the other van, where no light showed. Its doors then closed too.

At that moment people standing next to me snapped photos. Their cameras' flash lit my face. Momentarily blinded, I blinked to clear my vision. From the semidarkness below, a ghostly pale face stared up at me.

The blond man darted toward the steps that led to the Pincian Hill and the overlook. I had so little time to escape, I didn't call out for help. Explanations would take precious minutes. Strangers would hesitate. Then it would be too late.

There wasn't time to reach the trees of the park. They were too spread apart to provide much cover anyway. But if I stayed on the paths leading to Trinità dei Monti, I'd be out in the open, visible. I had to hide. All this I knew in an instant.

I stumbled toward the children's fair and reached the dark carousel, crawling between its horses and swans and peering from the shadow of a pink-painted elephant. The blond reached the top of the steps, no more than a hundred feet away. He scanned the plaza. Though I was as immobile as one of the plaster animals, my breathing was heavy, and my heart drummed so hard against the elephant's cool flank, I was afraid he might hear me.

He paced the overlook, making sure I wasn't mingling with the tourists. Now he ran past the children's fair. He was checking the path Capizzo had taken, which ended in a few yards where three streets came together. Even if he followed each of them a short distance, he would soon be back here. Then he'd search the fair.

The carousel left me too exposed. I stepped off the platform, keeping the elephant's body between me and the place I expected he'd emerge. Behind me were the twirling cups and saucers. I stepped through the outer ring of cups. My eye was on a cup close to the ride's hub. Painted dark green—nearly black at night—its open side faced the trees. The square's streetlamps didn't penetrate its interior.

I crawled into the cramped space under the shallow seat, a five-foot-six, 135-pound woman squeezed into a three-foot-long cavity. My height wasn't the problem. Lying on my right side, knees pulled up, I fit. But, as firmly as I pressed my back against the curving cup wall, and as tightly as I folded my legs, my calves and feet were fully exposed. I struggled to turn onto my back. In that position, my body was barely wider than the seat above. But I was twice as uncomfortable. My spine scraped the floor, and my shins were jammed against the plastic ribs supporting the seat, bone on bone.

With the dark clothing, I just might get away with it. The openings of the cups faced every which way. He would need to peer inside each one, and maybe he wouldn't. I maneuvered the cap over my face and worked the sweater sleeves over my hands so that no flash of pale skin would betray me.

Forcing my breath to quiet, using yoga breath—calm, steady—I held frightening thoughts at bay. The wool cap itched. I'd pulled a muscle on my left, broken ribs side. Pain shot through my torso. I focused on the pain, inhaled into it, willing it to subside. Slowly it retreated.

I desperately wanted to crawl out and periscope my head over the cup's rim. I told myself: Stay down, don't move, breathe. Stay down. Don't move. Breathe. Stay. Down. My new mantra.

Maybe because I couldn't see anything, my hearing was acute. Boots clomped nearby and faded; quick steps approached and faded again. Once the gravel crunched so close I was sure he stood within arm's reach. Then the heavy steps retreated and disappeared.

Meanwhile, my mind raced. That phone call. *Was it from Leo's office, or was it a trap?* If my pursuers did have my medical record, they had Leo's name from that business card. And something the woman on the phone said hadn't made sense. I'd been too excited to think it through. Now I replayed her words until she said, "Have him call me."

Him. If she was from Leo's office, wouldn't she know Officer Torre was a woman? And why didn't he call me himself? And why couldn't Capizzo get any information?

And Leo, supposedly so concerned with my safety, would he have asked me to come out at night like this? OK, supposedly he sent a car. But what happened to it? And why couldn't any of us reach him? Didn't he carry a radio? Capizzo and Torre did.

None of it made sense. I was curled up, cramping, cold, trying not to move. The blond man could be out there watching and waiting. If only I hadn't sent Capizzo away. And where the hell was he? Maybe Leo wasn't at the church, and Capizzo was trying to find him. If this was a trap, of course he wasn't there.

For god's sake, think about something else. That shiny thing they moved between the vans, what was that? Why did it look familiar? I tried to remember the many places I might have seen such an object. Too many. Too many questions.

Again I concentrated on calm inhalations, on slow exhalations, on not panicking. The surrounding area remained quiet for several minutes, until someone called my name. Thank god! Capizzo. Or was it? The men pursuing me knew my name too. The man called again, urgently. Was it Capizzo or not? I'd hardly spoken to him, and with the blood pounding in my ears, I couldn't be sure.

Footsteps crunched the pea gravel near—too near. The man called again. No, he didn't sound like Capizzo. I squeezed myself as small as possible.

CAPIZZO

Capizzo's cell phone vibrated a minute or two after leaving Genie behind. He was a newlywed, and Carmella was a nervous bride. When he worked late, their apartment was visited by strange noises and shifting shadows. And if Carmella was unhappy, so was he. He cajoled her as he strode along, but soon he stopped, rested his foot on the low wall skirting the street, and tried to calm her. Without his realizing it, almost ten minutes elapsed.

When he approached Trinità dei Monti, Leo jogged to meet him. "Where is she?" Leo asked through clenched teeth.

"*Signora* Clarke led us through the park, but she was winded by the time we got to the Pincio. I left her there."

This had made sense at the time, but he saw now it was a mistake.

"You left her?" Leo stared into the dark and empty street.

"She wanted me to come tell you we're nearly here and then go back for her. She had to catch her breath."

"Were you followed?"

"Definitely not. The route we took, anyone following us would have been obvious. And a good number of people are in the square." Capizzo's voice betrayed his growing agitation.

"The men I want her to see are eating dinner." Leo glanced at the restaurants below. "They won't stay forever. Bring her as fast as you can."

This time, Capizzo ran through the park. Infected by Leo's anxiety, when he arrived at Napoleon I Square and Genie was nowhere in sight, it was not surprise he felt, but rather the realization of his worst fears.

A few tourists lounged at the overlook. A blond man headed down the stairs to the street below. A handful of pedestrians crossed the plaza. But the benches at the children's fair were empty. He walked to the lineup at the parapet and asked people if they'd seen her. He called her name and called again from the middle of the square. He went a short distance down the nearest pedestrian paths leaving the square, Viale Valadier and Viale dell'Obelisco. He walked in and around the fair, and checked the carousel's swan boats. He stood in the middle of the rides and called a third time, voice cracking with desperation.

GENIE

Except for the murmur of tourists at the overlook, I heard nothing for perhaps ten minutes. Should I stay where I was, or go? I didn't believe the blond man would hang around, leaving his pals waiting in the van below. He wasn't the type. But might they have left him behind to search for me? Well, he hadn't found me.

Whoever had called my name had stopped, and the footsteps had gone away. It might be safe to slip out of my hiding place. It pained me to abandon the idea of meeting Leo. I'd never arrive in time now. Not even if the phone call was legitimate, which I seriously doubted. Maybe the blond had sneaked ahead to Trinità dei Monti to wait for me.

My shins and back ached, I was cold—shivering—and I needed to pee. That clinched it. I squirmed out from under the seat and unkinked my body, dangling my legs out the cup's open side. I took a minute to breathe.

According to my watch, I'd lain compressed under the seat for almost thirty-five minutes. It seemed like hours. I raised myself onto one elbow, came to sitting, and adjusted Andy's cap. I slowly raised my head until I could peer over the cup rim. People at the parapet, one or two pedestrians crossing the plaza, a bicyclist who headed down the path. No one poised like a lookout, no one I recognized. Shakily, I pulled myself to my feet.

LEO

When Capizzo appeared alone the second time, Leo raced to him, and they met a block short of the church.

"She's gone," Capizzo panted. He bent forward, hands cinching his waist.

"Gone? Impossible! Did you look for her?"

"I went to the overlook, I talked to people standing around, I went a ways down the two main exits. Why would she—?"

"Something frightened her. We have to check every street, the paths. There must be some clue to where she went." Or was taken, a thought he kept to himself.

Leo sprinted away, Capizzo right with him. As they ran, Leo pulled off his tie, stuffed it in his pocket, and unbuttoned his shirt collar. When they arrived at the square, it looked absurdly normal. The scattered pedestrians, the gawking tourists, the silent fair.

They combed the fair and the park surrounding the square. They buttonholed everyone in the area. Leo hardly spoke to Capizzo while they searched, afraid of what he might say.

It was nearly midnight when they returned to Agostina's apartment. A police vehicle was stopped in front of the building, and Leo's palms flashed damp, but it was the car picking up Officer Torre at the end of her shift and dropping off her replacement. Capizzo's shift was over too, but he insisted on staying.

Agostina met them at the door. When she saw they didn't have Genie, she cried, "No!" and clapped a hand over her mouth.

"Tell her," Leo said to Capizzo, who recounted the hurried trip through the park. He stumbled when he described how he left Genie to catch her breath while he went to find Leo. Agostina wiped her eyes with the back of her hand. Leo hunched over, head in hands, fingers clenching and unclenching beneath his thick hair.

"Many possibilities." Leo raised his head. "Worst would be if the men trying to find her did so." The words came in a rush. He couldn't have said them otherwise.

"I swear we weren't followed," Capizzo said, a feather of anxiety tickling his voice.

"And certainly they wouldn't be looking for her there, in the park. At night. Yet, if she left the square on her own, something or someone panicked her. She could be in the park, hiding. Or maybe she went down into the city. Or she may still come here."

Agostina shook her head. "It's a long uphill walk. She was tired, and she's not as strong as she thinks she is."

"But she is strong in will," Capizzo said.

"That she is." Leo walked toward the hallway and Genie's room, and the others followed. "We should see whether she has her passport and wallet. If she has money, she has options. Does she have her phone? If so, we can keep calling."

"I'll get her handbag," Agostina said and opened the bedroom door. "*Oh! Dio mio!*"

MARCO

A little after midnight, across town in a commercial neighborhood a few blocks from Santa Maria Maggiore, Umberto raised the door of the garage halfway. Marco drove his motorbike in, cut the engine, and jumped off. He rolled his shoulders to dislodge the sensation of still having Umberto plastered to his back after their forty-minute ride.

Before he hid the van, Marco had left Umberto and his motorbike at an empty office building in a suburb that itself was rarely visited. Then he drove another two blocks and parked the van behind a row of abandoned shops. He rolled up the plastic from the van floor and seats and walked back to the bike. The plastic they deposited in a trash bin miles away. Then they returned to their garage.

"A clever hiding place for the van," Umberto grudgingly acknowledged. "It won't be found for weeks."

"If we're lucky."

"And the tire tracks of the bike will never be found."

Marco grunted.

"Where are those *testoni*?"

"They'll be here."

After handing the reliquary over to Madoor's men, Nic and Lama returned to a club they frequented. If anyone inquired into their whereabouts that evening, they'd be remembered. The patrons were unlikely to notice the brief period they *weren't* there, right around ten o'clock.

Umberto tossed his key to the garage into an overflowing trash bin. "Not coming back to this dump."

After a long uneasy silence between him and Umberto, Marco cocked his head at the whine of a Vespa, growing louder. Soon his cousin pulled into the garage. Nic climbed off, waving a plastic bag. Glass clinked inside.

"*Festeggiamo!*" Nic hollered.

"Shut up!" Umberto snarled, as Marco hurried to roll down the garage door.

"Hey, man! I didn't mean anything." Nic rolled his eyes. "We did good. So I brought chianti."

"Put it over there." Umberto gestured to the workbench.

Nic held out the bag to Lama who took it and stepped away from the two men. Marco kept his wary gaze on Umberto.

"What's with you, man? I said we did good."

"Are you drunk?" Umberto asked, closing in on Nic.

"No, man! I had a few, but I'm not *drunk*." His glance slid to Lama.

"He's just feeling good," Lama said.

"Well, I'm not," Umberto said, right in Nic's face. "I'm feeling bad. I'm feeling bad because I'm working with stupid people." Specks of saliva hit Nic's face.

Nic's hand slipped into the pocket where he kept his knife.

Marco saw and took a few steps toward them. "What's the problem, Umberto?"

"This motherfucker takes off right in the middle of the job. Where he's gone, what for, is he coming back, who knows?" Umberto backed Nic against the wall.

Marco closed his eyes and, if he were a praying man, he would have launched a plea heavenward: Keep that damned knife in your pocket.

"I told you," Nic whined. "I saw the American bitch watching us. I wanted to finish her."

"And did you?"

"She was gone when I got up there." Nic tried to wriggle away, but Umberto kept him pinned. "So I came back to the van."

"You mean you missed her. Again."

"Lama and I had to get back to the club. Like you told us. It was a couple minutes. Worth a try."

Umberto grabbed him by the front of his jacket and slammed him into the wall. "How many times have you fucked up by trying? You keep trying, but you keep fucking up."

"I didn't have much time, man." Nic said, hoarse with rage.

"Leave him alone," Marco said. "We've all tried to kill her one time or another. She's a slippery bitch." He wondered whether Nic had really seen her. Or just another mirage.

"*I* haven't tried," Umberto said. "And I could make our meeting very enjoyable." He spat on the floor and walked away, toward the workbench. "Let's see if this asshole can at least buy a decent bottle of wine."

GENIE

A low voice drew me toward the surface, but the water was too deep. Slippery fingers of emerald sea grass ensnared me and pulled me down into the warm dark. Again the muffled sounds. Calling me. Calling my name. Why did my own name frighten me so?

"Genie, can you wake up?"

Something trapped my hand.

"*Cara?*"

My eyelids fluttered and closed. I went under again.

"Genie? Are you all right?"

The low voice plunged after me, trying to catch me before I drifted deeper. No! Let me go. The question swirled around me, barely audible through the roaring in my ears. The place, the day, the time, I was unmoored from everything, floating. No, not all right. Everything all wrong.

Something cool brushed my forehead. Presently, slowly, the gentle touch revived me. A hand, a cool hand. My eyes fluttered open. People. Agostina and Leo, indistinct in the low light. Agostina stroked my forehead. Leo held my hand.

She tried to speak, but the words jammed in her throat. "Where have you been?" she whispered.

"In a teacup," I mumbled.

Leo and Agostina exchanged alarmed glances.

"I know what she means!" The voice came from across the room. Capizzo. Yes, Capizzo. "She's talking about the teacup ride at the children's fair. I didn't search every one of them ..." Leo and Agostina turned to stare at him. He took a step backwards. "It was so unlikely—they're so small. Very." His hands described their size—impossible as a hiding place.

Agostina laid a damp cloth on my forehead. More awake now, I tried to hold it in place. I pulled myself to sitting and winced at the pain in my side. Leo steadied me, to let Agostina arrange my pillows.

"Did you call me?" I asked Capizzo. Lingering exhaustion muffled my words.

He came closer. "At the Pincio, yes."

"I'm sorry I didn't answer. I wasn't sure … and I meant to tell Agostina I was home, but I needed to rest just a minute. So tired, and …"

Leo kept his arm tight around me and spoke softly. "Can you tell us what happened? What frightened you?"

"How did you know that?"

Agostina switched on the lamps and brought a glass of water. I drank it all. I was fully dressed, except for my shoes and the cap and sweater jumbled next to the bed.

"Our gallop through the park?" My eyes found Capizzo's.

"I told them."

"You were so patient about my shortcuts. We made good time. I sent him to find you," I told Leo. "He didn't want to go. I had to catch my breath, sit. A minute. But I went to the overlook, you know, the one by the—"

"We know," they said in chorus.

"I was admiring the city when down below, men were moving a big carryall from one van to another. Something big and silvery inside. One of them saw me, and I saw him." I shuddered. "The black leather jacket, the spiky blond hair, it was him. The guy who attacked me."

Agostina's hand flew to her mouth.

"He ran for the stairs." I told them how I hid. Capizzo scratched his head. And how I heard the man's heavy footsteps and someone calling me, but I couldn't recognize the voice. And how I wondered whether the telephone call from Leo's office was a trap. "I was so confused." And how I snailed my way home.

"But, Genie, how did you get in?" Agostina protested.

"I was afraid if they really do have this address," my eyes pleaded with Leo to forgive me, "they could be watching the front, so I found the side door to the garden. My key worked!"

"What door?" Leo and Capizzo said together.

"It's never been used in all the years I've lived here. I totally forgot about it," Agostina said.

"It's very well hidden. I noticed it in my endless circuits." I pointed toward the patio door, where leaves and twigs were strewn over the floor tiles. "I did some damage to your landlord's vines."

"We'll have to watch that side wall," Leo told Capizzo, "unless we can persuade the landlord to seal it up."

"Genie," Agostina handed me a postcard from the bedside table, "is this what was in the carryall?"

I recognized the picture at once. "The crib? It was about that size and had lots of—how do you say 'embellishments'?" I said in English. "*Decorazioni,*" I tried. "I suppose it could have been." I peered at the postcard. "Wait a minute, is the crib—*missing*?"

"Stolen early this afternoon," Leo said.

"Is this what I overheard those men talking about?"

"Perhaps."

"Wow." I collapsed against the pillows, fading fast.

Leo squeezed my hand and rose, motioning to Capizzo. They conferred by the patio doors, and Leo borrowed his phone. He called headquarters and asked for a forensic team from *La Polizia Scientifica* to cover the ground under the overlook. He told them about the dark vans. That would be a long shot. The thieves had a head start of several hours. He left messages for Sal and Bracci, then came back to me, saying reassuring words.

Agostina brought a small broom and brushed the leaves and debris into a pile she chucked into the wastebasket. She made sure the door was locked, slightly opened a window so the fresh night air could slip in, and, in a contradictory action, closed the heavy draperies so the morning light could not. She took Capizzo's arm, and they melted away.

Left alone with Leo, I managed a smile. He brushed the hair from my forehead much as Agostina had done and promised to return in the morning. "We need to talk. But for now, *cara*, sleep well."

CHAPTER—12

Friday, October 26

Genie messaged Robbie:

> *Living with a local, highly recommended. Fabulous meals!*

LEO

Sal tapped on Leo's open office door early the next morning. "We were stuck at the basilica until nearly midnight," he said. "They asked us to finish so they could reopen this morning. Fine, but the echoes gave me the creeps."

"What did you learn?" Leo asked.

"One of the art experts from the TPC answered a load of my questions. She says the crib is more valuable than we thought."

Leo exhaled sharply. Not what he wanted to hear.

"The Vatican and TPC guys need to talk to you." Sal handed Leo their business cards.

"Any links between the theft and *Signora* Clarke?"

"Not yet. The thieves left tools and stuff behind, but no prints so far. Complete lab reports later today. You left a message about a possible lead?"

Leo described Genie's experience the previous night.

"Where was she, and where were the vans?" Sal asked.

"She was at the Pincian Hill, the overlook. They were on the street below."

Sal frowned, thinking. "And that street is Viale Gabriele D'Annunzio. Remember those words we couldn't figure out? *Signora* Clarke heard 'Gab'-something 'Danzio,' and we thought it might be a person's name? That's it! Gabriele

D'Annunzio. These guys always intended that street for the handoff, and they always intended it to be at ten at night, exactly like she said."

Leo pictured Tati defending that argument in court. Tricky.

Sal handed him a large envelope. "These are the blowups of Marco with the priest. The lab says he was holding a thermal imaging camera."

"Really? That's worth thinking about. Thanks. Meanwhile, the funeral? Do you have time?"

"When is it?"

"Eleven. At Cimitero del Verano."

Sal whistled. "I thought that place was full."

"Some powerful strings were pulled to get this *ragazzo* in there." He showed Sal several photos of the dead man.

"I'll go. Who is he again?"

"The gangster strangled in his bed Monday night. Snake tattoo. Not like the one Genie drew. Still, I'd like to know who shows up and why the rush. They barely had time to sew him up after the postmortem. Is the family hiding something? Or do they just need to get home to—" he searched his brain "—Modena?"

A few minutes after Sal left, Emilio Bracci settled into the chair opposite Leo.

"I sent your men on a wild goose chase last night," Leo said.

"So I heard."

"And got put in my place."

"Oh? Pacino was it?" Bracci's suppressed smile said he'd heard that too.

"I was out of line. I shouldn't have—"

"Heat of the moment. Forget it."

"Did they follow the men from the restaurant?"

"Yeah. They went to a disco, where they danced and tried to pick up women until four a.m. Drunk as monkeys. Apparently, my two tried to keep up with them."

"As it happens, the men we want were just down the street." He repeated Genie's story.

"Why are we sure the blond is the one who attacked her?"

"Aside from her eyewitness testimony?"

Bracci shrugged. He was right to discount it, Leo knew. Even assuming Genie was right, if the men were mafia connected, they'd have lawyers who specialized in introducing doubt. They'd turn any hairline crack in her testimony into a canyon-sized credibility gap.

"He gave it away when he took off after her so fast," Leo said.

"Not simply because she was watching them?"

"I don't think so." Leo repeated Sal's theory about the street name.

"That whole transcript was a piece of swiss cheese."

Leo pursed his lips, annoyed. But Bracci was right. His logic chain was plausible, but weak, and it could crumble under the attack of a smart lawyer. A theft this size would have serious sponsors, guaranteeing phalanxes of smart lawyers. As much as he wanted this case wrapped up, they needed stronger evidence.

"Let's lay out what we've got for Tati and see what he thinks," Leo said. "Come with me when I meet him this afternoon."

"Regrettably, there's a complication," Bracci muttered. "Shouldn't Gilletti be brought in? If she did see the reliquary, our case overlaps with his, and that skinny son of a bitch will try to fuck us up just because that's the kind of guy he is."

"Right. Somehow, we have to get hold of his case before he realizes we care about it. Maybe Tati can help."

"But does he know Gilletti like we do? He'll say we already have our hands full."

"He'll be right. But we can't let—What if we let Genie talk to Tati, tell him first-hand what she saw?"

Silence. Then, "How *is Signora* Clarke? She's unhurt?" Bracci asked.

"Exhausted last night. I'm meeting her and Agostina this morning to go over the whole situation. Come with me? Judge for yourself whether she's credible."

"Sure. Give me a few minutes."

Waiting for Bracci, Leo called the other police services, finishing by the time Sal stuck his head in the door. "Let me play this on your computer," he said. "It's the bank security DVD." Leo moved aside and Sal inserted the disc. "So, fast-forwarding through … there's the flowers by the van. Vehicles pass by without stopping. Here's a motorbike. Stops for the light. Two men in black leather. Passenger glances toward the flowers. Taps driver. They both look. Traffic blocks our view. Clears. Vespa swings into the alley; tall man in back is off, sprints to the van, grabs the flowers … he's on again. Bike backs into the street. Light changes, they speed away. Laughing."

"I'll bet."

"Now the van driver comes out of the shop. Looks around. Hands in the air. Cursing like crazy." Sal laughed.

"The cost of those flowers came out of his pocket."

"I know. But he *is* comical."

They watched again in slow motion. Although the riders' helmets hid their faces, the driver's ponytail was clearly visible when he turned toward the alley. Sal noticed something stuffed in the tall one's back pocket. "Baseball cap? I'll get a blowup to make sure."

Leo and Bracci parked their car and strolled along the curving street. They ignored the whistling gardener trimming hedges in front of an apartment building across the way and the window on the building's first floor, where a half-closed curtain shimmered as if a hand brushed against it.

They found Genie reading a newspaper story about the stolen relic. A huge photograph of the reliquary, a duplicate of her postcard, covered half the front page. Its screaming headline contained a crucial detail Leo had not mentioned.

"That poor priest," she said. Her coffee cup rattled in its saucer. "This *must* be the crime I heard them discussing. And now it's claimed two lives we know of and gotten me—and Agostina—into so much trouble!"

Bracci sent the man stationed inside the apartment out to watch the street, and the four of them clustered around the dining table. Leo unloaded materials from a folder, Bracci started his laptop, Agostina poured coffee, and Genie studied her own list of questions.

As they'd agreed, Leo asked Bracci to run through everything. He needed to make sure every one of them understood recent events the same way.

"Starting with the Sunday you're attacked," Bracci began, "you overhear a conversation among four men—one blond, one with a shaved and tattooed head, one with dark hair in a ponytail, and an older man who seems to be in charge."

As he proceeded, he laid their documentation on the table, starting with Sal's version of the overheard conversation, and her drawing of her assailant's tattoo. "You're in the hospital several days, leaving on Thursday and coming here."

"Thank god," Agostina said.

"That night, Gemma Capuano is murdered, apparently by men who deliver flowers to her room." Leo pulled out the bank DVD and handed it to Bracci, who loaded it into his laptop. They watched the replay of the flower theft.

"Notice anything?" Leo asked.

"The driver has a ponytail," Genie said. "And a black leather jacket, pants, gloves, the whole outfit."

Leo handed Bracci another disk. "Now this one, which you've seen, made from the hospital security tape. Here two men cross the lobby carrying flowers. Are they the same?"

The women murmured, "The flowers look the same."

"Same vase too," Genie said.

"No fingerprints, nothing left behind except the flowers themselves and the crumpled note with your name and room number," Bracci said. "Three days later, on Sunday, the media broadcast Gemma Capuano's name, and that night your medical record disappears."

"Which may answer one nagging question," Leo said, glancing at Genie to see whether she understood the implication.

"How they knew my name and room number on Thursday," she said. "They have access to the hospital's records. Maybe a person on the inside."

"So it appears. The head of medical records says it can take as much as a day for a chart to receive all the necessary sign-offs and find its way downstairs to them."

"And I left late Thursday morning. So meanwhile, my room was cleaned and given to Gemma."

"When your chart *does* arrive, no one's looking for it. Because—" Bracci's bushy eyebrows merged in a frown, and he shifted in his chair.

"Because they think I'm dead."

It pained Leo to hear her say it.

"Yes, and with *all* your records gone, the disappearance of the chart itself is less prominent. The details of your stay become confused, including the extent of your injuries at their hands."

"Aren't they afraid the missing records will tip you off?"

"They know we're aware of the attack," Bracci said. "Without the records, it's harder for us to do anything about it."

"Other events occur Sunday too," Leo said. He laid out the photographs from Santa Maria Maggiore. "The man we think is Marco visits several churches. Here he has a camera out of its bag. Genie noticed this camera is odd, so we had the photo enlarged." He showed them that picture.

"It's a thermal imaging camera," Bracci said. "Because he has it out suggests he used it down in the crypt. But for what exactly? This kind of camera reveals sources of heat. Good for identifying ..." Bracci stumbled. Leo guessed he'd been about to say, "a decomposing body" but tactfully switched to "... a person hiding in a dark building or behind a wall, certain chemicals—anything that creates a temperature difference."

"Electrical wiring?" Genie asked. "Was he checking the alarm system? Can the camera do that?"

"Good question." Bracci made a note.

Genie pushed the photo across the table. She pointed to Marco's hands. "See that? It reminds me of—" she grabbed her drawing from the growing pile "—this."

"Are you saying *he* is the man who attacked you?" Bracci asked.

"No, the tattoo's on the wrong hand. And he's not blond. But the way it covers the back of the hand, that's similar."

"Can we blow this one up further?" Leo asked.

"We can try." Bracci made another note.

This was exactly what Leo wanted. The more Genie understood the details of the case and the connections between them, the easier it would be to accept what he would require her and Agostina to do next.

"Still, there's good news," Bracci said. "So far, my people don't believe anyone else is watching this building or especially interested in it. Last night, you give this impression an unexpected test. No one tails you and Capizzo into the park.

"Earlier, as you know, a priceless relic was stolen from Santa Maria Maggiore, and a priest who presumably interrupted the thieves was fatally stabbed. A narrow-bladed instrument, the medical examiner says."

Genie paled. After a pause, she said, "It's odd, they don't use guns. I know guns. The havoc they wreak can feel remote. But knives, like the one he was going to stab me with … they're … intimate. Personal." She shuddered.

Leo gave them a moment to refocus, then said, "We believe the theft is connected to what went before," he gestured to the pile of documents and photos, "but we can't prove it yet."

"There are two vital connections in our theory," Bracci said. "First, what you saw last night at the overlook—something silver in the kind of carryall the thieves took out of the basilica—yes, we've confirmed that with two witnesses who spoke with the fake workmen. It's also important that you described the silver item and the carryall *before* you knew about the theft. And second, the fact that on that first Sunday, you heard a few words we couldn't understand. Given later events, they fit exactly the time and place of the hand-off—ten o'clock at night on Viale Gabriele D'Annunzio."

Leo listened and watched. Now he looked for weaknesses in the logic, like Bracci had earlier. And, they needed to observe Genie's reactions. Although she was calm, she looked tired as she studied her own list of questions, making check marks by a few. The detectives waited.

Eventually, she said, "I see I'm the weak link here. Everything you've laid out makes sense, and in the two key places you mentioned, your argument depends on me. The transcript from that first day? As we know, I missed a lot. And the possible street name? A fragment. It fits now, but … after-the-fact logic, you know? Always vulnerable."

"As for last night, you have only my word about what I saw. Lawyers could tear apart my testimony in many ways. They would say it was dark—by the way, the streetlamps seemed to be out." Bracci added a note to his list. "They could say it didn't have to be that the blond man recognized *me*, specifically, but that anyone committing a crime, if what happened at the Pincio *was* part of a crime, anyone would want to eliminate witnesses …"

Leo's heart wrenched.

"Really, it would be his word against mine," she continued. "There aren't any other witnesses—those people on the parapet were tourists and will be scattered around the world before you can find them. Anyway, they weren't paying attention to him *or* me."

As she spoke her manner grew firm. "If I weren't so sure it was the same man—when he looked up at me, my whole body knew *exactly* who he was—if I weren't so absolutely positive, I would say last night's link is terribly weak too."

Few victims could move from their emotional state to the strategy for making a case in court. But Genie intuitively grasped how vital she was. Cubellis would too.

MADOOR

Late Friday morning, Amit Madoor visited his suburban warehouse. Arrayed on the floor were the molds his men were using to create five prancing fiberglass horses, three-quarter size, and the head and neck of a sixth horse. They would fill the horses' hollow legs and bellies with sand to give them credible weight and cover them with metallic paint before mottling on shades of gray, charcoal brown and teal. With the shiny surface underneath exposed here and there, the colors would create the perfect illusion of patina.

Two workmen were building wooden crates for the finished horses. Though the crates were identical on the outside, the interior of the sixth crate, for the horsehead, was different from the others. It contained a sealed hidden compartment in which the reliquary would travel.

"How long to cure?" Madoor shouted to his Malaysian foreman over the combined roar of the building's exhaust fans and four dehumidifiers placed around the work area.

"About nine hours for three layers fiberglass. After, we can paint."

"And ready to ship?"

"Sunday morning good. Tomorrow, Nino visit farm of his brother and get straw. We pack early Sunday. Make sure paint dry." The foreman tested the tackiness of one of the horses and gestured to another worker, a Christian from South Sudan, that it was ready for the next layer of fiberglass.

A Brazilian came to stand beside Madoor. "The brackets for the horses are finished," he said, "and for the other." He gestured to where the reliquary rested on a wooden pallet, its shine visible even under layers of clear plastic film. His rough fingers caressed his elaborate silver and ebony crucifix.

"*Bom trabalho*," Madoor responded in Portuguese and clapped him on the shoulder. "Are you going home next week?"

Twice a year, Madoor paid for his workers' trips to their home countries, scattered around the world. These trips reminded them how his generous pay improved their families' lives, pay that came with just a few strings attached, one of which was to maintain absolute silence about him and their unusual jobs.

"My son will be twelve," the man said. "Almost a man. I want him to be proud of his father."

SAL

Sal squeezed through the crowd of mourners gathered for Gianni di Landri's graveside service, a minicam dangling inconspicuously from his keychain. Black-clad family members perched on flimsy folding chairs: an older man and woman curled with grief, a young woman who might be a sister whose husband or boyfriend was barnacled to the back of her chair, and a trio of large young men who resembled Gianni—his brothers probably—squirming uneasily.

At the front of the press of people closest to the grave was what appeared to be a greatly extended family. Beyond them, mostly younger people, cousins or friends, were packed into the narrow spaces between monuments. Heavy perfume from mounds of white flowers and burning incense mingled with the smell of fresh-dug earth. Sal discreetly took a few pictures.

Eventually, the priest leading the service introduced a tall, distinguished-looking man, Gianni's cousin, to give the eulogy. The man seemed unaccountably nervous, as he mouthed platitudes about "lost potential" and "the importance of family." When he finished, he quickly returned to his place alongside a stunning woman in a black designer suit.

After the service, Sal hurried to catch up to the handsome woman. "Great eulogy," he said.

She scanned him up and down. "You're joking."

The eulogist came alongside, saying, "Mama's riding with them. We need to hurry." He strode toward a short line of parked cars. Only the elderly and those with pull drove to the service; the young and healthy were expected to walk. "Your husband?"

"Ex. Star of a very lackluster family."

"No church service?" Sal asked.

"What church would have Gianni?"

"But the priest?"

"The one benefit of a big Catholic family. There's always a cousin to do—whatever."

Her ex-husband walked around to the driver's side of a silver Mercedes and beeped the door locks. Sal opened the passenger door for the woman as the man bent inside and retrieved a large envelope from the driver's seat. He looked surprised to find it there and even more surprised at its contents. He quickly glanced up and flinched when his eyes met Sal's.

"Nice eulogy," Sal said and smiled, then returned to helping the woman. "I'm sorry for your loss."

She snorted. "I came only out of respect for Venieri's mother."

The man slipped the envelope behind the seat before she noticed it and hurriedly folded himself inside. Sal snapped a picture of the car's number plate then jogged away to join the departing parade of Gianni's friends.

GENIE

The ground Leo and Bracci had gone over that morning was familiar, while my questions were about "what was coming?" On a break, I walked outside, making a couple of circuits of the garden. The bedraggled vines around the hidden door were a reminder of how entangled I was in everything they'd described. I'd fought free of the vines, now I'd have to free myself from the rest.

When we reassembled at the dining table, Bracci said, "Now we must revisit these events from the perspective of risk. Or, that is, timing."

Here it comes, I thought.

"First, the mugging two Sundays ago. *Signora* Clarke is in the hospital on Monday, Tuesday, and Wednesday. Why isn't there any move against her for three long days?"

I felt queasy now, recalling how, for long stretches of time, I lay alone in that room. And until late Tuesday, I was unconscious. Totally vulnerable. I glanced at Leo. The muscles in his jaw were clenching and unclenching.

"We know they haven't lost interest in her—I'm sorry, in *you*," Bracci continued. "We can make a few educated guesses about the delay. It may take a day or so to find out which hospital you're in and to identify a friend on the inside or put one in. They know you are badly injured, and they may assume the hospital staff is keeping a close watch initially. Maybe you even have a police guard.

"In the face of these uncertainties, you are safe. By Thursday, they put it together and—"

"Genie got out just in time," Agostina said.

"Yes, because Thursday evening they act. On Friday, Saturday, and Sunday, until the media reveal the victim's identity, well, those three days she—I mean, you. Again I apologize—" he bowed slightly, "you are safe."

"For all the wrong reasons," I said.

"Truly. But Sunday they learn they murdered the wrong woman, and within hours it seems they have your medical record. While they don't find this address, they do have Detective Angelini's name and your doctor's name. On Monday you keep your doctor's appointment. It is a potential risk, but as far as we know, nothing comes of it."

"We were not followed," Agostina said.

Bracci acknowledged her. "Again, they are a little slow. Then Tuesday."

I groaned and put my face in my hands. The ill-fated trip to the Spanish Steps.

"Tuesday, our luck may have run out. Agostina's observation of the man with the ponytail worries us most. If he *was* the man Marco, and if he was close enough to see the plate number—" his expressive eyebrows queried Agostina.

"He was."

"—almost certainly they know where we are even now."

Bracci's step-wise logic was utterly convincing. Unbidden, my hands crossed my heart.

"Again for three days they do nothing. Why not? With the benefit of hindsight, we know they have planned a crime—an unbelievable crime, a crime worth millions of euros. That crime is planned for Thursday. Would they risk trying once more to get to you before then?"

Working it out, I said, "If anything went wrong, if you had surveillance, if one of us called the police who arrive too fast, if an alarm went off—anything at all—it could jeopardize their *Progetto*."

"Yes. So, unlikely though it may seem, though they know exactly where you are and though we know how far they are willing to go, you have been safe. Except that you almost fall into their hands up on the Pincio. But last night your pursuer has more immediate concerns—"

"—and abandons his search," I finished.

"Yes. He knows he can find you later. Meanwhile, last night, they must be thinking of themselves as master criminals. Probably they believe the police don't have a clue about their audacious theft." He and Leo watched me closely. "Except one. You. Today they'll sober up, and doubts will creep in. Did they leave behind any evidence? Did they stray in front of a security camera?"

"But most important, what can they do about the American at the top of the lookout—the same woman who eavesdropped on their planning? What did she hear? What did she see? The theft is behind them, it's time to deal with her at last. Will they try?" He paused, and none of us breathed. "Based on thirty years of police work, I believe that is a certainty."

LEO

Leo watched Genie's pen, poised over her list of questions. He knew exactly what she would ask next, and she did.

"So, what do we *do* about it?"

"This afternoon, Bracci and I would like you to meet Maximilliano Tati." During their break, the detectives had agreed she was ready for this. "The theft opens new lines of inquiry, and we may have more photos for you to look at soon," Leo said. He sounded upbeat and positive.

"Umm. That is, *if* you are planning to stay in Italy." There. Bracci raised Leo's biggest concern.

"Yes, I'm staying," Genie said. "I don't want those men to get away with—to get away with *murder*. Anyway, *Dottor* Immormino hasn't released me yet. I'm staying."

"Once you've helped us identify them, you can go home, if you're well enough, but we hope you would return if they go to trial."

"Of course I would."

"All right. But our first priority is to move you, immediately. We agree this location is compromised. You need to be somewhere we can keep you safe," Bracci said, in his typically cheerful, but decisive manner. "Agostina must go with you. We can't have them trying to get at you through her."

The women looked stunned, but weren't objecting. Bracci continued, "We will find a secure place for the two of you, even if you must sleep at police headquarters under my desk."

Leo's eyes widened. That wouldn't be his top choice for safety.

"What about the hotel where I stayed before, near the Spanish Steps?" Genie asked. "The staff were so helpful. It's small. A busy neighborhood, and an existing police presence in the area."

"That is a good idea," Leo said. "Small *is* better. Fewer people to check out, and fewer to go home and gossip. I met the manager when I picked up your suitcase." He kept the worry out of his voice.

"I'm sure you understand that we cannot delay," Bracci said. "How soon can you be ready to leave?"

"I can be packed before my doctor's appointment. It's at eleven."

"I'll drive you there," Leo said.

Bracci said, "While you do that, I'll take charge of Agostina. At least until the hotel employees are cleared," Bracci said.

"And so?" Leo asked, walking Genie to the car after her appointment. She seemed to have drifted into private thoughts. "What did *lo stimato dottore* say?"

"Not much. He took out the stitches on the back of my head. That wasn't fun. He says my ribs are still 'healing nicely,' but he won't release me until I'm totally off the pain medications. I have a lower-dose patch starting tomorrow."

"How long will that take?" He kept his voice neutral. Despite what she'd promised, when Immormino said she could leave, she might.

"A week or so. My body is used to the drug, and he doesn't want me to have withdrawal symptoms, especially on an airplane. Me neither!" If she had any other reason to be in no hurry to be released into the sky like a slightly bedraggled homing pigeon, she did not say.

"I talked to the hotel manager. He says his employees are accustomed to people who want their privacy, a few of whom even have their own bodyguards. He'll give you and Agostina a suite on the top floor. Access will be extremely limited. Have you met my young colleague Sal Riccobono?"

"You've said so much about him, it's like I know him. Bright. Brave. A ladies' man."

Leo chuckled and nodded. "That's Sal. He and Capizzo are checking out the hotel staff. They'll do a thorough job."

"When does Capizzo sleep?"

"I don't think he does. He's a newlywed."

She laughed. "By the way, Father Harmon and I have been trying to get together. Would it be OK to invite him to the hotel?"

Asking his opinion, his permission in fact. That was a change.

She glanced at him. "You look very 'cat that swallowed the canary.'"

"I'm sorry. The cat—what?"

"You don't have that expression? It means 'excessively pleased with yourself.'"

"Oh, I am. I'm very pleased you like my friend. Having him visit is a fine idea. You and Agostina will need distractions."

He bought panini and drinks at a local shop, and drove to the Giardino degli Aranci, an out-of-the-way park, where they ate on a bench under the bitter orange trees. He explained again what Tati would need to know. "You were perceptive when you said how much depends on you. If he is going to believe in this case, he must believe in you, as Bracci and I do."

Leo left her in Tati's outer office while he and Bracci told the prosecutor about the previous night's developments. He immediately asked the key question: "*Signora* Clarke, she is positive about the man last night?"

"Her story is remarkably consistent," Leo said. "And, if she is right about seeing the crib, we've landed in the middle of that other case."

"Who is in charge?"

"Gillo Gilletti," Bracci said, failing to hide his annoyance.

Tati made a dismissive noise. "No chance you could work together on this?" Seeing their expressions, he said, "I thought not; the man is a fool. *Signora* Clarke is here? I have looked forward to meeting her."

Tati buzzed the intercom. His energetic young assistant Dante brought Genie into the office and moved a chair in front of the desk for her.

Tati shook her hand, saying, "So, here is the American who has created for us such a golden opportunity."

"How do you mean?" she asked.

"We would have no decent place to begin our investigation of the stolen reliquary, *Signora*, if your story were not running in parallel."

"I see."

"Yet, at the same time, the problem of keeping you from harm grows larger." He glanced inquiringly at the detectives.

"*Signora* Clarke will be at a small hotel with a trusted friend—an extremely capable nurse—and a posted guard," Bracci said.

"Pick that guard carefully," Tati said. "Now, *Signora*, please tell me in your own words what transpired last evening."

She gave a straight recitation of events, leaving aside the fear and the physical difficulties. Tati leaned back in his chair, hands folded on his chest, and watched her face. When she finished, his casual demeanor evaporated. "You are certain the man last night is the one who attacked you?"

"Yes, absolutely."

"Why is that?"

"Because every night he appears in my nightmares."

After a few more questions, he asked, "How confident are you it was the crib reliquary they were carrying?"

"I had a glimpse, no more. The men moved it carefully, as if it were awkward, difficult to handle. When the covering pulled away, I saw silvery metal …" She searched for an Italian word and settled on "ornamented."

"*feci belli* on the top and sides."

She's doing well, Leo thought.

More questions, including, "Will you stay in Italy and help us with our prosecution, if it comes to that? Or fly back here, if necessary?"

"*Signor* Tati, I cannot forget innocent Gemma Capuano, how we lay in the same bed, how we stared at the same walls. My thoughtless eavesdropping was responsible for her murder, yet her death gave me a few days of protection. I understand these men are dangerous; that's why they must be stopped. I hope you can do that. Please believe I will do whatever I can to help."

There's your answer. Mine, too.

Tati switched course. "Are you still taking narcotics?"

"Yes. My physician has prescribed fentanyl patches since I left the hospital."

"And, do the drugs cloud your perceptions?"

"They did at first. The drugs and the pain together. The concussion too, I suppose. But my body became accustomed, and the pain is much less now. My mind has been completely clear for almost a week."

"I see." After a moment, Tati stretched his arm over the desk to press her hand. "I am delighted you are recovering. Thank you for visiting with me." His manner in no way suggested they had just concluded a conversation that would determine the fate of his prosecution.

When the office door shut behind her, Tati said, "Fine. Now to our other problem." He punched in a telephone extension. "Good afternoon, Fausto. Max here. Is it remotely possible you could come to my office for a brief consultation? … This very moment, if you would … Most appreciated."

To the detectives he said, "He will be the answer to your prayers." He leaned back with a slight smile.

Ah. "The cat that swallowed the canary." I get it.

Soon Dante admitted a man approaching eighty. His short stature and slight limp typified many people of the wartime generation, when families lived on the smell of baking bread and shared a single apple among five. Now he carried a belly round as a basketball. Tati introduced him as Fausto Scarpatti, another public magistrate, one neither Leo nor Bracci knew.

Tati said, "Fausto received the Santa Maria Maggiore case this morning."

Scarpatti sighed and settled into Tati's sofa. His drooping eyelids sagged lower.

"We have an interesting situation here, Fausto. Two cases may be converging. May I tell you about mine?" He gave a concise review.

Scarpatti said, "That is the lovely American waiting outside?"

"Yes. I have talked to her."

"And?"

"Credible. Very credible indeed."

"Now you want me to give you the basilica theft and murder so you don't have to deal with that *imbecile* Gilletti."

"In a nutshell," Tati said.

"If he is involved, your case is hopeless."

"Our view exactly."

"But, how to do it so he doesn't create difficulties."

Struggling to keep a straight face, Leo didn't dare catch Bracci's eye. Behind Scarpatti's sleepy demeanor was a sharp and devious mind. The man didn't speak for such a long time Leo worried he actually had fallen asleep. Then Scarpatti said, "I notice on the roster of case assignments you have the murder of a young gangster."

Tati picked the dossier on Gianni di Landri's murder out of a short stack.

"We will trade," Scarpatti said. "My office will handle the paperwork. And Detective Gilletti." His rotund body lifted out of the thickly cushioned sofa in stages, like a hot air balloon struggling to rise.

"You are giving away an important case," Tati said. "Are you sure?"

Scarpatti limped to the desk and took the folder. "Too important for an old man, maybe. Gilletti's spoiled my cases several times. I never expected such an enticing opportunity." His laugh came close to a cackle. "No, Max, I'm sure."

Leo said, "How are you going to—?"

"You must be surprised."

AL PACINO

The *Polizia di Stato*'s Al Pacino look-alike dipped his brush in a can of umber stain and continued painting the trim of the garages outside Agostina's building, whistling an unrecognizable tune. He paused when an impressive black Mercedes sedan pulled into the garage apron and nearly knocked over his stepladder. Four men piled out. Black suits, dark ties, sunglasses.

"*Attento!* Careful there!" Pacino yelled. The men ignored him, and he waved his loaded brush at them. "Going to a funeral?"

"Just came from one," said a tall man with a tattooed head, tilting it to see the man on the ladder.

The painter roughly crossed himself, brush in hand. "Sorry. At least it's a pleasant day. I hate a funeral in the rain."

The tall man stared. "Did anyone ever tell you that you look just like—"

Pacino rolled his eyes and the older man who acted like the group's leader growled, "Leave him." The men moved in a tight cluster to the sidewalk gate, and the leader rang the bell. No answer. He rang again, glanced side to side, and jimmied the lock. Three of the men walked to the apartment building, the fourth stayed out front, watching the street.

Pacino's screwdriver clattered to the concrete and rolled down the drive. He swore loudly and chuffed down the ladder to retrieve it, securing it in a loop of his coveralls. By the time the men returned, he'd moved his ladder to a spot farther from their car. Grumbling among themselves, they marched toward him.

"Who are you looking for?" Pacino asked.

"None of your business." The leader sneered.

"Sorry. I thought I might be able to help."

They clustered around the ladder.

"Is an American staying here? Maybe with another woman?" asked a man with spiky blond hair. The leader growled.

"An American? I don't think so. A couple of years ago we had a Frenchman. Or, wait, maybe he was Belgian."

"Well, are there any women living together?" The blond persisted.

"No. A single man. Couples. No children, thank goodness. Little criminals, you ask me." He yawned. "But they're all out. No one's home."

"Why didn't you say so?" the leader said.

"I'm not the butler." He stayed on the ladder, forcing them to crane their necks.

"When will they be home?" asked a ponytailed man.

"What time is it now?"

"One-thirty."

"Hunh." Pacino studied the position of the sun. He moved his lips, as if making an obscure calculation. "The last one went out before I had my lunch. Every day I eat at noon exactly."

"Where?" The leader glared.

"Today? Right there." Pacino pointed to a bench in the well-trimmed front garden.

"Where did *they* go, idiot?"

"Work. Shopping. Mass. Out. How should I know? They don't discuss their plans with me."

Swearing, the men climbed into their car. After it curved out of sight, Pacino's gaze drifted to the building opposite. A curtain moved, as if by a current of air, behind which Pacino knew a camera watched. Pacino had given his colleague plenty of chances to use it, with its nice long lens.

LEO

Bracci tilted one of Leo's office chairs back onto two creaking legs. Sal stood against the rear wall. Through the window blinds the slanting late afternoon light striped the papers on the desk, including the blowup photo Sal had brought showing the flower thief's jeans pocket, baseball cap stuffed inside.

"They said they'd just been to a funeral. Maybe the one Sal went to." Bracci turned to the young detective. "Show Pacino your pictures."

"Tell me about the hotel," Leo asked.

Bracci said the women were in a two-bedroom suite occupying the entire top floor. The hotel was too small to have a restaurant and served breakfast only, but the neighborhood offered many restaurant choices. The suite even had a dining table, and the women would eat there. Managing their meals would help occupy Agostina.

"Staff security checks?" Leo asked Sal.

"Finished. No problems."

"Still, we should limit their exposure to the staff."

"That's the plan," Bracci said. There was no elevator, and hotel visitors had to climb three twisting flights to reach the top. The service stairs were narrower yet, and the hotel would keep that door locked on the fourth floor. Only the maid and people with business there would be going up. When they did, Bracci's officer posted in the short hallway would greet them. "Plain clothes. No point advertising a police presence."

At that moment, Gillo Gilletti barged in as if the doorsill were too hot to stand on. "Well, comrades, I'm afraid I have to dump my work on you."

He had the detectives' complete attention. "We'll do our best," Leo said. "Why, what's happened?"

"I'm being kicked upstairs," Gilletti said, hollow chest puffed with pleasure. "No new title, special detail. Working directly with one of the senior magistrates."

"Who?" Bracci asked.

"Fausto Scarpatti. The best."

Leo allowed himself a smile and an impressed murmur. "Congratulations! And you'll be doing ...?"

Gilletti lowered his voice to a "between us" level and leaned toward them. "The mafia buried one of their own today." Behind him, Sal covered his grin. "Scarpatti thinks it was an inside job, dissension in the ranks. Cubellis is getting old. If his so-called family is breaking apart, Rome will have a bloodbath. My job is to prevent it." He straightened, inflating even more. "And, it's solo—Scarpatti insisted—no big team to tip them off. 'Only one man for the job,' he told me. I develop the leads, and he brings in the antimafia mopes later. Very hush-hush." He gave a lizard-like wink.

When Gilletti retreated out of earshot, Bracci said, "One thing for sure. He knows nothing about Cubellis."

Sal laughed. "I'll burn another disc with the funeral pictures and leave it on his desk. Anonymously. Give him something to think about."

"He'll announce a major breakthrough," Bracci said.

"So you're getting Santa Maria Maggiore?" Sal asked.

"Yes, we are," Bracci said, folding his hands across his stomach and again tipping back the protesting chair.

"Tati wants to see us tonight at six to discuss the theft from his end," Leo said. "Tomorrow morning we'll talk to whoever's on it over the weekend and to the whole team Monday morning."

"I begged off today," Sal said, "but can I get back on board?"

"Without question."

Bracci's chair creaked ominously as he shifted position. "Unfortunately, we may run right into Gilletti again, if Sal's funeral victim was involved."

Leo shrugged, hands raised. "Even worse, we can't continue ignoring the mafia connection—those men at Agostina's apartment, their car's fake license plate, an insider at the hospital, the size of the theft, how quickly they unloaded the goods. This isn't the work of a few punks. Which means we'll not only be tripping over Gilletti, but whole mafia units—ours, the DIA, the *carabinieri*—maybe the *Guardia di Finanza,* since the crib is big money."

"Vatican security," Bracci added.

"TPC," Sal said.

"Poor Tati. That's a lot of meetings," Bracci said.

"Just so he keeps us out of them. And, Sal, one more thing. Another link in the logic chain. We've never figured out how Genie's medical record disappeared from the hospital. Find that leak."

GENIE

I rested my forehead on a folded towel at the edge of the hotel suite's dining table. Agostina had placed a basin of warm water and a pile of cotton balls nearby. The sharp odor of rubbing alcohol filled my nostrils. Over the last nine days she had gingerly cleaned that scalp wound, not wanting to disturb the stitches. With them finally out, she was doing a proper job.

"The alcohol won't make a spot on my clothes, will it?" I had on a navy sweater and slacks. "I'll go change."

"It will be fine." Agostina pressed a hand on my back, preventing escape.

After a perfunctory knock, Officer Torre walked in. "*Madre de dio*! It smells like a hospital in here. What are you doing?" She came over to the table.

"That looks disgusting," she said.

I couldn't disagree. I'd viewed the long, livid pink scar in a mirror, and the shaved strip around it looked like a man's three-day beard.

"Agostina is a saint." My voice rose from under the table.

"I'm bored to death out there! And the phone reception sucks," Torre said. "I came in to use the toilet."

Officer Torre wasn't hiding her annoyance at being assigned to guard us again. Agostina said the bad mood might have to do with Torre's new boyfriend. Based on the innumerable cell phone conversations Agostina overheard, he was coming on strong.

"Would you mind taking those towels in with you?" Agostina asked. The maid had left a pyramid of white terry cloth perched on the corner of the sofa. "I'm in the middle of this ..."

The policewoman grabbed the towels, then walked to the bathroom, back-kicking the door shut. A cell phone on the table vibrated, and a piece of wet cotton landed on my new red peep-toe flats.

"What—" I started to ask, but Agostina shushed me.

When Torre emerged a few minutes later, Agostina was again dabbing with the stinging alcohol.

"Unh!" I complained, as she found another raw spot.

"You had a call," she said to Torre.

"And?"

"And, thank you for moving the towels. I have to finish this before Detective Angelini comes."

"He's not—" I started to contradict, but Agostina's sandaled foot pressed on mine.

"He'll be here a little later," Agostina said. To me, she said, "This may sting."

The moment the hall door closed, I lifted my head. "What?"

Agostina was writing on a scrap of paper.

"We need Detective Angelini here as soon as possible," Agostina whispered. "You must call him." She handed me the paper and brought me my yellow bag.

"Why? What's the matter?" I rummaged for the phone.

"That Officer Torre is up to something. I looked at her phone to see who called her. Right on the screen, it said 'Marco.' That's the number."

I looked askance at the paper. "That doesn't make sense. How would Officer Torre know Marco? A common name, isn't it? Do you really think—" I picked up the phone. "No. What we *think* doesn't matter. We can't take the chance."

I punched in Leo's cell number and left a worried message. I tried Bracci's office. "In a meeting," a man said and switched me to voicemail before I could protest. I left another urgent plea. For good measure, I sent them texts:

Call me. Big problem.

Though no text message could convey how my heart was fluttering.

We stared at the phone, willing it to ring. Five thirty. "Where can they be?" At five forty-five, I said, "We can't just stand by. Remember, Detective Bracci said he would have an officer on the street? Can you find him?"

Agostina said, "I can try. Maybe he can reach Leo on the radio or come up here himself. I'll tell Officer Torre I'm going shopping for later."

"It was brilliant to say Leo's coming." I patted her back, the stinging on my scalp forgotten.

Agostina left the door ajar when she spoke with Officer Torre, describing her errand, even asking whether she could bring the woman anything. Once she left, shutting the door behind her, our suite was eerily still.

I closed the draperies and paced, staring at the closed door. There was no point in locking it. The officer stationed in the hall had an emergency key. It would even open the deadbolt. I quietly slid the flimsy chain lock into place, aware down to my fingertips that Torre—*the traitor!*—was only an arm's length away.

The plumbing on a lower floor knocked, loud as a gunshot. A shout came from the street below. I was sure I heard footsteps, then sure I hadn't. Whispering, or maybe not.

How long ago did Agostina leave? It seems like forever.

The clock read ten minutes after six. Surely she would have found the outside officer by now. The ghostly footsteps and elusive whisperings slipped under the door and drifted around our room like smoke.

To occupy myself, I capped the alcohol bottle, bagged the unused cotton balls, and gathered the towels into a pile. I picked up the water basin to carry it to the bathroom. From the hallway came a sudden confusion of voices and a sharp noise. Agostina! I started toward the door to unhook the chain.

The door flew open a few inches, hit the chain, closed again, and burst open, pieces of chain flying. Not Agostina. Two men wearing dark suits and ski masks charged into the room. I threw the basin of water at the tall man in front and streaked past him toward the door. I dodged around the second man, but he caught me from behind. He jerked my arm up my back, and pressed a hand over my mouth. The tall one taped my mouth closed. I twisted and kicked, but there were two of them, and my struggling earned me a hard punch in the stomach. I doubled over but they pulled me upright.

"Stop it!" the tall one hissed. "Stop it, or we'll kill you right here."

A black hood was pulled over my head, followed by some kind of enveloping shroud. The last thing I'd glimpsed was Officer Torre, mouth open in shock, holding her shattered mobile phone to her heart, a crumpled body at her feet.

LEO

Waiting outside Tati's office, Leo and Bracci retrieved their messages. Two heads jerked up. Leo yelled to Dante, "Have to go! I'll call!" As they pounded down the stairway to the parking garage, Leo tried to reach Genie, then Officer Torre. Bracci called the officer patrolling outside the hotel. No response.

Leo's car careened through the streets, siren pumping, scattering traffic. They spoke hardly a word, so much of the same mind about the significance of Genie's terse summons.

Maledizioni! Maledizioni, he kept muttering. *Dammit!* Repetition of this profane mantra crowded out other thoughts, especially thoughts of what they might find at the hotel. He pushed the accelerator harder.

Bracci called the hotel manager. "Agostina's in the lobby," he relayed to Leo. "She came in with a man who went upstairs. He hasn't come down again."

"Get backup," Leo said as they neared the hotel, but Bracci was already on the radio to dispatch.

The car's squealing brakes shattered the peace of the pedestrian street. He'd made the ten-minute trip to the hotel in a nerve-wracking seven.

Agostina sat immobile in the breakfast area. "Talk to her," Leo said to Bracci, and halted at the front desk where an agitated bellman whispered to the manager.

"Well?" Leo said.

With a glance at Agostina, the manager responded quietly, "I sent him up to check. He says there's a man lying on the top floor landing—dead, maybe. The suite door is open. He thinks it's empty."

If she's not there, they took her. Alive. There's a chance. If we can find her.

"Right. Call an ambulance." Then Leo called to Bracci, "Upstairs." He charged up the twisting stairway, Bracci a few steps behind. They found their officer at the top. Not dead, unconscious, next to a broken chair.

"Is that his gun?" Leo asked, pointing to a police service revolver that had skittered under the chair.

"He has his gun. That must be Torre's. Where the hell is she?"

They made sure the man's airway was open before leaving him for a quick search of the suite. Genie was gone. Bracci called in a request for a crime scene unit. "And hurry!" He fetched a blanket from the bedroom and laid it gently over the officer.

Bracci recounted Agostina's suspicions about Officer Torre and her search for his man outside. "She found him," he gestured with his head to the hallway, "but it took a while. He told her to stay downstairs."

"When?"

"Maybe fifteen minutes ago. We just missed them." He walked into the bathroom and called out, "Agostina wrote down the phone number of Torre's caller—Marco. Ours maybe? She gave it to *Signora* Clarke."

"Let's hope she left it." Leo glanced around the room for the note. He regarded the litter on the table, the wet spot on the carpet, the overturned basin, the lingering odor of rubbing alcohol. "What were they doing?"

"A little nursing. Agostina was cleaning *Signora* Clarke's scalp wound. The stitches came out today."

"I knew that," Leo said, under his breath, the trip to Immormino's office flashing through his mind. Genie in the car beside him, touching her sore head, smoothing her hair. He mimicked the gesture, skimming his hand over a bunched-up towel. Paper crackled. When he lifted the towel, the scrap with the phone number fell out.

"Got it."

"Go to the lobby," Bracci said. "Forensics will be on our asses if they find out we were in here so long." An ambulance siren wailed closer. "I'll stay with him."

"How did they get in and out?" Leo said. "They didn't pass the front desk."

"If Agostina is right about Officer Torre, she could have unlocked the service stairs door for them."

That door was indeed unlocked, and the dusty stair treads showed numerous scuffmarks. "Forensics," Bracci insisted, holding Leo back.

"I'll check down below." Leo took the main stairs two at a time, flattening himself against the wall near the bottom to let the ambulance team pass.

"Show me where the service stairs come out," he called to the manager.

The manager led him toward a door with a small square window at the rear of the breakfast area.

"Wait," Leo called. He squatted by Agostina's chair, the better to see her drooping face. He squeezed her shoulder. "I'll come talk to you in a few minutes."

He followed the manager through the old building's maze of interior hallways until they found a door with a similar square window latticed with chicken wire. "The service stairs," the man gestured.

"And the outside exit?"

"There." He pointed to a heavy fire door straight ahead.

Leo opened the exterior door, which led to a narrow alley, too narrow for cars. Numerous rear doors serving the surrounding buildings provided many places to hide or pass through to another street. "No alarm?"

"Not until the night shift. Our deliveries come in this entrance. Workmen use it. And the staff."

Maledizioni! We overlooked this.

Bracci came up behind them, pocketing his phone. The two detectives peered out, filling the doorway. "No vehicles?" Bracci asked, his voice mingling worry and excitement.

"They park on the street at that end of the alley," the manager said, pointing to the left. "There's no exit the other direction."

Leo said, "Tati's waiting. I'll call and explain. Bracci, you direct the forensics team. Have them scour that alley before it gets dark. And try to find witnesses."

Leo scanned the blank walls of the buildings that crowded the narrow passage. It was near sunset, and the thin daylight penetrating the space already dimmed. Genie could be miles away by now. They could be torturing her or—

He shook his head. He couldn't think about that. He'd find her.

Leo punched in Tati's number. Waiting for him to come on the line, the prosecutor's advice from earlier, "Pick that guard carefully," lacerated his brain.

When Leo explained the situation, Tati took a long time responding. When he did, his words cut like a steel blade: "What are the chances of finding her?"

"It isn't dark yet." Leo struggled for straws. "We may get a clue from the scientific police, any witnesses, Officer Torre when we find her, or Agostina may be able to tell us more …" He envisioned Tati's office, the thick carpeting, the armchairs, the photos lining the walls. Genie had been right there only a few hours ago. How could she have been so close beside him then and now utterly gone? His insides kinked and he thought he might split open.

Tati said, "Obviously, we must work fast. Now that they have her, there's no percentage in delaying their plans." The euphemism was excruciating. "She's not a candidate for ransom. Unless …"

Leo lifted his head.

"I apologize," Tati said. "I am thinking out loud. Can we offer them something? Immunity? We'd need the crib returned, but maybe I wouldn't prosecute them for it. Assaulting our officer? I could let that go, assuming he recovers." He sighed. "But the priest and the Capuano woman? No, we could not forgive them that."

"But could you negotiate with them a while—even one day—to give us time to find them?"

"Detective Angelini, recall whom you are dealing with. You yourself have told me how little evidence they leave behind at every step. This tells us they are smart or at least experienced. They did not become experienced by being easily caught. They will see no need to negotiate with us and risk a trap."

"One piece of information we do have," Leo reminded him. He fingered the scrap of paper in his pocket. "The number of the cell phone that called Officer Torre."

"Yes. Perhaps our best chance. My office will investigate that number, and if it is good, we must consider carefully how to use it. Such terrible timing."

"Why?"

"Because the people I must pull together to work on this problem, from your *Polizia di Stato*, the DIA, the mafia divisions of the other police services, the Vatican and TPC, and the American FBI will regret the necessity of a Friday evening meeting. But we must not delay. Even so, it may be too—"

A small, indistinct sound escaped Leo.

"—I made a list while we talked," Tati said, "and already Dante is summoning them here." After a short silence, he said, "You must recognize that, except for the FBI, these other law enforcement agencies are not interested in *Signora* Clarke. But they do want the crib. Or a path to *La Mafia*. For them, she is at most a means to an end."

Leo considered the implications of his words. These other officials wouldn't be invested in keeping Genie alive, not like he was. That would influence what they would propose, what they would agree to. Then Tati said, "Are you sure you should be part of this?"

Tati missed nothing. But Leo couldn't simply stand aside, not knowing exactly what was being done to rescue Genie. He was determined to extend every ounce of his intellect and energy in that effort. Yet he took a deep breath and said, "If you believe I am not helping—or my judgment is affected—"

Tati cut him off. "I have every faith in your judgment. None of us fully appreciated the risk to *Signora* Clarke until yesterday's lamentable events at Santa Maria Maggiore and last night when she saw her assailant again. But the case is moving fast and has many parts. My question is, can you deal with *all* of those parts?"

After a moment Leo replied, his voice at its usual strength. "Every part of it leads to the men we are after. Nothing is more important." *And those men lead to her.*

When the call ended, he went in search of Bracci, who reported his officers had found a witness, a storekeeper whose shop faced the passageway leading to the hotel's back entrance. He said a large black luxury vehicle had parked there a few minutes after six, when the Limited Traffic Zone controls went off.

Leo and Bracci went to talk to him. He said the driver stayed in the car while two dark-suited men hurried into the passage. In ten minutes or so, they reemerged from between the buildings, a woman wearing a burqa between them, her face obscured. They pushed her into the car.

"She stumbled along." The storekeeper had a prunish expression, and he muttered, half to himself, "*Per forza che*, wrapped up like a mummy."

"Clever," Bracci said. "No one would see her face, and no one would interfere."

"Another woman was with them—youngish—but she walked on."

"Torre," Leo said.

Bracci consulted his watch. "If Torre appears at her apartment, Sal will be waiting. That's *one* woman who won't be glad to see him."

"Will we be done here by seven? To meet with Tati?" Leo asked.

"Easily. As usual, they didn't leave much to work with."

GENIE

I was in a car, a heavy one with a smooth ride, but I was far from comfortable. Strong tape, digging into my wrists, bound my hands behind me. My face itched under the tape covering my mouth, and the black hood blocked all light. The cloth they'd swaddled me in should have been stifling. But I was freezing.

I didn't need to see to know we were still in the city, that rush hour wasn't over. The car's slow progress, jerking stops, and the honks and squeals of other vehicles revealed that much. Someone was in the back seat with me. The leather upholstery creaked when he shifted positions. The air sang with tension, though my kidnappers kept an ominous silence.

I thought of Robbie, the distance between us never greater. And Leo. Nearer, yet equally beyond reach. Would I ever see either of them again? Agostina. Was that her body on the landing? Might have been. My father, whose idea of "the good guide" I'd adopted as the pattern for my life. I'd guided myself right into a death trap.

What else had my father taught me? I remembered another ride, a ferry trip we'd taken from Busan to Osaka. A sudden storm. The wind and waves made the ferry yaw and creak. I wanted to scream then too, until my father said, "Concentrate on one thing, Genie. My coat button. Look at my shiny brown button. Think only about it; push everything else away." He told me to remember that, whenever I was frightened, if I could do something about the situation, I should do it. But if I could not, the important thing was to control my fear. "Quiet your mind, and wait for an opportunity."

To see Leo and Robbie again, to help Agostina, I had to survive. Surviving would take all my concentration now.

I pulled my thoughts into order. The longer this car ride, the better. *As long as the car is moving, I'm OK.* Even though it put more distance between me and Leo, it gave him more time to find me. I knew he was trying to.

Traffic became lighter, the rumbling road noise diminished, the car sped up. Now it stopped. Panic flooded me. *Are we there? Wherever 'there' is? No, we're moving again.* My heart continued to jump around. *Stop it!* I told myself. *If you want to get out of this, you must, must, must control yourself.*

I forced my mind to find and take hold of a still point, a pinpoint of nothingness, empty of fear and regret. As my father taught me, I concentrated on it. I held it in my mind and my heart, and breathed around it, slow and steady. The waves of panic receded like an outgoing tide.

After a time both endless and much too short, the car veered right, bumped steeply downhill over crunching gravel the distance of a city block, slowed, and stopped. The engine shut off.

This is it. Car doors opened, fresh air rushed in. Three doors slammed. Someone opened the door next to me. He pulled me out and hurried me across uneven ground. Three other people then? The two who came to the room and a driver?

Long grass brushed my ankles. Country smells— vegetation, dirt. Dry leaves of trees rustling overhead. I grabbed every scrap of information I could about that place in case it gave me even a tiny advantage if, if, if.

They halted. What lay in front of me? Footsteps on something solid, concrete, maybe. A plastic-sounding tap.

"Come on, come on," a man said.

The man gripping my arm said, "Hit it again."

Another tap, followed by the buzz and release of an electronic door lock. A door squealed open, and stale air enveloped me.

I'm not going inside! I'll die in there! I refused to move. "Bitch," a man said. "Grab her other arm." Strong arms lifted me, and my toes dragged, up and over a low door sill. Electrical switches clicked. A ventilation system coughed and groaned into operation. *Locks, lights, air.*

I was inside this place now, whatever it was. I shivered. The outdoor sounds cut off when the door clanged shut behind me, its echo suggesting space and emptiness. *No hiding places.* A smell of damp concrete.

I counted twenty-three steps from the door to where the men pushed me into a straight-backed chair. It was metal, according to what my numbing hands told me. I banged my shin on something to the right. *Table leg? Don't tie me to this chair!* I silently pleaded. They didn't.

Now they talked freely. Perhaps they didn't know I could understand them. *No, they don't care.* Three male voices.

"I'm calling Umberto," one said. I heard faint tapping. "Shit. Voicemail." He left a cryptic message:

"Your American is waiting."

"Where is that asshole?"

"Fucking his mistress. He doesn't trust the phone. He won't answer. He'll stroll in at eleven, as planned. He doesn't care how long we have to wait."

As they continued to talk openly, I gleaned they'd intended to take me from Agostina's apartment, but arrived too late. Officer Torre told them about the hotel—*That traitorous bitch! Agostina was right!*—and they decided to grab me there. When Torre said Leo might come later, they rushed the job. *That's why Umberto isn't here.* As the conversation dragged on, they bragged about a policeman they'd assaulted, but didn't mention Agostina. *Maybe she's safe then. One less thing to worry about.*

"What are we waiting for, man? We know she talked to the police," said the whining man too close behind me.

"Back off. Umberto wants more. Exactly what she's told them and whether they're putting things together."

"What if she won't talk?"

"Why do you think we brought her way out here? He'll get it out of her, but it won't be quiet."

"Just so she's mine at the end," the man behind me said, a tremor of anticipation in his voice.

I forced back a new rush of panic. I wouldn't— couldn't—think about this Umberto. Instead, I tried to figure out why they were suddenly so talkative. Did they think talking in the car was risky? If they believed the car might be bugged, the police might be hotter on their trail than I'd imagined. A sliver of hope?

I needed to be inside their heads, see what they saw, anticipate their reactions. I imagined I was a sparrow, spiraling toward the ceiling, alighting on a rafter, observing. From this vantage point, I saw myself down below, sitting on a chair in front of a piece of furniture, possibly a table. I was bound and draped in some kind of fabric. I wished I knew the color.

My thoughts darted crazily: *Maybe it's black. In mourning already. No. Or blue—sky blue. Men like blue. That was a desperate thought! White—no—too much like a shroud.* The vision of my bright blood staining a big white garment was too shocking. *Not white. And not red, either. Blue, a nice, friendly blue.*

From my imagination's high perch, the woman below came into focus.

Where are the men? Who are they? When we arrived, the warehouse seemed unoccupied—*no one greeted them*—and they switched on the fan and, presumably, lights. The one I threw the water at was tall, taller than whoever came in behind him. I didn't get a good look at him. *Were they Gemma's killers? The tall one and pony-tailed "Marco"?*

The man off to my right smoked. He seemed to be maybe fifteen feet away. Footsteps approached, and the furniture in front of me creaked and shifted a fraction. Yes, a table, small and light. Wool and cigarettes, a man's smell. A man who sat on the table, inches away from me.

Most frightening was the third man. The one pacing behind my back. He wore heavy boots and nudged my chair each time he passed. Back and forth, back and forth. With each bump, the hair on the nape of my neck responded. *Too close! Trying to intimidate me.* He smelled of old leather. The spiky-haired blond? *The one who wants me "last."* He's the one who stayed with the car.

Was that all of them? It seemed so. From above, I pictured a cavernous, mostly empty space, me on a chair twenty-three steps from the building's exit. A blue lump seated at a small table. Three men. The pacer, threateningly close behind, the smoker to my right—not terribly near and, as far as I could tell, not too invested in all this. And the mysterious man perched on the table.

Time passed, the tableau didn't alter. The smoker yawned and lit another cigarette. I pictured him standing amid a growing litter of butts. What I couldn't picture was any way out of there.

A cell phone on the table vibrated. *Umberto.* The pacing stopped, as did my heart. The seated man answered.

"She's OK," he said. His tone was suspicious, hostile. The smoker approached, the man behind me pressed forward. "No! No picture. Call again in five minutes." He slid off the table, needing only four steps to come around to my chair. "Get this thing off her."

"Who is it? Who's calling?" Two voices asked together. "Cops."

"How do they have your number?"

I know the answer to that one: Agostina. So, the mystery man is Marco after all. I pictured him—dark, ponytail, suit.

"From Torre? From her phone? How the hell do I know?"

"What do they want?"

"To make sure she's safe. They wanted a picture. No way. They want to deal to get her back. We'll tell them what they want to hear, but we don't negotiate without Umberto."

There will be no deal. They've gone too far for that. Leo is buying time.

The man behind me said, "Umberto will shit when he finds out the cops have your number."

"Yeah? Well, maybe you won't tell him."

The smoker said, "My ribs are still fucked up from the last time. I say we keep our mouths shut."

Could I use this? Umberto surely won't negotiate with me. *But maybe, if there is treachery within his group?*

"Come on, get this thing off her," Marco repeated. "So she can talk to them."

They pulled me, wobbling, to my feet. They cut my wrist restraints and pulled the cloth garment over my head. A hand groped under the hood to rip the tape off my mouth—*it felt like it took skin with it*—and pushed me back into the chair. I kept my hands quiet in my lap, hoping they wouldn't retape them, but they did, in front this time. *Better.* I flexed my shoulders to release the muscles. *Ouch.*

With the cloth garment gone, I could see through the black hood, ever so slightly. Shadows, anyway.

Meanwhile, the man I thought was Marco instructed me. I should tell the police I wasn't hurt, they shouldn't try to find me, I'd be free in a few hours. *That's was a lie*. And, he said, I couldn't talk long. *I knew that. Leo would try to trace the call. Maybe that's why they asked for a picture. Hoping for a clue to where I am, yes, and to keep the connection open as long as possible.*

I sensed them close around me. In my bird's-eye view, the scene changed. No longer a cloth-draped lump, I was a woman in a navy blue pantsuit, red shoes, and a black hood, crowded by a trio of jittery men. One of them was Marco, the man behind me was probably the blond, and the smoker must be the tall one with the tattooed scalp.

Even though they expected the call, the blond yelped when the phone buzzed. Marco grumbled threateningly, pausing between each word, "Tell them you're OK." He pressed the phone to my ear.

"*Pronto?*" I tried to sound calm and steeled myself to hear Leo's voice.

"Genie, are you all right?" His deep voice reached me through the cloth and wrapped around my heart.

"Yes. I'm OK." I purged my response of inflection. "Don't try to find me." A flat, mechanical tone is not easy in Italian, I found. Something pricked the right side of my neck and pressed against the skin. "They will release me soon."

On Leo's end, people were arguing in the background. In a calm voice, he instructed, "Genie, if you're really OK, tell me a number between one and three."

I considered how to answer. "*Sei*," I said. *Sei* could mean several things. One of them was six.

A muffled shout of "No!" came from Leo. To me, he said, "*Capisco.*"

Marco snatched the phone away. "We will call you later." He must have disconnected, keeping it short.

But they wouldn't. The sharp thing at my neck went away.

With realization, Marco said, "You *do* speak Italian."

"Of course. It's the world's most beautiful language."

"So you understood us. At the *caffè*."

"Wait a minute—you tried to kill me *twice* and weren't even sure I could understand your language? Anyway, you're wrong. I did *not* know what you were talking about. There was no reason to come after me. Or for—this."

A snort from behind.

"That's not for you to say. Maybe you heard more than you pretend."

"It's true I speak Italian, standard Italian. I don't know your slang." *Gergo.* I learned that word from Leo.

He left it there. From above, I envisioned him sitting on the table, watching me. A light, rhythmic slapping sound was him, tossing the phone from hand to hand.

"I'm turning this fucking thing off," Marco said. The slapping stopped. "Umberto's not calling, and the cops might trace it."

They are already trying.

"How will Umberto get ahold of us then?" the man behind me complained.

"Fuck him," said the smoker.

The dangerous blond remained so close to my chair I could feel his body heat. His knife had pricked my neck. It stung. The smoker wandered away again. A lighter clicked, and he muttered something around the cigarette in his mouth, excitement floating on his voice like the sheen of oil on water.

If it were possible to make any kind of move, it would be easier now with the cloth thing off and my hands bound in front. I might be able to raise my arms—the right one, anyway—and snatch the hood off. I visualized doing it.

The biggest threat was the blond. I might kick the chair backwards and trip him. And, if I knocked the table over, it could briefly protect me from the other two. At the moment, Marco was sitting on that table. But if anything unexpected happens—the police barge in, the lights go out, any sort of miracle—he will stand up. Leo had said, "I understand," and his voice was tinged with hope. I sent him a telepathic message: *Leo, I'm ready to do my part.*

Across the room, the smoker's stomach rumbled. The others laughed. "I'm hungry, assholes." Before long, they persuaded themselves there was no point starving while they waited several more hours for Umberto. They would bring in food, wine.

I didn't like that idea. A little drunk, they'd be even more dangerous. Maybe they'd send the man behind me. *Please!*

They prowled around the space now, bored and restless, and I tracked them, as they circled their prey—me! Their hunger produced an elaborate and confusing food order.

"Who can remember all that? Make it fucking easy!" said the one I thought was Marco.

"And I need cigarettes." Obvious who said that.

"*Che cazzo*! You always need cigarettes. Forget it." The man behind me.

"Then I'm going." The smoker.

"But you don't know what I want." Behind me.

"Fuck's sake, both of you go." Marco.

"I'll stay with her." From behind.

"Nic, no goddammit, you're not. Umberto wants to talk to her, remember?"

The smoker's foot made a scraping noise, snuffing another cigarette, and he said, "Anyway, you blew another chance last night."

Marco made a disgusted noise.

Nic. The blond was Nic. The name brought him into focus.

In the end, two of them would go, leaving Marco—my heart forgot to beat when they confirmed the name—to guard "the American bitch." They obviously believed one guy, one of *them*, could handle a woman sitting immobile, blindfolded, hands bound, in an empty building far from anyone's hearing. *Don't bet on it*, I thought.

Grumbling, Nic moved toward the door. "You drive," he said to the smoker. "I'm sick of that *mostruosità*." Keys jangled.

A click, a draft of cool night air. The door slammed, metal on metal.

Alone with Marco. My odds had greatly improved. I took comfort in that, though he must have a weapon or maybe more than one. What did I know about him? *The motorcycle and leather clothing, the stolen flowers, Gemma Capuano, the church visits, the crazy camera, the ponytail, the smudge on the back of his left hand that might be a tattoo, the call to Officer Torre, his new girlfriend.*

How were kidnap victims supposed to behave? What had I read about that? I'd been acting like a nonthreatening pile of cloth on a chair. *That's a mistake. Make him see you as a person, an individual. Engage him, get him to relate to you.* Even though he couldn't see my face and I couldn't see him at all.

You don't know me yet, Marco, but I know you.

"*Che stai facendo?*" I asked Marco in a clear voice, in response to his rhythmic grunting. "What are you doing?"

The unexpectedness of the question must have surprised him into answering. "*Addominali.*"

Crunches. I rolled my eyes. Probably he exercised every spare moment. I knew this type from my gym. He'd be in good shape. And might love to talk about it.

"Do you work out?"

"Yes." He sounded bored.

"Well, can you do them this way?" Without waiting for a reply, I rose slowly from the chair. No sudden movements. "I'll show you." *Nothing to worry about. It's just the two of us.* I sent encouraging thoughts his way. *What can it hurt?*

I couldn't know what his reaction was, but I crossed my ankles and lowered myself to the floor in one smooth movement—a trick that required good knees. I lay on my back on the cold floor and raised my legs to forty-five degrees and levered my torso up, my body making a V-shape. I kept my legs in the air and, counting to five, lowered my upper body to the floor. An inhale and I rose again. I thought it might kill me. I hadn't practiced this move since the attack, and it was harder without the use of my arms. My muscles were screaming. Only sheer nerves propelled me, but I persisted. It was life or death. *V for victory*, I told myself.

"Nice," he said, sounding interested, maybe.

I lowered my legs to thirty degrees and repeated the exercise a few times. Best to stop before I faltered. "Good for the lower back too," I enticed him. I thought he might be attempting it, because he was puffing. I remembered the first few times I'd tried that exercise. Practically impossible.

"Hard," he said.

"Especially good for the abdominals."

I turned on my side, facing him, stacked my legs, and angled them slightly forward. "What about this?" I lifted the top leg to point at the ceiling and made large *rond de jambe* circles in the air. My form was off, but he wouldn't know the difference. "Also good for the abdominals." *And for getting the blood flowing to my legs, in case I need to run.* "Try it! Hold your stomach in, tight as you can." I spoke as if he were following along, and I was coaching him. He grunted. *Maybe.*

I ran him through a few more exercises and, if he actually was following, his hip joint and upper thigh would be burning. Mine were, and I'd done these moves for years. But I would recover faster. I tried bicycle pedaling, but kicked the chair. "Ouch!" I jerked my foot away.

"Here," he said and came close. He removed the hood. Shirt collar unbuttoned and sleeves rolled over muscular forearms. Snake tattoo on the left. Ponytail.

I knew those things about you, Marco. Of course it's you.

The cavernous room mirrored my mental picture, except the table was bigger than I expected, with another chair on the side opposite mine. His suit coat, a tie draped over it, hung on it. Too bad he had on the totally wrong trousers for what I planned for him. Piled next to my chair, the crumpled cloth garment. Black. I shuddered.

"*Grazie.* You ever do yoga?"

"No," he sniffed.

"You think it's easy? Try this." Standing slowly, I set my feet and legs for the Warrior One position. The front knee bent to ninety degrees put considerable pressure on that thigh. I raised my bound hands overhead, as high as I could, engaging my upper body. "Hold your arms straight up, by your ears." I let him stiffen in this position before revolving my torso into Warrior Two. My bound hands wouldn't let me demonstrate the arms, so I said, "Arms out to each side, and look toward your right hand."

He followed my instructions, more or less, snickering at their simplicity. But I held the pose. He took two massive inhalations. And I held it. "Go deeper with every exhale." The thigh of my bent leg rebelled, but I willed it not to shake. "Left arm higher, parallel to the floor." And I held it. "Deeper … strength below, length above." Muscle training, adrenaline, and willpower cemented me in position.

In this pose, I faced the warehouse door. To its right a credit-card-sized green rectangle glowed. The exit button! I would have to hit that green square to release the door's electronic lock. Those twenty-three steps might as well be a mile, but the glowing green rectangle felt like a promise.

I didn't let him quit. "Now bring your right forearm onto your right thigh, and stretch your left arm toward the ceiling." His thigh was suffering; it quivered. "Look up at your left hand." He didn't expect that turning his head would so disturb his balance, and he almost toppled over. I pretended not to notice.

"Top ribs rotate backward; bottom ribs forward." Thanks to *Dottor* Immormino, I was well acquainted with the word for "ribs." I demonstrated, imitating the supportive, hypnotic tone of my yoga instructor, whose words alone maneuvered her students into ever-stronger positions.

"Other direction." I took the Warrior One position, followed by Warrior Two, staying in each as long as I could stand it, then a little longer. My injured side throbbed and was frustratingly weak. But I could hold each position much longer than his inexperienced muscles found comfortable. He was tiring. Perspiration slicked his arms. But of course, he wasn't going to show a woman his weakness.

"Good," I said, meaning something different than he probably thought I did. "I'd like to show you an inversion. A shoulder stand. Excellent for the heart—and the brain."

If I can persuade him to lie on the floor ...

I would do what I could and do it full-out, praying he'd go along. I sighed extravagantly. "But I can't. I need my hands to support my lower back. Let me see one of your favorites."

"Can you do this?" he said.

Push-ups. Of course, with those arms. "Sure," I said. "Not now, lucky for you."

"Too tired?" he mocked, though he was flushed and shaky.

"No." I indicated my bound hands.

I was cross-legged, sitting like a pinioned Buddha, calm gaze fixed on the floor in front of me. I projected as benign and nonthreatening an aura as I could. This was the pivotal moment. He'd accept my challenge or he'd step out of the yoga zone.

"Why not?" He walked over to me, pulled a knife from his pocket, and cut the tape binding my wrists. "For a few minutes."

I'll make the most of them.

I stretched and rotated my hands, keeping every trace of joy off my face.

Focus. No mistakes now.

True, he had a knife, but I'd inspected him from all sides and did not see a gun tucked in his waistband or strapped to his ankle. It could be in his coat pocket, over on the other side of the table. How fast could I run to that door? I had to get out before the others returned, but what would I find outside?

"Inversion first, OK? I need to warm up my arms and shoulders before doing push-ups." I demonstrated the Plow position, lying flat and vaulting my legs over so that my toes touched the floor behind my head. The pressure on my sore side was excruciating.

"That looks ridiculous."

Am I losing him? "Yes," I said, "but it makes it easier to do this."

I lifted my legs into a shoulder stand. "Sarvangasana, Candle pose. Some people do this every day. Blood to the brain. Helps you think better. Very healthy."

He snorted.

"You'd be surprised."

He snorted again.

"If you want to try, I'll spot you." I let myself down, giving him time to consider. "It isn't as difficult as it looks."

"It does not look difficult."

"Well then, up you go." I dragged the chair to sit beside him. "Remember not to turn your head, or you could injure your neck."

Was he going to do it? He was at least lying down, knees bent, but his eyes darted around the room. I kept my voice low, calm, encouraging. "Focus. Lift your legs so that your feet point to the ceiling." I guided him into it. "Now I'll help you lift your waist off the floor. Excellent. Use your hands to support your back. Perfect. Straighten your legs. Steady." I stood and held his legs in a vertical position. "If you need more back support, move your hands—"

A commotion erupted outside the door. *They're back! If they see this—*

Shouting and banging. "Police!! Open the door!" *Oh, my god!*

Marco was already lowering his legs and rolling away from me. I grabbed the chair, lifting it as high as I could, and lunged toward him. As he scrambled to stand, I swung the chair into his chest. His raised arms deflected the blow. Stepping aside, he tripped me, and my momentum took me to the floor. As I fell, I twisted, trying not to land on my broken ribs. My right hand managed to hold onto the chair. I rolled onto my back, ready to fight.

"We're coming in!" a voice outside yelled.

"Don't shoot!" I screamed as Marco landed on top of me, pinning me with his knee and a hand on one shoulder as I tried to squirm from underneath him. I wanted to scream again but didn't have the breath.

I slid the chair around hoping to grab it with both hands, but my left side was too weak. I couldn't reach far enough. Marco's free arm waved wildly, making it almost impossible to hit him. He reached behind him, just for a second, opening a space in his defenses. This was my chance. I swung the chair, grabbing it with my left hand in midair, and crashed it over his head. His grip on my shoulder loosened, and I pushed him off me. I leapt up screaming, "Don't shoot" and ran to the door.

"It's me!" I yelled. "Don't shoot!" I hit the green button and the lock clicked. I flattened myself against the wall, shouting my own name. The door swung open, and the muzzle of an automatic rifle entered the warehouse, followed by a nervous looking policeman, then another. The first policeman kept his gun aimed at Marco, while the second took aim at me.

Wearing a big grin, Bracci pushed past him, and wrapped me in an embrace. Over his shoulder, I saw Marco, sitting, dazed, head in his hands. The warehouse filled with blue-gray uniforms. Bracci held me away from him and looked into my eyes, his tangled eyebrows raised, questioning.

"He's the only one here," I panted. "Dinner run. And they're waiting for ... for ... a man called Umberto." Realizing *what* they were waiting for, not whom, made me falter.

"Then we will wait for him too."

"He's supposed to come around eleven."

He kept an arm around me and called to a sergeant. "Get him into a car," he gestured toward Marco, "and move the rest of our vehicles out of sight." To the officer pushing a handcuffed Marco out the door, he said, "Take *Signora* Clarke with you. To the magistrates' offices, Maximilliano Tati."

Bracci pulled out his phone. Car engines revved outside. Waiting for the call to connect, he said, "Be quick. We have to get you out of here," and into the phone, "Leo? Someone to speak to you."

"Leo?" I couldn't manage more. The fact that I was now safe took the starch completely out of me. My whole body shook, and I returned the phone to Bracci.

"She's not hurt." Bracci looked to me for confirmation and I nodded. "Only one of them was here—Marco—and he's ours now. We'll wait for the others. She let us in. I don't know how. She'll have to explain." With a touch on my back, he moved me toward an officer standing in the doorway. "We're sending her to you so I can organize a welcoming committee."

A half hour earlier, all I wanted was to survive. Now I wanted a lot. I wanted the ride to the city to be over with, to put the terror of the evening behind me, to make sure Agostina was all right, to see Leo. If the ride to the warehouse seemed long, the return trip seemed endless, even though rush hour was over, even though the blue lights flashed and the siren wailed, and even though my driver believed traffic lights and speed limits barely rated as suggestions.

When at last he pulled the car into the courtyard of the *questura*, he said, "Come inside? I have to turn over custody of him. It may take a few minutes."

"I'll wait here." Being surrounded by official metal felt safe, cocoon-like after the cavernous warehouse. The officer opened the rear door to take Marco out, and I turned to look at him. Our eyes met. I expected anger from him, but his expression was hard to read.

"Can you really do push-ups?" he asked.

"Not at all."

And he was gone.

I unfastened the seat belt and brushed cement dust from the warehouse floor off my slacks, not very successfully. I huddled in the corner where the car's seat met the door and closed my eyes, not wanting to move, not sure I could. In the warehouse, I'd had a tight focus, the sparrow on the rafter. Now that my thoughts could wander anywhere, they kept returning to that huge empty space where I was a vulnerable black lump, not a blue one. "Umberto wants to *talk* to her" echoed in my head.

The door I leaned on clicked and opened, and I jerked upright. Leo bent down and put his warm hands on my cheeks. He pulled me out of the car and wrapped his arms around me. The dam of tension burst, and I sobbed against him. When a thin cloth brushed my face, my hand flew up to tear it away, but it was only his handkerchief.

Tati greeted us at his office door. The men he'd convened to discuss my fate had either gone home or to police headquarters to await the prisoners, except for the FBI man, Agent Tesone. I hadn't met him before, and as he gripped my icy hand, I managed a relieved smile just to be near a fellow American.

Almost at once, Tati's assistant Dante arrived, bringing *panini*, fruit, rum cake, and espresso.

"I haven't eaten since noon. Dante, thank you!" Tati said.

The rest of us grumbled appreciatively and reached for the food. I thought I could manage only a few bites, but I was wrong.

"While you're eating, why don't I tell you how we found you?" Tati said. "I will summarize."

A sandwich stopped halfway to my mouth. "Please, I want the details. Don't feel you must spare me."

Leo gave a quick nod, and Tati took a deep breath. "All right, then. About seven thirty this evening I brought together the different branches of law enforcement involved in this—this incredible case. The circumstantial evidence was so strong that your captors were the same men who stole the crib that I could not omit the Vatican police or the TPC—you know what that is?"

"Stolen cultural treasures."

"Yes. By now the several antimafia forces are involved. Also your FBI. They assist whenever an American is kidnapped outside the United States."

Tesone grunted assent, mouth full.

"We needed to make a number of difficult decisions, in the face of significant unknowns," Tati said. "We had a few things in our favor—first, the phone number the woman Agostina wrote down. When Dante traced the owner, we believed he was the Marco of interest. About that time, Officer Torre arrived home and found a detective waiting for her."

"Sal," Leo said.

"She appeared genuinely distressed by the attack and the violence of it. Although she said she did not know where you were, she might have revealed more, if we needed her to." A ripple of horror washed over me, as I considered the means they might have used to gain that information.

"Detective Angelini had anticipated the gangsters might visit the apartment building where you have been staying, which they did, earlier in the day. One of Detective Bracci's men was ready for them. As was I, taking care of the necessary paperwork." Tati smiled. "His detective planted a tracking device under their car—the same vehicle they used this evening. When you were abducted, Bracci ordered the device activated. He didn't tell Detective Angelini—"

"He was afraid it wouldn't work," Leo broke in. "He didn't want me to pin too much ... on it."

Across the table, our eyes met. The missing word, I guessed, was "hope."

"Correctly so. But when we needed it—" Tati raised his arms like a magician showing off an especially clever trick. "When the car stopped, we knew where they'd taken you. As Bracci and his officers raced north, we used the phone number. We wanted to confirm you were there, because it would affect how they entered the building."

"You needed to know if I was alive."

Tati gave me a penetrating glance. "Yes. We heard many opinions about how the phone conversation should go, and we had Detective Bracci on a secure line. I regret our discussions delayed your rescue."

Tati stirred his coffee, his forehead corrugated by recollection. The debate would have been between those who wanted to storm the warehouse—with me as potential collateral damage—and those who wanted my rescue. Leo and Tesone—Tati, maybe—against the others. I remembered Leo's "No!" and fortified myself with a sip of espresso. So many powerful strangers had a say in my survival!

"In fact," I said, "if Detective Bracci had arrived any sooner, the men probably would have killed me at once. The one with the knife would have done so, gladly. Even Marco might have."

Tati blew out a long breath. "We also hoped the phone call would buy a little time. I kept Detective Angelini here, because … we needed someone you trusted available to talk to you."

More than that, I thought, he wanted someone who'd speak for me.

"Just as Detective Bracci was ready to strike, the GPS indicated the car was moving, leaving the warehouse. We didn't know whether you were in the car or still in the warehouse. Bracci left most of his men hidden in the woods above the building, and he and an officer discreetly followed the car. It went to a *trattoria* a few kilometers away.

"The manager knows his regular customers and gladly pointed out a tall stranger who ordered food to take out. He doesn't like the type, and he's not set up for takeaway service. But the man paid a big overage, so the manager went along to avoid an argument. Bracci asked him to slow the kitchen as much as possible and returned to the warehouse."

"No arrest?" *Two of them had been practically in Bracci's hands!*

"Too risky. The restaurant was full of people, the man may have been armed, and Bracci had only one officer with him. He judged it would be better—more incriminating—to arrest him at the warehouse, and he and his officer hurried back there to wait." Tati paused. "He didn't express this, but I believe he also had another priority."

Me.

"And the rest you know." Tati took a sandwich. "But now, we want to hear your story, *Signora* Clarke. Notes, Dante, please?"

Dante opened his laptop.

I told them about the masked intruders in the hotel room, how they taped my mouth, put the black hood on me, and swathed me in cloth.

"A burqa, a witness said."

Of course.

I described the silent drive. The lively discussion once they reached the warehouse. Their attempt to call Umberto. Their other conversation, mostly trivial.

"The crib?" Tati asked.

"They didn't mention it. Marco *is* the man with the ponytail, and the man who paced close behind me—his name is Nic. He's the blond who attacked me, I'm almost positive. I could smell that leather jacket." My nose wrinkled. "As to the other two men from the caffè, I think the smoker is the tall one with the tattooed scalp—I didn't catch his name. And the man who seemed in charge, he could be Umberto, the one they were waiting for."

I told them how surprised the men were when Leo called, and how they had to take the burqa off me and untape my mouth so I could talk. That was why they wanted a callback. I described how they decided to bring in something to eat and drink. And Marco's yoga lesson. The four men burst out laughing. Dante stopped typing.

"I couldn't believe it, either," I said. "But once he seemed engaged, I kept going. When Detective Bracci arrived, Marco was in Candle pose, balanced on his shoulders with his legs straight up in the air. That gave me the chance I needed."

Tati regarded the gallery of violent characters he'd put in jail. "I wish I had a picture of that," he chuckled.

I felt their amusement tainted my accomplishment. "Yoga is actually hard, you know, if you do it right," I said.

"I'm sure." Agent Tesone wiped a tear.

"You men don't believe it *is* hard. You think it's something women and foreigners do. And I'll bet Marco's people think the same. Even more so. *We* know about him and the yoga, they don't. Keeping such a secret might be worth something to him. Would he want them to know he so lost control of the situation that I could open the door for the police?"

The laughter stopped. "*Signora* Clarke, you are quite the strategist," Tati said.

I continued, "Despite his role in Gemma Capuano's murder, of the three of them, Marco was the least, I don't know, the least bought into the violence. The yoga thing would never have worked if he hadn't gone along with it. He could have stopped me at any time, but he didn't. It would *never* have worked with Nic." She recalled Marco's enigmatic last glance. "I can't explain this exactly, but the others were excited about Umberto's arrival. Marco seemed almost … offended by it. By what was going to happen. In a way, I think, he felt sorry for me."

Leo's cell phone rang, interrupting the dark thoughts filling the room. "Are you on your way here?" Leo asked. "Good."

Umberto was in custody.

Bracci strutted in an hour later. For the first time, I heard Leo call his detective by his first name, Emilio, as he muttered a gruff "*grazie.*" Beaming, Bracci shook off their congratulations.

The burn-off of adrenaline had left us all sagging at that late hour, but Bracci deserved our attention. "We were ready to blow that door, then *Signora* Clarke opened it," Bracci said and grabbed *panini.* "I was astonished. But she had it under control."

"I was afraid one of you would shoot *me*," I said.

His mouth was full, and he shook a finger at me. Soon he continued, "When the dinner delivery arrived—arms full of bags—that arrest was easy, and we made short work of it."

"The food, too, *lo credo*," Leo chuckled.

"Part of the clean-up operation. When we heard Umberto's car, we doused the lights. Opening the door to a dark warehouse confused him just long enough." Bracci hadn't stopped grinning.

"Fine work tonight," Tati said. "Speaking for myself, I would like a little sleep. But that's more than Umberto and his friends will get. Your people from the *Polizia di Stato*, the mafia unit, the Vatican police, the TPC were all waiting for them. Their list of questions is not short, though their patience is."

"Those three are in for a long night." Bracci laughed.

I frowned. "What did you say? Who's in for a long night?"

"Our prisoners."

My voice quavered. "You said three." I ticked them off. "Marco, Umberto, and the two who went for food."

"*Two*? Only one came back."

"There were two."

Leo raised a calming hand and studied the notebook in front of him. "Describe the man who brought the dinner."

"Tall, with the tattooed scalp *Signora* Clarke has mentioned before," Bracci said, his voice filled with anxiety. "His name's Lama Rinaldi."

"The smoker," I said.

"Pestered my men for cigarettes."

"Suit. Was he wearing a suit?" I asked.

"*Certo*."

I clapped a hand over my mouth. Bracci glanced from me to Leo and back again.

"That means the man Nic is on the loose," Leo said. "We think he's the blond who attacked Genie. He was at the warehouse and went to the restaurant with Rinaldi, but he wore leather."

NIC

A Few Hours Earlier

"Let me out," Nic said to Lama, as the car slowed at the head of the warehouse driveway. "Gotta piss."

He watched the Mercedes taillights, flashing between the trees in the dark patch of woods, jiggle down the hill and stop. Nic zipped up and regained the driveway when an unexpected noise erupted inside the building. He dropped to a crouch and worked his way forward. There were people below. Too many people. *What in hell—?*

The warehouse door opened, releasing a shaft of light, and a police car raced around from behind the building and parked by the door. Lama was brought out in handcuffs and shoved inside. Two officers rode in front. *How'd this shit happen? Did Umberto rat us out?* Nic could believe that. Almost. Marco wouldn't have snitched—this whole project was his big play. But where *was* Marco?

The car raced up the hill. When it reached the road, it turned left, toward Rome. Another police car followed. After enough time for them to reach the highway, sirens started. Police officers passed in front of the open doorway. Three or four in uniform and a heavyset man in a suit. No sign of Marco or the American. The door closed, extinguishing the light. They were inside now, waiting. For him? For Umberto? If they knew he was out there, they'd be searching the woods already. Had to be Umberto.

His phone read nine thirty. They'd be stuck in there another ninety minutes, if Umberto kept to schedule. Enough time for him to hike a few miles toward the city, hitch a ride. *No. Something better.* He crept uphill through the woods and at the road, he turned in the direction opposite the one the police had taken. He could be back at the *trattoria* before ten. A hundred yards past the driveway, he phoned Umberto and left an urgent message, then loped away, alone.

At a table on the hillside *trattoria's* deserted patio, the woman in the violet dress gazed into the distance. A few strands of pasta remained on the plate pushed to the center of the table, and her wineglass held a last sip. It was her third at least. She'd had her second with him an hour before, while Lama waited inside for their dinners. She was old, maybe thirty-five, and weighed thirty pounds more than she should have, but he'd flirted with her to pass the time.

"It's you, Carlo." Her eyes widened in recognition, the pupils large in the near-dark. In the few seconds it took him to recall the name he'd given her, he glanced over his shoulder. *Merda. Had she noticed?* Her smile said no.

He signaled the waiter for more wine and dragged a chair alongside hers. Past low shrubbery, the lights scattered across the valley mirrored the stars. The cool air, still as a held breath, made the moment feel outside time and full of possibilities.

"I shouldn't have left you," he said, leaning into her shoulder. He inspected her full lips, a little greasy, and the ample breasts puffing out of her low-cut neckline. They reminded him of two unbaked loaves of bread, the snowy dough risen and ready for the baker's attention. His right arm lay on the table.

"Your tattoo." It was almost a question.

Instead of holding out his hand for her inspection, he wrapped it around the long stem of the wineglass and revolved his wrist toward her, creating the illusion the snake wound up to the bowl. She shivered.

He took off his leather jacket and, draping it over her shoulders, brushed against her nipples, tantalizingly erect beneath the straining purple fabric. "Is your husband at home?" He kept his left arm around her and let his right hand drift down and land on her thigh, light as a moth.

"We're separated. Three months to go."

He squeezed her shoulders. So, nine months without a husband, and who knows how long before the divorce could be finalized. Perfect. "Not much fun for you." He moved in closer and stroked her thigh with a slow, circular motion. The silky material slid under his hand.

"Oh, Carlo. A nightmare." She took a large gulp of wine. Her wide, shining eyes fixed on the valley lights.

He nuzzled her neck and whispered in her ear. "Is there someplace we could go?" He lowered his head so his warm breath fanned her breasts.

She hesitated. He took his hand from her leg and drew away. His warmth went with him.

"My apartment?"

He leaned in again. His hand on her knee played with the hem of her skirt. Now on top, now touching the inside of her bare thigh. Her legs separated, ever so slightly. His fingers sought the tender skin, higher, then a little higher. She took another drink. "My apartment." Her voice was husky.

"Your apartment," he breathed into her ear. He unwrapped his arms and made a show of fumbling for his wallet, in no real hurry, and by the time he worried it out of the pocket of his jeans, her little brocade purse gaped. She dropped a few bills on the table.

On their way to her car, he said, "I missed dinner tonight. I need something good to eat." He licked the skin behind her ear. She put perfume there. It smelled like roses but tasted bitter.

Her laugh became a giggle.

CHAPTER—13

Saturday, October 27

NIC

Nic woke Saturday morning in a tangle of unfamiliar sheets. The smells of coffee and breakfast filled the bedroom. He stretched and got out of bed in one smooth movement. Too lazy to lift the toilet lid, he peed in the sink, splashed water on his face, and grinned at himself in the mirror. He walked into her kitchen stark naked.

She was washing the previous night's dishes. She wore a colorful silk kimono patterned with umbrellas the size of dinner plates. It didn't flatter her, yet the sight of her aroused him, her roundness, top and bottom. He pulled her to him and kissed her, long and hard. The pan she was scrubbing sank into the water, and she lightly ran her soapy hands up and down his bare back, shoulders to thighs, and kneaded his buttocks. His erection pressed against her soft belly.

"Oh, you," she said, scolding a naughty boy. Her pelvis tilted toward him.

They didn't manage to cross even the short distance to the bedroom and had their morning fuck on the living room floor in the narrow space between dining set and sofa. Sheer orange draperies billowed with breezy morning light from the open balcony door.

"Good morning, Carlo," she said afterward, as he lay on top of her.

He groaned.

"Before you fall asleep ... *mio caro* ... a shower, we'll eat. Then ... again?"

He laughed. She wasn't a beauty, but she was convenient and pliable. And she could cook. He slid off her and sauntered to the bathroom.

Late in the morning, they walked to the outdoor market in the town square to shop for their dinner. The police in a sleepy town like Riano would be dusty with disuse, Nic figured, surveying the predictable line of storefronts leading to the market. Pharmacy, doctor's office, cameras and computers, and their first destination, the butcher shop. Totally boring.

"Breakfast tomorrow?" she probed, as they joined the line at the meat counter.

"*Certo.*"

"And dinner tomorrow?"

"Why not?" He gave her round ass an encouraging pat. "Cigarette."

He stepped outside and fired up his phone, a coiled cobra imprinted on its bright red vinyl skin. He risked a quick call to Marco. Lama. Umberto. Voicemail everywhere. Even if the police had arrested them, at least one of them should be out of custody by now. Cubellis's lawyers would have swarmed police headquarters all night, and Nic had known them to pop men out of jail who were in much trickier situations.

He should have slit the American bitch's throat when he had the chance, and they'd have been far from the warehouse long before the police arrived. But Umberto wanted his fun. Now he'd been out of touch an entire day.

He had to find out what was happening and placed another call.

LEO

Leo arrived at the lair of the police department's technology freaks, just as one of them swore loudly. Bracci, dozing in a chair, startled. "Got something?" He ran his fingers through his hair, massaging his scalp awake.

"Your guy's using his phone at last," said a young man wearing headphones. "But the calls are too short. We can't get a fix on the location."

"He's calling the others. He'll get through to someone eventually," Bracci said.

Leo stepped into the room. "*Buon giorno,*" he greeted Bracci with feeble heartiness. Leo had circles under his eyes, but Bracci was a wreck. "Tati wants to meet at nineteen hundred. Tell me what's happening, then go home and sleep."

"*Signora* Clarke?" Bracci asked.

"Recovering."

"I can't do too many more like last night," Bracci heaved himself out of the chair. "It's like I've been chained to a fucking roller coaster. These guys," Bracci cocked his head toward the technicians, "got Nic's number off the others' phones. He was quiet until now."

"Go. I'm on it."

Bracci trudged away without a good-bye.

Three young officers, two men and a woman, were stationed at computers with extra-large screens. The one in the middle introduced himself as Silvio. He wore a headset and was connected to Vodafone, whose technicians were tracking Nic's phone. "North of town," Silvio said, repeating what he heard through the headset, "in …" The others held their hands poised above keyboards. "Riano."

"Riano? There's nothing there," Leo said, then recalled it was only a few kilometers from the warehouse where the kidnappers held Genie.

"Maybe that's why *he's* there," Silvio said, already tapping keys, "or his phone is."

"Here's the map," the other man said, pointing. He clicked a satellite map, and the view zoomed closer, showing Riano's few downtown streets and the roofs of its buildings.

"He's near the corner of Via Giovanni Pascoli and Giuseppe Mazzini," said Silvio, as the phone company's information became increasingly precise.

"On the map that's a parking area." The man pointed to a spot where several streets converged, creating a small public square. Nic was right there. The detailed satellite picture showed parked cars and dots that were pedestrians. The officer switched to a street-level view, and they could see the cars, the people, and the surrounding buildings. It was as if they stood among them. Leo bent down for a closer view. "Is this real time?"

"No. Recent, though."

"This is," the woman said and pointed to her screen.

He stepped behind her. Long lines of stalls for vendors of fruit, vegetables, and baked goods replaced the cars. "A market?" Leo put his hand to his forehead. "It's Saturday, right? Where's this coming from?"

The woman gave him a quizzical look. "Public webcam. Lots of places have them. This one's at an electronics store. The picture's live."

"But no one's moving."

"It will refresh. How often depends on how it's set up. There. That's a new picture."

"*Oh mio dio*. There he is!" A young man with spiky blond hair idled in front of a butcher shop, talking into a cell phone. In his other hand, he held a cigarette, and his bare arm bore a sizeable tattoo.

They stared at their quarry. The woman hit 'Save.' 'Print.'

"When is he going to move?" Leo said. He gripped the woman's chair.

"Wait …"

"He's off the phone." Silvio pulled off his headset and rubbed his ear.

"… There." The new picture showed Nic from behind, walking toward the market stalls. His right arm draped the shoulder of a heavyset woman who teetered on high heels. "Shopping," the young woman said. "She has a string bag with a couple of brown-paper packages. From that butcher, probably."

"I can't believe we're watching him like this," Leo said.

"Don't you have a computer?" said Silvio, surprised. "This isn't exotic stuff."

The picture changed. Nic and the woman had moved a few meters farther from the camera, frozen in the act of selecting a tomato.

"What do you think?" Leo asked.

"Buying their dinner," the woman said. "So he's planning to stick around a while."

"Can we keep watching? Find out where they go?"

"If they keep moving in that direction, they'll be out of view soon. Riano has only the one webcam."

"See that? There's a street patrolman." Like a frustrated puppeteer, Leo's hands and fingers moved involuntarily toward the screen. If only they could swivel that patrolman around and propel him toward the departing couple.

Silvio snapped the headset on and called the Riano police. He talked to the duty officer and asked about a patrolman in the market square. Yes, the man had a radio. The Riano station summoned him. In a moment, the patrolman was pressing a radio to his ear.

Silvio relayed information from Rome and Leo's instruction: "Don't do more than find out where they go."

They waited. The next picture showed the patrolman's back, and in the next he'd traveled halfway across the piazza, moving fast between camera shots.

"Would you stay in touch with the Riano station?" Leo asked Silvio. "Here's my number. I'm going up there."

"Here," the other officer said and handed him a printout of the Riano street map and directions to the police station.

VENIERI

Pietro Venieri and Chung-Lee Kim—Cubellis's "scientist" Venieri scoffed—met at ten Saturday morning on neutral territory, the Lancisiana Library. Its impeccable collection of works on the history of medicine was so esoteric, Venieri could count on remaining undisturbed.

He handed Kim the top sheet of a short stack of papers. "The formula's chemical components. And a summary of the process,"—he waved a five-page document—"which I will describe to you then answer any remaining questions." He consulted his watch. "We should finish mid-afternoon." *By which time, Kim's brain will be spinning back toward Korea.*

"One moment," Kim said. He scanned the list of chemicals and paged through the summary, then launched into detailed questions about the manufacturing process, grilling Venieri on possible alternatives to his methods. He asked to see the results of the most recent computer runs. A few of Kim's questions fired ideas, and intellectual excitement overcame Venieri's habitual secretiveness. He logged onto Sapienza's computer network and slid the laptop in front of the Korean.

Kim silently pored over the screens for almost an hour. When he got to the end, he went through them again quickly. Pointing to one diagram, he said, "You build the molecule by linking these two novel compounds, so as to enhance neurotransmitter function, particularly acetylcholine, through this branch here. So far, so good. But your stabilizers are weakening the methylene's ability to penetrate the blood-brain barrier. Ultimately, your molecule's function is so degraded it produces a negligible effect. If you substitute a different stabilizer, a new form of polyvinylpyrrolidone, you avoid the weakening effect."

The chemical name flew off Kim's tongue. Venieri was too surprised to attempt it. "PVP has a new form?"

"I developed it for Mr. Cubellis," Kim said, offhandedly, and sketched the molecular structure on a pad.

"For Cubellis? Why?"

"To create a stronger heroin." Kim yawned.

"Where did you say your laboratory is?" Venieri realized he didn't know.

"I trained at Sejong University in Seoul. They're into polymeric stabilizers. Now I have a fellowship at Stanford University, in Palo Alto, California."

Of course. The little shit. Boosting heroin right under their snooty California noses. Venieri closed his laptop, and the men divided the papers. "Your idea may have potential.

I'll think about it over the weekend." Venieri attempted to mask his excitement. "Otherwise, you have what you need?"

"I know what to do."

CUBELLIS

Cubellis relished his midday meal, as always. His sister lived with him and cooked whatever he wanted. Today, veal and peppers. Vittorio Cima joined him, and the older man asked after Cima's three young children. Cubellis never paired his food with discussions of business.

After they settled in the study, a dark-paneled room full of substantial chairs and well-padded sofas, he said, "You have news."

"Yes. Madoor says the reliquary is sold. We wanted a hundred million; he negotiated one twenty-five. He'll receive the money Thursday in Pula and start transferring it to our accounts."

"Pula?" Cubellis tried to remember where Pula is exactly.

"Madoor owns an apartment building on the Croatian coast. He can stay there as long as necessary."

Cubellis wasn't curious about the buyer or the crib's whereabouts. Cima wouldn't have asked, and Madoor wouldn't have told him if he had.

"On another matter," Cima said, "the *Polizia di Stato* have started an investigation that might touch us. It's small, so far, centering on Gianni di Landri's murder."

"Nothing to do with us."

"We know that. But they see a wedge."

Cubellis exhaled like a steam train stopping. "Who is in charge?"

"Gillo Gilletti."

"Forget about it." He barked a wheezy laugh and slowly shook his head. "The things they will do to amuse an old man."

"Nicola called a while ago. He saw Lama arrested, but he doesn't know what happened to Marco and Umberto. Or the American."

"What did you tell him?"

"They're in jail, but our lawyers will pry them loose."

Cubellis offered Cima a cigar, and they fussed with lighting them. "The American woman. A thorn in our side from the outset," Cubellis said.

"I'm working on it. I contacted New York, as you suggested." Cima puffed and a cloud of smoke rose. "Though we may have a weak link at the jail. Marco used a woman to get close to the American. A *poliziotta*. They arrested her too."

"Who is she? What's her name?"

"Barbara Torre."

"'Barbara?'" Cubellis's mouth constricted as if he'd bitten an under-ripe plum. "What's wrong with a good Italian name?"

Cima chuckled agreement. "We don't know how much she knows."

"Marco is clever. She'll know little. But you're right to keep an eye on her." Cubellis's mind wandered. "Barbara Torre ... Isn't she related to Enzo Torre? I think so. I recall a little barbarian in his family. If she is, tell Enzo to take care of it."

"I'll talk to him after we finish. *Dottor* Kim is coming?"

"An early dinner, yes. He may stay for the meeting with the lawyers. Mention Gilletti tonight. But I am most interested in the problem of the men in jail and, you will understand, the American."

NIC

Nic had scored the perfect hideout. His friends didn't know about his new female companion, so even if they talked to the police, which he doubted, they couldn't give him away. No one would hunt for him here in brain-dead Riano. Even the Saturday market didn't attract much of a crowd. Still, not being able to talk to Marco made him nervous. Vittorio Cima had shared almost no information, and that grudgingly. "Stay strong," he advised.

The woman said something as they approached a crowded *trattoria* at the edge of the market stalls. His thoughts still on his conversation with Cima, he didn't respond.

She patted his arm. "Hungry?"

"No." He needed to be careful about money. He would get what he needed from her, but not yet.

"You don't say much, do you, Carlo?"

"What?"

"You're a quiet one."

"Deep thoughts," he said. He whispered in her ear, "The deeper, the better."

She giggled. Nic rested his hand on the small of her back. The warm touch and her movement against him brought the shopping mission to an abrupt end and a hurried return to the apartment.

She set the groceries on the dining table and stepped to the balcony door to slide the curtains closed. For a moment she gazed into the street.

"I'll just put the food away," she said.

Nic yawned.

When she walked into the bedroom, Nic was stretched out naked on the unmade bed. "Come here," he said. He roughly undressed her, and she laughed when the pearl buttons of her blouse flew across the bed and pinged against the walls and hit the floor. He lifted her heavy breasts and buried his face in them, massaging the nipples with his thumbs. He pushed her onto her stomach and lifted up her hips. This position seemed to surprise her, and she responded eagerly. Soon she was flushed, wanting more.

Afterwards, she lay with her head on his shoulder. "I want to show you Riano's castle," she said. "You'll be impressed."

He doubted it. He jerked up, and her head bounced onto the pillow. No messages yet on his phone. What was happening?

"*Il quotidiano?* Did you get the newspaper?"

"I didn't know y—"

"I need it."

"I will get dressed and—"

"I'll go." He was already out of bed, pulling on his jeans. No underwear. She shivered and rubbed her arms. She pulled her kimono around her and followed him into the living room. He was tying his boots.

"It's so gloomy," she said, and pushed the curtain aside. The morning had been sunny, but now thick clouds covered the sky. "I hope it won't rain."

Nic jogged into the bedroom. "Wallet."

"Funny," she said. "*Signora* Biondi's son is still standing there. I noticed him a while ago, before … a while ago."

He returned, working the wallet into a back pocket. "You're a nosy one." The words came out cold, harsh.

She let the curtain fall. "It's because he has his uniform on. I thought he was on duty."

Nic instantly came to her side. "What?"

"His policeman's uniform." She lifted the curtain. "See?"

"You know him?"

"I've known him his whole life. He's my neighbor's son, Tommaso. It's hard to think of him as a police officer. A sweet young man, but not very bright."

As if he knew they were talking about him, Tommaso Biondi glanced up at the apartment, and they took a guilty step back.

"Stay here and keep an eye on him." He hurried into the bedroom once more.

"Now the shopkeeper is talking to him," she murmured.

"Where can I get a paper?" Nic interrupted her.

"Go back toward the town square. There's a *farmacia*, and a couple of—"

"Good enough."

"Don't be long." She fidgeted with the curtain. "Carlo." He closed the door before she finished whispering his name.

Nic crossed the street and trotted away. A glance behind revealed Tommaso looking after him, head cocked to one side. About halfway down the block, Nic tossed his phone into a trash can.

LEO

Leo and Sal agreed to approach the woman gently, obliquely. Her name was Rosetta, and they knew enough about her from the Riano patrolman and enough about Nic to guess the situation. When she opened her door to them, she wore jeans and a fuzzy pink sweater with a daring V-neck.

They introduced themselves. "The man who left here a while ago?" Leo asked. He couldn't let her see his frustration.

"Carlo? He went for a newspaper."

They let her think a moment. Then she said, "But he's been gone too long. For that."

"How did you meet him, Rosetta?" Leo asked.

Something about the question surprised her. She blinked, then whispered, "He never called me by my name." Her face reddened. After a moment, she said, "I'm sorry, what?" She started to cry, and the tears left a trail of mascara on her rouged cheeks.

"How did you meet?"

She told them about the restaurant and perhaps too many glasses of wine. She noticed Sal had Nic's red phone. "How did you get that?" she asked, before remembering. "I saw him throw it away."

"Did you give him money?" Leo asked, his tone suggesting it was a thing one might do. No judgment.

"Absolutely no."

"Are you sure?" It wasn't an accusation, merely an acknowledgment of everything we don't know about our own lives.

"*Certo.*" She blinked several times "We'll see." She stepped into the bedroom and came out carrying her bag. "We'll see." She pulled out a little brocade purse. From the way she examined its compartments, one after the other, they knew what she found. She put her head in her hand.

"How much?" Sal asked.

"Almost a hundred euros," she wailed. "What was I thinking?"

"Please, *Signora*, there's no fault in meeting an attractive stranger," Leo said. "And, if he is not who he says he is, shame on him for having secrets he wants to keep from you."

"I believed—" She didn't continue.

"Of course."

Sal laid his business card on the table. "If he calls you again, or comes here, find a way to let us know."

Leo added, "But be extremely cautious. He is a dangerous man."

SAL

Late Saturday afternoon Sal slapped his badge against the locked glass door of *Ospidale Fatebenefratelli*'s medical records department, and a buzzer gave him entry. A young woman with midnight hair staffed a reception counter she could barely see over. Lively blue eyes appraised him. It could have been Sal's extravagant smile or merely a welcome diversion, but, when he asked, she seemed delighted to do a little public service.

She introduced herself as Angela, and Angela had skin like the petals of one of Sal's grandmother's roses. She worked weekends and attended the university during the week. She was on duty the previous Sunday and knew about the missing record. "Eugenia Clarke, the American."

Behind Angela marched row upon row upon row of shelves filled with patient records. Sal shook his head. "How do you find anything in here?"

"There's a system, naturally. That record really *is* missing. It was here Sunday, ready for processing, but gone the next day. I came in after they couldn't find it and helped them search. We almost never lose one. We call it M.O.R.—misfiled, on a desk, or 'R' for 'removed without being checked out.' Eventually, they come home, like little lost sheep."

"Unless the wolves get them." Sal leaned on the counter and gave her a wry smile. "It's been missing almost a week now. How about 'S'—for stolen?"

Angela flinched.

"Do you know why we're worried about it?" Sal asked.

"*Dottor* Immormino needed it."

"Sure. *Signora* Clarke is his patient. But it's important to us detectives too. Remember the woman who was murdered?"

"How could I forget!" Her sparkling sapphire eyes never left his.

Though the two of them were alone in the huge room, he dropped his voice. "*Signora* Clarke was in that same bed earlier in the day. We think she was the intended victim."

"Oh, my god."

"And if so—" Sal let Angela's imagination work.

"The record may help them find her!"

"Clever girl." She blushed, and Sal continued, "Between us, please. We need to find out who took it without tipping them off."

She gave him the full picture. Weekdays, the department's door was left unlocked, eight to eight, because the records staff was present. Weekend hours were noon until seven, and a single person was on duty. "Since I'm here by myself and sometimes I leave this desk, I keep the door locked. People with cardkeys—doctors, mostly—can access the records room any time. They rarely come off-hours, though. They would have to find a file themselves."

She angled her computer screen so he could see it. She called up an administrative file, titled *Access Record*. "Our director created the security system himself. We didn't check this file, at least not Monday while I was here, because he believes the record was—is—M.O.R."

"What's that file, Angela?" He walked around the end of the counter to stand behind her, presumably for a better view. Leaning in close, he received a whiff of gardenia. He smiled.

She scrolled down the entries for Sunday, October 21, showing when various people, including *Dottor* Immormino, came in and out. Then they found an anomaly.

"Late Sunday night, someone came in and left again two hours later. Card 1158, but there's no name."

Sal scented a dead end and made a disgusted sound.

"Don't lose hope, we *are* a records department." Further e-sleuthing revealed the owner of card 1158, a woman who'd erased every trace of herself but one. Angela clicked on a file called *Personnel* that required a separate password. "Lucky for you, they made me a superuser, since I'm by myself on weekends."

"Very lucky." From above, Sal watched her ears turn pink.

"OK, she's new to the department, but not to the hospital. She transferred here ten days ago."

A few days after the attack on Signora *Clarke.* He said, "This woman—or whoever she gave that card to or whoever stole it from her—may have located the physical record, but that doesn't take two hours." He was thinking. "You know, *Signora* Clarke's information is missing from the hospital's electronic files too. Even billing."

Angela's eyes glittered like sun on sea. "No way."

"That could be how your visitor spent her time." Sal would ask Leo to turn their cybercrime expert loose on the records department computers. "So, you finish work at seven, right?" He tried to sound casual.

She was busy closing administrative files. "Are you asking me to dinner?"

Sal, not shy himself, was taken aback. He laughed. "I might be."

"If you do, I'll say yes."

CUBELLIS

While his sister finished their dinner preparations, Cubellis listened to Chung-Lee Kim describe his meeting with Pietro Venieri.

"Would your ideas work?" Cubellis asked.

"Undoubtedly. And I could organize a manufacturing facility for you here in Italy, as we've discussed." He paused. "If I might suggest an alternative?"

"Of course."

"As a long-term strategy, an established pharmaceutical company in the States or the EU should manufacture and market the drug legally."

"Say why."

"My industry contacts could rapidly move this drug into phase II trials. The approval process might take five years, but after that, it's an outrageous moneymaker, with decent patent life."

"For the company, yes."

"You stay in the game as a partner, by underwriting the testing. An effective, legitimate Alzheimer's drug will have a huge market in every country in the world. If you broker an ongoing percentage, even a modest one, it will pay dividends for years. And for your organization? Completely risk-free."

Cubellis would prefer not to bother with government drug regulations, but he knew about big pharma profits—*criminale*, in his opinion—so, perhaps ... "I will consider it." His sister knocked on the study door, and he said, "Please, accompany my sister to the dining room. I will meet you in a few moments."

Now more than ever, the American woman remained the biggest problem. She was the only witness who might link his people to the crib. He didn't know how much she'd really seen. Definitely she'd seen Nic. She'd talked to the police, yes, but without her, their case was built on guesses. They'd have to drop it. And he needed them to drop it before they started wondering what happened to the millions the crib would bring in. Once that money got this pharma project going—however he decided to handle it—it opened the door to a fortune, and she stood squarely in his way.

Cubellis's people gathered well before the hour appointed for their meeting. His top lieutenants, heavy and silent as bears, took their accustomed places in the study. The four lean lawyers squeezed in where they could. Chung-Lee Kim sat quietly on the sidelines.

Cubellis drummed his fingers on the desktop and eyed each of his lieutenants in turn. "Three men in jail." He assumed everyone in the room knew what happened the night before. Nevertheless, he asked Cima to summarize.

"Why'd they leave the fucking warehouse, expose themselves like that?" a lieutenant asked.

"To get something to eat," a lawyer said and studied his shoe tips.

The older men squirmed, growling about the younger generation's weaknesses.

"When Lama came back to the warehouse with the food, the police were already inside," Cima said.

"How'd they get in?" another lieutenant asked.

Cubellis answered, his voice betraying a simmering anger only a degree or two below full boil. "They were let in, by Marco or the American."

The men continued to grumble. They grew up as men of action, and this situation seemed to call for it.

"Do the cops connect us with the crib?" one asked.

"They can speculate, but they have no proof unless one of our people talks," Cubellis said.

"They've been asking about it," a lawyer said, "persistently." Everyone in the room would know what that meant. *Not politely.*

Cima said, "The American may have convinced them she saw the hand-off Thursday night. Because she definitely saw Nicola." The grumbling intensified.

Cubellis began what at first sounded like a digression. "When Marco and Gianni approached us with their idea, it seemed far-fetched. They said they could get the formula for a new Alzheimer's drug. They said it could bring a fortune. Yet, it would require a substantial investment to produce such a thing or buy a legitimate company to make it."

"And many bribes," an older man said.

"We did not know whether the drug would work," Cubellis said. "In the worst case, we would be selling hope. There is always a ready market for hope. *Dottor* Kim will say where we are with that project now." He turned to Kim, "And he has a recommendation I'm considering."

Kim rose and bowed. He told the men the original drug was nearly useless, but a key adjustment in the formula would likely make it effective. "I suggested to Mr. Cubellis that he arrange for a legitimate company to produce this drug. Your money would support testing, and the company would handle red tape, manufacturing, and marketing. Mr. Cubellis would negotiate a percentage of profits. Your organization would get a smaller piece, but the pie would be much, much bigger. Entirely legitimate."

"Tell me the size of the market for this drug again?" Cubellis knew, but his men needed convincing.

"Ten to twenty billion dollars a year—about seventeen billion euros."

"Even one percent of that would be a hundred and seventy million a year—legitimate down to the last euro," Cima said.

"Previously, we expected to make the drug ourselves, keep the profits, and get them sooner. *Dottor* Kim and I will continue to discuss that possibility," Cubellis said. "This is a costly venture, no matter how we proceed. That's why we told Marco and Gianni to find investment capital."

"They've succeeded," Cima said. "Because they are young and their plan was risky, I put Umberto Ricci in charge of that part of the operation. Gianni and Marco, especially, didn't like that, but they went along."

"Until last night, perhaps." Cubellis's fingers tapped.

"Now, Gianni's dead. We don't know who killed him," Cima said. "Marco has played his part well, but he and the American were alone at the warehouse—"

"That bitch is a problem," a man interrupted.

"It's her word against theirs," a lawyer said, "and even if the police believe her, they need more."

Another lawyer added, "We're arguing that Umberto didn't know anything about the American. He'll be out soon. Lama, too, maybe. Although she did not see him, his cigarette butts prove he was at the warehouse before the police arrived."

"Such a bad habit, smoking," Cubellis sighed.

"But Marco is stuck. The police found him there with her. No deniability."

"What the police care about at present is the crib," Cubellis said. "The American is an excuse to hold our people while they try to break them down."

A man sitting in the shadows next to Chung-Lee Kim said, "If we get rid of her, we solve a lot of problems."

"Yes," Cubellis said. "Time is not on our side. When Umberto gets out, she must be his first priority."

A little later, when Cima described Gillo Gilletti's new investigation, the men broke into derisive laughter. But Gilletti was a momentary distraction. What hung in the air was Cubellis's "Yes."

TATI

While Cubellis was conferring with his lieutenants and lawyers, Tati also convened a strategy session regarding the Santa Maria Maggiore theft. The atmosphere was thick with discouragement. Nearly round-the-clock questioning of the three suspects had proved futile so far.

Umberto's lawyers claimed he drove out to check on the warehouse, one of his employer's regular places of business, because the security system indicated unusual after-hours activity. They said Umberto knew nothing about an abduction or why the men at the warehouse would have mentioned him, if they did. Unless the authorities could shake that story, they would have to let Umberto go. Even preventive detention had its limits.

Marco and Lama were equally closemouthed. "The bitch is lying," is all Lama said.

"We had a line on the fourth man—Nicola Bertaloso. We know he spent the night in Riano, but he's disappeared again," Leo said, his frustration evident.

Someone asked, "What about the woman, the *poliziotta*?"

"Also not talking. Though we don't think she knows much. Nothing about the crib," Bracci said.

"As a *Polizia di Stato* officer, you'd think she'd be more cooperative," the *carabinieri* representative said, happy to skewer another service. "Why didn't she use her gun, for example, when the American was grabbed?"

Bracci tried hard not to sound defensive. "Because one of the kidnappers was her boyfriend. She was shocked to see him there, shocked they assaulted the other officer, and they acted fast to disarm her. They left her gun behind and forced her to leave with them."

Tati went to the wall and tapped one particular photo from twenty years before. A woman being escorted from a police car, her free hand shading her eyes against the news photographers' flash. "Has she had visitors?"

"Only family," said a man from the unit overseeing the jail.

"Who, precisely?"

"A cousin. Also Torre. Enzo Torre."

Bracci slapped his hand on the table. "That's that! You won't get anything more out of her. You're talking the *malavita* now. Enzo Torre is … a bad actor in every respect. *Merda*! Her cousin?"

Tati wagged his pen. "Anything else?"

"A witness to the abduction, but he cannot say who was under the burqa. Plenty of people noticed the two 'workmen' at the basilica, but their disguise was clever. They were seen, but not seen."

"We have a lead on how *Signora* Clarke's medical record went missing," Leo put in. His and Bracci's priority was keeping Genie safe and bolstering her testimony, but this was of little interest to the others.

"*La Polizia Scientifica*?" Tati asked.

"No forensic evidence from the basilica. Or from the overlook. Or the hotel. Marco's fingerprints and Lama's cigarette butts from the warehouse, but then, we have the men themselves," Bracci said.

Tati protested. "We believe these men have been involved in multiple serious crimes, beginning with the attack on *Signora* Clarke, the murder in the hospital, the murder and theft at Santa Maria Maggiore, the assault on your officer at the hotel, and *Signora* Clarke's abduction last night. Forensics can help with none of these?"

"Not so far."

"What about the van?" the Vatican representative asked.

"We believe it was stolen that morning from a delivery service, and we are searching for it, but ..." Bracci looked doubtful.

"We may as well assume the van will be clean too, when we find it," Tati said. Silence accumulated along with the dead ends. "I have another idea. Recall *Signora* Clarke's perceptive words of last night. She said she believed the man Marco cooperated in her escape—if not cooperated, at least allowed it to unfold."

"We haven't gotten a thing out of him."

"No," Tati said, "but she might."

"Send the American in to talk to him?" the *carabinieri* liaison objected.

"Is she up to it?" Tati asked.

"We can ask," said FBI agent Tesone. "She's waiting outside."

GENIE

I skimmed the newspapers in Tati's reception area while representatives of the various police agencies met to strategize. The prosecutor wanted me there in case one of them had a question for me. I closed *la Repubblica*—not a word about my abduction in it. Was that good or bad?

I took a look at Facebook. My friends' birthdays and kid pictures. A new puppy. A couple of friend requests. I resisted responding to anything, no matter how enticing.

Then a direct message in Italian:

A morti e a sorta stannu arretu a porta.

I needed a few seconds to work out a translation and a few more seconds to process it:

"Death and fate stand behind the door."

What is that about? Genie thought.

As if on cue, the door to Tati's office opened. A grinning Dante stepped out to accompany me inside. The men stared and shifted to make room for me to sit at the crowded table. I slipped the phone into my sweater pocket and clenched my hands in my lap.

Tati asked me to relate my impressions of Marco. With difficulty, by speaking slowly, I controlled my voice and matched his businesslike tone. My intimation that Marco was an unenthusiastic member of Cubellis's team was met with muttered disbelief.

"Would you be willing to talk to him?" Tati asked.

Surprised, I darted a glance at Leo. He studied a paper in front of him, lips pressed tightly together. "What do you want from him?" I asked.

The Vatican police official slapped the table, exasperated. "That should be obvious."

"There are no restrictions," Tati said. "We want him to begin talking. Everything he says makes it easier to say the next thing. If one of our prisoners doesn't talk soon, we will have to let them all go. Except Marco. Him we can hold, and he knows it."

"The crib! Ask him about the crib," the Vatican police official blurted, his fist pounding the table. He threw his hands in the air and gazed at the ceiling.

"Incapace," the *carabinieri* representative mumbled. *Hopeless.*

Except for Leo and Bracci, maybe Tati and Tesone, the men's expressions were skeptical, even hostile. Bracci frowned, and Leo stared holes in the table. I could tell he opposed the idea as much as the others did, but I suspected it was for different reasons.

"A morti e a sorta stannu arretu a porta." Was it death or fate they were offering me? Was my fate an awful one, or was I fated to take up their challenge?

Or was Leo worried I might somehow damage the case he was trying so painstakingly to construct? That was the last thing I wanted. I absolutely could not disappoint him again.

The Facebook message was a reminder—wholly unnecessary by this point—that danger surrounded me, that my cell phone number could be found by people who wouldn't stop looking for me. If the investigators remained stymied, Leo would have no case, no matter how hard he worked. There was only one way not to disappoint him.

"I'll do it."

CHAPTER—14

Sunday, October 28

GENIE

"Why did they send you?"

A steel table separated Marco and me. His right wrist was handcuffed to a chair bolted to the floor. Nothing in the interrogation room captured the attention of his flitting eyes. Gray walls and floor, a claustrophobic six square meters, it held the table, two straight chairs, an empty wall plug for a recording machine, and a dirty tin ashtray.

His white-heat hostility was so different from the chilly antagonism of the police officials the night before. Now they watched from behind a one-way mirror, just waiting for this interview to fail.

"To talk. A little." It was early Sunday morning; I'd brought coffee.

"Why would I talk to you?"

I pushed one of the paper cups in his direction. "That's up to you. I owe you."

Marco, either weighing my comment or uninterested, didn't reply. Silence settled between us like ash. When the police officials had laid out the questions they wanted answers to, my task sounded so simple. But how could I get a conversation going? They didn't tell me that. And my mind was blank.

What did I know about him that might give me an opening? That might startle him into a response? At last I said, "I saw a picture of you with the priest at Santa Maria Maggiore. Did you kill him?"

Again he didn't respond. The impatient men behind the mirror were right. I had no idea what I was doing. I was wasting everyone's time, abusing Leo's trust, while Marco merely stared at me. Then, something changed. Behind his impassive expression, I thought I detected a glimmer of interest.

"Well, did you?" Eyebrows raised.

His black eyes locked on my uncertain ones. "I didn't kill him. Do you have cigarettes?" As his left hand cradled the warm paper cup, the sinister snake circled it.

"I don't smoke."

"Shit." He slouched in the metal chair and tucked the thumb of his shackled hand into an empty belt loop. He watched me through half-closed eyes.

"Who did kill him, do you know?"

"The one who wanted to kill you."

"Umberto?"

He spat out a laugh. "Umberto is the one who was *going* to kill you. Eventually."

Nervous perspiration prickled my underarms, but I kept my voice steady. "Nic then?"

"Yes, Nic. Nic loves to hate. I'm astonished you're alive."

"I may not be for long."

"The Fates cut the string whenever they wish." His fingers made a scissoring motion.

"Or, Nic can, with his knife. He escaped, you know."

"*Did* he?" Interest at last. "In that case, you must be very careful. What did you mean, you 'owe me'?"

"You could have killed me Friday night."

"And, if I talk to you, what do I get out of it?"

"The police—the *pubblico ministero*—may ask for a lighter sentence if you cooperate."

He snorted. "You speak Italian, *Signora*, but you know nothing of Italians. I'm talking to you because, why not? Already I'm a dead man."

"Because I was rescued on your watch?"

"Yes, and because they will know why."

"And why is that?"

He hit the table with his fist and almost shouted. "Because I can't fucking do it anymore!" More quietly,

"For me, Morta took out her scissors the moment they murdered the priest. I saw he was a fool. But, when I was a child, the priest in my hometown told us to be 'fools for god.' He was that too.

"And what happened to that woman, the one we thought was you. In the hospital. What Lama did …" He shook his head.

Lama. The tall one.

"My fucking cousin." He studied his hand, opening and closing the fist. Abruptly he leaned across the table and looked straight in my eyes. "You remind me of my mother. The dark red hair. But her eyes were brown, not cats' eyes, like yours."

I waited. My heart skipped ahead. Maybe this would work.

"Not just the hair. The spirit. She never gave in." He paused between each word of his last sentence. "And in the warehouse, neither did you. You didn't cry. You didn't beg. You didn't give us anything."

"I cried later."

"She might have too, but never so *he* could hear it."

"Your father?"

"No, the head of the 'Ndrangheta in Stilo, where I was born."

"The head of *what*?"

"'Ndrangheta, the Calabrian mafia. The dead priest was from there. Around there. He had the accent." He rubbed a fingertip on a spot on the table, as if locating the town on an invisible map. "That mafia pig had his eye on my mother and nagged her constantly, but she gave him no encouragement. I learned this only later of course. She said nothing to my father, to protect him. Perhaps she hoped the man would lose interest."

"But he did not." I imagined the men behind the mirror losing patience.

"No. One night he came to our front door. Drunk, bellowing for her. I was eight years old. She pushed me into a cupboard. There was a crack between the boards, and I saw everything. When my father opened the door, the swine knocked him aside and rushed into the house, waving a gun. He ordered my mother to come with him. My father leapt across the kitchen table to defend her. The man hardly bothered to aim, he just fired."

"He killed your father!" I cried, in shocked sympathy with a child whose father's life exploded in front of him.

"No." Marco studied his tattoo. "He shot her … 'Coward!' My father screamed. To him, hurting a woman was the worst act of a coward."

"And your father?"

He shifted in the steel chair. "The man dragged him out to the yard, and some of his people came to help. By sunrise, my father did die in the field behind our house. The longest night of my life. I slipped away to the neighbors' house—a family my parents knew since they were children. I ran inside, leaving footprints of my mother's blood, and they wept with me to hear my father's screams. They could do nothing." His hands trembled. "Yet they did one thing. They hid me until my uncle—Lama's father—came from Rome to take me away."

"That's a terrible story."

"In the hospital room … the woman …" He glanced away distractedly. "We thought she was you. We agreed you had to die. That was necessary."

I swallowed hard and waited him out.

"But when he cut out her tongue and throat. That was not necessary. That was being a coward."

My hand flew toward my neck, but I aborted the gesture and instead pushed my hair behind my ear. When I spoke, my voice had an edge: "You were there. You didn't stop him."

Marco's expression hardened, and he didn't respond.

"Did you plan the theft of the crib?"

"I helped."

"Don't be modest."

"Not fucking likely. A job like that is complicated. 'Important people' are brought in. Shit people." He jerked his chained arm as if testing the limits of the restraint.

"Umberto?"

He didn't answer.

"You say Nic killed the priest. But were you with him? Again, merely a bystander?"

"No. I wasn't there."

"Someone was. Lama?"

He didn't respond, and I sensed diminishing interest. "Where's the crib now, do you suppose?"

"Long gone. We don't know where."

"Who did you give it to Thursday night?"

"So it *was* you?"

"On the overlook? Yes."

"Nic said it was. We figured he was crazy. He's obsessed."

Somehow, I kept my voice even, mechanical. "You transferred it to another van."

"Belonged to the fence."

"And?"

"We didn't talk to them. I don't think they even speak Italian. We're not involved in that side of the business."

"Who *is* involved?"

He didn't answer.

"Did you see me at the restaurant? And our car? Did you get the license plate?"

"Yes."

"But you didn't follow up on it."

"I had a better idea."

I could guess what that was. "Was Officer Torre—Barbara—your girlfriend all along?"

"Nah. I picked her up after we saw her with you that day."

"How did you—?"

"I recognized her. Her cousin's a friend." A strange smile spread over his face, and he stabbed his finger toward me. "Now him, you *really* don't want to meet."

"And she told you where I was?"

"No. She told me where *she* was. She was as surprised as you when we got there."

"She hasn't talked."

"Do you expect her to? Lama told her he'd kill her. Him and Enzo. And they would. She is in no doubt of that."

I had run out of questions and was too exhausted to think of more. After a few moments of silence, I said, "Maybe we'll talk again."

"Bring cigarettes."

A police officer came into the room to return Marco to his cell.

"What was his name?" Marco asked, over his shoulder.

I was confused for a few seconds, then I knew what he was asking. "Maratea. Father Nunzio Maratea."

When the security doors at the end of the corridor clanged behind Marco, Leo and Bracci entered the interview room. I stared into my empty cardboard cup.

"Good job," Leo said. He might have said more, but for the one-way mirror and the men behind it.

"You didn't tell me everything about Gemma Capuano," I said.

"No."

"I'm glad. If I'd known …" I inhaled deeply and straightened my spine. "Anything else you're not telling me?"

"No."

"Hunh." I wasn't convinced.

"We got a lot to work on from this," Bracci said briskly. "And Marco's right about one thing. He's a walking dead man in here."

MADOOR

The poet Gabriele D'Annunzio was born in Pescara, on Italy's Adriatic coast, a coincidence Amit Madoor contemplated as he strolled along Pescara's beach. Sand grains dusted the trouser cuffs of his bespoke suit, and tiny tan polka dots danced on the toes of his expensive black wingtips.

He was waiting for his men, and they were late. They were supposed to leave Rome early that morning, cross the peninsula, and arrive well in advance of *Petra*'s ten-thirty a.m. sailing. The trim white passenger vessel rocked quietly in the marina.

He passed the sun umbrellas of the upscale resorts, where early risers—families with young children—were claiming the best places. At last an unmarked truck crawled along the quay toward the customs shed, and he met up with it there, heartily greeting the official in charge.

Although the port of Pescara required few customs formalities, Madoor possessed all the necessary papers, two sets of them. One, not accurate in every detail, described six fiberglass horses, contemporary manufactured products that could leave the country without the exacting inspections and delays—and bureaucratic near impossibilities—involved in shipping genuine antiquities. This set would be approved easily.

With an apologetic shrug, he passed the customs officer a second set of papers, which described the horses as ancient Etruscan bronzes.

"These papers are … for the buyer."

A crafty expression clouded the official's eyes like cataracts. He was familiar with the creative methods of antiquities smugglers. Madoor knew him well too, an Italian citizen born of Turkish parents, who held his job through the intercession of *Signor* Cubellis. While he was without doubt a man who could be paid to look the other way when Italy lost a portion of its precious heritage, Madoor intended to focus his gaze in the wrong direction entirely.

Madoor's men unloaded six wheeled crates from the truck's cargo box and rolled them into the customs shed. Madoor and the Turk watched as they opened the crate marked #1 and unwound yards of bubble wrap to expose an exquisitely crafted prancing horse bearing the patina of millennia.

"How is your son?" Madoor asked the Turk, admiring his hairbrush mustache.

"He does brilliantly in school and plans to enter university next year. I only hope I can afford to send him." The man sighed.

"You must be very proud."

The Turk murmured assent. In silence they watched the laborious uncrating, unwrapping, and careful rewrapping of the horses in crates 2 and 3. The official yawned. He examined the two sets of customs papers. "Beautiful."

"I have a gift for your son." Madoor slipped a thick envelope into the Turk's jacket pocket.

The man made no attempt to demur. "He will be grateful, as I am."

They inspected the horse from crate 4. "But these horses," the smiling Turk pressed, with a lift of his eyebrows, "will your buyer be persuaded the price was fair? By these?" He shook the false papers.

Madoor replied softly, "Let me put it to you this way, my friend. I sold them to *un greco*." A Greek.

The official threw back his head and laughed. "Then my questions are finished."

They approached the fifth crate. "So, here's another one." The Turk passed by without waiting for it to be fully unwrapped. Madoor gestured for his men to move to the final crate.

"And the last." He rested his hand on top.

The truck driver stepped to Madoor and said, "Apologies, *Signore*, but we ran out of packing materials. Nino packed this one in straw." The workers pried away the top two boards, pulled out some of the straw, littering the shed floor with it.

"What?!" Madoor made a face, and he and the Turk stepped away. "It smells like manure!" He took another step. "Filthy straw!" Another board came off, they pulled out more straw, and the horse's head became visible.

The Turk waved the men off and hollered, red-faced, "Pack it up. Get it out of my shed!"

"A thousand apologies, my friend." Madoor said, as his men scurried to repack the crate. To them he shouted, "Get it out of here, quickly. Quickly!" He jabbed at a mound of straw with his foot.

Madoor put an arm around the Turk's shoulders. "Please forgive them. They don't know ... this is why we need more young men like your son." He glared over his shoulder at his workmen and shouted, "Men with brains in their heads!"

Inside the paper-strewn customs office, the Turk stamped and signed the two sets of shipping documents. He and Madoor then boarded *Petra*, dazzling in the morning sun. The Turk, his good mood reviving, handed the documents to the captain—a jovial man secretly in Madoor's employ. Once at sea, the captain would shred the papers claiming the horses were antiquities.

The captain offered them espresso and pistachio-laden baklava. The three men talked comfortably, hardly noticing the occasional thumps as Madoor's men loaded the crates into unused staterooms. The sixth filled a special climate-controlled compartment, its precious cargo sealed against barnyard dust and sea air alike.

Shortly after the visitors disembarked, the water surrounding the ship churned, and the crew loosened the mooring lines. Precisely at ten thirty, *Petra* glided out of the slip, gently turned, and moved into open water, sailing for Singapore.

Madoor watched her from the coast road until she dissolved into the haze hugging the horizon. Seven hours later, he drove through the border crossing into Croatia.

THE BRAZILIAN

Madoor had closed the Via in Selci shop and given his workmen a month off to visit their families. Yet, on the evening he arrived in Pula and for several days thereafter, his Brazilian foreman—the tan-skinned man who wore the distinctive ebony and silver crucifix—labored until well after dark. He had set himself a difficult job for one man alone, even with the aid of plaster molds made in secret. It required a substantial quantity of Madoor's silver and gold too, supplies he would replenish out of his own savings many days before they could be missed.

LEO

Leo and Bracci silently contemplated each other across Leo's desk, where the crumbs of their lunch lay as scattered as the disconnected pieces of the investigation.

The phone rang. "Well, find someone who does!" Leo covered the mouthpiece and said despairingly, "You don't speak English?"

"Sal does."

"Get him." And, into the phone, "We may have somebody. Take the number and tell him we'll call back."

Soon Bracci hurried in with Sal. "Caught him at the elevator."

"Yeah. I remembered it's my day off."

"What?" Bracci said. "'Day off?'" He queried Leo.

"No idea." Leo told the police operator to place the call. "*Signora* Clarke's brother called me. What's the English for '*collega*'?"

"Colleague," Sal said.

A phone in Virginia rang and was answered immediately. "Hello?"

"*Buon pomeriggio*," Leo said. He looked helplessly at Sal, who mouthed "good morning."

"Goood moarning," he said, as if making the words longer would make them clearer.

"*Signor* Angelini?"

"*Sì. Leo Angelini.*"

"I'm Eugenia Clarke's brother, Robert." The man also spoke slowly, and Leo understood the words, but the tone of his faraway voice revealed much more. Something was wrong.

"'Brother,' *sì. Un momento. Mio* 'colleeeg.'" He rolled his eyes in tongue-tied embarrassment and handed the phone to Sal. "Put him on *vivavoce*."

"Hello?" said Sal, in American English. "I'm Sal. I work for Detective Angelini, and I lived a couple years in Chicago. I'm putting you on speaker, OK?" He listened, then punched the button. "You talk, and I'll translate."

Robert spoke, and Sal said, "His sister mentioned Leo's name ... he makes an apology for not speaking Italian ...

something happened yesterday ... awake all night ... probably nothing ..."

The story emerged that Robert ran a farm stand where he sold produce, mostly to locals. A stranger came by the day before and, idly chatting, worked his way around to talking about Italy. Robert said his sister was in Rome, and the man—"very casually but persistently"—tried to find out where exactly. Robert knew he'd made a mistake the moment he mentioned her and summed up, saying, "Something wasn't right."

"Good instincts," Bracci said. "Like his sister."

"I don't like it. Was he American?" Leo asked.

Sal translated the question.

Yes, American, but could be Italian American. New York accent. He drove a rental car, and Robert gave Sal the plate number.

Apparently Genie hadn't told her brother much. Robert knew she hurt her leg and was recuperating—Sal shrugged as he relayed that information—but he didn't understand the secrecy regarding her whereabouts. She didn't call Friday when she said she would, and when she did text him on Saturday, she was evasive.

"He wants to know what's going on," Sal concluded.

"I understand," Leo said, "but I cannot break *Signora* Clarke's confidentiality. If she does not want to tell him—"

"You hear him. He's worried."

"Ask him to try her one more time. And tell him ... tell him we are doing everything in our power to keep his sister safe."

Sal raised his eyebrows at this, and spoke into the phone. Robert was silent a long time. The three detectives exchanged glances. From a farmhouse kitchen thousands of miles away came a gruff *"Grazie, Signore."*

When they disconnected, Sal said, "Do you think that will satisfy him?"

"No, I do not." Leo gazed out the window. High overhead a silver airplane caught the sun in its sparkling descent to Ciampino airport. "I hope not."

Leo tapped the desk with the eraser end of a pencil as his face went through a series of expressions. "I don't like it," he repeated.

"Potential hostages?" Sal asked.

"Or simple blackmail. 'We know where your family is.' Let's not tell Genie about Roberto's call, not yet, but we must end this. I am calling Tati."

LEO

Leo and Bracci stopped by the hotel that afternoon. Genie and Agostina had remained at the same hotel, but refused the suite. A regular room would have to do. They found Genie pacing the small space.

"I've been thinking," she said, "and I might have kind of an idea."

"I would like to hear it," Leo said.

"I'm thinking we shouldn't wait for Nic to come up with a plan—time and place of his choosing. We should get ahead of him, draw him out. We believe he's trying to find me. Let him see me again, and maybe he'll make a move."

"Out of the question." Leo could envision a hundred ways such a plan could go wrong.

"Where would we try this?" Bracci asked. "We don't know where he is."

Leo stared at him, shocked he would entertain this idea for even a moment.

Genie said, "We know where he's *been*—Spanish Steps, Piazza del Popolo. He's found me there before. And, since I'm staying close by, you already have police around. All those plainclothes officers in the lobby."

"*That's* what we should have asked Marco," Bracci said, "where Nic is likely to be."

"I'm worried about Marco," she said. "Believe it or not."

"We've taken extra precautions. We moved him to a smaller jail, and very few people know where," Bracci said. "I drove him there myself."

In response to Genie's skeptical expression, Leo said, "Cubellis will assume we'd pick a *higher* security facility, not a small local jail with only a couple of guards. Even if he figures it out, finding Marco will take time. But why are we even discussing this?"

"And does *he* believe you're acting on his behalf, protecting him?" she asked Bracci.

"So maybe he'll do something for us in return? You want to talk to him again? Ask where Nic might be?" Bracci actually seemed to be considering her crazy idea.

"Absolutely not!"

"Leo, please think about it," she said. "I know it's a risk, but now, everywhere I go and everything I do is a risk. I showed you that Facebook message. It wasn't the only one." She handed him her phone.

"Keep this damn thing turned off. Except in emergencies."

Bracci said quietly, "She's right about 'time and place,' Leo. And you're right, we need to end this."

MARCO

It was early evening when Marco next met Genie, and the circumstances were entirely different. These rural police didn't put restraints on him, and the room where she waited for him was where they ate their meals. Through the partially open window, he could see scattered lights from houses and farms. Fresh air and the scent of the countryside bathed the room. He could almost forget the policeman leaning against the wall behind him and the tall detective from Rome—Angelini—standing guard outside.

Genie pulled a pack of *MS* out of her sweater pocket and laid it on the table.

He flashed her a look and drew the pack toward him. "Why are you here? Again."

"You need cigarettes. And there *is* something important you can tell me. If you're willing."

He grunted.

"Where do you think Nic is? Would he stay in Rome?"

"Why would I tell you that?"

"Because you're angry that what you planned as a simple theft, the others have turned into a bloody mess."

He blinked. *Too smart for her own good.* "I wouldn't say 'simple.'" He took the cellophane from the top of the pack. Genie waited. Marco tolerated the silence as long as he could. "The theft wasn't the point," he said. "We needed money."

"We?"

"Me and *mio compagno.*" He sniffed the pack of cigarettes, filling his lungs with the aroma. "Cubellis liked our idea well enough, but he wouldn't give us the cash to get it going. We had to figure out how to pay for it."

"The crib was the means to an end."

"Yeah."

"What was the idea?"

What the hell. I'm as good as dead. "My friend's uncle or cousin or whatever invented a new drug for Alzheimer's disease, and we were going to get it. It would have made billions, so my friend said. So his auntie told him."

"Billions? Really?"

He shrugged and briefly met her eyes. "Now my friend is dead, and I'm here. Sometimes I think he might have made it up. Not the whole thing. He has hundreds of relatives. He might have one who works in a lab. Some kind of lab. But a relative of Gianni's, a scientific genius?" He laughed bitterly. "He—he always wanted things to be more than they were, you know?"

After a moment, she said, "Even so, the crib is gone. And Cubellis will get your money."

"Yeah." He shifted in the metal seat.

"Do you think he will pursue it without you? The Alzheimer's thing?"

He glared darkly at the cigarette pack. "No reason not to."

"But if you weren't sure about this relative, why did you go along?"

"I wanted to see if we could fucking do it! Then it was too late for such questions."

"And they brought in Umberto." She pushed a pack of matches across the table. "Oh, go ahead."

Marco took his time lighting the cigarette, never taking his eyes off her. He screwed his mouth sideways to blow the smoke away.

"So, where's Nic?" she asked again after he took a couple of drags.

"No special place. He doesn't have a real home. Keeps some stuff at my place. He crashes with friends or picks up a woman and stays with her a couple of days or weeks. Tourists, usually. Never lasts."

"Where does he find them?" She sounded skeptical, and Marco didn't blame her.

"Spanish Steps. Keats Museum. He says it attracts the sensitive type, the ones who want to mother him." In a thin, mocking way he said, "The pale waif." *The pale psycho.*

Again the silence grew, until Marco said, "He might be at the garage."

"Garage?"

"Where we got ready for the robbery and where we took the crib after."

"Where is it?"

He told her. "Nic had a key. We all did. I threw mine away, and I know Umberto tossed his."

"Would he risk going there now?"

"Why not? Rent's paid. It's what he knows. Like violence is what he knows." He tapped his forehead with the fingers of the hand holding the cigarette. "Not many new ideas up there, you know?"

"I appreciate everything you've told me. It's helpful. But why?"

Asking myself the same fucking question. "If I thought I'd get out of this alive, I wouldn't tell you a goddamn thing. Like I said before, I can't do it anymore. I'm done with them, and, *Signora*, I'm betting my life they are done with me."

CHAPTER—15

Monday, October 29

Genie's message to Robbie:

Why not answering my texts! Where are u?

SAL

Monday morning, Sal dashed into the detectives' office, late for the team meeting on the Santa Maria Maggiore theft. Speeding through the reception area he noticed a tall man whose red sunken eyes suggested a sleepless night. His arms slumped on the handle of a rolling suitcase. An American by his clothes and vaguely familiar.

Sal backpedaled a few steps and spoke to him in English. "Excuse me, sir, but are you … Robert Clarke?"

Relief passed over the stranger's face. "Yes! But how did you—?"

"Sal Riccobono." Sal stuck out his hand. "We spoke on the telephone yesterday. You've come to see Detective Angelini?"

Smiling, Robert pumped his hand energetically. "I don't know where my sister is, but I knew I could find the police station. I called her, like the detective suggested, but she wouldn't tell me anything. I could tell there's more going on than an injured leg." His voice acquired a thick coat of worry. "Then two FBI men came—they didn't explain anything, either—said they couldn't—but suggested it would be a good time for a vacation. That was the last straw—do you know the phrase, 'the last straw'?"

"Sure," Sal said. "Detective Angelini will want to meet you ASAP." He grabbed Robert's suitcase and signaled the grateful desk officer he was taking charge of the foreigner.

Leo's meeting had just begun when Sal halted in the doorway. He gestured to Robert behind him, and said, "*Il fratello.*" Leo hurried over, beaming. Sal, sandwiched between the two tall men, made introductions and told Leo about the visit from the FBI.

"Tell him I know he has been worried, and I will take him to her in a half hour. Put him in my office. Get him coffee. Then come back. I'll wind this up as soon as I can."

On the ride to the hotel, Leo and Robert surreptitiously sized each other up. They were almost desperate in their desire to connect, and Sal did his best to keep the halting conversation going. *It's hard to talk when so much needs to be said.*

"Wish I'd slept." Robert gazed out at the shop windows decorated in orange and black. "Halloween. I didn't know you celebrate that here."

"Coming up Wednesday. Always a busy night for us," Sal said. He asked about Robert's trip.

"Haven't used my passport in more than thirty years. But I keep it up-to-date. For emergencies."

Sal translated.

"Well, this is one," Leo said, under his breath.

"Do you want me to tell him that?"

"No."

GENIE

Agostina and I were expecting the hotel bellman to bring our late breakfast and were glad when the knock came. But when Agostina opened the door several people entered, and I glanced up from the newspaper.

"Oh!" I jumped out of the chair, newspaper flying, and ran. I threw my good arm around Robbie's neck, and received a massive bear hug. "Oh my god! Not so tight! Oh my god."

He rested his head on top of mine, repeating my name. We had a rapid conversation in English, faces nearly touching. "What are you *doing* here?"

Someone said, "*Il fratello,*" and Agostina said, "Oh. OK." Robbie drew his head back to study my face. His thumb traced the livid pink line down my cheek.

"Hurt your leg, huh?"

"Oh, it's so much better than it was." I chuckled and gave him another squeeze. After a long moment, I broke off the embrace and wiped my eyes. I looked for Leo and caught his expression—pleased with himself. "*Grazie. Grazie mille.*"

His smile didn't erase the furrows between his brows. He hurried to introduce the young man with them, Sal Riccobono.

"Your boss is full of your praises," I told him, one arm still around Robbie, my head on his chest.

"He was our translator," Leo and Robbie said in two languages.

This second-floor room had only three chairs. Sal offered to leave, since his translating services weren't needed with me there. Leo asked him to stay.

The bellman knocked, ready to wheel in the table and lay out breakfast.

"Chairs, we need two more chairs," Agostina took charge. "And more food."

"Sal and I will grab chairs from across the hall," Leo said. The police had installed themselves in a room there, which they used intermittently.

The awkwardness of the crowded room with the two big men and the tiny table broke the ice, and breakfast was surprisingly jovial. Afterwards I told Robbie the whole story, beginning with the mugging, while Sal quietly translated. I kept trying to reassure him, patting his arm, but I didn't sugarcoat the situation. Rooted to his chair, he clamped his hand to his mouth, as if to hold back his words. It seemed to me he barely breathed.

When I got to the end, Robbie took my face in his hands. "The strain you've been under." He shook his head. "I don't understand, though, why are you in *this* hotel? Where they kidnapped you?" He turned to Leo, "Why are you keeping her here?"

"You would find a new place for her?" Leo asked through Sal.

"Undoubtedly."

"They also will think that. They will not expect her to be here, though they may check to be certain. For that, we are ready. The big hotels—security is difficult. Too many people. The staff here is small, already investigated thoroughly. The alleyway door is always bolted now, you can be sure. A different small hotel—it takes time to do the background checks. Agostina's apartment—impossible, of course."

"Gangsters are so much better prepared for this kind of thing. With their safe houses," I said, trying to kid him into a less anxious mood. "Going to the mattresses."

"I saw that movie too." Robbie threw me a line: "'In Sicily, women are more dangerous than shotguns.'"

"We'll see about that."

Looking puzzled, Leo continued, "We've needed her close to help us identify the men she overheard. That's less important since the arrests, you understand, but she must visit her doctor, our prosecutor may have more questions, we need her to help us with Sal, if we go forward with a new plan—" He made a gesture suggesting further unstated reasons. I wondered what they might be. "The list is becoming shorter."

"Meaning?" Robbie asked.

"Soon we may be able to move her out of Rome."

First I'd heard of it.

Arms crossed over his chest, Robbie contemplated the flowers in the carpeting. "I want to take you home," he said.

"I can't, Robbie. I just can't." I gave Sal a quick headshake, and he didn't translate. Or need to.

Robbie sighed. "Of course you can't. I know what you're thinking. You have a responsibility here. Anyway, is home any safer?"

"Tell her about the FBI," Sal said, and Robbie described the Saturday encounter at the farm stand and the FBI's visit.

"Robbie! Where are Andy and Susan?"

"Susan went to stay with her sister in Baltimore. Andy's still in Morocco on that student exchange. Hard to track either of them." He sounded tired, running on empty.

"You need a nap. We can talk more later." For what's coming, I thought, he needs his rest.

LEO

Leo and Sal returned to the hotel in the early evening, bringing Bracci. They found Robert awake, talking with his sister. They assembled in the policemen's room for a change of venue and because it contained a convenient sofa. On the table was an enormous basket of fruit.

"Guess who visited us?" Genie asked.

"Someone you were glad to see," Leo said, happy she was smiling. He gestured to the basket. "A fruit-seller?"

"The manager sent that. Probably thought we needed a pick-me-up. Or hopes I won't sue him over that unlocked alley door."

"Sal," Leo said, pointing to the fruit, and Sal proceeded to take out and examine each piece of fruit, all the tissue paper underneath, and finally, the basket itself.

Genie and Robert exchanged a look. She said, "Oliver Harmon came by. He's very entertaining." Robert laughed when he caught what Genie was saying. "He *is* a nonstop talker, but Robbie was so glad to meet him. My savior. Oliver wants to help. He said he's going to keep an eye out."

"For what exactly?" Leo said, doubtful.

"I don't know. He's close by. He takes walks. He may have a different viewpoint than your police."

"That I am sure of," said Leo, charmed by her enthusiasm. Maybe his old friend could add a bit of divine intervention too.

When they were settled, he directed his remarks—translated by Sal—to Robert. "We want to tell you about a plan we are developing." He was afraid his own doubts would be obvious and this conversation would not go well.

But it was their best idea at the moment, and it needed a fair hearing.

Bracci began. "We released Umberto late this morning. He's the one in charge of the reliquary theft, though our evidence was too weak to hold him. Before we let him go, we let him overhear some disinformation, which was that we believe Nic is long gone and it's safe for *Signora* Clarke to go out to busy places—the Vatican, restaurants and shops on Via del Corso, Via dei Condotti, and the like."

"That's this neighborhood," Sal added to his translation. "Fancy shops. Spanish Steps."

"The garage Marco mentioned—it *is* being used. By Nic, maybe. The foot patrol will keep checking it. So he may still be in the area, which adds to our sense of urgency."

"Tati agrees the outreach to the States is a bad sign," Leo said, and waited while Genie explained who Tati was. "Someone highly placed is serious about getting to Genie. Generally, Cubellis likes his people to clean up their own messes, so probably both Umberto and Nic will be searching for her." He arrived at the difficult part. He looked squarely at Robert. "We'd like to draw them out rather than wait for them to pick 'time and place.'"

Robert got it. He interrupted Sal's translation. "You're not setting her up to—"

"We have to," she said. "Please, Robbie," she glanced around the room. "I can't keep living like this. Until they're caught, I'm vulnerable, no matter what. So is Agostina. So are you, maybe. Waiting like a prisoner for them to make a move—it's getting to me."

Leo guessed the others also heard the stress in her voice, Robert most of all. "She will not be alone out there. Sal will be close by. And many of us."

Robert went to the window and studied the pedestrian street. "Things are so different here." He let the curtain fall. "I have only one sister."

"That is why we must catch them," Bracci continued quietly. "The older man, Umberto, we've suspected of certain crimes in the past, but we've never been this close."

He didn't elaborate on the shockingly violent and sadistic nature of those crimes. "The younger one, Nic, is about Sal's age. He attacked your sister in the churchyard. Murdered a priest. Chased her at the Villa Borghese. He was a half-step ahead of us Saturday, and we missed him again yesterday at the garage. He won't quit."

"Why do they still care about her?" Robert asked. "You have two of them in custody and know who the others are. You know who stole the crib. Hurting her would only bring more pressure on them."

"The trial," Leo responded. "When they find out Marco talked, like he said, he's as good as dead. We will try to protect him, but he may never testify. And, even if he does, the others will have smart lawyers who will blame everything on him. Genie is the only witness who overheard all four of them plotting, who saw Nic at the overlook, who can recognize their voices from the warehouse. She is the glue in the whole case. They know that."

"But can't you get them on the murders?" Genie asked. "What about Gemma Capuano?"

"We have circumstantial evidence, but it points to Lama *and* Marco, and Lama could swear he left the room after they delivered the flowers and deny everything else."

"But, Father Maratea?—the priest murdered at the basilica, Robbie, remember?—Marco wasn't even there, or so he says."

"No one at the basilica can give more than a vague description of the two phony workmen. Plus, we have photos of Marco with the priest. These, unfortunately, would go against him."

She worried her glass beads. "But what about the kidnapping?"

"Yes, we might be able to make a convincing case they were involved—"

"Of course they were involved!"

"Your word against theirs, I'm afraid," Bracci said. "Marco is the only one we found with you. And he's the one who called Officer Torre; the phone records prove that. Umberto says he didn't know about the abduction. And

Lama says all he did was ride along out to the warehouse. He didn't know who you were."

"What about Barbara Torre?"

"She won't talk."

"The witness who saw them shove me into the car?"

"He can't identify you. Even if he could, a lot can happen between now and a trial. He might disappear. An accident. Sudden wealth."

"But—" She twisted in her chair and was silent a moment. "It's a labyrinth. You think you see a way out, and it becomes a blank wall, a stairway ends at a mirror."

And one wrong turning could be fatal to people in this room.

Robert swore in frustration.

"You see our predicament. We're *not* saying that making our case will be impossible," Leo said, "though it will be more difficult than you imagine. The kidnapping shows they believe Genie has valuable information. That hasn't changed. To really protect her, we have to get our hands on Nic and Umberto. Tie them to the theft or …" He stopped, mentally adding, *or to a more serious charge, like attempted murder.*

"One point in favor of this plan," Bracci said. "They came up as street fighters, and they continue to work that way. Close. That lets us also stay close. No rooftop snipers. No bomb-throwers."

Genie broke into Leo's uneasy thoughts. "When can we start?"

NIC

Nic made ready to abandon the garage. A shame, since they'd paid rent on the place for another three days. It had been a convenient den until someone found him, and the tang of human waste now mixed with the gasoline and motor oil reek of the place.

Footsteps sounded in the alley. Nic pulled his knife from its sheath and sidled to the window. A man leaned on the door frame, unrecognizable behind the oily glass. He tapped on the door. Nic pressed himself against the wall. The man knocked again lightly and said, *sotto voce,* "Umberto."

Nic opened the door a few inches and put the knife away. "I figured you'd show."

Umberto slipped inside. "Cops let me go right before lunchtime. *Bastardi!* They still have Lama and Marco." Nic returned to the old auto bench seat he used as a sofa. Umberto grabbed a metal chair and ran his hand over the seat checking for grease.

"Fuck's sake, what happened?" Nic asked.

"*Cazzata.*" Umberto spat. "The warehouse was dark when I got there. Cops waiting inside."

"Answer your fucking phone sometime. I could've told you."

"How'd *you* get away?" Umberto countered, his eyes narrow.

"Hid in the woods. I got out of the car to piss and saw the cops drive off with Lama, but I never saw Marco or the American bitch. Where were they?"

Umberto shook his head. "A guy on the inside"— meaning one of the jail guards in Cubellis's pocket—"told me the American visited him. Now he's disappeared."

"No shit." Nic lit a cigarette. "What's he up to?"

"Nobody knows. Cima will take care of it."

Umberto surveyed the dimly lit garage. "That wasn't here before." He pointed to a dark lump amidst the scattered junk.

"Cop came by about an hour ago. He won't be reporting in."

"You killed a fucking *sbirro*?"

"He interrupted my lunch, man." Nic toed the fast-food wrappers wadded on the floor.

"Are you crazy? Don't we have enough problems?"

Nic yawned. "That's why I'm leaving." He got busy again. He shoved some scavenged T-shirts into a plastic bag, and put his trash in a paper sack, along with cigarette butts and spent matches he scraped from the concrete. "I might get out of town, anyway, as soon as I kill the bitch."

Umberto snorted. "Where will you go?"

"Cousins in Naples. But meantime? You tell me."

"Not my place. My wife won't have it." Nic didn't bother to ask about his girlfriend's apartment. "You have money?"

"Not much." *Rosetta's.* "But I'll need it, after."

"Jesus Christ." Umberto thought out loud. "How about the storage lockup?" They rented one in a grim part of town. "For a night or two."

"Listen, doesn't Cubellis have a safe house? The hotel?"

Umberto barked an incredulous laugh. "You want to ask a favor? Now?" He jerked his head toward the policeman's body.

"Storage lockup," Nic agreed.

In the car Umberto said, "Before the cops let me go—finishing their goddamn paperwork—they put me in a waiting room. I overheard them talking about your American. They think you're somewhere north, and she's safe now."

"Riano." Nic grinned.

"*Ehi,* they argued about it. She's going stir-crazy, so they decided to let her out a little. Busy places. If you lay low a couple of days, they'll relax their guard."

A mirthless smile slowly lifted the corners of Nic's mouth. "They're making it too easy."

VENIERI

Pietro Venieri took a break from solving the problems with his formula to gaze out his office window and reset his perspective. In the past two days as he hammered away at the revised drug formula, a new concern arose. What if the mafia backed out of the agreement? Cubellis said he had a way to manufacture the drug. And he had Kim. Did they still need him? What if they left him high and dry?

He watched a battered Alfa Romeo pull into the no-parking area in front of his building and stop. The driver door opened. *Security will be on top of that.* Sure enough, the elderly guard was hobbling toward the vehicle, vigorously pointing toward the visitors' parking lot. The driver was a pale, skinny man in an ill-fitting gray suit. He flashed some kind of identification and sauntered away, as the guard scowled, hands on hips.

"Jerk," Venieri muttered and returned to his computer. He'd been a scientific whirlwind since Saturday's conversation with Chung-Lee Kim. Cubellis had said a list of ingredients wasn't enough, he also needed "the recipe." Well, Venieri was refining that recipe right now. He'd create Cubellis's damn sister's damn angel cake this time for sure.

He would need to run *in vitro* tests, but the computer models were producing amazing results. He was ready to tweak a vital input to one of his subformulas when a peremptory knock sounded, and someone opened his office door.

"Yes?" he said, attention on the screen.

"Pietro Venieri?" The man's challenging tone hinted Venieri might try to deny it.

"Yes, what?" He continued painstakingly entering parameters.

"Police. I need some answers from you."

Venieri stopped typing. His visitor was the thin, pasty-complexioned man he'd seen below. The illegal parker.

"Please." Venieri hit "save" and indicated the visitor's chair. "You are?"

The detective snapped his business card onto the desk and glared. "Detective Gilletti. I'm investigating the death of Gianni di Landri."

Venieri's stomach churned alarmingly. *Dead because of me.*

"Your cousin," Gilletti prompted. "Murdered last week."

I know that, you buffoon. "Yes. I gave the eulogy."

"I talked to his sister today."

"Carla?"

"And her boyfriend."

The Hoverer. To Venieri's relief, his phone rang, and he could suspend this uncomfortable encounter, even for a moment. *Think.* "Excuse me," he said. "*Pronto?*"

The gravel-strewn voice was unmistakable. A police detective glowered on the other side of the desk, and here he was, talking to Italy's most dangerous man. His heart rate increased alarmingly.

"I'm sorry, what did you say?" Venieri assumed Cubellis rarely needed to repeat himself.

"*Dottor* Kim was most satisfied with your conference Saturday. We want to give you what you have earned."

"I'm glad." He tried to sound cheerful, but his attention stuck on the ambiguity of "give you what you have earned." Maybe Cubellis *did* know about his new identity documents and planned to finish him off.

Cubellis named a meeting place for Friday night. Venieri started to write it in his datebook, but the steely-eyed detective watched, so he merely circled the appointment time. Even that seemed risky. What if he were followed? The pen slipped out of his sweating hand and clattered onto the desk.

"Please say that again?" Misery made his voice high and unnatural. He had to commit the address to memory, right then, while his thoughts scattered in tiny windblown pieces.

"Thank you, *Signore.* I appreciate your consideration." He ended the call with a flourish and returned attention to the detective. "I'm sorry. Where were we?"

"Was your cousin involved with organized crime? The mafia?"

Venieri recoiled. Was it possible the detective knew who his caller was? Would arrest him on the spot, lead him away in handcuffs? "I spent hardly any time with him. Big age difference."

"Who killed him?"

"I have no idea."

"The sister is hiding something. Who's she protecting?"

"Really, I had almost no contact with him, with them." Venieri swallowed audibly.

"You have to—" The telephone interrupted again.

"So sorry. A moment." Venieri answered. "*Pronto.*"

"Venieri, it's you!" No mistaking Rosa Lisi's voice, either. "I hate talking to your operator. I don't believe she gives you my messages." Frantic though he was, he could detect sarcasm.

"How may I help? Is it quick? I have a visitor." He tried to smile at Gilletti.

"I met the most interesting man." Venieri's foot under the desk tapped in staccato. "We attended the same lecture this morning, at the Center for the Health of the Elderly, your rival institution."

He might have known he couldn't hurry her. "Rosa—"

"You should be out and about more, Pietro. I felt like a real doctor again." She laughed. "The man I met is an American. Well, Korean, really, but an American now."

His foot froze. Dread shooting up from his toes seized his chest.

"*Dottor* Chung-Lee Kim. He says he knows you. We're having dinner tonight. I wondered whether you'd like me to pass on a greeting."

Yes, tell him to fuck himself. "How kind, Rosa." *And fuck you too.* "Please give him my good wishes. Now, I really must go. So sorry." *Why was she yanking his chain?*

"Who's she protecting?"

"Who?" The image flashed through his mind of beautiful Rosa Lisi and Kim, heads together, in an elegant dining room. *She lays on the charm. Questions, questions— another glass of wine?—you're so brilliant—and the starstruck Korean, goddammit, tells her everything.*

"Yes, who?" Gilletti interrupted this disturbing vision.

"Who's protecting someone?"

"Carla! Your cousin." Detective Gilletti, who lacked Rosa Lisi's interrogation skills, almost shouted.

Venieri scurried to gather his guilt-riddled thoughts. "She's upset, naturally. After all, a murder in her own house … her brother … Bianca killed …"

"Who?"

"Bianca. Her cat." Venieri silently berated himself for this idiotic digression. "I'm so sorry—" He flushed.

Gilletti snapped his notebook shut. He wagged it at Venieri and scowled. "You, *Professore,* don't understand how serious I am."

Before Venieri could concoct a mollifying reply, the detective stormed away.

CHAPTER—16

Tuesday, October 30

SAL

"Good news!" Sal greeted Leo early Tuesday morning, before noticing his boss' glum expression.

Leo pushed aside the papers he was signing. "I need good news. What is it?"

"What's wrong? What's happened?"

"The patrolman checking Marco's garage yesterday didn't return to the station. Last night they found his body inside—and Nic's gone."

Sal made a restrained, private sign of the cross. "How?" he asked.

"Stabbed in the gut." A straightforward answer to a more complicated, possibly unanswerable, question.

Sal sank into a chair. "That bastard." He gazed over Leo's head, needing a minute to regroup. It didn't matter whether he knew the dead policeman. They were one piece, he thought, a fragile net over the city. Nic had torn a strand, had sent a quiver through the entirety. Could they still snare him in it, with all its gaps and tangles?

Something different about Leo's office pulled Sal back into the moment. The familiar photograph of his wife was missing. With her wistful expression, she had seemed another helpless observer of Leo's loneliness. He didn't want to read too much into this, but perhaps now, only the present mattered.

"I'm reconsidering our plan," Leo said.

"We have to get him! More than ever."

"That's what Genie says." Leo rubbed his forehead. "The dead patrolman isn't the only reason. Tati tells me his wife's friend, the television journalist Rosa Lisi, called him with some gossip. Actually, a very specific threat. Tati asked who she heard it from, and of course she wouldn't say. She did say, and I quote Tati exactly, 'What you need to know, Max, is the mafia is serious about getting rid of this woman.' And, her source indicated they're in a hurry. Days, not weeks."

"You believe this is credible?" Sal asked.

"According to Rosa Lisi, her source heard the discussion firsthand."

No wonder Leo looked like he hadn't slept.

"I understand your caution," Sal began slowly. "There is a risk, but we knew that."

"Yes, we did. And possibly being in a hurry will work against them. Increase the chance they'll slip up. We, of course, will have to be even more vigilant." Leo sighed, and tossed a pile of signed papers into the outbox. "Your news, then? You promised it's good."

"OK," Sal said, changing gears. "Our telecommunications guru spent time in the hospital records department yesterday. Supposedly as a consultant. Sure enough, one of their computers was used after hours on the twenty-first, like Angela's file showed—"

"Angela?"

"The weekend records manager I interviewed." Sal tried unsuccessfully to suppress a grin. "Someone accessed every one of the departments *Signora* Clarke's information disappeared from—billing, radiology, the works. We identified kind of a suspect—"

"We?"

"Me and Angela." Now Sal was flustered. "Our investigator asked for the suspect's help on a problem. She says the woman definitely has the skills to delete those records. And cover her tracks—almost. The other staff people, no. She'll have her report to you by tomorrow. Want me to bring the suspect in?"

"Not yet. No tip-offs that we're getting closer. *If* we are. When do you go to the hotel?"

"Eleven."

"Have your vest? One for Genie?"

"I do."

Leo rubbed his stomach, as if trying to soothe a deep ache. "This worries me, you know."

"I know. But we're going ahead?"

"Only a test for now."

GENIE

Robbie and I were playing our own version of poker—a game whose complicated rules mystify everyone who watches us at it. We invented it when we were kids, and its principal aim is to keep the action going. I was the more strategic player, as if strategy mattered in a game so dependent on blind luck, and Robbie was the more brazen bluffer. When Sal knocked just before eleven, the stacks of euros in front of us were roughly equal.

I answered the door and turned to Agostina, who was sewing. "Agostina! Our victim has arrived." I laid my cards facedown and gave Robbie a warning look. She and I huddled with Sal in the doorway of the bathroom.

"Agostina bought everything you need. Take a bath, shave everything that will show with a dress on. We have two—one blue and one beige—both with long sleeves and high necklines. Pick whichever."

Sal's backpack slid to the floor.

"Underwear is in the shopping bag. Stuff the bra with tissues." Sal cocked his head. "Twelve-year-olds can do it. Give yourself a close shave, and when you come out, Agostina will fix your makeup and wig."

Sal looked askance at the tub. "I haven't taken a bath since I was six."

"Hot water makes shaving your legs easier. Lather up and take your time. You don't want to bleed to death in the bath."

"Old Roman custom," Sal said.

"Nevertheless."

Before long the bathroom door opened, and the shopping bag, now full of Sal's clothes, flew out in an explosion of fragrant steam. I'd resumed my card playing. "When should we tell him about the bikini wax?" This made Robbie laugh. After another hand, I said, "I'm going downstairs for coffee. Anyone else?"

Agostina, bent over her mending, declined, and Robbie said, "Nope. I have half a cup. You sure it's safe?"

"The ground floor is crawling with police. I'm surprised you aren't insisting I go, since it's your deal." And in Italian, "Agostina, watch him with the eye of a hawk, and make sure he doesn't deal from the bottom of the deck."

In the lobby, I scanned the newspaper headlines. I couldn't tell which of the loiterers were police and which were hotel guests. I took a newspaper and read the front page as I slowly climbed the stairs. On the first floor landing, I stopped. Heavy footsteps had started up the curving stairway below, and the hair on the nape of my neck quivered. Above, a door opened. "Genie?" Robbie called.

Staff used the service stairs. Maybe the footsteps belonged to one of the hotel's few guests, but maybe not. I didn't have time to wonder. The guest rooms would be locked, but a maid's closet was two doors ahead. I flung open the door. Too shallow to hide in. I dropped the newspaper and coffee to the floor, snatched the maid's white nylon sweater from a hook, pulled it on, and grabbed a rag. The man arrived on the landing as I went to my knees and snapped the rag on the baseboard. Head bowed, I crawled slowly backward toward the stairway, wiping vigorously. The man's shiny black shoes and the cuffs of his trousers passed by. He walked to the end of the hall, stopping to listen at doors, and returned. The shoes stopped under my nose. They smelled strongly of polish.

"Is there a guest here, *Americana*?"

I kept my head down. "*Nu prea vă înţeleg.*" As long as he didn't respond in Romanian, I'd be OK, since the only Romanian I remembered meant "I don't understand." Fitting. "*Nu prea vă înţeleg.*"

"*Maledetto* foreigners!" He kicked my half-healed ribs with venom.

I let out a gasp and clamped my left arm to my side. Cowering like a dog accustomed to blows, I wiped harder. He muttered another curse and slowly climbed to the second floor. A door opened. If it was Robbie, they must see each other. *Please, Robbie, don't call out again!* He didn't, the door closed, and soon the man climbed to the top floor. Only one room up there, our former suite.

I bolted downstairs to the lobby, bumping into Leo at the bottom. He steered me through the breakfast room and into the rear hall. We watched through the small window and soon the man descended the last few steps to the lobby.

"Umberto," he said.

Umberto glanced around the breakfast room at the few remaining people, intent on their newspapers or laptops, two women poring over a guidebook, no one taking any notice of him.

"When I came in, they told me he'd gone upstairs," Leo said. "He's checking things out. Probably making the rounds of all the area hotels."

"You knew he was here? Why don't you arrest him?"

"On what charge? First, it would tell him where you are. And second, we want him and Nic out of action permanently."

A man sitting by the front door yawned hugely, zipped his laptop bag shut as Umberto passed, and followed him out.

Leo watched the lobby, making sure Umberto was gone. "It's clear."

"He was on the landing with me."

"I know. One of my people followed him, but backed off when she heard him going on upstairs." He pointed to the dust rag.

"I decided to dust the baseboards." I grinned. Then I caught his eye. "He kicked me."

His return look was full of sympathy. "And he didn't recognize you?"

"I kept my head down, and so far as I know he's only seen me once, that first day when I crossed the Piazza del Popolo. Then I had on a hat."

We were so physically close, peering out the small window. I wanted his strong arms around me, but I backed away. Pressing my back to the wall, I picked fuzz from the sweater. "Leo, I have to say this. I know I made a big mistake when I took Agostina to the restaurant a week ago." He tried to shush me. "No, I can't forget it, I want you to know you can count on me …"

He lifted my chin. "I never doubted it. And I do count on you. More than you know. A dozen times I've considered canceling this operation. But because I do count on you, I've decided we should go ahead. You can't live in danger forever. We have to bring this situation to a close while everyone around you is on high alert."

I pulled my chin away, retreating from the thing I most wanted. I brushed the shabby sweater. "Nobody ever notices the maid."

"I do."

Nail polish fumes assaulted Leo and me at the hotel room door. Sal lounged in a silk robe, smooth legs elegantly crossed, makeup and wig in place. The effect was startling.

"Wow!" I said.

"I've always wanted to work undercover," Sal said. And, to Agostina, "My dress?"

Hands on hips, she said, "Please. Let your nails dry."

In English, I said, "You're gorgeous."

Leo coughed. "Not bad."

"A shady character was in the hallway a few minutes ago," Robbie said.

"Umberto. Checking things out. He's gone."

"Did he see you?"

"Me? No." *Truth, of a sort.*

"We need to get out there." Sal fidgeted.

Agostina made him wait another five minutes before fastening on the body armor, and I helped him shimmy into the cornflower blue dress. I handed him a pair of flat shoes with a secure velcro strap. "No stilletos for us. Can't run in them." I was still put out that I'd lost my favorite sandals fleeing Nic way back when.

Robbie said, "Sal, a word of advice? Stay out of bars."

At last we let him see himself in the bathroom mirror. We heard a muffled "*Cristo!*" In a moment Sal emerged, glided to an armchair, gracefully lowered himself, crossed his legs, and said, "Are we ready?"

"You are. Most certainly," Leo said, "but the rest of our people won't be in place until noon. That gives us time to discuss something. Agostina, Roberto, and Genie must be out of Rome as much as possible until these criminals are off the streets."

"But I have to do my part—"

"Aside from that. Yes, you must do your part."

"But where can we go?" I clung to Robbie's arm, missing Leo already.

"I have a suggestion as crazy as one of yours." At least he smiled when he said it. "Perugia, with my parents. They live far out in the country, hard to find. They would be thrilled to have American visitors."

"Leo, that sounds—" *Awkward*. But I realized he wanted us with people he trusted one hundred percent. It must be hard to live like that. Never sure of people.

"We have the trial run this afternoon. This evening, I will drive you there."

"All of us?" Agostina asked.

"Of course. Cubellis and his men are not above using you or Roberto to get to Genie. Putting you out of the way is safest for everyone."

"Is that OK with you?" I asked Agostina.

"For me, it's perfect. I would enjoy seeing them so much. I've known them forever, remember?"

"What about our plan? With Sal? Sally?" I amended.

"A car will bring you back tomorrow afternoon. It's Halloween. Crowds out at night. People in costume. Confusion. A likely time for them to make their move."

"Tomorrow is—*what?*" I'd lost track of the days.

"Halloween. All Saints' Eve. The day after is All Saints' Day—a holiday. Spend it in the country. You can come back to Rome again in the evening, if necessary."

"Friday I have an appointment with *Dottor* Immormino. Isn't that sort of a holiday too? All Souls' Day?"

"What day?" Robbie asked.

"Day of the Dead. Ghastly coincidence."

Leo caught the word. "In Umbria, you will be far from such things." In English, he tried, "Coincidences *and* incidences."

"I don't know—"

"This plan requires traveling, but under two hours each direction. It keeps you mostly out of Rome and Roberto and Agostina away *del tutto*."

While the prospect of meeting Leo's family simultaneously intrigued and intimidated me, what mattered was what would keep all of us safest.

"OK. Perugia," I said. "Beautiful. A beautiful plan."

"It's noon," said Sal.

In the last week, the lines of Leo's face had deepened, and he sounded tired. "Genie, put your body armor on. As you walk around, know we are nearby. You remember the signals?"

"Yes," Sal and I said together.

Leo shook Sal's elegantly manicured hand.

My job was to act naturally. Strolling, making myself visible on the crowded shopping streets, while Sal loitered a half block behind, his eyes hidden behind enormous dark glasses, watching for trouble. For anyone approaching too fast, too close, too interested. Other police were doing the same. I didn't recognize them, though, and it felt like no one noticed me at all. That was not reassuring. Just the opposite. It made everyone equally dangerous. *You just have to get through these few hours.*

For an afternoon with so little excitement, Sal and I were exhausted by the time we returned to the hotel.

"My feet are killing me," he said.

"He's a natural, don't you think, Agostina?"

Sal continued, "How do women stand it? The wind went right through this dress! The shawl strangled me, and my bra straps kept sliding off. Everything I'm wearing itches or pinches or both!"

"You're right," I said. "There *should* be more women saints."

Sal disappeared into the bathroom, emerging in jeans and T-shirt, greatly relieved. He was saying good night when Leo arrived.

After a quick dinner in our hotel room, we were on the road. As the highway penetrated Umbria, the lights of hill villages appeared and disappeared in the rhythm of its curves, and, eventually, the faint glow from Perugia and its surrounding villages persisted in front of us.

With every kilometer, I felt like I relaxed just a little. Leo's idea to spirit us away from Rome was more than a safety measure, it was an act of mercy. Our eyes met in the rear view mirror, and I grinned in gratitude.

Well before we approached the town, Leo turned off the highway to follow a series of progressively narrower and less traveled roads sketched across the countryside. "At last," he said and steered the car into a tunnel of trees. The entry drive opened onto a flood-lit farmyard, with a collection of sturdy barns and sheds on the right. To the left, more discreet bulbs glowed against the sand-colored stones of the house. A huge black dog raced in front of the car, joyfully barking, and stopped on the driver's side.

The house's front door flew open, releasing a stream of light. A man emerged, tall for his generation, and crossed to the car to embrace Leo, both of them talking and laughing at once. They were mirror images of each other, thirty years apart. Without doubt he was Leo's father Paolo. He pressed my hand and greeted Agostina with a delighted shout. He and Robbie shook hands, tussling good-naturedly over the privilege of carrying the bags.

From the doorstep, a woman waved, calling Leo's name. Renata wore a flowing caftan on her thin frame, and many gold bangles sparkled on her arm. She would look as much at home in fashionable Milan as on a farm in Perugia. But, like any good Italian mama, she wrung her hands with excitement as her son approached. He leaned over to hug her, and they shared a whispered conference. She received Agostina as an old friend and acknowledged Robbie before greeting me. She gave me an intent appraisal and gently took my arm to lead me inside.

The men deposited the suitcases at the bottom of the staircase, and we stopped there too, slipping off jackets and getting our bearings. The house's main level consisted of two enormous rooms with a stone floor running throughout. To the right of the stairway lay the kitchen and an informal seating area filled with brightly cushioned sofas and chairs and lamp tables crowded with photographs. A large counter and stools let people monitor progress in the kitchen. A door led to the long covered porch, I'd noticed when we drove up.

Paolo and Renata guided us into the room to the left of the stairs, which served as living and dining room, about thirty feet long and almost as wide. This room was darker, but not gloomy. Thick, roughly planed wood pillars supported the upper story, providing a pleasing rusticity. The dining table with ten tall chairs carved of black wood stretched across the front of the room.

Numerous sofas and armchairs, arranged in comfortable groupings, bore dents and creases in their chocolate brown, leather-covered cushions, proof the family spent much time there. Squat lamps sent cones of light over the furniture's thickly padded arms, and tempting piles of books and hand-knitted afghans urged visitors to settle in. I chuckled at the contrast between this cozy room and our hotel room, with its perennial shortage of places to sit.

Leo zigzagged through the furniture to his father's old-fashioned oak desk in the far corner and locked his gun in one of its drawers. The rest of us were drawn to a wide stone fireplace where Renata had set out espresso and pastry on a low table.

Leo and Agostina were accustomed to my fading bruises and healing skin, but the scrutiny of Leo's parents made me acutely aware of them. I lifted a hand to my face and hid the scar. "Still healing," I said, laughing awkwardly.

Leo said, "You're doing very well, compared to the pictures."

"Pictures? You've seen them?"

"Well, yes, it was a crime, so there are pictures. And, no, you don't want to see them."

Oh, yes, I do. Were these pictures of my face or my whole battered body? After all, I had scrapes and bruises everywhere. I flushed. In the presence of Leo's parents was not the time to find this out. Had he already seen them when we met in that awful hospital room? Was that only thirteen days ago?

His father was speaking to me."*Scusami*? I asked about your brother. Leo tells me he's a farmer too?" He sounded hopeful.

"Yes, he has a large organic farm—" I broke into English—"Robbie, how big is Hilltop View?"

"Ten acres."

I mentally calculated then switched back to Italian. "His farm is about four hectares. It's sixty kilometers west of Washington, D.C."

"Who is taking care of it?" Paolo said, real concern in his voice.

I conferred with Robbie then said, "The twins who help him out with his restaurant deliveries every day. They are continuing that. If they run the farm stand too, he lets them keep what they earn. Robbie says there's never any vacation when you are a farmer."

Paolo laughed. "In the morning, would Roberto like to see my farm?"

"I'll ask, but I know the answer." Robbie's enthusiastic reaction didn't require translation. "It would be more a question of trying to stop him," I told Paolo.

"You grew up in this house?" Robbie asked Paolo, with me translating.

"Yes. It has been the family home since my father's father. It used to burst open with people. Now, the two of us."

"It's the world we live in," Renata said crisply. "Children scatter and make their poor old parents worry."

Leo quietly chuckled. He'd heard this before. "Mama, I think Genie is tired. We all are."

We climbed the stairs to the bedrooms. From my window, I watched Leo pull his car into the big barn, slide the doors closed, and lock them. The exterior lights switched off. After Rome, the night was too black and too quiet for sleep, and I lay awake thinking about Italy, Leo, his family. Hours later a strange noise woke me. A rooster. I rolled over and slept again.

CHAPTER—17

Wednesday, October 31 - Halloween

GENIE

The aroma of morning coffee lured me to the kitchen. Outside, the barn door was open and Leo's car gone. I perched on a stool at the counter next to Agostina. Renata rinsed vegetables that looked just picked.

"Paolo and Roberto have been outside for hours," Renata said. "Prode is with them, tearing around like a wild animal."

"*Prode*?"

"Leo's dog. He gave him that name in the hope he *would* be 'brave.' But I'm afraid even the field mice have little to fear."

I laughed. "You had a similar hope when you named Leo, yes? And with more success."

Renata smiled at the compliment to her son and assembled an egg and toast for me. Colorful plates were stacked on the center island, its butcher-block top crosshatched with use. Baskets of fruit and eggs and hanging bunches of herbs testified to the farm's prosperity. The contrast with the way Leo had described Gemma Capuano's farm—lonely, untended—gave me an uncomfortable pang. Here I was, alive in this beautiful setting, when Gemma had spent her days in a forlorn place, a cheerless gray smear on the landscape of my imagination.

Agostina returned upstairs, and I said, "You and Agostina must have been catching up."

"We've known her since she was a child. Her mother worked many years for my sister."

"She is a treasure. So capable."

"She speaks well of you."

I swallowed. "I'm afraid I've brought her nothing but trouble."

"You've made her feel useful." Renata wiped the gleaming countertops.

"And she's always cheerful. She's been so good for me." Another thing Leo had counted on.

"You are frightened." Renata watched me closely.

I returned her gaze. "Yes." I longed to let down my guard, to succumb to the glowing autumn day, the pull of the timeless hills and ripe fields weaving out of view beyond the windows. I longed to write about this part of Italy, to share with my readers the peace I felt here.

But I couldn't. Out there also, beyond what I could see, beyond this bright day, this comfortable moment—out there somewhere—lurked a treacherous future. All I could manage to say was, "I'm not—I can't be … myself, really … until this is over."

Renata brought more coffee. Her eyes resembled Leo's. Painfully so.

I said, "I'm afraid for him too. These people are—" *No need to finish.* "I'm sorry."

Leo's mother returned to the sink. "We will pray it ends soon."

I'd been living with this anxiety for two weeks, and it was almost unbearable. Renata had lived with it day and night since Leo joined the police.

Heavy shoes stomping on the porch outside and Prode's excited barks announced the men's return. Robbie burst into the kitchen. "It was great!"

"The language difference?" I asked.

"No problem. We spoke farmish."

I translated and Paolo laughed, "We forgot about it. Yet, we seemed to understand each other completely."

"They have pumpkins! Paolo calls them *zucca*," Robbie said. "Carving contest?"

I loved that about him. Up and doing. Always useful and fun.

"Great idea!" My mood lifted. "I'll get dressed. I want a tour too. But no scary pumpkins, please. Wacky grins."

Later we gathered around a wooden table under the canopy of an ancient oak, a mountain of string-tangled pumpkin seeds on newspapers in the center. Robbie created two or three smiling jack-o'-lanterns to my single, more artistic attempt. His apprentice, Agostina, followed his simpler model and received extravagant compliments. "When we light them, they will be incredible!" he said.

"If I were going to write a blog post about this place," I said, "I'm afraid my readers wouldn't believe me. It's so perfect."

"Well, don't," Robbie said. "Being overrun with tourists would spoil the effect."

Around eleven, I carried two pumpkins, each the size of a large grapefruit, into the kitchen. "May I make pies?" I asked Renata.

"Delightful! I want to see how you Americans do it."

Leo's sister Elena arrived at lunchtime with her two children. Rolling out piecrust, I overheard her greet her mother. "I couldn't wait any longer to meet—" I heard muttering. "She speaks Italian?" In a stage-whisper, *"Mea culpa!"*

Elena flew into the kitchen and introduced herself. I said, "I saw your children running to the barn. They are beautiful."

"Please," Elena's voice approached a whine, "may we speak your English? I much need the practice."

I glanced at Renata, not wanting to be rude. "If you wish." I asked Renata's advice about the oven, and as we slid the pies onto a rack, I said, "A taste of home."

"Homes," Renata said, "yours and ours."

I washed the flour off my hands, dried them, and held out a damp hand to Elena. "Now we can meet properly. How old are the children?"

Elena's hand lay limp in mine. "Seven and ten. The boy Enrico is seven, Dona is ten."

I put a hand to my heart. Robbie and I were eight and ten when our parents were killed. But I smiled at the children's mother. "Lovely. Shall we walk outside and meet them?" In Italian, I repeated this suggestion to Renata, who checked her daughter's expression and declined.

As I told Robbie later, Elena was "a bit of a pill." A half-buried complaint lay in every remark. Meanwhile, the children delighted in the farm. They already adored Robbie, who swung them into hay piles and resurrected his son Andy's favorite barn games. He was tired before they were and came to stand close to me. "Their ages, it's … you know …"

"Yes." I slipped an arm through his. Though we were surrounded by the tan and gold of the nearby fields and the soft gray-green of hillside olive groves, my mind—and his too, I suspected—filled with the memory of a jagged white landscape.

"My driver is coming at two," I said.

He gave my arm a squeeze. "Too bad. Paolo and I are going pheasant hunting, and you always get more than I do."

"Just making sure I have enough to eat," I teased. "But you're a pretty good shot, yourself."

"I'm fair. You're the family Hawkeye."

I laughed. Reenacting *The Last of the Mohicans* was a favorite pastime in Aunt Stevie's attic. At that moment, a real sparrow hawk, as if conjured by Robbie's remark, slowly circled the peaceful yard.

A sudden noise sent me to the kitchen window. A red sports car flew into the yard and skidded to a stop, scattering gravel. The children shrieked and ran to it, and even Elena rose from her seat under the oak and walked over.

"My son, Camillo." Renata rolled her eyes, smiling.

Camillo strode in bearing an armload of fall flowers wrapped in orange tissue for his mother and wreaths of smiles for everyone else. The room seemed too small to contain him. Ten years younger than Leo and even more handsome.

"So, here she is," he said, checking me out, head to foot. "She's beautiful!" he said to the others. "My brother has outdone himself!"

I gave an embarrassed laugh. What was that supposed to mean? I didn't read into it; Camillo seemed the type to make a flattering remark even if I'd resembled a bat-eared Roman gargoyle.

The children pulled their grandfather indoors, each clinging to a hand. He hugged his younger son and received a stream of compliments on the state of the farm. Camillo greeted Robbie in English, but with such a thick accent, for a moment he didn't recognize our own language.

"Agostina!" Camillo cried. He picked her up and twirled her around. "Are you still helping out that brute, my brother?"

She giggled. "Put me down!"

The adults crowded into the space between the kitchen and sitting area, except for Elena. "Where's Gloom-and-Doom?" Camillo asked.

"Cigarette," his mother said. "Her husband is supposed to arrive around six. We'll see."

"And Leo, my brother, my idol?"

He said it cheerfully, but Genie detected the distant clatter of sibling swordplay.

"Not today. Important business in town."

I looked away.

"It's all important, isn't it? So he says." He rummaged in his leather satchel and pulled out two bottles of red wine. "But we are here. Family and friends."

"Here's Genie's car," Robbie said. A black sedan crunched into the yard.

LEO

The remoteness of the Angelini farmstead made it easy to set up unobtrusive surveillance of the nearby country roads. Of course, if Leo believed Genie was in any real danger, he wouldn't have taken her there. But Tati had insisted on a perimeter, and Leo kept this potentially worrisome information to himself.

Leo phoned Officer Capizzo, who was Genie's driver that afternoon, and asked him to pass the phone to her. When she answered, he asked, "Where are you?"

She conferred with Capizzo. "He says we'll be at the hotel in forty minutes."

"I'll meet you and Sal there." *I can't wait to see you.* "I hope my father didn't bore Roberto, inspecting every plant and bug on the farm."

"Robbie loved it! It's so beautiful! We carved pumpkins; I made pumpkin pies. Your sister and her charming children came for lunch. And Camillo arrived." She had every reason to be anxious about what the evening might bring, yet happiness danced in her voice, lifting his spirits too.

"The whole tribe."

"Except your brother-in-law."

"Right. Except him. So forgettable. Did you say you made pies?"

"Yes."

"In my mother's kitchen?"

"Yes."

"Was she out on an errand—to Albania, perhaps?"

"Your mother was most welcoming. It was fine. I didn't break a bowl or spill the flour or anything."

"I'm sure it was fine, but it was a first." He laughed.

"She asked me if I'm Catholic."

Ma! That was bold! "Are you?"

"No."

"Oh."

"A surprise though."

"One of many."

GENIE

Genie's Note to Herself:

Rome Halloween: Devils & togas & assassins, oh my!

That afternoon, I spent time at the Keats-Shelley house—supposedly Nic's preferred pickup spot. I dawdled, took photos of the bedroom where Keats died at age 25, bought a poetry book, and lingered on the Spanish Steps a while, reading it. A crew was constructing a low stage near the foot of the steps, and I watched them lug amplifiers and speakers into position and snake electrical cables to a row of portable generators. The afternoon was getting late, and I was losing the light.

For a while, Sal sat two steps below, wearing the beige dress today. Another detective—*without doubt the one they call Al Pacino*—joined him.

"*Ciao, bella,*" Pacino said, grinning. "Like to party?"

"Shut up." Sal smiled sweetly.

"Pretty girl like you, you must have your pick of guys."

I bit my upper lip to keep from laughing.

"Go to hell." Sal smiled again.

"Oooh. Temper too. Come on, *bella,* let's go somewhere private."

"Only so I can shoot you."

Sal blew a kiss and sashayed away, leaving Pacino to keep watch a while.

As twilight came on, I sauntered toward the restaurants with the outdoor umbrellas. Though I loved *Il Girasole*, the cheaper, red-umbrella restaurant was more Nic's style, and I went there.

I caught a waiter's eye and waved vaguely in the direction of several vacant tables. He let me pick. I sat near a woman wearing a beige dress and asked for mineral water. My mouth was bone dry. Nerves. I anticipated a frustrating series of false alarms—a rush of terror, followed by the letdown. Exhausting. Yet, surely Nic would appear eventually. Nic or Umberto. Or both. Soon? Or never? At that moment, I couldn't have said which I preferred.

I rummaged in the yellow bag for my phone and called Robbie. "Everything OK so far." Laughing and excited voices came through from his end. "What's going on?"

"I lit the jack-o'-lanterns. The kids are hopping all around. The adults are pretty delighted too. Yours looks amazing!"

"Send me a picture!"

"I will. Stay in touch," Robbie said.

I smiled to see the photo—pumpkins glowing cheerfully in the dark farmyard—and had an aching desire to be there myself. What was I doing here? I shook my head. Not the time for doubts.

The restaurant tables were gradually filling. Couples, mostly, a few foursomes—tourists and groups having a drink after work. A constant stream of pedestrians squeezed through the path among the tables, more and more of them in costume. Masks, wigs, and disguise paraphernalia were so easy to get this time of year, Nic could easily change his appearance. Leo said it wouldn't be how Nic looked, but his body language, his way of moving, that would give him away.

I stiffened when a man approached my table from the side. Just the waiter, bringing the mineral water and delivering wine to a nearby table. On the Spanish Steps, a noisy group of costumed people cavorted—witches and vampires and ghosts—and the band members drifted onto the stage.

Parading past were people dressed as Renaissance princes and streetwalkers, in harlequin silks—*Arlecchino*—beggars' ragged cotton, the inevitable togas. A few had painted their faces red or black or half of each. Most joined the crowd gathering near the band. Someone came up behind me, and I flinched. The waiter again, bringing bread.

Streetlights created long shadows that played tricks on me. Daylight savings time had ended a few days before, and the evening seemed darker than it ought to be. The whole scene was off-kilter, confusing. That was the point, I supposed. A tiny woman with a curling moustache swirled by, wearing a black top hat and scarlet-lined cape.

I finished the water, bitter with some unfamiliar mineral combination. The waiters clustered in the shadows by the restaurant door. They chatted and swung the white napkins they draped over their arms. So many of them! Dark hair, big moustaches, which one was mine?

I blinked, trying to clear my vision. After a prolonged stare in the waiters' direction, at last one made eye contact, detached himself from the group, and came to the table. He brought me more water, and I ordered linguini with white clam sauce. I ate a piece of bread to settle my stomach and counteract a vague dizziness.

Don't let stress get to you now, I chided myself.

At the Steps, the musicians warmed up. Their speakers blasted discordant notes—irritatingly loud. I hoped dinner would arrive quickly. The noise would be deafening once the band got going. People making their way to their tables bumped my chair, which reminded me of that awful night at the warehouse.

Why had I thought this was a good idea? It was unbearable. And the constant commotion set my teeth on edge.

Red devils waving their tails and bats with outstretched wings pranced menacingly at the restaurant's periphery. Costumed pedestrians with contorted faces blurred past. A leering matador was followed by five women wearing tan bodysuits and bull masks. A lachrymose clown. A bearded Brunhilda with straw braids and kitchen-funnel breasts.

The waiter brought the water, and I emptied half the glass at once. Perspiration broke out all over my body. Simultaneously hot and cold, I felt a monster headache on the way. I needed to get some food into my stomach. My arm felt unaccountably heavy as I lifted the glass to wash down another mouthful of bread. Where was my dinner? An ear-piercing squeal from the band's sound equipment made my brain quiver.

Here was my waiter again. *At last.*

He slid the plate in front of me. His thumb with its grimy nail was right in my food. The napkin slid off his forearm, and I saw the snake tattoo writhing out of his sleeve. My head jerked up. Black hair, bushy moustache, and Nic's unearthly silver eyes.

"Bitch!" he hissed.

I tried to stand, but my knees buckled. I grabbed the table for support and pulled myself upright. I could barely stand. I weaved, panicking. He was so close. His hand dove into his pocket. I lost my grip on the table and began to crumple.

Someone yelled Sal's name. As I fell, Sal was lunging across tables and chairs toward Nic. Then the table blocked my view. I yelped as I bounced off chairs and landed hard on the concrete. I glimpsed a beige skirt.

"Knife!" I screamed a warning.

I flung my arms around Nic's legs to pull him off balance, away from Sal. He landed on top of me, elbow in my stomach. Uttering a vicious oath, he grabbed my throat, squeezing hard. Where was the knife? The next few seconds were a tumult of gunshots, yelling, overturning furniture, and shattering china. I gasped for breath.

I grabbed Nic's hair, full of greasy black stuff. My breath nearly gone, I pulled as hard as I could, jerking his head one way then the other. Against the force of his grip, I twisted my own head. The knife lay a few feet away. I flung my arm toward it. It was just out of reach. I squirmed to get closer. Now I touched it. Now I had the end of the handle in my fingers.

I needed air. I fought against the blackness that would come at any moment. Hold on. Just a few more seconds. *Until Leo comes.*

LEO

While Genie awaited her dinner, Leo hovered in an unlit doorway a half block away. A man dressed as a priest approached him.

"Oh, it's you!" he said to Oliver Harmon. "All these costumes!"

Harmon spoke quickly. He'd seen Genie in the restaurant and noticed one of the waiters acting strangely.

He thought the man put something in Genie's water glass, but he wasn't sure …

Leo didn't wait. He took off running, dodging pedestrians, never seeing them. As he reached the restaurant's outer tables, Genie wobbled to her feet, a waiter alongside her. Umberto emerged from the shadows on the right and walked toward her, forearm extended, hand draped in a napkin. She grabbed the table for balance as her waiter plunged his hand into a pocket.

Leo plowed through the crowd of diners, who, confused, leaned back in their chairs, slowing his progress. Genie began to collapse just as the waiter drew a knife. Sal leapt over a chair and slid across a tabletop toward the man. Leo yelled, "Sal! Knife!" Someone else hollered a warning too.

Umberto was closing in on Genie. Bracci approached him from behind, moving fast. Sal struck the waiter in the shoulder, knocking him off balance. Sal spun away from the man's thrust, and the knife tore through the side of his dress. The waiter stumbled, falling on top of Genie. The knife slipped out of his hand and skittered across the pavement.

The restaurant patrons screamed and scrambled away, upending chairs and creating chaos. Plates and glassware flew. A shot. And another. Bracci reached Umberto just as the man fell, arm still outstretched.

Sal was out of view. The waiter was choking Genie. She was fighting him off, one-handed. He couldn't see her other arm, blocked by the table. He crossed the distance between them, and shoved the waiter off her. The man's head banged on the concrete. Leo pinned him there.

"Drop the knife, Genie."

She had a wild look. Did she recognize him? Her chest heaved. She clutched the knife and looked to where the waiter lay.

"Genie. *Cara*. Let the knife go."

After what seemed like a long minute, she dropped it. "Nic," she gasped. "He's Nic."

"Sal!" Leo cried from atop the dazed Nic. The bedlam around them buried the response, if there was one.

Breathing heavily, Genie crawled under the tables toward Sal. The young detective lay unmoving.

For a few seconds, all sound seemed to cease. They were an island of quiet while the commotion rippled away. As abruptly, more feet pounded up, and shouting resumed. Leo could see shoes and blue-gray pant legs but would not slacken his hold on the man writhing underneath him. His forearm pinned Nic's neck to the ground, and it took all his willpower not to press a little too hard.

Officers dragged tables and tumbled chairs out of the way. Turning his head, Leo counted seven people on the ground, including himself and Nic. He flipped Nic over, knelt on his back, and handcuffed him. Nic swore and spat blood.

A few feet away, Genie cradled Sal's head in her lap, crying.

Bracci got to his knees, shaking his large head. He rolled Umberto over. A red stain blossomed on the man's white shirtfront.

"You got him?" Leo called. Umberto's dead hand still held the gun. Bracci kicked it away.

"No. Capizzo did. Then Umberto shot him."

Wordlessly, Leo queried the officer who squatted by Capizzo. His expression carried the message quicker than his words: "He's dead."

Another officer jerked Nic to his feet and hustled him, yelling and cursing, to a patrol car rolling up nearby. Siren yelping, an ambulance moved through the crowd. Leo crawled to Genie. Sal lay motionless. He found a pulse, irregular and weak. Bracci joined them and ripped open Sal's dress. He examined the bulletproof vest and discovered a hole on the left side. When he pulled his hand away, his fingers glistened with Sal's blood.

"Ambulance!" Leo shouted, but medics already hurried toward them.

"We'll take him to *Fatebenefratelli*," one puffed. "Closest. Quickest."

"Know it well," Leo muttered. "Too damn well."

The medics applied a pressure bandage then lifted Sal onto a stretcher. Bracci kept a hand on Sal's chest. "He's young. Strong," he said to no one in particular.

"I wanted it to be over, and now it is," Genie whispered. "'Be careful what you wish for.'" She choked back a sob. "You made me drop the knife."

"You might have used it. And regretted it ever after."

"I'm not sure I would have," she said. "Regretted it."

He put his arm around her and squeezed. "You would have."

The medic jerked his head toward Umberto and Capizzo. "Them?"

"Dead. Leave them. The scene investigators will want to see this."

Leo moved to Capizzo. The officer's eyes, wide open and horrified, might have been watching the bullet speeding toward him. Leo closed them, took off his suit jacket, and laid it over Capizzo's face.

"He was a good man." Genie shivered. Tears spilled down her cheeks. In a hoarse voice, she said, "He followed me through the park, he trusted me, he called my name, and I didn't answer." Adrenaline had only temporarily overpowered whatever drug she'd been given, and now she was shaking. Bracci helped her into a chair. She waved off the medics. "I'm fine. Just need some time."

"Not good enough," Leo said, and sent her to the hospital too in one of the squad cars.

A cordon of uniformed officers guarded the crime scene. Others corralled witnesses while a detective bagged weapons, including Nic's knife. At the restaurant's edge, waiters righted chairs and straightened tables and one swept up broken glass and plates. Most of the crowd slipped away toward the Steps, where the band's warm-up resumed. It was a while before Leo and Bracci could leave, and they had more work to do.

The two detectives stopped at the *questura* to gather incident report forms. "We may as well fill them out at the hospital," Leo said. "Make the waiting shorter." As they entered the squad room, Gilletti was lurking near Leo's office.

"For Christ's sake," muttered Bracci. "Can't we just abandon him in the wilds of Sardinia wearing a big sign: '*Polizia*'?"

Leo chuckled. "Stay close. Keep me from doing something I may regret."

"I was planning to help you," Bracci said, working his jaw. They strode across the room and into Leo's office, Gilletti sidling in behind.

Leo opened a drawer and pulled out manila folders of forms and slapped them on the desk.

"What a day!" Gilletti said. For a brief moment, Leo thought he might be commiserating about the loss of Capizzo and Sal's injury. But no. "I've talked to Gianni di Landri's sister *and* the university hack. Been studying my notes for two days. Had to brief Scarpatti this afternoon."

What the hell? Leo assembled packets of forms while Bracci glared at their colleague.

"The sister, she's hiding something. Don't know what yet." Gilletti gazed up into Leo's fluorescents and scratched his chin. "The cousin, the so-called scientist—Venieri— he's a slippery customer. He's a big deal in the family, though. Gave di Landri's eulogy. Supposedly he's a big Alzheimer's researcher, but he can't keep two thoughts together. Must have caught the disease from one of his patients." While he laughed at this joke, Leo met Bracci's glance, and they slowly focused attention on Gilletti, two field artillery pieces adjusting the direction of fire.

"Alzheimer's?" Leo asked.

"Yeah. It's a brain thing."

"Your scientist, his name is what again?" Bracci asked.

"Pietro Venieri. Gianni di Landri's cousin."

"And he does research on Alzheimer's disease?"

"Yeah. Big shot. But, I'm telling you, he's got it himself. I had to stop the goddamn interview. I went to his office to talk about his cousin's murder—the first sign of the unraveling of the fucking mafia—and this imbecile was telling me about a dead cat, even the name—Bianca." Gilletti spat it out.

"Bianca?" Bracci said.

"The fucking cat!"

Bracci murmured in sympathy. A smile slowly spread across Leo's face.

"You are doing an amazing job, Gilletti. Formidable progress." Leo joggled the sets of forms on the desk. "Emilio and I have to finish this paperwork, so …"

Unaccountably, Gilletti took the hint and retreated. "*Ciao*. Late night for me."

"Right." When Gilletti ambled out of earshot, Leo muttered, "I've got those funeral pictures here somewhere." He switched on his computer and, while he waited for it to boot up, flipped through several files. "The cousin who gave the eulogy is the one who got the surprise package in his car. There's a shot of them driving away. Believe it or not, Gilletti may have stumbled onto something useful."

He found the photo showing the license plate and quickly ran the number through the motor vehicles database. Pietro Venieri.

He gathered their forms. "Bracci, I don't care what you say, Gilletti is a genius."

Sal's family lived in the north, and the people in Rome closest to him were his fellow officers. By the time Leo and Bracci arrived, at least a dozen police paced the corridor outside the surgery waiting room or talked in quiet groups. Genie appeared, a few scrapes bandaged. "They gave me something and said I'll get a good night's sleep. Not to worry."

When Tati briefly joined them, they told him about the Venieri lead. "At last, we may be seeing the whole of their plot," Tati said, "and now we have to destroy it. An interesting challenge."

Leo took him aside and muttered, "Cubellis may still send people after her."

"Certainly. His desire to do that is another thing we must crush."

"I can talk to him."

"And say what? You have no power over him. I, however, might."

"But—"

"Detective, either we are a team or we are nothing. Tomorrow Fausto Scarpatti and I are planning our next moves. Rest assured, *Signora* Clarke's safety will be a prime consideration. You must let me do my job."

He said good night absently, already deep in thought, leaving a frustrated Leo behind.

When the surgeon emerged through the swinging doors, Leo and Bracci rose to meet him. The men clustered around.

"Detective Riccobono was lucky," he said. "If the blade had penetrated any deeper, he would have bled to death before we got to him. We gave him stitches inside and out, and he will be sore. We will keep him a day or two, but most likely he will have nothing more than a scar." He held up his thumb and index finger about a centimeter apart.

"When can we see him?" Bracci asked.

"He should be alert enough for visitors by noon tomorrow."

The men murmured relief.

"We will move him to a room in a half hour or so."

Bracci signaled two of the officers and told them to set up a rotation. "We need a twenty-four-hour guard on him. And, *dottore*, keep his information out of the hospital records system until late morning. Other than your team, no one must know he's here. Please tell them not to talk."

The doctor's face showed he had questions, but he said, "I can do that. At the best of times, we are not as efficient with our records as we ought to be."

Leo phoned the department's computer whiz and told her to draw up a warrant for the medical records leaker. "With Nic and crew neutralized, there's no need to hold off. Arrest her tonight."

It was past eleven, and he and Bracci had one more job to do. He unfolded a paper and checked the address. "It's up north. Forty minutes."

"Are we ending today or starting tomorrow with this?" Bracci said. "Lousy, either way. Take two cars? When we're done, you and *Signora* Clarke go on to Perugia. Enjoy the holiday. I'll call you."

Leo studied the paper. "Carmella. Capizzo's wife is Carmella."

CHAPTER—18

Thursday, November 1 - All Saints' Day

LEO

"Sitting down?" Bracci asked when he phoned Leo in the early afternoon, his voice bubbling with good news.

"Yes." Leo, at the kitchen counter, was eating the last piece of Genie's pumpkin pie. She sat next to him reading the newspaper. Fresh bruises marked her neck and arms, but she looked relaxed and cheerful.

"We got a call this morning from Santa Maria Maggiore," Bracci said. "Some new problem. So I went over there. Somebody left a big cardboard box by the service door. With what happened last week, they called us before they'd haul it inside. 'Bombs are small, unobtrusive,' I told them. 'Open it up.'

"What do you suppose was in it? The crib! Goodnard— the fainter—almost toppled over again. It isn't the *real* crib, but one so like—it's unbelievable! No clue where it came from."

Genie looked up and smiled to hear Leo laugh.

"At first Goodnard was outraged. 'Sacrilege,' the whole thing. But I could see him thinking about it, and the longer he thought, the better he liked it. By the time I left, he was considering moving it into the crypt, he said, 'so as not to disappoint our visitors.'"

"Any old pieces of wood in it?"

"No. Whoever created it is leaving that decision to higher authorities. I'm betting it will be in its niche by vespers. And, if the TPC and the Vatican never locate the original, there it will stay. People may eventually forget it's a copy."

"Sounds about right." Leo chuckled.

"And, I saw Sal. The doc was as good as his word. Medical records didn't find out about Sal until shortly before noon. Since it's a holiday, the records department has weekend hours and weekend staff. *Signorina* Angela. Sal interviewed her, remember? Well, she was already in his room when I got there. Sitting on the bed, bringing cold cloths, massaging his temples. Quite a lovely little medical records clerk too. So, watch for signs of malingering. I couldn't tell how he really feels—brave front, with Angela there—but he'll be fine."

"And Nic?"

"I was trying to keep to the good news. Just like the others, not a word out of him. But he's not having a good day. Oh, and," Bracci's voice became serious, "we're taking a collection for Capizzo's widow tomorrow, when everyone's here. A couple of the guys are helping her organize the funeral. Will you be a pallbearer? Monday."

"But of course."

"And, Genie, how is she?"

Leo glanced at her, half-hidden behind the newspaper. "Couldn't be better." He ached to put his arm around her, but the timing still seemed so wrong. The more he cared for her, the harder he had to work not to let his desires override his duty.

It isn't over yet.

He thanked Bracci and after they disconnected, relayed the gist of the conversation to Genie.

"I know it's not the real crib," she said, "the original one, but does that matter?"

"Of course!"

"Really? Do you think it actually contained pieces of a 2000-year-old manger?"

"Symbolically, yes."

"Can't the new reliquary be the same? Symbolic of the original, and as powerful?"

Leo's mouth twisted. "I see what you are saying ..." She wasn't talking about the crib.

"The lost reliquary has intrinsic value, *certo*—the materials involved, the workmanship—but isn't most of its real value the meaning attached to it? If people transfer that to the new one, then—?" Leo did put his arm around her now. She said, "I wonder, can a replacement ever be as good as the original?"

He had to get his answer exactly right. "Oh, yes. Because having lost a treasure, we realize how precious it was and value the new one even more."

Prode bounded into the room and was extravagantly petted by them both.

"So, what do you think of my home, my family?" Leo asked. "Like your many loyal readers, I am interested in your opinion."

"It is—they are—beautiful! Your parents do everything they can to make Robbie and me comfortable. And this place—" She made an Italian gesture of unqualified approval.

"My brother and sister?"

"Super. Though I sense some tension between Elena and your mother."

He laughed. "An old story. She's never forgiven mama for saying her Raimundo would be a worthless husband."

"Surely after so much time …"

"Elena isn't angry because mama opposed the marriage, she's angry because mama was right. And living with Raimundo is a daily reminder."

Genie unsuccessfully stifled a laugh.

"Very human, no?"

At that moment, Renata came in from the garden. She set flowers aside and filled the sink with greens, humming happily. Everyone in the household, except perhaps Camillo, was aware of the tension of the past few days, and now that it had lifted, if only a bit, it pulled their spirits up with it. Leo hadn't burdened them with reminders about the ongoing danger. There would be time enough for that.

"Are you going to the cemetery tomorrow?" he asked. It was the family's annual All Souls' Day ritual.

"In the morning. Elena and Camillo are going with us. And you?"

"Not this year." Leo needed to be in his office on Friday, and Genie was scheduled for what she hoped would be her last visit with *Dottor* Immormino. "The dead will just have to wait." *It's the living who worry me.*

CHAPTER—19

Friday, November 2 - All Souls' Day

THE PROSECUTORS

Tati went to his office early on Friday to confer with Fausto Scarpatti. The two prosecutors devised a modern variation on the tried-and-true strategy of Imperial Rome: *divide et impera.* Divide and conquer.

At ten, Carla di Landri and her boyfriend entered Scarpatti's waiting room in response to his summons. The elderly prosecutor limped out of his office and greeted them warmly. He invited her in. The boyfriend tried to follow. Scarpatti raised his heavy lids and waggled a warning finger at him. "I promise I won't steal her from you."

The young man smirked and stepped aside.

With the door closed, Scarpatti guided Carla to a cozy green sofa. The low table in front of them displayed large framed photographs of his family, including a close-up of a fluffy white cat.

"Oh," she said and held out her hand.

"*Nebbia.*" He sighed, a wheezing, old-man sigh. "An apt name for her, 'fog.' She could appear and disappear like magic. She lived to twenty-one. Old for a cat."

"I had a cat." Carla spoke wistfully and held the photo in both hands.

"What was her name, my dear?" Scarpatti patted her arm.

In an hour, he knew everything.

He walked Carla to the door, his arm around her shoulder, and thanked her profusely for coming. The boyfriend was gone.

He walked to the table and turned the picture frame over. He pulled out the image of a white cat he downloaded from the Internet that morning, revealing the face of his Bergamasco shepherd, bright eyes barely visible among coal dreadlocks, pink tongue lolling, laughing back at him.

VENIERI

On Friday morning, Pietro Venieri paced his home office, debating whether the police or the mafia would get him first. Cubellis's ominous phrase "give you what you have earned" echoed ever louder in his mind as their appointment approached.

Venieri was equally haunted by the visit from the police detective. "Deep. Read me like a book," he muttered. And, the man had talked to Carla. Who knew what she had said? She hadn't made sense for weeks. And he'd mentioned the goddamn cat. Nerves, pure nerves. He might as well have confessed on the spot.

And Rosa Lisi and that Korean. Another incipient disaster.

The telephone interrupted him with an unexpected summons to the office of public magistrate Maximilliano Tati. The man's assistant wouldn't reveal what the meeting was about, just that his immediate attendance was required.

Venieri set the envelope containing his incriminating new identity on top of his briefcase and stared at it until he could bear the guilt no longer. He snatched it up, stuffed it inside, snapped the latches closed, and hurried to his car.

From the moment Gianni was murdered, he should have known word of his plans would get out. Forgery, false documents, fake identity. Dangerous offenses in this security-obsessed age. *Especially when they precipitate murder.* As he crossed the Tiber bridge he considered flinging the briefcase and its tainted contents into the river. *Except I may still have a chance to use them.*

"All right, all right," he yelled to a honking driver who momentarily commanded his attention. "Fuck off!" He sped up.

Or, maybe this Tati knew about his deal with Cubellis. *But that's—how did Cubellis put it?—"sharing an idea with a friend," and the idea may not even work. Right, an abandoned project. A dead end.* He shuddered. Should that be his tack? *Almost too bad the drug probably will work now, thanks to Kim.* Whatever he said about it, he shouldn't mention Kim. Chatting with another scientist would sound suspicious. *But could it lead to prison?*

His heart pounded wildly. He couldn't imagine himself in a place like Rome's Rebibbia prison. *A death sentence.* Even Cubellis wasn't as frightening as the bowels of Rebibbia. After all, he might escape Cubellis. Using his phony documents.

Maybe this Tati didn't know all his secrets. Maybe he didn't know any of them.

"Thank you for coming." Tati guided Venieri to a chair. He gestured toward a man seated across the room. "My colleague, Fausto Scarpatti." Scarpatti's hands were folded across the sphere of his stomach. The old man looked ready for a nap. Venieri dismissed him from his attention. He composed himself to listen.

"I must tell you, Dr. Venieri, we know about your doomed plans," Tati said.

So. He knows about the false papers. My escape. Gianni's death sentence!

"In fact, I'm meeting with Mr. Cubellis this afternoon to discuss them."

No, he means the Alzheimer's formula!

"Perhaps you didn't know what a dangerous situation you fell into when you made your arrangement with your cousin."

The false papers.

"Lucrative for you, no doubt. But there might be a hidden price."

The drug formula.

"I should warn you, by the end of the afternoon, that project will be *finito*."

My three and a half million euros? He would have had them tonight. Or, he would have been "given what he had earned" in a currency harder than cash. Like a toy sailboat, he was prey to every puff of air—from Cubellis, Rosa Lisi, that clever detective, and now this man.

Tati leaned back in his chair and put his fingertips together. "But I have a different deal to offer you. The new deal requires you to tell us everything you know about Mr. Cubellis and his intention to manufacture and sell your drug."

"And about your cousin," Scarpatti interjected.

The false papers and *the drug formula. Rebibbia.*

Venieri's eyes flitted around the office. He'd be reasonable. He wouldn't sound like a criminal. "When you put it like that … *Signor* Cubellis wanted the formula and the process, which *Dottor* Kim—"

Already a false step.

"Please, more slowly," Tati said. "From the beginning."

Venieri swallowed. "My cousin Gianni came to my office about two weeks ago. He worked for, well, you probably know, he worked for Cubellis's organization, a very low-level position, I'm sure. We weren't close." He glanced at Scarpatti. "He hinted Cubellis has Alzheimer's disease, and he wanted a new drug I've been working on, though it's far from ready for human patients. I told him that. I was very clear."

Venieri crossed his legs, then recrossed them the other way. It was as if he could still feel the jabs in his backside from Cubellis's ancient sofa. "A few days later—" *the night of the disastrous* Telegiornale *interview* "—Gianni arranged for me to meet Cubellis. Not something you can say no to."

Tati's eyebrows raised.

"I didn't observe any impairment in the man. But then I met him only once. Briefly. He reiterated that he wants my drug, and I said I don't know yet if it's effective—or safe. And of course I emphasized it isn't officially approved. Even so, Cubellis wanted the 'recipe,' he called it—in case he ever needed it."

Venieri's recitation sped up, relieved to be telling this. "The manufacturing process is complicated. I thought he'd never be able to replicate it, so what was the harm? Especially if I abandoned the project, which seemed likely at the time."

"And he'd pay you, naturally."

Venieri studied his hands, which in a few hours should have held a fortune. Almost inaudibly he said, "Yes."

"How much?"

"Three and a half million euros." Less the paltry one percent Venieri had given Gianni.

"Did you receive this money?"

"No, not yet."

"Do you know where it was coming from?"

"From his accounts, his other … business dealings, I suppose." Everyone in Italy knew what those other business dealings were. Venieri's face flushed. "I would be putting his money to good use, you know. Medical research—"

Tati interrupted. "The money wasn't coming from anyplace special?"

"I don't know. My interaction with him would be at the outset, and if things didn't work out, I …"

"Would be gone," Scarpatti prompted.

"You know?"

The false papers again.

"It's obvious."

"Cubellis wanted me to meet someone, so I could explain the process. No, first, he gave me a deadline for making my decision. And, I did decide to do it. I wasn't sure I could refuse." Venieri's voice climbed several defensive notes.

Tati addressed Scarpatti. "The analytic mind is impressive, no? So this person he wanted you to meet, he is—?"

"*Dottor* Chung-Lee Kim. From Stanford University. In America. He does scientific work for Cubellis. Biochemistry." The magistrates sat up, looking surprised. "Heroin," Venieri clarified, and they relaxed.

"But could Kim handle a product as complex as yours?"

"Yes. He suggested a way around a certain difficulty." He coughed. "With this minor change, the drug may actually work, and—"

"*Dottor* Venieri, please remember that what interests Cubellis is not a health program, but a profitable venture."

"Kim said as much. He said the cost of the ingredients—even taking into account the expense of outfitting a manufacturing facility—was so low, the drug would easily make many millions. Many." *Billions, in fact.*

"Where is *Dottor* Kim now?" Tati asked.

"He was in Italy on Monday. He had dinner with Rosa Lisi. Maybe she knows."

"Rosa? The television doctor?"

No, Rosa, the shifty bitch.

"And your cousin's interest in this?" Scarpatti asked.

"Gianni wanted to boost his standing in the organization. He was so pleased with himself."

"So, what did you ask him to do for you?" Scarpatti asked. He gave the impression he expected an answer and would wait for it, if necessary, forever.

"False papers—a passport and so on. Just in case. I gave him thirty-five thousand euros. I—I had to get away from Cubellis." *See? I'm not really a criminal.*

"And this is what you found in your car after your cousin's funeral? The 'passport and so on'?"

Venieri's surprise showed. The briefcase on the floor felt warm against his leg. "Yes."

"You have them?" Tati asked.

"Yes." Venieri pulled the case onto his lap. He took out the envelope and held it to his chest.

"May I see it?" Tati asked.

Venieri reluctantly handed it over. The magistrate studied the documents inside. "Nice," he said. "These will save us time and trouble." He called in Dante and gave him the papers with a scribbled note of instructions.

"Well!" Tati slapped the desk, startling both Venieri and Scarpatti. "It's good you have these papers; you're going to need them. Yesterday I arranged with my colleagues in the U.S. Federal Bureau of Investigation to include you in their witness protection program. You must leave Rome before evening. Dante will give you a boarding pass for a flight to Milan as you leave my office.

"I was afraid you'd have to stay there a few days while we obtained the necessary documents, but you may as well use the ones you have already paid for. When you land in Milan, your ticket to the States will be waiting, in your new name. As I said, I'm meeting with Cubellis this afternoon, and what I will tell him will make it dangerous for you to remain in Italy."

"But are my papers good enough?"

"They are fine. Expert. You were prepared to use them before. You must trust them now. And they keep us out of it. Our big, leaky bureaucracy. Gianni must have paid plenty for them."

After a long pause, Venieri said, "With his life."

"What do you mean?" Scarpatti asked, alert.

"I never believed they would kill him." He remained a toy boat racing the wind, his thoughts tacking from one direction to another so many times in the last hour he could no longer judge the risk of his revelations, and he wailed, "Just for those papers?"

"What are you talking about?" Scarpatti said. "Carla's boyfriend killed Gianni. He was mad at Gianni for upsetting her—letting the cat escape so the dog could kill it. She says he shot the dog too. The barking drove him crazy. Carla thinks Gianni's murder is *her* fault. And she's scared to death of the boyfriend. But we've taken care of him."

Venieri was incredulous, "A *cat*?"

"Poor little Bianca."

Several minutes elapsed before anyone spoke, though Scarpatti suffered a coughing fit.

"There is one thing you could do for us," Tati said, gazing at the ceiling, avoiding the eyes of his fellow magistrate.

"Ye-es?" Venieri said.

"I believe Detective Gilletti visited you, asking questions about your cousin's death."

"Ye-es."

"Before you leave Rome, would you please visit the *questura* and tell the detective the full story—Gianni's letting the cat escape, the vicious dog, the upset sister, the short-tempered boyfriend, in custody now. In a nutshell, tell him Gianni di Landri was killed because of a cat."

"Ye-es." Venieri sensed he was missing the point, but the request seemed simple enough. Since he'd already mentioned the cat to Gilletti, it might possibly make sense.

"We will be most appreciative. Are we done here, Fausto?"

"I am," the older man answered sleepily.

Tati walked Venieri to the door but didn't shake his hand. "My friends in the FBI will meet your flight to the States. You must return to Italy and testify against Cubellis, you understand, if it ever becomes necessary."

Dante returned the envelope containing his identity documents. Clipped to it was an airline boarding pass. "One question. After Milan, where am I going?"

Tati was skimming his phone messages and distractedly said, "Didn't I say? California. San Diego, California."

TATI

Tati watched the scientist scuttle to the elevator, clutching his briefcase. "Dante, make an appointment for me with Mr. Cubellis. I'll go to him. Today, if possible. And get my wife's friend Rosa Lisi on the phone."

He patted the departing Fausto Scarpatti on the shoulder. "You were right, Fausto. The envelope in the car did contain new identity papers. An impressive leap."

"Obvious," the old man said and limped away in the direction opposite the one Venieri had taken.

Tati shut himself in his office and made a slow circuit of the photos lining his walls. He might have been an art gallery patron in the way he paused and studied certain images, brow furrowed, bent slightly forward. What engaged him was not the images themselves, but what they represented regarding strategy and the precise, almost mathematical balancing of opposing forces. Except for a few short telephone calls, he remained mired in this contemplation until time to leave for his appointment.

Tati's driver stopped at Cubellis's steel gate and announced him. A camera eye examined them, an invisible security guard pushed a button, and the gate retracted. Vittorio Cima stepped out of the house to meet Tati and escort him to Cubellis's study.

"Thank you for seeing me on short notice," Tati said to Cubellis, who was seated behind his large desk, wearing an expression of polite interest. "It's time we reviewed where we are, in light of recent events."

"I am interested in your perspective," Cubellis said, his rough voice a contrast to Tati's smooth one.

"Our detectives have worked hard and in a coordinated way across agencies—" Tati emphasized these last two words "—and they have developed much evidence. Evidence I, as a prosecutor, would be confident taking before any court in Italy."

Cubellis's hands were folded on the desk. He appeared to await information of interest.

"In a nutshell, we have Umberto Ricci, the leader in kidnapping the American and theft of the Santa Maria Maggiore crib, who killed one of our police officers two days ago. Unfortunately, as you know, he is in one of our medical examiner's large refrigerators, beyond reach of our questioning.

"We have Marco Rinaldi." In a restrained, matter-of-fact manner, Tati ticked off Marco's crimes: "murder of the woman in the hospital, Gemma Capuano, assault on an officer at a hotel, kidnapping, and accessory to the theft of the crib. We have photographs of him in the basilica holding a thermal imaging camera. An expensive item. We didn't find it in his apartment. Perhaps you own one?"

Cubellis shrugged.

"We have Lama Rinaldi: murder of Gemma Capuano and mutilation of her corpse, murder of the priest, Father Nunzio Maratea, theft of the crib, assault of the officer at the hotel, kidnapping, and theft of a delivery van, which we located last night, by the way.

"And, we have Nicola Bertaloso: kidnapping, theft of the crib, murder of the priest, murder of a policeman—you are surprised? The dead officer found in a garage in the center city four days ago. The theft of cash from a woman in Riano—a small matter, but large to her, I assure you. The vicious mugging and several attempts to murder an American tourist. And the attempted murder of a young detective of the *Polizia di Stato*, for which we have numerous eyewitnesses and the testimony of the victim himself. Not to mention the video a tourist made with his cell phone. A one-man crime wave, your Nic. If you believe any of these men will be out of custody quickly, you are mistaken."

Cubellis appeared to reflect a moment, then pressed forward. "Is that it? I presume these people you mention have lawyers. Their view of events may be quite different."

"No doubt. But my view will prevail. The evidence is, as I said, overwhelming."

Cubellis sharply expelled a gust of air, as if to blow Tati's evidence away.

"Plus the confessions." Tati risked overplaying his hand. They had Marco's admissions, but that was all.

Cubellis's eyes narrowed. Confessions would be a more serious hurdle, yet even they could be dealt with, Tati knew, given the alarming suicide rate in Italian prisons.

"Remind me why you are here, *Signor* Tati. What does any of this have to do with me?"

Tati's big play was coming, and he made Cubellis wait for it.

The Alzheimer's drug. Venieri had admitted he'd only belatedly signed the university's paperwork and that Chung-Lee Kim had made a key change to his formula. The argument over who owned this new version was guaranteed to keep the university's patent attorneys tied up for years, with no guarantee they would eventually prevail. Tati couldn't start down that path.

He said, "My concern is a crime-in-the-making, if you will. We know, to a certainty, you are engaged in a conspiracy to manufacture a new drug for Alzheimer's disease. A drug you would sell to thousands of desperate people, even though it is not approved—a significant crime of itself. And even though there is no proof the drug would work or be safe, which is also a moral crime against the Italian people."

Cubellis's expression remained impassive.

"The particulars of this crime were discussed with you personally, not with your hirelings. Your confederates *will* testify," Tati said, "and you will not find them."

"A bureaucratic matter." Cubellis waved the problem away. "If the drug seemed promising, my new company would send it through the proper approval channels."

"Too late for that, I'm afraid. I know your implementation schedule. Money from the sale of the crib would cover the expense." Cubellis couldn't mask the twitching nerve next to his left eye. "You planned to begin production almost immediately, and you expected profits in the second quarter of the new year."

During the ensuing silence, Tati silently praised the wiles of Rosa Lisi and too much red wine. Together, they'd extracted this vital information from Cubellis's biochemist. Then he continued, as calmly as before. "I phoned an old friend today to ask his opinion on whether we should pursue this matter. He happens to be the new president of the *Corte Suprema di Cassazione*. You'll recall that Italy's Supreme Court elected a new president two weeks ago, after the tragic death of the previous president, his father. The family is devastated." Tati clucked his tongue in commiseration. "A terribly long and difficult illness."

"And he died of ...?" Cubellis was quick.

"Alzheimer's disease. Sadly, yes. My friend tells me he is deeply interested in this prosecution. He has no specific control over the lower courts, but what interests the President of the Supreme Court will interest them. Conspiracy cases do tend to drag on mercilessly. Not a pleasant way to spend the next eight to ten years." He stopped talking and let the elderly man consider his options.

After a long silence, Cubellis said, "I sense there is a way to avoid this."

"There is. First, any plans to illegally manufacture, sell, or distribute this drug must cease. And, second, every attempt to harm the American woman, Eugenia Clarke, or her family, or her other connections, here or in the United States"—Cima's chin lifted a centimeter—"must end immediately. No harm must come to her or them. Otherwise, Alzheimer's will be the death of you, one way or another."

Hands folded, Tati waited. Finally, to restart the conversation, he said, "The crib. I assume you have no idea where it is."

"None."

"Or how to find it?"

Cubellis shook his head sadly. Tati could push a deal only so far and must claim success where he could.

"In that case, we must pursue that mystery with our own resources. But the drug and the American …?"

"The men you mentioned. They had a kind of *vendetta* against her. She is of no interest to me."

What you mean is, continuing to pursue her while your men are in custody would point attention right back at you.

Cubellis continued, "And the drug? Why would I manufacture it here in Italy, when I can help an American company do so legally? Let them handle all that government red tape. Bah! More trouble than it would be worth to an old man."

"So we are in agreement on those two points."

Good luck finding a legitimate foreign drug company to work with, once they know where your tainted cash came from. As I will make sure they do.

"Absolutely." Cubellis rendered a crocodile smile.

"Well. I will leave you to enjoy your afternoon."

In the car once again, he closed his eyes and leaned his head against the seat. Much had been accomplished. Cubellis would keep his word—and so must his men—because it was so much to his advantage to do so.

He pulled out his phone and made a call. "Detective Angelini? Tati here. Would you meet me in my office in—" he caught his driver's eyes in the mirror.

"Thirty minutes," the driver said.

"—thirty minutes? I have news that will interest you."

GENIE

When Leo pulled his car into the farmyard, we could see Renata and Agostina busy in the brightly lit kitchen, and the men in the room beyond, ignoring its comfortable chairs, engaged in a conversation punctuated with vigorous gestures. At the front of the house, the pumpkins glowed.

Prode bounded to the car.

"Someone's glad to see me," Leo said.

"Everyone will be glad to see you tonight."

He parked the car in the barn, alongside the sweet-smelling bales of hay, while Prode danced for joy.

Inside the house, we received a boisterous greeting. Agostina smiled unceasingly, preparing the vegetables for dinner, aided by the clamoring children. Only Elena kept apart, a glass of wine in her hand and no husband in sight.

"Sit. I know you are tired," Renata said. "Orangina?"

"Actually, I'll have a glass of that Valpolicella. *Dottor* Immormino says I've healed *so* nicely and the morphine is so completely gone from my system, I'm off the wagon."

"Off the—?"

"Sorry! I can enjoy wine again. And I plan to."

I swiveled the stool to watch the lively group of men. Leo grinned to see the glass in my hand. He looked a decade younger.

"I have good news," he announced. "As you might imagine, we feared Genie and Roberto and his family might remain under threat from *La Mafia*, despite the recent arrests. Today, our public prosecutor, Maximilliano Tati—" he lifted his glass, and everyone followed "—solved that problem for us most cleverly. The mafia will back off, here and in the United States. Our American friends are safe. They and Agostina can go home in peace. Maximilliano Tati," he toasted.

Everyone chimed in, and Leo said, "Also, Tati has reason to believe the unlikely combination of university and criminal scientific minds may actually produce an effective—and legitimate—Alzheimer's drug in the foreseeable future. Not the usual outcome of a *Polizia di Stato* investigation and not something to broadcast yet, but a distinct possibility." Another round of raised glasses.

I stood. "On a more personal level, today the long-suffering *Dottor* Immormino released me into the wild, and I can honor Leo's success properly." I raised my wine glass. "Thank you, Leo, for dedicating so much—" my voice started to get husky "—for working so hard—to protect me. *Cin cin.*" Everyone chimed in, even the children.

But Leo's mention of going home had startled me. It made real the day I knew was coming. Didn't he want me to stay? I hoped he didn't notice the wine's trembling surface as I held up my glass.

"It took all of us," Leo said, "Tati, Fausto Scarpatti, my detectives, every person in this room, but mostly, Genie, you and your good brain and your courage. When you learned about Gemma, at the Pincio, when they kidnapped you, interviewing Marco, Halloween night. I could never have done it without you." He addressed the others, again raising his glass, "To a brave and sagacious spirit. *Cin cin!*"

LEO

After dinner, Leo and Agostina bent over the dishwasher. She whispered, "What are you going to do about Genie? She can fly home now. Her editor is pestering her."

Leo had thought of little else all evening. He didn't want her to go. But, really, she had a full life before she met him. Why would she upend all that? After his wife died, he didn't believe he would ever fall in love again. Then this lively, independent, capable, thoroughly attractive woman hurtled into his life. Was it selfishness to want to keep her?

"How can I stop her? She's so accustomed to traveling everywhere, to her independence. She will come back if there is a trial, I am sure, but why would she want to be tied down here?"

Agostina laughed. "Must I answer that? And why isn't Rome a suitable home base? We have airports."

He knew Genie held him in high regard, that there was appreciation, even affection. But was it more than being thrown together in such intense circumstances? He hadn't approached a woman *in modo romantico* for many years and desperately feared a misstep. He watched her talking with Camillo and his father, laughing and confident. "She doesn't need me now."

Agostina rolled her eyes. "Please."

There was something else. On Halloween night, Genie waited in the car while he and Bracci went to Capizzo's apartment. Seared in his memory was Carmella Capizzo's expression when she saw them on her doorstep. How she sank to the floor, sobbing. He had tried to protect Genie from so much. By not pursuing her, he could protect her from that too.

"It isn't a good life," he said.

"It's *your* life." She put her hand on his arm. "Leo, despite the terrible anxiety of the past few weeks, I haven't seen you so … so fully yourself since … you know."

Across the room, Robbie brought a chair to where Genie sat, and they talked, heads together. "She is a prize that keeps slipping away. Sometimes these last weeks I've thought she can never … we can never …"

"Only she can tell you that. Talk to her."

Elena brought them her coffee cup, and they silently made room for it.

GENIE

Camillo handed me a cup of espresso. "So, you are a free woman now?" I sat on the end of the sofa next to Paolo, while Camillo was in a chair alongside.

"Free of so much. I can't quite get used to it. But …"

"But?"

"I will always blame myself for Gemma Capuano's death and the … desecration. That's why we were late, Paolo. Did Leo tell you?"

Leo's father shook his head.

"We made a detour coming home"—the word slipped out—"by way of Sommati. We put All Souls' Day flowers on Gemma's grave. There's no stone and probably won't be, but the groundskeeper told us where to find her. That actually helped a little. It showed someone remembered, that she was connected to us. We to her. Sounds silly, I guess."

"Not to me," Paolo said, taking my hand. "It will be hard to put everything that has happened behind you."

"It was so kind of Leo to do that for me."

"And what are you doing about him?" Camillo grinned.

I met his eyes, so much like his brother's. "Doing? About Leo?" I twisted toward the kitchen, where he and Agostina loaded the dishwasher. "I don't know what there is to *do*, actually."

"We all see how you feel. How you both feel," Camillo said. His expression was filled with delight, as if he were revealing the world's most poorly kept secret.

"He's never said ..." My hands fluttered distractedly.

"Is that necessary?"

It was not, not since he made me give up Nic's knife. Yet, was I ready to abandon my defenses? Become vulnerable in some new way? "I don't want to compete with a ghost. Especially, so I hear, a most charming one."

"You are so different," Camillo said.

"*Not* charming?"

He laughed. "Just as charming, in your own unique way. Genie, my brother is ready for a new chapter." Paolo, listening carefully, murmured agreement.

Before I could respond, Robbie pulled up a chair. "Why didn't you tell me how much fun travel is!"

I tapped his knee with an admonishing finger. "Now I know you never read my articles. I always suspected it."

"I'm having a wonderful time!" he said. "Everything is great—the countryside, the farm, the house, and the people! And with Camillo translating, it's been terrific. I love it!"

I laughed, thinking how tenuous was Camillo's grasp of English. "There's no telling what you agreed to today."

In English, Camillo said, "We have been sharing high tales."

"High tails, like 'hightail it out of here'?"

"He means 'tall tales,'" Robbie said, chuckling. "Growing up in this house, where his family has lived for generations—it was hard for him to imagine our childhoods before—you know. And Aunt Stevie's."

"Peripatetic."

"*Peripatetico*," Camillo echoed.

"Perfect word." Robbie grew thoughtful. "You know that poem you always liked so much? T.S. Eliot? I've been thinking about it."

"'Burnt Norton'?"

"That's the one."

"I was sixteen, Robbie. And I bet I know where you're going with this. You and Camillo have been conspiring. Rather transparently." I felt my cheeks flushing.

"Maybe it's the long view a place like this inspires," he said, ignoring me. "'Time present and time past' all around us. You read that poem to me every day for months."

I could smell the sun-heated wood timbers of Aunt Stevie's attic and see the dust motes dancing to the rhythm of the words. "Not months. Weeks, maybe. Days."

"There's that line near the beginning. It always made you cry … as I recall, it was something about the road we didn't take, the door we didn't open. Well, that's the gist of it, anyway. That always stuck with me."

The memory of these melancholy reflections pierced me. Was I facing a door I could try to open? Our imminent departure was calling the question. But was I ready? Was he?

I gave Robbie and Camillo a hard look. "The two of you … absolutely shameless."

Robbie laid his hand on my arm. "Genie," he said, "I hope you know how proud I am of you. I know you'll do what's totally right." He leaned over and kissed my forehead.

I carried my cup and saucer to the sink. Leo dried his hands, cleared his throat, and said, "Shall we take a walk?"

"*Certo*," I said, and set the cup down before it could rattle. I grabbed a sweater from a peg by the door, and Leo told Prode to stay.

We walked to the front of the house for another look at the glowing pumpkins.

"Roberto and Camillo have become great friends," Leo said.

"They have had a good time together."

"Roberto told him something, something you've forgotten."

"Really? What?"

"About your parents. The disaster."

"Ah." I hugged my elbows.

"You said you don't remember how you and Roberto got off the mountain. But he remembers clearly."

"We never talk about it." I didn't want to talk about it now.

"You did it. You led him to safety. You marched down the mountain holding him by the hand, encouraging him all the way. He says you saved his life."

"I really don't remember. I guess it just had to be done." After a moment, I spoke brightly. "Your father has night-blooming jasmine in the garden. Maybe we can find it."

"We can try. Follow our noses."

The air was chilly, with a slight breeze. He put an arm around my shoulders. We crossed the brightly lit yard toward the barns and the dark garden beyond.

"One thing more, about what Roberto said. I am not surprised. And yet, you are a surprising woman."

We reached the open barn doors, where Leo's car nestled among the hay bales. A snapping sound from the direction of the big oak halted us at once.

"What?"

"Wait." His arm tightened.

The fear that had filled the last weeks flooded back. We were fully visible in the farmyard's bright lights, while anyone beyond the glare, if there *was* anyone, was lost in blackness.

Another sound came from beyond the tree, and we pulled each other, diving, into the protection of the barn. A flash and a rifle's report came almost instantly. We lay between the driver's side of the car and the barn wall. Shouts erupted from the house, and the kitchen lights went out. Leo groaned, face drawn tight. He motioned for me to swing open the barn's side door, facing the house, and he shouted, "Stay inside!"

I held his face. "Where?"

How could this be happening? We're supposed to be safe!

"Right shoulder." He coughed out the words. "We're too exposed. I'll have to cut the lights." His face contorted when he tried to move.

"I'll do it. The switch next to the barn door?"

"Yes," his voice a croak. I guessed that part of his pain was that I had to take that risk.

I tried to sound calm, reassuring, though my nerves sparked like fireworks. "Easy."

I crept forward, shielded by the car. In one lightning motion I leapt up, hit the switch, and dropped to a crouch. A bullet whistled inches over my head. Way too close. The shooter had a good scope. Maybe night vision. I hoped not.

Now that we knew he was there, he—or, god forbid, they—didn't try to move silently. I could hear him slowly approaching, still near the tree, more than fifty yards away.

"My gun's in the glove box. Can you—" He gasped. "Key in my pocket."

"OK." If I opened the car door, the dome light would come on, and the shooter might see Leo lying there. "We have to move you back." I spoke firmly. No time for discussion.

Leo groaned as he dragged himself onto his knees and left arm. I supported his injured side, and we scraped along the dusty floor. We left a trail of blood, black in the scant light entering the barn. The amount of it made my mouth go dry.

Near the front of the car, he stopped, panting, unable to continue. I grabbed his jacket and, using strength I didn't know I possessed, dragged him a few more feet. The effort left me shaking, but now he was in front of the car, the whole heavy vehicle between him and the barn door. I stripped off the sweater and balled it over what appeared to be the source of the blood, somewhere near his collar bone. If he was lucky, it missed his lung.

"Press this on it. Tight."

Leo laid his left hand on the wadded sweater. Best he could do. He was on his back, breathing heavily. I retrieved the keys and duckwalked to the driver's door. It would have been easier to access the glove box from the passenger side, but that would put me squarely in the shooter's view.

In the near dark, it took a moment to identify the correct key. I clenched it between my teeth. I opened the car door, threw myself inside, and awkwardly swung my legs in, pulling the door behind me. Momentum closed it far enough that the interior light turned off. Although it had sputtered on for only a few seconds, a bullet shattered the car's rear window into hundreds of tinkling pieces and exited the front windshield with a crack.

"My head is down, you creep," I muttered.

For a few precious seconds, I fumbled with the key, but managed to open the glove box. I retrieved Leo's revolver and a box of cartridges.

I swiped unsuccessfully at the overhead light with the gun butt, but the angle was bad, and I couldn't spend more time on it. I shoved the keys deep into my jeans pocket. Getting out of the car with the gun and the ammunition was going to be harder than getting in. Leo and Sal carried their guns against the small of their backs. I didn't dare. It might slip out, and I'd have no time to grope around for it. As I squeezed my shoulders between the steering wheel and seat, I bumped the horn. With my every nerve on alert, the sound was deafening. My heart skittered. I swore, knowing how it must have startled Leo.

I eased the driver's door open far enough to drop the gun and cartridge box on the barn floor, then pulled it closed. Once more, the interior light flashed, and the rifle fired, puncturing another hole in the windshield. In a burst of scrambling movement I propelled myself out of the car and kicked the door shut. Two more shots, aimed more to the left. Shards of the driver's side window rained on my back and pricked my neck.

Crouching, gun in one hand and ammunition in the other, I returned to Leo's side. His right arm shook uncontrollably. No more than five minutes had elapsed since he was shot, but he'd lost a lot of blood. If he went into shock, I didn't know what I'd do.

I pushed this possibility away and concentrated on my next steps. "Got it. Is it loaded?"

"No. You have to—"

"I know how." Hours of firing range practice paid off, though my trembling hands slowed me down. Leo might not have realized it yet, but I would have to do the shooting too. Eight shots, all I'd have. I was grateful for the gun's six-inch barrel. It would improve my aim.

"Ssss," Leo said.

"What?"

He pointed, and I leaned down to peer beneath the car. A man's figure, black and indistinct, crept across the dark yard. The faint starlight reflected off the barrel of the rifle tucked under his arm, and in his other hand he carried something squarish.

"Give me the gun," Leo whispered. His left hand gestured slightly.

This gravely injured, wonderful man wanted to save me again. But this time I'd deal with the bastards myself. For him. For us both.

I kissed his forehead, and whispered, "It's OK. I'll do it."

"Don't leave me." He reached for my arm with the hand that had been holding the blood-soaked sweater.

I took his hand and pressed it back on the sweater. "No, Leo, don't you leave me."

Scuttling along the barn wall, I kept the car between me and the approaching gunman. Broken glass crunched underfoot. From inside the house, Prode barked steadily. Timed to that noise, I cocked the revolver's hammer. When

I reached the car's rear wheel, I peered underneath. The man was much closer, but the car still hid me.

He dropped the rifle and advanced to within five meters of the door. I darted across two feet of open space and flattened myself against the wall next to the barn door. Busy fiddling with a long stick, he hadn't seen me. Liquid glugged from the square object. The sharp smell of gasoline floated across the yard.

At once I pictured Leo, lying helpless, as burning bales of hay engulfed the barn in flames. *Not happening.* Stepping away from the wall's protection, I dropped to my right knee. Both hands held the gun in front of me. As he lit a match, I fired, steeling myself to absorb the noise and the recoil. He staggered toward me. I held steady and pulled the trigger again. And again.

He cried out as he crashed forward and launched the burning cloth-tipped stick toward the barn. But he'd come up short. I walked toward him, gun held out, ready to fire again. I kicked the burning stick away and scuffed dirt over it. He was only semiconscious, the rifle lying nearby. I kicked that away too.

I held the gun muzzle to his temple as I slipped my hand under his jacket to check for a handgun and found it. He was in too much pain to stop me. I checked his ankles and pockets. No more weapons. I tightened the cap on the gas can and flung it, end over end, across the yard. Not as far as I would have liked, but he'd never get to it. He wasn't going anywhere.

I picked up the rifle and ducked into the barn. Squatting beside Leo, I laid the rifle and two handguns on the floor.

Cars raced up the long driveway. Flashes of headlights between the trees strobed the yard.

"Now what?"

"Police, I hope," he said through gritted teeth. "Tati's perimeter guard. What about—"

"Out of commission. Couldn't miss at that distance."

"I smell—"

"Gasoline. Taken care of."

"Amazing." His deep voice was rough and weak, but he managed a sort of smile.

LEO

Men in cars, more on foot. When she made sure it was the police, Genie turned the yard lights on.

"It was one guy," the sergeant in charge told them, while one of his men radioed for ambulances. "We found his car and followed him here. We kept our distance in case there were more of them. I'm sorry he got farther ahead of us than he should have."

"You're sure there's no one else?" Genie asked.

"Positive."

"Then let me tell them." She ran across the yard to the house. The lights inside came on, and Paolo and Robert accompanied her back to the barn. Renata and Agostina followed with blankets and a clean towel. As the bloody sweater rolled to the floor, Renata's lips tightened.

"Let me," Agostina said, pressing the towel to Leo's wound. "You put those blankets on him."

The sergeant continued. "We heard shots, but we didn't have visual, so couldn't tell what he was shooting at. When we heard the car horn, we knew somebody was in the barn, so some of my men swung around to come at him from the side. And keep him away from the house."

"I was scared when I bumped that horn!"

"Good thing you did. We were nearly in position when he stopped advancing."

"Fixing his torch."

"Yeah. We sure saw that with the infrared. Then we heard more shots, and he went down—and we were, what the hell?—because none of us fired yet."

"Is he—?" Leo asked.

"He'll make it," the sergeant said. "Three of my guys are standing over him. He's not going anywhere."

Leo muttered, "*Incredibile*!" Then to the sergeant, "Help me up. I'm OK, I'm OK."

"You are not," Agostina protested.

The sergeant leaned over and pulled Leo to his feet with one strong arm. Wincing, Leo leaned into him. "Go into the house, mama. You too, Agostina." He gestured with his head that his father and Robert should follow them. He was about to tell Genie to go too, but they exchanged looks, and he knew she wouldn't go. They were in this together. He didn't even ask.

With the sergeant's aid, Leo hobbled to where the gunman lay, conscious now and moaning. He nudged the man's leg with his foot. "Who sent you?"

The man swore and gritted his teeth. "Nobody."

"You shot a cop, asshole," the sergeant said. "You'll be in our hands a long, long time. Answer the question."

No response.

Leo nudged the man's bleeding leg again, harder, and he screamed. "My idea," the man said. "Cubellis wants the American dead."

"Cubellis called that off."

"I didn't know." The words came panting out, ending in a moan. "I heard about her in Rome a few days ago. No one could find her. I've been up here since." He gulped air. "*Sono Perugino*. I knew I could find *you*." He spat.

In the distance, ambulance sirens wailed.

CHAPTER—20

Saturday, November 3

GENIE

Saturday morning, word went from Tati to Cubellis about the attempted assassination. Within the hour an expensive display of flowers arrived in Leo's hospital room with this note: "It won't happen again. C."

"*Strelitzia*," I said.

"That's one flower whose name I know," he chuckled.

I stayed at Leo's bedside for most of the three days he was in the hospital, but the combination of frequent visitors and drug-induced sleep meant that the conversation between us, which seemed about to happen Friday night, never took place. There was no predicting how that might have gone, and maybe I was relieved.

Somewhere in there, I messaged my editor Wally:

Home in a few days. Boy, do I have a story for you! Unpublishable, tho.

Sunday afternoon, Tati called. Lama had confessed to sending Genie the threatening text messages and, most important, the worst of the crimes Marco was directly involved in—the murder of Gemma Capuano. In exchange for a guarantee that Marco would testify against the others by video, Tati found him safe haven outside Italy.

"But where?" I asked. "Where could he be safe, really?"

"Tati is the only one who knows. He has his ways."

"Remember how you said the violence children witness can affect their later lives? I think that's what happened to Marco." I surprised myself then, saying, "I really hope he *is* safe."

"And takes up yoga?"

"It would help him." I laughed.

The local police chief, a friend of Leo's, stopped by on Monday to tell us that the man I shot was killed by a sniper as the police transferred him from the hospital to jail. "No leads," the detective said. I wondered whether they even planned to investigate.

Monday afternoon, I was keeping the bedside watch when Leo woke. "What are you reading?" he asked.

"I'm finally finishing this crime thriller. *Il Testimone Valoroso.* It's what I was reading the afternoon I overheard—now I know their names—Marco, Lama, Nic, and Umberto."

"Enjoying it? *The Valiant Witness*?"

"Kind of hard to get into it again. Too much reality has interfered. Look at us." I made a head-to-toe gesture. "Real blood. Real broken bones. Real scars."

"But healing nicely?"

"*Certamente.*"

CHAPTER—21

Tuesday, November 6

GENIE

Leo looked pale and tired when Paolo brought him home from the hospital. While we all tried to make small talk, his glance kept returning to the window. Out in the farmyard sat a hired car, the driver leaning against it. Its gaping trunk had already swallowed three suitcases. Robbie's and my flight was booked for the next day. I felt low, and from what I could tell, everyone else did too.

"We have to get home before I abandon my farm and move next door to Paolo," Robbie said, and when I translated, they chuckled.

"Do it!" Paolo said.

"I'll return to Rome in a few days myself," Leo said. "The *questura* will send another driver."

Renata clucked. "I'll keep him here as long as I can."

"They took your car to get the windows replaced," Paolo said. "And cleaned up my barn." Shattered glass and his son's blood.

"Good," Leo said. He caught my eye, and I moved to the sofa to settle on his uninjured side.

Silence descended again. Agostina stood and grabbed her handbag. "I'll make sure everything's in the trunk."

Renata and Paolo muttered something about instructions for Agostina regarding the box of plants they were sending home with her, and Robbie shook Leo's hand, saying he wanted one last walk through Paolo's garden.

Leo and I were alone. "I want you to stay," he said. With his good arm, he pulled me close.

"I want to stay." I rested my head on his shoulder. "But I need a little time. I've never had three weeks like this, Leo. I have to be sure I'm thinking straight." I kissed the knuckles of his hand.

"I'll miss you." He kissed the top of my head.

"Robbie was wrong, you know. I'm not going home. *This* is home."

"I told you you'd like Perugia!" His voice rumbled, deeper than usual.

"Not Perugia. You. Home is with you."

All the confusing emotions of the past weeks untangled and evaporated with the long kiss we shared.

"You saved my life, you know," I said.

"And you saved mine."

"Didn't you tell me those are forever obligations?"

"*Certo.*"

"*Bene.*"

THE END

About the Author

Victoria Weisfeld's first mystery-thriller, *Architect of Courage*, published June 2022, is fast-paced, twisty, and highly recommended. More than 45 of her short stories have appeared in leading mystery magazines and anthologies, including *Busted: Arresting Stories from the Beat, Seascapes: Best New England Crime Stories, Quoth the Raven*, and one is included in *The Best Private Eye Stories of The Year: 2025*. Her work ranges from Sherlock Holmes adventures set in 1880s London to current-day stories unfolding in Sweetwater, Texas. She has won awards from the Short Mystery Fiction Society and Public Safety Writers Association and is a member of those groups, as well as Sisters in Crime and Mystery Writers of America. She blogs regularly at www.vweisfeld.com and reviews new mystery, thriller, and suspense novels for the popular UK website, www.crimefictionlover.com. She also reviews New Jersey theater for the Manhattan-based website, TheFrontRowCenter.org.